THE LOST CAUSES OF
BLEAK CREEK

CROWN
NEW YORK

THE LOST CAUSES OF
BLEAK CREEK

A NOVEL

RHETT McLAUGHLIN & LINK NEAL

WITH LANCE RUBIN

This is a work of fiction. Names, characters, places, and incidents either are the product of the author's imagination or are used fictitiously. As you might have guessed, Rex and Leif are based on us as teenagers and Bleak Creek is loosely based on our hometown of Buies Creek. And Ben is a tribute to a very close friend. Otherwise, the rest of the book is strictly a result of our wild imaginings. If there is any resemblance to actual persons, living or dead (or undead), events, or locales, it is entirely coincidental.

Published in the United States by Crown, an imprint of Random House, a division of Penguin Random House LLC, New York.
crownpublishing.com

CROWN and the Crown colophon are registered trademarks of Penguin Random House LLC.

Library of Congress Cataloging-in-Publication Data
Names: McLaughlin, Rhett, author. | Neal, Link, author. |
Rubin, Lance, author.
Title: The lost causes of Bleak Creek: a novel / Rhett McLaughlin and Link Neal with Lance Rubin.
Description: New York: Crown, 2019.
Identifiers: LCCN 2019017895| ISBN 9781984822130 (hardback)
| ISBN9781984822147 (trade paperback)
Subjects: | CYAC: Humorous fiction. gsafd | BISAC: FICTION / Humorous. |
FICTION / Science Fiction / Adventure.
Classification: LCC PS3613.C576 L67 2019 | DDC 813/.6—dc23 LC record
available at https://lccn.loc.gov/2019017895

ISBN 978-1-9848-2213-0
Ebook ISBN 978-1-9848-2215-4

Printed in the United States of America

Book design by Debbie Glasserman

2 4 6 8 9 7 5 3 1

First Edition

DEDICATED TO OUR CHILDREN,
LILY, LOCKE, LINCOLN, SHEPHERD, AND LANDO.
KEEP QUESTIONING AUTHORITY
(OTHER THAN OURS, OF COURSE).

THE LOST CAUSES OF
BLEAK CREEK

PROLOGUE

THE BOY RACED THROUGH THE WOODS, BLOOD STREAMING FROM his hand.

He was growing faint.

Can't pass out. Just gotta make it to the fence.

He heard his pursuers yelling. They sounded as panicked as he felt.

He didn't know if the dizziness was due to blood loss or the shock of what had just happened.

They were gonna kill me.

He'd known this place was twisted from day one, when they'd stripped him of everything, including his own name. But even with all the vile things he'd seen, he had still assumed that the brutal punishments were designed to intimidate. Not exterminate. That's why he'd been so calm, willingly letting them guide him along blindfolded and gagged, right up until the moment they'd sliced his palm.

What if this particular test was no different? Maybe he was doing exactly what they wanted him to, running through the trees like a trophy animal. They had only cut his hand. No arteries. Plus, he'd somehow gotten away from the two men holding him, one of them enormous, much bigger than any of the other adults he'd seen there. Had they purposely let him go? No, he shouldn't sell himself short. He'd fought like hell.

The boy felt a flash of pride. All those hours of memorizing Jean-Claude Van Damme's moves had been worth it.

Can't wait to rewatch Kickboxer.

He struggled to move at a full clip, as branches, rocks, and logs snuck up on him in the sparse moonlight. He dodged the obstacles, hoping he was heading in a straight line.

Where's the damn fence?

He saw it just before he collided with it, the grass of the pasture on the other side of the chain links glowing a dull gray under the night sky. He started to climb without thinking, pain exploding as the metal wire slipped into his open wound. He stifled a scream, hoping to conceal his exact point of escape. While clenching his jaw, summoning the resolve to hoist himself up the ten-foot barrier, he saw it: a cut section of fence not five steps away.

Lucky.

As he pushed his way through the flap and stood in the pasture, he heard the roar of an engine to his left. A pickup truck was hurtling across the pasture in his direction.

They were trying to head him off.

He broke into a sprint toward the cover of trees bordering the pasture, his shadow sprawling in front of him as the headlights shined on his back. He was confident in his speed. Ninety-ninth percentile in the President's Challenge Shuttle Run. He'd timed himself.

But they were closing the distance, fast.

Get to the tree line.

He knew there'd be a barbed-wire cow fence at the edge of the field. He'd have to clear it in stride.

In only a matter of seconds, they would be upon him.

He was steps from the trees.

The headlights lit up the short fence, helping him judge his distance. He stutter-stepped to set up his leap, then threw his lead leg in the air.

A clean jump.

He heard the truck skid to a stop on the wet grass behind him, the doors opening. Men screaming.

He knew this stretch of forest well; there was barely a patch of nature around town he hadn't explored. Another hundred feet or so and he'd make it to the clearing.

He broke into the lane cut through the forest, a grassy corridor that followed the sewage line along its lazy descent to the water treatment plant. He heard the chasers clumsily moving through the woods, crashing into branches and grumbling to themselves.

Morons.

Randomly choosing a direction, he dashed down the clearing, reaching a manhole in less than fifty steps. He grabbed a nearby stick and jammed it into the notch on the cover, just as he'd done a thousand times before, no longer thinking about his throbbing hand. The weighty metal disk lifted, releasing an acrid smell. He raised the lid on its edge and swiftly descended into the rank darkness below, skittering down the iron rungs as fast as he could.

The disheveled men popped out of the trees no more than ten seconds after he'd dropped the manhole cover in place.

The boy listened as their cursing voices passed him.

He waited in stinking silence for another five minutes.

Thrusting open the cover, he emerged into the damp air.

The boy fled deeper into the woods.

1

THOUGH REX MCCLENDON KNEW THAT HE AND HIS BEST FRIENDS were about to attempt something audacious, he never could have anticipated the category-five suckstorm that would spin out from the next hour of his life.

As he scanned the crowd for Leif and Alicia, his dad's camcorder heavy in his backpack, the muggy August day hit its first sour note as Rex realized he'd forgotten to put on deodorant. He stuck his nose under the collar of his No Fear T-shirt to get a sense of exactly how dire things were.

It was awful. Almost horselike.

"Stop smelling yourself in public, sweetie," Martha McClendon whispered. "People are staring."

Rex pulled his nose out of his shirt. If his mom thought this was bad, she was going to hate his plans for the afternoon, which hinged entirely upon people doing just that: staring.

"Let's see if we can find your father." Rex's mom led him through the masses gathered in the parking lot of the sole strip mall in Bleak Creek, North Carolina, pragmatically named the Shopping Center. It was home to a majority of the local economic powerhouses: Piggly Wiggly, C.B.'s Auto Parts, the Fish Fry, Thomble and Sons Hardware, Morris Coin Laundry, and the living testament to Bleak Creekians' year-round appetite for celebrating Jesus' birthday, Cate's Christmas Cave.

Every few steps, Rex and his mom returned the customary polite smiles and *hey*s doled out by familiar faces. His shoulders tensed up as they made small talk about the weather with Sheriff Lawson, whose mirrored aviators and perennial look of disapproval did nothing to stem the mounting feeling that maybe his dad's camera should stay zipped in his backpack. There was still no sign of Leif or Alicia.

They arrived at a massive barbecue smoker resting in front of the laundry. In Bleak Creek, it didn't take much to justify cooking a pig. Today's excuse was a Second Baptist Church fundraiser to replace the copper pipes that had been stolen from the church's organ (for the second time— it had happened just six years before, too). Everyone knew who had taken the pipes (Wendell Brown, again), and everyone knew why (to fund his cough syrup addiction), but in a way, people were appreciative, because it had been three weeks since the last "pig pickin'."

Rex spotted his dad in his usual white shorts about ten feet from the barrel-shaped smoker, staring at the grillmaster Wayne Whitewood with a combination of awe and resentment. Whitewood and his mane of perfectly coiffed white hair were beloved in Bleak Creek for many reasons, one of which was his opening of the Whitewood School, a reform school for wayward youths, in 1979. The school was seen as the primary reason Bleak Creek had made it to 1992 unscathed by the "Devil music and crack pipes" that plagued the big cities. That alone would have cemented Whitewood's status as a pillar of the community, but he was also considered to be one of the town's premier pork gurus.

Rex's dad had worked hard on his own barbecue stylings for the better part of a decade, but he'd never been bestowed that great honor, the highest a Bleak Creek man could receive: being asked to cook a pig for a town event.

"I think it's because I'm a mortician," he'd say. "People don't like the idea of me touchin' people then pigs." Steve McClendon was the owner and operator of the McClendon-McClemmon Funeral Home, formerly known as the McClemmon Funeral Home. When Martha's father, Mack McClemmon, died in 1984, Martha had convinced Steve to move the family back to her childhood hometown and try his hand at the funeral business. The result: a funeral home with a name few locals could correctly pronounce on the first try.

Today's choice for chef was a no-brainer, as Wayne Whitewood was also Second Baptist's organist, the player of the very instrument for which this entire event had been planned.

"We gotta get Whitewood his pipes back!" said Mary Hattaway, the secretary at Second Baptist, a thin woman with highlighted hair that spiked in the back, giving her an unintentional resemblance to Sonic the Hedgehog. She repeated her mantra as each new person arrived at the pay table, raising one bony fist in the air.

"Picking up any tips?" Rex said, attempting to break his father's trance.

"Huh?" Steve said, recoiling as if Rex were a door-to-door salesman before realizing it was his son. "Oh, no, not really. I know most of these techniques already."

"Right, *of course*," Rex said. It was unclear what techniques his dad was referring to, as Whitewood was just sitting there reading the *Bleak Creek Gazette* while the grill did its thing.

"You ready to join us, honey?" Martha asked Steve. "You're probably makin' Mr. Whitewood nervous."

"Oh, it don't bother me," Whitewood said, surprising all three McClendons, who hadn't realized he was listening. "I'm flattered you care that much." He returned to his paper.

"Let's go, Steve," Martha said. "Nice to see you, Wayne," she lied.

"You take care now," Whitewood said without looking up, turning a crumpled newspaper page.

"Yessir," Steve said. "You too. Can't wait to eat your meat."

Wayne Whitewood shot his ice-blue eyes at Steve without moving his head from the paper, staring at him for a few uncomfortable seconds. Despite his small stature, Whitewood was remarkably intimidating. He seemed to be waiting for Steve to correct himself.

Rex's dad took the bait and stammered, "Well . . . *the* meat. *That* meat. The barbecue."

Whitewood's mouth cracked a smile, his eyes unchanged. Martha grimaced and tugged Steve's arm as Rex put a guiding hand on his back.

"What was that?" Martha whispered to Steve once they'd put some distance between themselves and the grill.

"I don't know! I'm just tryin' to make a connection!" Steve shout-whispered back.

"Yeah, I think he definitely got that impression."

Rex was glad his parents were distracted by their own drama, as it meant they'd be slower to notice the carefully manufactured drama he was about to shoot—using all the fundraiser attendees as unsuspecting extras—for the film he'd been making all summer with Leif and Alicia. He again checked the crowd for his collaborators, wondering if Leif would have a Speed Stick in his bag whenever he showed up. It wasn't impossible. Leif was always bragging about how prepared he was. Probably the more appropriate question, though: Even if he did have some, would he let Rex use it? Leif could hardly share a can of Mello Yello—no way he'd okay indirect armpit contact. Rex gave himself another sniff, hoping that his proximity to the smoker might have helped to mask his odor.

Nope. It actually smelled worse.

"All right, folks," C.B. Donner, of C.B.'s Auto Parts, said into a staticky microphone. "It looks like Chef Whitewood will be platin' up some of his heavenly pork in a matter of minutes, so get your bellies ready. And once we chow down, it'll be auction time!" Ever since C.B. and his wife, Diane, had divorced earlier that year, he'd made a point of emceeing as many town events as possible. "I'd also like to take a moment to remind all you ladies out there that my store's got a sale on air fresheners, and we just got a new scent in. It's called Pink Swan. Come by and smell of it all you want." He pointed down to his neck, where he was wearing one of the air fresheners as a necklace. True to the name, it was a pink swan. Rex wondered if it would solve his own scent problem.

"Hey, you ready?" a voice asked from behind him.

He turned to find Leif Nelson, at last, standing there in a white T-shirt and a clip-on tie, with his dog, Tucker, leashed next to him.

"Hey," Rex said. "Where've you been?"

"Sorry I'm late. I was getting Tucker ready for his scene."

"What does that mean?"

"Like, I was prepping him. Getting his mind in the right place."

"I still don't understand."

"That's because you don't have a dog."

"Oh, hey, Leif," Rex's mom said, smiling, for the first time all day, like she meant it.

"Nice to see you, Mrs. McClendon. Mr. McClendon."

"Good to see you, too," Rex's dad said, rubbing Tucker's furry head. "Those specs are lookin' sharp!" Leif had been wearing glasses for several months now, but Rex's parents had made a habit of complimenting him like they thought he was insecure about them.

"And I like that tie," Rex's mom said, pointing to the clip-on.

"Oh, thanks, it's for our—" Leif was about to say *movie* until he saw Rex staring him down. "Fundraiser. Well, not *our* fundraiser. But *this* fundraiser. That we're all attending now."

"Well, okay." Rex's mom had gotten used to her son and his best friend saying inscrutable things. "Is your mom comin' by?"

"No, ma'am, she's at work," Leif said. His mom had three jobs, which meant Leif was usually on his own. Rex loved this, as it meant Leif was always around to hang, as had been the case that whole summer.

"Looks like folks are startin' to sit down," Rex's dad said, wiping sweat from his bald head with his black and white McClendon-McClemmon Funeral Home handkerchief, and pointing to the two people who'd taken a seat. "Shouldn't be long now till we eat."

"Hey," Rex said to Leif under his breath as they walked toward the tables. "You got any deodorant on you?"

"Any what?"

"Deodorant." Rex looked around to see who was listening, realizing that maybe he wasn't so different from his mom after all.

"Why?" Leif asked.

"Like, to use."

"You want to use my deodorant?"

"Yes. Yes, I do."

"Oh." Leif stared at Rex as if seeing him for the first time, like he'd just discovered some long-buried truth about the best friend he'd known since he was six. Or maybe he'd just inhaled. "No. You think I just carry deodorant around with me?"

Rex said nothing as he began to absorb his fate for the rest of the day.

"And even if I did," Leif continued, "I probably wouldn't let you use it. Unhygienic. No offense."

"Excellent, thanks," Rex said, shaking his head. His parents sat down at one of the tables, but Rex and Leif stood a short distance away, where they could plot their film shoot out of earshot.

"Alicia's still not here?" Leif asked.

"Nah," Rex said. "Or if she is, I haven't seen her."

"Even when I'm late, she's even later," Leif complained.

Alicia Boykins had completed their friend trio when she'd moved to Bleak Creek in third grade. During recess on her second day at school, she'd asked Rex and Leif if she could get in on the drawing contest they were having. They'd given her a skeptical "Um, okay" and told her she'd have to "draw fast 'cause they were almost done." "That's not a problem," Alicia had said, taking a multi-pointed rainbow pen from her pocket and, within minutes, busting out a picture of a smiling girl clutching three human heads in each hand. Rex and Leif had looked down at their own creations—a dragon wearing a beret and a half turtle, half bear, respectively—and realized they'd found a friend even weirder than they were.

"She'll be here, don't worry," Rex said.

"The whole point is that the scene takes place at an outdoor event," Leif said. "So we need to shoot before it's over."

"We'll be fine," Rex said, unzipping his backpack and taking out the camcorder. "We still gotta figure ou—"

"What's up, fellas?" Rex and Leif turned to see Mark Hornhat next to them, in his usual polo shirt and khaki shorts and smelling like he had just showered in Eternity by Calvin Klein.

"Oh, hey," Rex said, trying his best to seem enthusiastic.

"You guys ready for some 'cue?"

Rex and Leif shrugged. Hornhat was one of those guys

they probably wouldn't be friends with if they lived in a bigger town and had more options. He lived in Heath Hills, the affluent, gated section of Bleak Creek, and, for Rex and Leif, he served as a walking representation of why being rich wasn't all it was cracked up to be. "I'm not going to make too much money when I get older," Rex had once said. "Don't wanna turn into a Hornhat."

"Can't believe freshman year's starting soon," Hornhat said. "High school, amigos."

"Yeah," Leif said, swallowing so loudly that it made a sound. He and Rex hadn't explicitly talked about it yet, but Rex knew they were both pretty nervous about high school.

"What's the camera for?" Hornhat asked, gesturing toward Rex's hand.

Rex raced to form the word "Nothing," but Leif spoke first.

"Our movie," he said.

Rex sighed. He had come to despise talking about their movie with other people, since it always seemed to suck the magic right out of the whole thing. He knew telling Hornhat would be no exception.

"Whoa, cool!" Hornhat said. "What's it called?"

"*PolterDog*," Leif said, stroking his dog's back. "Tucker's the lead."

Hornhat squinted at them. "So, it's a part chicken, part dog?"

"No," Rex said, tempted to hit Hornhat with the camcorder whack-a-mole-style.

"Then why's it called *Poultry Dog*?"

"It's not," Leif said. "It's *PolterDog*! About a ghost dog. Like *Poltergeist* but without the *geist*. And instead a dog."

"Ohhhh," Hornhat said, finally getting it. "You should just call it *Ghost Dog*. That's cooler."

"If by cooler you mean super obvious," Rex said. This was the exact conversation they'd had with at least ten other people. Though somehow it was worse with Hornhat.

"Wrap it up, Hornhat," Alicia said, appearing next to Leif as if out of nowhere. "We got a movie to make." Rex had to hand it to Alicia; she *was* always late, yet somehow her timing usually ended up being perfect anyway.

Hornhat seemed hurt for a moment before deciding to be amused instead. "Whatever, Boykins." He laughed.

"But seriously, man," Alicia said, "we do have to start shooting."

"Okay, yeah, no problem. I was on my way to get a root beer anyway."

"You enjoy that now," Alicia said as Hornhat wandered away. This was one of her greatest strengths in life. She could get away with saying things to people that Rex and Leif would never utter in a million years. "Hey, losers," she said, throwing an arm around Leif's neck and mussing up his hair.

"Hey hey," Rex said.

"You're late," Leif said, but he was smiling.

"What's that smell?" Alicia asked, brushing a swath of dark curls away from her forehead.

"Barbecue," Rex quickly answered.

"Rex forgot to put on deodorant," Leif said.

"It happens," Alicia said, mockingly pinching her nose and smiling at Rex. Somehow her blunt acknowledgment of his stench made him stop worrying about it. "So what's the plan? Have you figured out how to get Tucker to chase me yet?"

Leif raised his eyebrows and smiled, reaching into his backpack. His hand emerged holding a large plastic bag.

"Uh, what's in there?" Alicia asked.

"I present to you . . . the bacon belt!" Leif pulled out

what looked to be a wad of greasy bacon tied together with fishing line.

Tucker barked and lunged at Leif, who pulled his hand away just in time.

"See? He loves it," Leif said. "All you gotta do is put this on and he'll chase you anywhere."

"You want me to . . . wear that?" Alicia asked. "I'm not so sure bacon grease goes well with stonewash," she added, gesturing to her jorts.

"Maybe you can just put it through one loop," Rex suggested. "You know, more of a bacon tail."

"I guess that'll work," Leif said with a hint of disappointment. He'd obviously had big expectations for the bacon belt.

"Okay, perfect," Alicia said, running Leif's creation through the back loop of her jorts, not without some trouble. A piece and a half of bacon fell to the ground, which Tucker gladly disposed of. "Where's the script?"

"Here you go," Rex said, holding out two lightly crumpled pieces of paper, meticulously typed with Rex's dead grandpa's Smith-Corona.

"Lemme see," Alicia said, grabbing the pages. Rex leaned over her shoulder to refresh himself on the scene he was about to direct.

```
EXT. OUTDOOR BIRTHDAY PARTY—DAY

JESSICA (played by Alicia) and her DAD (played by
Leif) are at a birthday party.

                    DAD
     Whats the matter, sweetheart? Aren't
     you exited to be at Aunt Kate's birth-
     day party?
```

                    JESSICA
        Of course I am. It's just . . .

                    DAD
        You still thinking about Mr. Bones?

Jessica nods, tearry-eyed.

                    DAD
        I know. I wish that darn motorcycle had
        never hit him. Hey, here's a Frisbee.
        Why don't you go throw it around a bit,
        have a little fun?

                    JESICA
        Okay, Dad.

Jessica walks around the party. She throws the
Frisbee to no one, then stops in her tracxks when
she sees a dog.

                    JESSICA
        Mr. Bones . . . ? Is that you?

The dog barks twiice.

                    JESSICA
        Oh my gosh!! I knew you were still
        alive!

Jessica runs to enbrace Mr. Bones, but then he
tries to pounce on her!

                    JESSICA
        Mr. Bones stop! Why are you doing this?

Jessica notices that Mr. Bones now has a long white
tale.

                    JESSICA
        Wait a second . . . Your not alive, are
        you? Your a g-g- g-ghost!!! Ahhhhh!!! 1

Jessica starts to run, weaveing in and out of
people. Mr. Bones chases and barks evilly.

                    JESSICA
        Somebody help!!! My dog is a ghost!

She runs into the arms of DAD.

                    JESSICA
        Help, Daddy! Mr. Bones is back and he
        wants to kill me!

DAD looks. Mr. Bones is gone.

CLOSE-UP on Jessica, scared and confused.

"Okay, got it. Let's shoot this thing," said Alicia.

"Well, actually," Rex said, "I just had an idea. If we
wait to shoot until lots of people are sitting down, we can
get a really good reaction shot from them."

"Yeah, that'll be perfect," Leif said. Though they were
practically brothers at this point, Rex still felt proud when
Leif complimented one of his ideas. "In that quiet moment
after they say the blessing, Alicia will come by screaming,
with Tucker on her heels. It's gonna feel so real."

"Plus," Alicia said, "I'm gonna deliver a highly authentic performance. I won't be surprised if somebody steps in
to rescue poor Jessica from her ghost dog."

"*Polter*Dog." Rex and Leif corrected her in unison.

Alicia nodded and winked. "Right. *Polter*Dog. It won't

be long before people all across North Carolina are saying that."

The three of them looked at each other, their excitement palpable. The deadline for the Durham Film Festival was in three weeks, and though it would get a little trickier to find time to shoot (not to mention edit) once school started, they were still on track to get *PolterDog* finished and submitted just under the wire.

"All right, great," Rex said. "So let's save the dialogue for later and start with Tucker chasing Alici—"

"Rex, sweetie," Martha interrupted. "Are y'all gonna sit down and join us?"

"Oh," Rex said. "Yeah, Mom, in a sec, after they actually serve the food. We, uh, just have to film a quick shot for our movie." He knew it would be wiser to give some kind of heads-up, so it didn't seem like he was trying to pull one over on them.

"Now? Here?"

"It'll be really quick. People probably won't even notice," Rex said, unconvincingly.

"We've talked about this, son," his dad said. "You need to spend less time on your little movie and more time practicing, so that you're ready for basketball tryouts."

"I know, Dad," Rex said, a tightness settling in the pit of his stomach, like he was six years old again and had just wet the bed. "But it's not like I could practice here anyway."

"You can practice your defensive stance anywhere." His dad dropped into a squat and stretched his hands out to his sides.

"It's fine, it's fine," Rex's mom said, breaking the tension. "As long as you sit down with us once you're— Oh, hey, Alicia!" Rex watched his mom's mouth twist into the manufactured grin that Martha McClendon offered to people she had reservations about. "Didn't see you there.

How are you, hon?" She didn't dislike Alicia, but she definitely liked Leif more. She'd once said to Rex that she didn't trust "girls who make so many jokes." It hadn't helped that Alicia had been caught earlier that summer pulling down the pants of every mannequin in the display window of the Belk department store. Even though the only thing exposed was a series of smooth, mild bulges on the androgynous dummies, the store manager, Faye Johnson, had found the whole scene so scandalous that she'd fainted, toppling over a pyramid of pantyhose. Word had spread quickly throughout town that Alicia Boykins was to blame.

"Excellent! Thanks, Mrs. McClendon," Alicia said.

"We're gonna go get ready for this quick shot," Rex said, leading Leif, Alicia, and Tucker—Leif holding tight to Tucker's leash as he pulled and licked his lips at Alicia—away from the picnic tables. Hungry Bleak Creekians had already filled the seats and were patiently waiting for Pastor Jingle of Second Baptist to say grace, giving them the green light to gorge themselves on pig parts.

Rex surveyed the area, holding up his hands in the shape of a box like he had seen Martin Scorsese do in a picture from the set of *Goodfellas,* a movie he and Leif had watched after sneaking in through the exit of the Twin Plaza theater two years before. Rex still had an occasional nightmare where he was lying in a trunk and Joe Pesci would open it up and begin stabbing him. He never told Leif.

"All right," Rex said with a firm nod, trying to seem like he'd had some directorly epiphany. "I'll stay over here, just past the tables, and you guys head all the way back over there toward the parking lot entrance. As soon as Pastor Jingle finishes saying grace, I'll throw up my hand and you'll start running."

"I'll have Tucker by the collar until I see your signal," Leif said.

"Right. Then Tucker will run, and Alicia, you'll be screaming and saying your line."

"Yep," Alicia said.

"All right, all right." C.B. Donner's voice crackled through the sound system. "It's the moment we've all been waitin' for. Chef Whitewood, if you please . . ." C.B. pointed to Whitewood, who, with a flourish, lifted the cover of the grill. "His glorious pig hath been cooked!" C.B. said, to cheers from the crowd. "I'd like to introduce Pastor Jingle and our special guest today, Pastor Mitchell, from First Baptist. They're gonna say grace . . . *together.*"

A murmur rippled through the crowd. Pastor Mitchell's presence was notable, seeing as a main tenet of the Second Baptist Church was the silent judgment of congregants of the First (and vice versa), to which Rex and his family belonged. No one could remember why it had once seemed so necessary to start another church, especially one that held to the same precepts as the first, but that did little to temper the hushed rivalry. In fact, Whitewood's barbecue was likely the only reason that so many Firsters had shown up and donated six dollars to an organization they despised. This surprise tag-team blessing may have been Second Baptist's way of thanking them for coming. Or, it may have been more about establishing a subtle yet united front against the Presbyterian church that had just been built outside of town. Either way, no one had seen this level of cooperation between Pastor Mitchell and Pastor Jingle since they both insisted that the Bleak Creek High School chorus not perform John Lennon's "Imagine" at their regional competition.

"We gotta get going or we'll miss our moment," Rex said, trying not to be thrown by the dual prayer or by Sheriff Lawson, whom he'd noticed standing by the tables, his hands rubbing his bulbous gut like he was preparing his stomach for the imminent feast. Shooting a movie in public without a permit wasn't an arrestable offense, was it? Guess he'd find out soon enough. "Head over there, and as soon as I signal, you go."

Alicia nodded, and as they started to walk away—the pastors walking into position and C.B. Donner telling all the women in the crowd that leopard print seat covers were twenty-five percent off through Labor Day—Leif stopped.

"Wait!" he said. "We need to put the ghost tail on Tucker."

Rex frantically dug in his backpack, mortified that he'd forgotten something so vital. He passed Leif the white felt tail and a roll of Scotch tape and breathed a sigh of relief as he watched him stick it on, realizing how close they'd come to disaster. It wouldn't be *PolterDog* if the dog wasn't poltered.

After Leif used what looked to be half the roll of tape to firmly secure the tail, he and Alicia jogged with ghost Tucker to their starting spot as Pastor Jingle, a rail-thin man who blinked a lot, began to speak. "Hello and thank you, everyone, for being here today. As you may have heard, Pastor Mitchell of First Baptist has been kind enough to join us to say grace during this pipeless time." He gestured to Pastor Mitchell, a round, handsome man with a dark beard. (Rex had always thought he looked like a fatter, more conservative George Michael.)

"It is a blessing to be here as we unite for such an important Baptist cause," Pastor Mitchell said in his deep, familiar voice. The emphasis on *Baptist* was hard to miss. "Let us pray."

"We thank you, Heavenly Father," Pastor Jingle said,

"for this delicious barbecue and for providing us with so capable a grillmaster."

"Yes, Lord," Pastor Mitchell said, as Rex looked into the camcorder and adjusted the lens, zooming in and out on Alicia to properly frame the shot. "Though First Baptist has many capable grillmasters as well, we are grateful to be here to benefit from the talents of Mr. Whitewood."

"Indeed, since we all know Mr. Whitewood is the *most* capable," Pastor Jingle added. "And, Lord, we also ask that you open the hearts of those present and compel them to give generously, even beyond the minimum six-dollar donation, to help restore the wonderful sound of praise-filled pipes to your house."

"And, dear Lord, maybe even *more* importantly," Pastor Mitchell interjected, "we ask you to open the hearts of those at Second Baptist to installing a state-of-the-art security system like the one we have at First Baptist to prevent Wendell from stealing their precious pipes yet again." Rex didn't hear what Pastor Jingle said next, or what Pastor Mitchell said after that, because, as he took in the features of Alicia's face, he was distracted by a ping in his chest. He found himself fixated on the gentle curve of her lips.

He was snapped out of it, though, when he realized Pastor Jingle had just said Jesus, more than likely as part of the phrase "In Jesus' name," which was always the last thing said before "Amen." Rex went to throw a panicky hand in the air when he realized the pastors were still dueling.

Phew. It must have just been a random Jesus mention.

Rex couldn't believe how disoriented he'd gotten in such a crucial moment. And because of *Alicia?* He shook it off, knowing he needed to focus, and gave a confident thumbs-up to Leif and Alicia, like *Get ready* and also like *Everything's under control, I wasn't just distracted by the beauty of someone who's been my best friend for years.* Not wanting to accidentally forget later, Rex pressed the red record button, and, knowing the "In Jesus' name" was coming any second now, held his signal hand at the ready.

"And so," Pastor Mitchell went on, his voice shifting into a conclusive decrescendo, "we are so blessed to be here together, First Baptist and Second Baptist joined as one, as we consume this delectable bit of sustenance together. In Jesus' name . . ."

There it was. Go time.

Rex's hand was already in the air when Pastor Jingle, clearly desperate to get the last word, began to speak some more. "Yes, in Jesus' name, we now bless our food. And the Lord hears us. And He likes what He hears." *Seriously?* How many blessings were there going to be?

Rex yanked his hand down, but it was too late. Leif had released Tucker's collar, and Alicia was already sprinting and screaming. Rex wanted to explain his mistake to the crowd, but he had no choice but to keep filming. Sure, the three of them would probably get in more trouble than they'd anticipated—that was very clear when he panned over to the dozens of confused, angry faces staring at Alicia (*perfect* reaction shot)—but really, there was something even more authentic now: Tucker's powerful barks forcing the pastor to stop speaking.

"Somebody help!" Alicia shouted. "My dog is a *ghost*!" Her voice pitched higher on the last word, and it was gold. She'd completely nailed it. But Rex's triumph turned to concern when he saw that Tucker's performance was almost *too* convincing, his pursuit of the bacon tail transforming him into a seemingly rabid dog, inciting what looked like genuine terror in Alicia. Rex instinctively took his eye off the lens and saw Leif, already in a full sprint to retrieve his dog, his panicked face whiter than Tucker's fake tail.

"Now, what is this all about?" Pastor Jingle said into the microphone.

"You got some nerve, interruptin' the pastors!" a man with a goatee in a Garth Brooks T-shirt shouted at them, which inspired similar reprimands from others.

It was an accident! Rex wanted to shout, but he didn't want to taint the incredible take he was getting. He put his eye back on the lens in time to see Alicia zigging and zagging away from Tucker, whose age of eighty-four dog years was the only thing keeping him from closing the distance to Alicia and chomping the bacon lure. Rex figured he'd give it another few seconds before stepping in.

Leif wasn't on the same page. "Tucker!" he shouted. "Tucker, sit!" The collie, laser-focused on the prize, did not slow down. Then, Leif, apparently sensing the limits of human language, began making wild movements and animalistic sounds to get Tucker's attention, which only kind of worked. He had, however, in an impressive display of newfound post-pubescent speed, caught up with Tucker. Left with no other options, Leif awkwardly tackled his canine companion, who let out a startled yip. Alicia looked back midsprint, which is why she didn't notice that all her zigging and zagging had put her on a collision course with Wayne Whitewood, who was standing next to the open grill, ready to serve some pig plates.

"Watch out!" Rex shouted, for some reason still looking through the camera.

It was too late, though. Wayne Whitewood tried to sidestep the curly-haired hellion heading his way, but upon hearing Rex's warning, so did Alicia. She plowed directly into Whitewood, sending him reeling sideways, his sweat-covered torso landing on the cooked pig. He caught himself on the still-hot metal bars of the grill, searing his bare hands with a sickening hiss.

Whitewood let out an uncharacteristic shriek followed

by a long, guttural moan. The crowd, stunned into silence, could have heard the faint sizzle of melted pig fat falling onto the hot coals if it weren't for Whitewood's oscillating between gasping and groaning, now coupled with Alicia's repeated apologies.

"I'm so sorry, Mr. Whitewood! So, so, sorry!" Alicia cried.

Whitewood continued to breathe heavily, trying to gather himself. A crowd of about a dozen people, including Sheriff Lawson, had sprung into action and now clustered around the wounded man. Leggett Shackelford—a tall, wide man who, as the owner of the only other funeral home in town, was also Rex's dad's arch nemesis—put an arm on Whitewood's shoulder, then turned to Alicia.

"You, young lady, are out of control!" he yelled, his oversized mustache jumping up and down.

"What possessed you to do such a thing?" demanded Mary Hattaway, who had also come to Whitewood's aid.

Rex was incredibly grateful that he was still filming, but the gravity of what was happening to Alicia quickly overshadowed his enthusiasm for *PolterDog*. This wasn't good. It was an accident, sure, but Rex knew that wouldn't make a difference to everyone who'd witnessed it.

The crowd began to escort Whitewood to his nearby Ford Super Duty truck, perching him on the tailgate, where he held his red, blistered hands. Rex turned off his camera and ran to Leif and Alicia, who both looked shell-shocked. "Are you okay?" he asked.

"I didn't mean to do it," Alicia said.

"I'm sorry," Leif said, staring at the ground. "I underestimated Tucker's . . . enthusiasm."

"Just tell me you got the shot," Alicia said to Rex.

"Oh yeah. I got it. It was awesome. *You* were aw—"

"What in the world were you doin'?" Rex's mom asked as she rushed over to them. She was as angry as he'd seen her in a long time. "Interruptin' grace like that . . . have you lost your mind? And Mr. Whitewood is hurt!" She spun to Alicia. "Are your parents here?"

Alicia looked every bit as terrified as she'd been while Tucker was chasing her. "No, ma'am."

"Well, I'm gonna call them as soon as I get home," Martha threatened. She then headed toward Whitewood to survey the damage her son and his friends were responsible for.

Sirens cut through the air as both Bleak Creek ambulances pulled up to the sawhorses blocking Main Street. EMTs hopped out of the back and started rushing toward Whitewood.

"I think I might be in a lot of trouble," Alicia said.

Whitewood was quickly wheeled into one of the ambulances, conscious and alert and waving to the crowd.

"Nah, he looks totally fine," Rex said. "You have nothing to worry about."

"Yeah," Alicia said, but she didn't sound convinced.

Rex wasn't convinced either.

2

"WELL, BOYS," STEVE MCCLENDON BEGAN, "I THINK WE ALL KNOW why you're here."

Leif and Rex sat in two formal high-backed chairs in the McClendon living room. Rex's parents, along with Leif's mom, Bonnie, were lined up across from them on an antique wood-trimmed couch. Leif figured that the impending discussion would not be pleasant, as he'd only seen Rex's mother let two types of people sit in her living room: out-of-town guests she was desperately trying to impress, and children she was desperately trying to discipline.

"Yes, sir," Rex replied, which Leif quickly repeated.

Even though Alicia had been the one who'd leveled Wayne Whitewood, she wasn't present. As usual, Rex's parents had decided to treat the two boys as a unit, something Leif's mom had passively accepted years ago. Leif had grown used to receiving whatever punishment Rex did, and he didn't mind; enduring the same sanctions as his best friend somehow made them closer.

"What you two did," Rex's dad continued. "It was just so . . . disrespectful." There it was. The worst offense a Bleak Creek youth could commit: failing to show proper reverence for the institutions the town held so dear. And, in a sick twist of fate, because their stunt had rudely interrupted a prayer during a pig pickin', they had simultaneously dishonored the town's most sacred deities, God *and* pork. Double whammy.

"I thought we raised you better than that," Rex's mom said, looking over to Leif's mom, who put down one of the at-least-five-year-old Andes mints she'd picked up from the porcelain bowl on the coffee table. She nodded in an effort to lay on the collective condemnation.

"You did, Mom," Rex offered. "It was really stupid. And I can promise you that it won't ever happen again." Leif signaled his agreement by assuming the most contrite posture he could, pressing his knees together and drawing his elbows to his sides.

"Well, it won't happen again because I'm takin' my camera back. Your dog movie is over," Rex's dad said.

Rex and Leif exchanged a look like they'd both been punched in the stomach.

"No, Dad, please!" Rex pleaded. "We're almost done with it!"

"I was never comfortable with you makin' a movie about a ghost in the first place," Rex's mom said. "There's no such thing as ghosts. The Bible says 'absent from the body, present with the Lord.' That stuff is demonic!"

"It's just a movie, Mom. Please, please, please . . . don't take the camera! We've been working on this all summer." Leif thought Rex was going to cry, and figured it might help the cause.

"No, son. I'm sorry. You can finish it later," Rex's dad insisted. "Because, you know, your mother's right," he added, looking to his wife. "You're starting high school. This is no time to be messin' around with . . . demon stuff." Leif doubted that Rex's dad really thought *PolterDog* was Satanic, but figured he wanted to present a united parental front. "If you start behaving—not to mention begin puttin' some of that movie energy into gettin' yourself in shape for basketball tryouts—then maybe you can use the camera next year."

Leif looked to Rex, who sat quiet, resigned that arguing further would only make things worse.

"And . . . we think you should take a break from spending time with Alicia," Rex's mom added.

"What? No!" Leif had planned to stick to nonverbal communication, but he couldn't help himself. "It wasn't even her fault! We're the ones who made her run into Mr. Whitewood!"

"It doesn't matter whose fault it is," Leif's mom said, breaking her similar practice of letting the McClendons do the talking. "Between hitting Mr. Whitewood and that . . . mannequin situation, she's getting a bad reputation."

"That's right," Rex's dad said. "And you two are too. Would hate to have to bring the Whitewood School into this, but . . ."

Leif found himself short of breath. In all previous disciplinary episodes in this room, the McClendons had never mentioned the possibility of Wayne Whitewood's reform school. This was new. And terrifying.

Leif tried to steady his shaky knees as Rex began to speak again.

"Mom, Dad, Mrs. Nelson," he said, making eye contact with each adult as he addressed them. "We know what we did was wrong, and we feel horrible about it. We'll do whatever it takes to regain your trust. Even if that means not finishing *PolterDog* and never talking to Alicia again."

Leif nodded accordingly, though he was relatively certain his best friend was being strategic rather than sincere.

—

LEIF PEDALED IN the dark, his mind racing even faster than his bike. He'd convinced himself that Alicia running into Mr. Whitewood—and him no longer being allowed to be her friend—was all his fault. It didn't matter that Rex had given the signal too early. He had been the one to suggest the bacon belt. And he had been the one who had tackled Tucker, causing Alicia to turn her head at the worst moment. He kept running through the scene, each time hearing the humiliating moans of the usually composed Wayne Whitewood. What an absolute nightmare.

He'd also correctly guessed that Rex had never intended to keep his promise to his parents. Later that night, Rex had found the camcorder exactly where he knew his dad would hide it: the not-actually-secret secret cabinet in the garage. Rex had then done his Rex thing, telling Leif about the amazing destiny that awaited them if they could just finish the film.

"First, we win the Durham festival," he'd said, standing on the back deck overlooking the woods behind his house, his arms moving in sweeping motions, like he was materializing the future right in front of them. "Then we get into a big one. Maybe even Sundance. Then we get distribution. Next thing you know, we're getting coffee with Robert Zemeckis. Coffee with Zemeckis! Are you telling me you want to say no to that?" He was extremely convincing. Coffee with Zemeckis felt so possible. Plus, Leif had learned that once Rex set his sights on something, trying to dissuade him was futile.

That was why he now found himself barreling down the middle of Main Street after midnight, on his way to meet up with Rex and Alicia to film one of the last remaining scenes of *PolterDog*.

However, of the two restrictions they'd been given by their parents, not hanging out with Alicia was far more concerning to Leif than not finishing their movie. And this wasn't just because he was worried about the demise of their tight friend group. No. Lately he'd been thinking about Alicia in a very different way.

It had started during their first day of shooting *Polter-Dog*. Alicia and Tucker were cavorting in a field for an early scene meant to establish Jessica and Mr. Bones's easy, playful rapport before Mr. Bones bit it. Alicia wasn't an animal lover, but she *was* a great actor. As Leif watched her dote on Tucker for the first time in her life, burying her face in his shaggy neck on the same soccer field where Leif had made minor contributions to at least two rec league victories, a strange half-formed image sprang into his head: grown-up versions of him and Alicia sitting by a fireplace, Tucker sprawled in Alicia's lap as Leif worked on a crossword puzzle, mug of coffee by his side.

"Are the kids asleep?" Leif had imagined himself asking.

"I think so," grown-up Alicia had responded.

"But you're not entirely sure?" grown-up Leif had asked.

"No, no, I'm mostly sure."

This strange daydream about grown-up Alicia's uncertainty regarding their unborn children's consciousness was interrupted by real Rex asking real Leif if he thought that last take had enough face-licking.

"Uh, yeah. That's plenty," Leif had said with a false confidence.

He had tried to put these thoughts about Alicia out of his head, but that only seemed to intensify them. His distant-future visions had been replaced with present-day fantasies: the two of them tandem-biking through the woods, feeding each other popcorn at the Twin Plaza, eating a fancy dinner at TGI Friday's. And making out. A lot. Complete with serious, mouth-exploratory tongue action.

After a week of this, Leif had admitted to himself (and to his diary that he called a journal): *I, Leif Nelson, have a crush on Alicia Boykins.* Though it felt good to acknowledge, he knew he wasn't going to do anything about it. Yes, she was smart and funny and fearless and trustworthy and so pretty that he had no idea why he hadn't fully registered it before, but she was also part of his best-friend triangle, or, as Alicia had coined them, the Triumvirate. He instinctively knew no good could come of it, so he'd made a vow to himself (and to his diary) that he would tell absolutely no one. Not even Rex.

As an unspoken corollary of this vow, Leif had made sure nothing in his behavior gave even the slightest hint of his crush. At times, he'd swung too far in the other direction, harping endlessly on Alicia's minimal flaws (such as her inability to be punctual), seeming like he actually despised her. But he preferred that to revealing the truth, which would surely alter their trio's dynamic forever. Besides, the odds seemed good that Alicia didn't feel the same way, so what was the point of baring his soul for no reason?

Or, at least, that *had* been Leif's philosophy.

Until he'd been forbidden to see her.

Before the incident with Whitewood had screwed everything up, he'd convinced himself that he could carry his hidden crush around with him while still enjoying her presence, savoring the moments when she playfully put him in a full nelson, her hair brushing up against the back of his neck. He could live with that. But the thought of only being able to see her in secret as they filmed the last few scenes of *PolterDog* filled him with an electric desperation, like he *had* to communicate his feelings *now.*

Adding to the sense of urgency, Alicia had not only agreed to finish the movie, but insisted they shoot tonight. Maybe she felt the same connection between the two of them after all.

"Really?" Rex and Leif had said simultaneously, their heads pressed together to the earpiece of the phone at Rex's house earlier that evening, while both the McClendons and the Boykinses attended a back-to-school PTA meeting at Bleak Creek High.

"Yeah, really," Alicia had said. "We've got three weeks. Just a few more scenes and then the edit. We're cutting it close either way."

"We don't want to get you in even more trouble," Leif said.

"You don't get me in trouble, Leif," Alicia responded, grinning through the phone. "I get myself in trouble. And anyway, my parents and I had a talk, and they actually seem pretty okay about what happened. They know I didn't run into Mr. Whitewood on purpose. Plus, the idea of having some kind of secret friendship sounds pretty sweet. Like we're a secret society or something."

Leif couldn't help but smile. "Okay," he said.

"Yeah," Rex agreed. "Let's finish this thing. Meet you at your place at quarter past midnight."

"Word," Alicia said. "See ya."

In just a few short hours, Leif might be embarking on a clandestine romance with the girl of his dreams. A real Romeo and Juliet situation. He tried to convince himself that he didn't care about the outcome, though of course he was hoping Alicia might want to be his girlfriend and that Rex would be supportive. Crazier things had happened.

———

LEIF BROUGHT HIS bike to a stop a couple houses down from Alicia's (the appointed meeting spot with Rex, a dark patch in between streetlights) and waited. As he scanned the house in front of him—which belonged to a new family that had recently moved to town from Nebraska, a place that seemed so foreign as to be exotic—Leif flinched at the sight of a pair of eyes staring at him from only a few feet away. *Is that Rex waiting to do one of his classic jump scares?* he thought. *Or are these Nebraskans actually insomniacs who walk the streets at night?* But as his eyes adjusted, he saw it: a raccoon perched atop the Nebraskans' trash can. Leif let out a loud hiss, and the raccoon, seeming to understand it as the universal sound for "Get the hell out of here," darted away into the night.

Leif pressed the light on his calculator watch: 12:09. He was glad to be early—more time to rev himself up to make this happen. He figured the most appropriate moment would be after they'd picked Alicia up and made it to the woods. The woods, after all, were very romantic. While Rex scoped out the shots, Leif would open his heart to Alicia.

"Hey, dude," Rex said, gliding up on his foot-powered scooter.

"You're still riding that thing?" Leif asked. It was too dark to make out all the features of Rex's face, which, after his encounter with the raccoon, freaked him out a little.

"Uh, yeah," Rex said, "and I'm gonna be riding it for a while. They're predicting that by 1998, bikes will be practically extinct. No offense."

"Who is *they*? And objects can't go extinct."

"You know what I mean. Obsolete."

"Isn't a bike actually faster and more efficient than a scooter?"

"See, that's where you're wrong," Rex said, caressing the scooter's handlebars. "This puppy has serious speed. You're just not using it right."

"I've never ridden a scooter."

"Exactly. You just proved my point. Now let's go get Alicia."

Leif was not a fan of Rex's tendency to declare things

cool no matter what counterevidence was presented, or the way he took it upon himself to prematurely end arguments to preserve the illusion that he was right. But it didn't matter, because Rex had already sped ahead with a series of rapid Flintstones-style pushes off the pavement. Leif hopped on his bike and, even with the late start, easily caught up to him.

As Rex placed his scooter on the grass near the curb, Leif put down his kickstand, acutely aware of the pounding in his chest. Now that he was standing with Rex at the foot of Alicia's lawn, he was having second thoughts.

"Call her," Rex said, nudging Leif with his shoulder.

"Oh, right." Leif put one loose fist over his mouth and delivered one of his patented turkey mating calls, a sort of seductive gobble that he'd mastered a few years earlier at Baptist boys' camp.

They focused on Alicia's first-floor bedroom window, her lamp already on, illuminating the opposite wall, which featured her collection of posters showcasing her excellent taste in pop culture, including one of Larry and Balki from the TV show *Perfect Strangers*. Leif had always wondered if Alicia saw Rex and him as Larry and Balki, and in this moment, as he prepared to profess his deepest feelings for her, he realized that he was definitely Balki. He didn't know whether that was good or bad. Maybe his proclamation could wait.

Just then, the window opened and Alicia's dark curls emerged, blocking both Larry and Balki from view. She flashed a sly grin when she saw the dark outlines of her best friends. Leif grinned back, his second thoughts evaporating. He felt a serenity wash over him. He didn't need to work on his precise wording—he would let the rhythm of the moment guide him. It was all so much simpler than he'd—

Suddenly, Alicia screamed, as two hands grabbed her shoulders and attempted to yank her back inside.

Leif and Rex stared in the darkness, speechless.

"Get off me!" Alicia shouted, writhing back and forth.

"Her parents . . . ?" Leif asked, but Rex was already in a crouched run, his backpack sticking out like a turtle shell as he headed toward the window. Leif followed, but this time catching up was harder; he'd never seen Rex run this fast in his life.

It wasn't fast enough, though. Just as he got to the window (a full two seconds before Leif), Alicia's grip on the windowsill gave out and she disappeared.

"Rex! Leif! Helmmmmphsseh!" Alicia shouted from inside. Leif ignored the tiny voice in his head that wondered why she'd shouted Rex's name first. He peered in and shuddered. Two men in beige coveralls were lugging her out of her bedroom.

What the hell . . . ?

"Get off her!" Rex shouted through the window as he climbed in after them.

"Yeah!" Leif added, following Rex's lead and wincing as he felt the sting of a splinter from the sill dig into his calf. He had no idea what the two of them would do once they caught up to the kidnappers, but it turned out to be a moot question. Alicia's door slammed shut when they were halfway across the room.

Rex tried to open it, but it wouldn't budge. One of the men was blocking it. "Come on," Rex said to Leif. They threw their bodies against the door.

"Go home, boys," a strained but familiar voice said from the other side.

Leif and Rex stopped pushing. They stared at each other, dumbfounded. "Mr. Boykins?" Leif asked.

"I know you're trying to help Alicia," he continued, "but we know what's best for her."

"You don't understand!" Rex shouted. "Two guys just—"

"We know, Rex," Mr. Boykins said. "Please, this is hard enough as it is."

Leif heard a scuffling from outside and ran to the window, where he saw the men putting a still-writhing Alicia into the back of a white van parked at the curb. If Leif hadn't been so busy planning his stupid love confession, maybe he would have noticed it earlier. Rex vaulted out the window past Leif, shouting, "Get off our friend, you jerks!"

Leif threw himself out the window after Rex, but without deciding exactly how he was planning to land, ended up facefirst in the grass. He leapt up from the ground in time to see the van's back doors slam and hear the engine rev up.

"Easy with that lip, son," one of the men said, still standing by the closed doors. "You could be next." He popped into the passenger seat and the van took off. Rex had reached his scooter, which he picked up and began wildly propelling down the street with his giraffish left leg. It certainly looked like he was going fast.

Leif ran to his bike, flipped up the kickstand, and jumped on his pedals all in one motion.

"Don't follow them," Mr. Boykins said from the front porch, clad in a bathrobe, an arm around Mrs. Boykins as she wept into her hands. "Please, Leif. After what happened today . . . Don't make this any worse for Alicia than you already have."

"I'm so sorry," Leif said, and he suddenly understood that the Boykinses hadn't actually been okay with the whole pushing-Mr.-Whitewood-onto-a-grill situation, not at all.

Leif knew where Alicia was being taken.

He took off on his bike, Mr. Boykins shouting his name three more times before his voice faded into the distance. Leif was impressed with how far up the street Rex had gotten, but he was clearly out of breath, and the van was almost out of sight.

"They're taking her to the Whitewood School," Leif said.

"Oh, shit," Rex said between gasps. "We gotta go there!"

He continued to swing his leg around and pump his scooter down the narrow road after the white speck in the distance. Once again, Leif had no idea what the plan would be once they caught up to the abductors, but he knew they had no choice but to follow. He felt stupid for not seeing this coming; after you'd grilled the hands of a man who runs a reform school, chances were good you'd end up there.

Leif had always heard the stories about kids snatched away in the night, but, like most people, he'd dismissed them as urban legends, designed to scare them into being good kids who went with the flow. Seeing one of these snatchings up close, and happening to his best friend, was traumatic to say the least.

Leif looked for Rex, as he often did in anxiety-provoking situations, knowing that his calmer, less panicky energy would be grounding. But no one was there. Rex had fallen far behind. Leif experienced the briefest moment of satisfaction before rapidly U-turning.

"Leave the scooter," Leif said, pedaling alongside him. "Hop on my pegs." Another burst of intense satisfaction. Rex had been making fun of Leif's "unnecessary" bike pegs for years.

"No, you go ahead," Rex said. "It's not the scooter. I just haven't developed my scooter leg enough yet."

Leif couldn't believe that, even now, in hot pursuit of their kidnapped best friend, Rex refused to admit defeat.

"Your scooter leg?" Leif couldn't help but ask.

"Yeah, the pushing leg. It takes months to have a reliable scooter leg," Rex insisted.

"So I'm just gonna take these guys on alone?" Leif asked.

"No, I'll definitely catch up. My leg's about to get a second wind."

"We're wasting time!" Leif could no longer see any sign of the white van. "Just get on my pegs!"

Rex kept scooting.

"I agree it's your scooter leg and not the scooter," Leif said.

Rex abruptly hopped off his scooter and tossed it under a shrub on the side of the road. He stepped onto the two pegs jutting out from Leif's back wheel, his hands on Leif's shoulders. "Burn it."

And Leif did. He pedaled like he'd never pedaled before, rocketing forward even with the extra 150 pounds of lanky human freight. The fiery pain in his thighs was overwhelming, but as the boys rounded the last turn on Creek Road, the white dot reappeared ahead, and that was all the motivation Leif needed.

Soon the lights at the Whitewood School gate came into view, the only indication that there was anything behind the pine trees lining the road. On the rare occasion when Leif had passed by the school, secluded as it was on the far side of town, he'd been unsettled with how the utilitarian chain-link fence seemed much more like the gateway to a prison than to an educational institution. But that was the least of his concerns now. By the time he'd pedaled them to the entrance, one of the men was locking the gate, then hopping into the van and heading up the long driveway toward Alicia's new home.

"Alicia!" Rex shouted, hopping off the pegs and grabbing the fence, shaking it to punctuate his anger. Leif joined him, passionately rattling the links as headlights briefly illuminated one side of the three-story school in the distance before the van disappeared behind it.

Alicia was gone.

"We gotta get in there, man!" Rex said, reaching up as if he was about to climb the fence.

"And then do what?" Leif asked. "Alicia's parents sent

her here. If we somehow get her out, they'll just send her back."

"But . . ." Rex still had both hands and one foot on the fence. "So that's it? We're just giving up on her?"

"I . . . I don't know," Leif said, wiping his wet cheeks, grateful for the cover of night. "Maybe."

"Aaaargh!" Rex shouted, pulling himself away from the fence and violently kicking at nothing. Save for the light from the lampposts on each side of the gate, darkness was all around them.

Leif stared down the shadowy driveway, feeling like his heart had been injured. It didn't seem real that he wouldn't see Alicia tomorrow. Or the next day. She was right there in that building, just a bike ride away, and yet she might as well have been on the other side of the globe. Or in Nebraska.

"We should probably get back," Rex said, seconds (or minutes?) later. "I don't want my parents to realize it's my punching bag in my bed and not me."

"You think they'd fall for that?"

"No. That's why I'm saying we should get back."

"Yeah." Leif flipped his kickstand, let Rex step up on the pegs, and started pedaling toward home. "My mom had an overnight shift, so . . . she's not even home yet. You want me to drop you off at your scooter?"

"Nah. I'll get it tomorrow."

They rode to Rex's house in silence.

"Hey, Leif," Rex said out of nowhere, and Leif had the funny thought that maybe Rex had read his mind, that he was about to tell Leif what a great couple he and Alicia would make someday. "Good call on the bike pegs."

Or not.

Leif nodded and kept pedaling.

3

IT HAD ONLY BEEN TWO DAYS, BUT JANINE BLITSTEIN WAS ALREADY tired of Bleak Creek.

Things that had seemed charming and quaint during her childhood summertime visits now seemed, at best, out of touch and, at worst, annoyingly backward. It completely boggled her mind that her mother had grown up here. Then again, her mom had left town as soon as she could, so in that way it made perfect sense.

It occurred to Janine why this trip felt so different: It was the first one she'd made on her own. Every other time, her parents had been there to offer their commentary, which, once she and her brother, Jared, were teenagers, was usually her mom railing against the patriarchy baked into Bleak Creek's churches or the xenophobia hidden beneath the town's folksy demeanor, and her dad—a Jewish guy from New Jersey—voicing his wry befuddlement at pretty much all of it. But now, a decade or so later, the only commentary was inside Janine's own head. Her eighty-one-year-old grandmother, GamGam, certainly wasn't providing any. Which left Janine in a constant state of feeling slightly insane. And lonely.

"Tell me more about the first kidney stone you remember," she said now, one eye on the lens of her camcorder, making sure that her grandmother was still framed well.

"Ooooohhhhh, honey, do I remember it!" GamGam said, leaning slightly forward in her floral chair. "Though, I'll tell ya, Neenie, I'd like to forget it!"

"Uh, don't use my name, GamGam," Janine said, standing up from behind the tripod. "Remember, just talk to me like I'm a stranger who's never been to Bleak Creek."

"Oh, I'm sorry, sweetheart. You've told me that goin' on a dozen times now. Guess I'm not used to bein' a big movie star yet." GamGam winked. "Now where was I . . . ?"

"That first stone." This was Janine's second interview with GamGam, and she felt considerably less enthused than she had yesterday during the first. But she knew that if she asked the right questions, she'd find what she was looking for: confirmation that this project—the reason she'd flown down here to stay with her grandmother for a couple weeks—was a brilliant idea.

"Oh right, my first stone," GamGam said. "I named it Mildred."

"You *named* it?"

"I name 'em all! Name 'em after people that did me wrong. But I tell ya, it never matters what I name 'em— they all hurt like the Devil!"

Nope. It didn't seem brilliant yet.

"I wouldn't wish stones on my worst enemies," Gam-Gam continued. "Except maybe Evelyn Barber, the one who spread a rumor that I was a Democrat. All I said was that I thought Bill Clinton was a good-lookin' man, which is true! He's what you might call . . . sexy." GamGam made a clicking sound with her mouth, her go-to way of accenting anything she considered particularly edgy. "But I'm still a Bush lady all the way."

"Yep, can't get too much Bush," Janine said for her own amusement. "How many people do you know in

Bleak Creek who regularly get kidney stones?" She was trying to keep the momentum of the interview going, but it felt like rolling a boulder up a hill.

"Hmm, let's see," GamGam said, staring at the popcorn ceiling. "There's me, there's Evelyn,"—she rolled her eyes—"Christine Neally, John Reed, Harriet Logan, Ted Yarbrough . . ." As the list went on, Janine had a sinking feeling in her stomach. She probably would've been better off asking GamGam to explain why she found Bill Clinton so sexy.

The idea for this project had come to her less than seventy-two hours earlier, while on the phone with her mom, who'd been worried about GamGam's recent struggles with gout. "Along with all the kidney stones she's had," Janine's mother had said, "it's made her doctor concerned about—"

"Wait," Janine interrupted. "Kidney *stones?* Plural? I thought it was just the one."

"No, she's passed eleven this year alone. We've told you this, sweetie." Janine hadn't visited Bleak Creek since finishing undergrad, but she was ashamed to think she'd tuned out vital information about her beloved grandmother's health.

"*Eleven* in *one year?* That's a ridiculous number of kidney stones."

"Well, it is and isn't," her mother said. "For Bleak Creek, that's not unusual."

"What the . . . ?"

"I know, right?" Her mom laughed. "Growing up there, I got so used to people passing kidney stones, I didn't even know it was weird until I left."

"Yeah. It's definitely weird, Mom."

"You remember GamGam's friend Rose?"

"Nosy Rosy? Of course."

"She passed thirty-one last year."

"*Thirty-one* kidney stones? That's, like, one every couple weeks!" Janine hadn't been this curious about anything in months. "What the hell is going on in that town, Mom? Like, seriously!"

And that's when the idea hit her:

What the hell is going on in that town?

"Oh, you're making it sound way more dramatic than it is," Janine's mother said, chuckling. "It's still just kidney stones."

Janine barely heard her, though, as her future documentary's title dropped into her brain, a gift from the muses after three epic months of creative roadblocks: *The Kidney Stoners.* A funny yet intriguing doc about her mom's small southern hometown, a place with a bizarre and unexplained proliferation of kidney stones. This could be her very own *Vernon, Florida,* the quirky, small-town film from her cinematic hero, Errol Morris. It was perfect. Within twenty-four hours, she and her RCA ProEdit camcorder were on a Continental Airlines flight headed from JFK to Raleigh, ready to make the film that would kickstart her career.

"So, I don't know," GamGam concluded. "How many people was that I just named? Maybe forty?"

Janine continued to zone out for a couple seconds before realizing her grandmother had stopped talking. "Yeah, forty sounds right," she said, having no clue. "Wow. Since kidney stones aren't, like, contagious, why do you think so many people here get them?"

"I don't know, Nee—I mean: I don't know, *ma'am.*" She winked again. "Guess it's just something in the water! Dr. Bob says perfectly healthy people can get kidney stones. He's had a bunch."

"What does this Dr. Bob say about people passing more than thirty a year?"

"That it's painful as all get-out!" GamGam laughed.

"Woo, boy, kidney stones are not a good time. Did I tell you yesterday what they feel like?"

"You did, yes. In great detail."

"But did I mention what it's like as they're comin' out of you?"

"Uh—" Janine heard a click on her camera. She'd reached the end of another tape. An act of mercy, really. "We'll have to get it next time, GamGam."

"Aw, nelly, I was just gettin' started!" She'd been speaking for ninety minutes.

As if struck by an epiphany, but the bad kind, Janine suddenly knew:

She'd made a terrible mistake.

Why she had thought talking to older women about their kidney stones would make for a cinematic master-piece was beyond her. Clearly, it wouldn't. Even Nosy Rosy, who Janine felt confident would be the linchpin of the whole movie, came up short in her interview last night, clamming up when the camera was aimed at her, offering limp gossip that would barely sustain a public access tele-vision show, let alone a critically acclaimed documentary. ("Harriet Logan doesn't actually have kidney stones," she'd said, her eyes wide. "It's just *gas*.")

As Janine's mom had said: *You're making it sound way more dramatic than it is.* That was always what Janine did, and she felt incredibly stupid that she was twenty-six years old and still hadn't learned to listen to her frigging mother. It was a bunch of old people with a lot of kidney stones. Big deal.

"Well, I gotta say, makin' movies is a whole lot of fun, Neenie," GamGam said, rising gingerly from her chair and hobbling over to the kitchen. "And I think people are gonna love this one. Especially Dr. Bob."

"Yeah," Janine said, taking the camera off the tripod

and placing it on the kitchen table. "I guess we'll see." Dr. Bob wasn't exactly her target audience.

"Hey, I keep meanin' to ask," GamGam said. "How's that boyfriend of yours?"

Janine froze.

GamGam had uncorked the painful truth Janine had been trying to avoid. The real reason she'd jumped at the chance to leave New York and ended up in this godforsaken town.

Dennis.

"Oh, uh . . . we broke up," Janine said, blinking her eyes repeatedly in an effort to not cry in front of her grandmother.

"Oh no," GamGam said. "Did that just happen?"

Janine nodded as she let the tears flow. She'd been dumped almost three months ago, which probably no longer qualified as "just happening," but it was too embarrassing to admit she was still this sad after so much time.

"I'm sorry, Neenie," GamGam said, walking toward her, even though it was obviously a strain to do so.

"No, no, don't overexert yourself, GamGam," Janine said. "Please, I'm fine. I'm really fine."

She wasn't fine.

The night before Janine's big idea had come to her, she'd run into Dennis at a mutual friend's party. He wasn't alone. He was with Lola Cavendish, the actress who had starred in his grad thesis film. To say it stung was an understatement.

Janine was crushed. Devastated. Furious.

When she'd met Dennis almost three years earlier, during their first year at NYU's grad film program, she'd instantly dismissed him (along with his leather jacket and purposely ripped jeans) as a pretentious, insecure wannabe, even as she'd objectively recognized that he was gorgeous. As the year progressed, she was exasperated to see Dennis become the crown jewel of their class, because Janine saw through him. She knew his films were just a hodgepodge of stolen references with no actual heart: a pinch of Godard here, a dash of Kubrick here, and a small sprinkle of Kurosawa for good measure. She'd diplomatically expressed this during a class critique, and the professor, the TA, and several classmates had practically bitten her head off.

Meanwhile, Janine's odd, original film projects—like her riff on Kafka's *Metamorphosis,* in which a woman woke up one day to find she was a kangaroo—were met with lukewarm smiles and head-scratching. It was maddening. By the end of her first year, Janine was seriously considering dropping out.

But then something strange happened: Dennis asked her out on a date.

She'd scoffed at first, assuming she was about to be the butt of one of his attention-grabbing jokes. But then Dennis had continued: "I really like your films. They're unique. And I like what you said about my work that day. It really got me thinking." Janine was skeptical, and conflicted. No good Riot Grrrl needed validation from a boy. But she couldn't help but be strangely flattered.

Dennis's charms eventually wore her down. Before long, they were inseparable. They became the class power couple, and Janine loved it. Soon she was ripping her own perfectly good jeans.

By the time their third year of school rolled around, Janine was deeply intertwined with Dennis, both producing *and* running camera for his thesis film, *The Boy Who Became a Man,* and already planning the production company the two of them would start after graduation. They would call it Dennine. Janine cringed just thinking about it now.

Their hard work had paid off, though, as the entire faculty thought Dennis's film was genius, the head of the department going so far as to pass it along to some hotshot agent friend, who loved it and wanted to meet with Dennis in L.A. immediately. Janine and Dennis had done it. They were on their way.

Or at least Dennis was. The week after they graduated, he'd flown to California alone, explaining to Janine that he thought it would make more sense to meet with this agent one-on-one first and fold her into the mix later. "Okay, that's fine," Janine had said, "but I can still come with you to L.A. and just not go to the meeting." "I don't know," Dennis had said, grimacing. "It just seems easier for me to do the trip alone." He'd been uncommunicative his entire week away, and the day he came back, he dumped Janine over the phone.

"What? Why?" Janine asked, completely blindsided.

"I just had so many good meetings this past week," Dennis said. "I don't really have time for a relationship right now."

"We can make this work," Janine said.

"I don't think we can," Dennis said. "Best of luck with whatever else you make, though."

"What about Dennine!"

He'd hung up.

Best of luck with whatever else you make, though. Almost two years together had gone up in smoke with that hideous sentence.

Janine fell into a deep depression. She couldn't write. She couldn't think. She could barely eat. She moved into a Chinatown apartment with one of her grad school friends and cycled through a series of mind-numbing temp jobs, simultaneously searching out and avoiding any and all gossip about what Dennis was up to. The more time went by, the more she realized that she actually hated his ostentatious films, and also that in dating him, she'd all but abandoned her own passion, her own creativity, her own voice.

She would have to get it back.

And that is exactly what she thought she was doing when she'd, at long last, had a new idea all her own and flown down to North Carolina to make it happen. A decision that, coincidentally or not, would also get her far away from a certain leather-jacketed asshole and the not-all-that-talented new girlfriend he seemed to have plenty of time for.

And a decision, just like her entire relationship, that was a mistake.

She would call Continental and figure out the next flight she could book home. "You were too smart for that boy anyway," GamGam said, pulling Janine out of her own head. "Plus, at your graduation I heard him say he didn't like *Smokey and the Bandit*."

Janine smiled in spite of herself. GamGam had no patience for anyone who didn't recognize the genius of Burt Reynolds.

"You're better off without him," she said as she opened the fridge and slowly took out a plate of fried chicken.

"Yeah, I think you're right," agreed Janine, ashamed that she was still having trouble convincing herself of that.

The doorbell rang.

"Oh," GamGam said as she walked the chicken over to the table. "Would you mind getting that? It's your cousin."

"Donna?" Janine asked, seized by the sudden urge to go hide in the guest room.

"You got other cousins livin' in this town I don't know about?"

"Oh yeah, thousands," Janine deadpanned. "Aunt Roberta's poppin' 'em out all the time. But I just— You could have told me she was coming."

"Well," GamGam whispered, "guess I didn't wanna give you time to find a way out of it." She gave one of her trademark mouth clicks as the doorbell rang again. "Coming, Donna dear!" she shouted before returning to a whisper. "Neenie. Go get the door, please."

As GamGam well knew, Janine had been hoping to postpone any interactions with Donna for as long as possible. She could imagine few things more awkward and uncomfortable than spending time with her cousin.

"You're being ridiculous," GamGam said. "Donna can't even stay long. She's just sayin' hey real quick 'cause you're in town."

Janine sighed. She *was* being kind of ridiculous. She stepped out of the kitchen and into the living room, weaving her way past the floral chair and the plastic-covered couch toward the front door.

It hadn't always been this way.

When Janine and her family had made yearly visits while she was growing up, Donna—who was two years older—had been Janine's best friend, her role model, the funniest, weirdest, most creative person she knew. It was Donna who had sparked Janine's interest in film in the first place, ringleading their operation to slink into the now-shuttered drive-in movie theater to see movies definitely not intended for preadolescents. She remembered lying on the grass in the dark next to cars that were leaking the most sound (convertibles were a gold mine), staring wide-eyed as a teenage prom queen was doused in pig's blood in *Carrie,* and gritting her teeth as she saw Marlon Brando in *Apocalypse Now* utter "the horror . . . the horror" before succumbing to machete wounds. Those images were seared in her young mind, planting in her a desire to tell her own stories on screen one day.

Soon after, the two of them started making their own movies with Donna's Super 8 camera, a series of silent shorts called The Gnome Girls. Donna would make huge dialogue title cards on posterboard, regularly slipping in witty surprise messages just to crack Janine up. She also taught Janine how to sew costumes, how to authentically walk like a gnome, how to craft elaborate dioramas out of grass and random objects that when shot from the right angle looked like a vast, fantastical forest. She was amazing.

But when Janine visited town the summer after ninth grade, that all changed. Donna was notably quiet and withdrawn. Moody, even. She wanted nothing to do with Janine, and Janine had no idea why. They'd always sent each other hilarious letters during the year; maybe one of Donna's had gotten lost in the mail, leaving her waiting in frustration for a response from Janine that had never come?

When Janine worked up the nerve to ask Donna if this was the case, or if she'd offended her in some other way, Donna had just said, "No," before retreating into her room and closing the door. Janine was relieved, then instantly wrecked. Because if she hadn't done anything wrong, it meant she was simply not cool enough for her older cousin anymore. Maybe she'd never been. The feeling of rejection was new and all-consuming. And painful.

It only got worse the following year, when Janine received the awful news that Donna's dad, Uncle Jim, had died in a car accident. At the funeral, Donna was understandably as closed off as ever, and though Janine had made a few fumbling attempts at reaching out in the months and years that followed, she'd long since accepted the truth: She and Donna would always be cousins, but they would never again be friends.

And now she found herself looking at the door, her once-close cousin standing on the other side. No part of her wanted to open it, but she took a breath and did it anyway.

"Hey, Donna," Janine said.

"Hey."

It was hard for Janine to connect the person in front of her to the radiant human she'd once idolized. Donna had what seemed to be permanent dark circles under her eyes, and her deep brown hair—once lustrous and so long that it reached her waist—was unwashed, choppy, possibly self-cut. It was parted in the middle and hung down the sides of her face to her chin, giving the constant impression that Donna was hiding from something. Her loose-fitting flannel shirt and baggy jeans only added to that effect. She did not look well.

"It's great to see you," Janine said.

"Yeah," Donna said, staring at the ground. "You too."

For the first time in twelve years, Janine didn't feel angered or hurt by her cousin. She just felt bad for her. She wanted to give her a hug but wasn't sure how that would go over. "Come on in," she said instead.

Donna nodded and shuffled past her. "Hi, GamGam," she said as their grandmother met her in the middle of the room.

"Hi, Donna dear," GamGam said, kissing her on the cheek and wrapping her up in a big hug that made Janine regret not following her own impulse. "Oh, my two little granddaughters, all grown up and standin' in my livin' room together. Y'all have no idea how happy this makes me."

Janine felt an unexpected wave of emotion. They'd shot one of their Gnome Girls shorts in this very room, GamGam making a brief but memorable cameo as the Gnome Queen. Janine wanted to bring it up, but much like the hug, she didn't know how.

"Take a seat, girls," GamGam said. "I'll bring the chicken over."

"I'll get it," Janine said, concerned for her grandmother but also not wanting to have any alone time with Donna, who had already deposited herself onto the couch.

"Nonsense." GamGam slowly hobbled toward the kitchen table. "I need the exercise. I've been sittin' for my close-up all mornin'."

The plastic covering on the couch crinkled as Janine took a seat next to Donna, who was staring straight ahead at nothing in particular.

"So," Janine said. "Been a while."

"Yeah," Donna said. She seemed to be biting her nails, though Janine didn't know for sure since Donna's hands were concealed in her sleeves.

"What's . . . Uh, what have you been up to?"

Donna thought for a long moment before answering. "Not much. Work."

"Oh, cool. GamGam said you're still at Li'l Dino's, right?"

"Yeah." It seemed to be the main word in Donna's vocabulary.

"Great, great," Janine said. "Has their pizza gotten any better?" When they were kids, they'd joked constantly about how horrible it was.

Donna looked at her for the first time since she arrived. "Better than what?" she asked, completely serious.

"Oh, I don't know," Janine said. This conversation was somehow even more excruciating than she'd anticipated. "Better than it used to be."

"I don't really eat the pizza much," Donna said, turning away.

"Excellent," Janine said, nodding to herself. "Glad we've got that all sorted out."

"It's chicken time!" GamGam said as she placed the

plate of cold leftovers on the small table near them. "Eat up, my little chickadees."

Janine wanted to point out how gruesome it was to imagine little birds feasting on a chicken, but, once again, she didn't think it was the right audience. She grabbed a drumstick.

"You like dark meat. Just like me," GamGam said proudly.

"Twins," Janine said as she took a bite.

Donna took the smallest wing.

"See? Puttin' that plastic to good use!" GamGam said, pointing at the couch they were dropping crumbs on before grabbing a drumstick and lowering herself into the floral chair.

The room was quiet except for their chewing.

"So I went to film school," Janine said. "Did you know that, Donna?"

"GamGam said that, yeah." Janine had been hoping to see a flicker of something in Donna, but it was as if Janine had referenced a trip to the dentist. She was at a loss for what else to say. She was very ready to be back in New York.

"It's been wonderful havin' Neenie in town again," GamGam said. "She's makin' a movie, just like you girls used to do. You remember those, Donna?"

Donna shrugged.

"Oh, you must, dearie," GamGam said. "You two were always runnin' around here with cameras on your shoulders, causin' a ruckus. Just like those kids at the pig pickin' yesterday. That was a real mess!"

"What happened?" Janine asked, eager to talk about anything other than The Gnome Girls.

"Oh! Most excitin' thing all summer! Yes sir, poor Mr. Whitewood ended up at the ER . . ."

"I need to get to work," Donna said, jumping to her

feet like the couch had shocked her. Janine felt a palpable sense of relief. She didn't care what Li'l Dino's pizza tasted like these days; in that moment, she felt immense gratitude for its existence.

"It was great to see you," Janine said, rising from the couch to say goodbye.

"Now, hold on a sec," GamGam said. "I just thought of somethin', Neenie. You should get a ride with Donna over to Li'l Dino's with your camera, get some footage for your movie."

"Oh," Janine said as her insides screamed *GOD, NO!* "I don't think that's necessa—"

"No, listen," GamGam said, her voice rising and speeding up in that way it did when she got excited. "Big Gary—he's the owner over there—he just passed a coupla kidney stones last week! And they ain't his first. He'd be a perfect interview!"

Janine didn't have the heart to explain that in the last half hour, she'd more or less scrapped the entire project. Donna, meanwhile, was just standing there, her shoulders slightly hunched.

"Okay GamGam," said Janine. "Maybe I'll stop by there tomorr—"

"I haven't even gotten to the best part," GamGam interrupted. "He saves all his stones, Neenie! He's got 'em in a jar right there in the restaurant. Isn't that right, Donna?"

Donna stared, then gave a slight nod.

"Now *that's* somethin' you need in your movie!" GamGam concluded triumphantly.

Janine sort of wanted to throw up, both at the idea of a bunch of kidney stones in a jar and at the predicament she'd found herself in. "Um . . ."

"I'm sure Donna wouldn't mind givin' you a ride, right?"

"Yeah," Donna said, which made it sound like she *did* mind, but GamGam wasn't having it.

"Great! You girls go, have a fun time together."

Janine really didn't want to, but she saw the earnest, hopeful look on GamGam's face and knew she had no choice. "Um, okay, I guess that works," she said, a hard knot forming in her chest as she followed Donna toward the door. This would be the last destination on her Failed Kidney Stone World Tour. Fifteen minutes at Li'l Dino's and then she'd get out of this town as fast as she could.

"Wait!" GamGam shouted. "Your camera!"

"Oh, right," Janine said. She grabbed her camcorder off the table and zipped it into its case. "Thanks, Gam-Gam. This should be a blast."

"I'll say!" GamGam raised her drumstick in the air and shook it like a maraca.

By the time Janine stepped outside, Donna was already in the car.

4

REX AND LEIF SAT ACROSS FROM ONE ANOTHER IN SILENCE, EACH perched on his own rock on a tiny island in the middle of the Cape Fear River. They'd been coming to this place for a couple years now, ever since their parents had given them permission to visit the river without supervision.

This miniature isle, with its natural privacy from the low roar of the nearby rapids, was the setting for many of the most significant moments in their friendship. It was here that Rex had shown Leif the calendar he'd found in his grandfather's garage, entitled "Snow Bunnies," featuring women wearing mittens, scarves, and nothing else. It was here that they'd discussed whether or not Matthew Jenkins was going to Hell because he believed in evolution. And it was here that they had first conceptualized their now-very-much-in-question masterwork, *PolterDog*.

The idea they once could not shut up about was now the reason for their silence. They didn't remember who had first suggested making the movie, which was both comforting and frustrating, as it left them to share the blame for Alicia's current predicament.

Leif had slept a total of forty-two minutes the night before. After he'd dropped Rex off and returned to his empty home just past two, he'd lain in bed, eyes open, as still as a corpse, his mind cycling through the events of the past day, Alicia's voice the looping soundtrack: *Rex! Leif!*

Helmmmphsseh! At one point, he'd found himself whispering aloud, "I'm racked with guilt!" This habit of vocalizing inner thoughts was something he'd developed the year before while memorizing vocabulary words for eighth grade English. He wondered if there was any other situation in which one could use the word "racked"? Could you say that you're *racked* with happiness? Or donuts? It seemed like you should be able to, but Leif didn't think he'd ever heard it used that way. He'd then realized he was casually questioning word usage while his best friend and secret crush was trapped in a creepy reform school, which made him feel even more guilty and ashamed. This pattern continued for hours. It was a long night.

Rex had fared better, his sleep logging in at three hours and fifty-one minutes. Though a part of him may also have been guilt-racked, most of him was angry. Angry at the Boykinses, angry at Mr. Whitewood and his stupid school, angry at himself. After Leif had dropped him off at home, he'd peeked into his parents' bedroom and found them both snoring loudly. Good. They hadn't noticed he was gone. Rex had then gotten into bed, not even bothering to remove the human-sized punching bag that had been his sleeping substitute. In fact, he'd begun to punch it. And kick it. And scream under his breath at it. When he'd abruptly realized how idiotic it was to pummel a punching bag while lying in bed next to it, he'd jumped up and walked out the front door, figuring his parents would be out cold for at least another five hours.

Rex had walked the streets of Bleak Creek, reliving Alicia's abduction and their failed attempt to save her. He'd stopped when he'd reached his destination: the bush he had left his scooter beneath. It wasn't the right bush. The one next to it hadn't been right, either. "Come on!" Rex had shouted angrily to no one.

After nearly an hour of fumbling blindly beneath

bushes, he'd finally found his scooter, by which point the fury of searching for it so long had commingled with the Alicia fury to create a sort of superfury.

Rex had channeled that into his scooting. He'd powered down street after street, this time with no clear destination, thinking only one thing: *Work that scooter leg.* If it had been up to snuff earlier, maybe they would have caught up to the van. Maybe Alicia would be with them right now. Rex wasn't sure how long he'd rage-scooted, but by the time the sky started to turn purple, the first sunlight peering past the horizon, he knew he was exhausted. He'd gone home and fallen asleep seconds after his head hit the pillow.

"Do you think she's gonna be okay?" Leif asked now, not looking up at Rex, who was sitting on the larger of the two rocks on the river island. Last year, they had established a conversational system in which the person sitting on the smaller rock could only ask questions, while the person on the larger rock could offer answers or original thoughts. It seemed cool at the time, but had since become a bit of an unnecessary hindrance to communication.

"Yeah, definitely," Rex said, staring out across the river. "She's Alicia. She's unbreakable."

"But what about the kids who . . . died?" Leif hadn't wanted to think about, much less talk about, the three kids who had passed away at the school since it opened in the late seventies.

"Those were accidents," Rex said. "Kids being where they shouldn't. Freak mishaps. Alicia is the least accident-prone person I know. That's the last thing we should worry about."

Leif nodded, trying his best to let Rex's certitude comfort him. It only half worked. "Okay, but even if she's safe, how do we know she won't . . . change?"

The Whitewood School was known to be very intense and very effective in its reform mission, but there were conflicting reports about what actually happened inside. What Leif and Rex both knew well, though, was that pretty much every single kid who had gone there had come back . . . altered. Tommy Dowd had been sent to Whitewood in fifth grade when, during career day at Bleak Creek Elementary, he'd snuck into Anna Coleman's dad's police cruiser—which Officer Coleman had been proudly showing off to the kids—and blasted a cassette of N.W.A.'s "Fuck tha Police" on the car speakers. When Tommy came back four months later, he was no longer listening to N.W.A., but he also never really did anything else interesting. Two years ago, Katie McQueen had been taken to Whitewood after calling her mother a bitch in front of several customers at Loretta's Beauty Salon. It didn't matter that her mother was widely known to fit that description perfectly; Katie went away for an eight-month stint at Whitewood. After getting out, she always respected her mother, but the once-gutsy girl was now just compliant.

"I mean," Rex said, ignoring the shiver running down his spine, "at the end of the day, it's still just, like, a school. Maybe the teachers are stricter, but . . . she'll still be, like, learning stuff. Just in a different location." He knew his words reeked of denial.

Leif thought of Alicia losing her Alicia-ness and his eyes filled with tears. He quickly turned his head away, pretending to inspect the water rushing past them. Even in his fake watching, he couldn't help but observe a decomposing leaf float by, following it with his eyes until it disappeared into the mild rapids below them.

As his eyes returned to his towering best friend on the Big Rock, lost in his own river gazing, it occurred to Leif that it might feel good to tell Rex about his profound crush on Alicia. Sure, it wasn't the same as telling *her,* but it was a way to get it off his chest, and he knew Rex would probably have wise insights. "You know what you need to do?" Rex might say. "Write her an epic love poem." And Leif would say, "Good idea, thanks." And Rex would say, "No problem, that's why I'm here." And Leif would smile and feel okay for a moment.

Of course, this was all impossible because Leif was sitting on the Small Rock. They needed to switch places.

"Hey, man," Leif said, beginning to stand, "I—"

"I've got something funny to tell you," Rex interrupted.

Leif sat back down.

"You'll probably think this is weird," Rex continued.

Leif decided he could momentarily deal with the interruption. Rex's stories that started this way never disappointed.

"So . . ." Rex said. "When we were shooting at the fundraiser . . . No, actually, *before* we started shooting at the fundraiser . . . Like, while we were preparing to start shooting, you guys on one side and me on the other, I was, um . . . I was looking through the camera to frame Alicia, and I just, like . . . really noticed her lips. Like *really* noticed them."

Leif stared at Rex, expressionless.

"I know, I know," Rex said, feeling completely insecure. "I told you it might be weird. But . . . I mean, I don't know. If she wasn't just, you know, taken away or whatever, I probably would have ignored that moment or forgot all about it. But now that she's gone, I just feel like . . . I think I have a crush on Alicia. As of yesterday. I know it's weird. But, I mean . . . *is* it weird?" Rex caught himself violating the Big Rock rule of no questions. "I mean, I'd like to know if you think it's weird."

Leif felt frozen, unable to fully process what he'd just heard. From the word "lips" onward, he'd plunged into some kind of out-of-body experience, as if he were suddenly underwater, staring up at Rex from a great distance. And desperate for oxygen.

"Yeah, I knew you'd think it was weird," Rex said, shaking his head.

The words brought reality crashing back to Leif, whooshing him up into himself again. He blinked and adjusted his glasses as he tried to think.

Rex *also* had a crush on Alicia.

As of a day ago.

This was a painfully unfair turn of events.

Leif started to speak but was barely able to form a word. "I—"

"Let's go to the Tree," Rex said, standing up, then stepping off the island and steadying himself in the knee-deep water. He was feeling embarrassed and wanted a change of scenery.

Leif remained paralyzed. Why did Rex get to confess his crush first? He hadn't even let him sit on the Big Rock at all! And Leif was the one who'd been grappling with his crush for at least a month. His feelings had actual *substance*—it wasn't just about one time when he liked looking at Alicia's lips. Geez!

Rex turned his head. "You comin'?"

Leif slowly stood up, almost involuntarily beginning to follow Rex to the giant tree they'd found two summers ago, a hardwood so enormous that Rex, Leif, and Alicia couldn't hold hands around it. They checked every time the three of them visited to see how close they were getting. Just a week ago they were still one foot short.

Leif carefully worked his way through the river, which was never more than waist-deep at this spot during late summer. He caught up to Rex as they reached the silty bank, even in his stupor still keeping an eye out for the moccasins that loved to bask along the water's edge.

As they began to walk into the woods lining the river, Rex noticed that Leif wasn't okay.

"Look," Rex said. "I know there are things about Alicia you find super annoying, so you probably could never imagine her this way, but—"

"No, I could," Leif said, sensing an opening. "I really could."

"Oh, you could?" Rex asked, surprised.

Leif's heartbeat quickened. Here it was. For better or worse, they were both going to lay it all out there. "Yeah," he said. "I could." His whole body tensed as he waited for Rex's response.

"Thanks, man," Rex finally said, putting a hand on Leif's shoulder. "Thanks for supporting me like that and not thinking it's weird. Even if Alicia does really irritate you sometimes."

Wait! No! For weeks, Leif had been imagining the joyful moment when Rex would give his blessing to the Leif and Alicia coupling, and now somehow it was Leif giving a blessing to *him*? Everything was spinning out of control. He had to undo this.

"Not that it even matters," Rex said. "Since Alicia is off at Whitewood. Man, it sucks so much. We can stop talking about this, but thanks, dude. Telling you that felt, I don't know . . . freeing or something."

"Um," Leif said. "Wait, we can . . . Uh, let's talk about it a little more."

"Really?" Rex said. "I didn't thi—" He stopped midsentence, his head pivoting sharply to the right. "Did you hear that?"

"Hear what?"

"I thought I heard a twig snap." Rex scanned the area with laser focus.

"I didn't hear anything," Leif said, his sleepless body already exhausted from the waterlogged walk to the Tree, which was now only thirty or so feet away. He wondered if Rex's sudden concern with a snapping twig was just another case of him employing his sophisticated subject-changing tactics. "Might have been a raccoon or something."

"Raccoons are nocturnal," Rex said.

As they emerged into the small clearing that surrounded the ancient hardwood, they immediately noticed something different since last visiting the Tree. There were branches leaning against the oversized trunk, covered in mud and leaves, making a crude shelter. In front of the lean-to, a ring of rocks surrounded a fire that had only recently died, red-hot coals still glinting. Beside the fire, on a flat rock, lay a freshly peeled squirrel skin.

Rex and Leif knew that deer hunters used these woods alongside the river, but this didn't look like any deer blind they'd seen, and they were pretty sure hunting season was still at least a month away. This was someone's . . . *home*.

They looked at each other, instinctively knowing not to speak.

Rex slowly walked toward the shelter, Leif wildly but silently expressing his disapproval of his friend's decision to investigate. There appeared to be a collection of belongings under the leafy roof, and Rex figured they held clues as to the identity of this mysterious forest-dweller.

He knelt down at the mouth of the shelter.

"Halt!" a squeaky voice shouted from behind them. They turned their heads to see a boy, probably close to their age. His face was covered in dirt, and he was barefoot, though you may have first thought he was wearing brown shoes given the mud that caked his toes. The only thing unsoiled was his lightning-blond hair, giving him an almost angel-like appearance. He had some sort of animal pelt—maybe rabbit, maybe possum—over his shoulders. In one hand he held a homemade spear, and in the other, a stick skewering a half-eaten squirrel carcass. He took a step forward, his wooden spear not exactly pointed at them, but not exactly *not* pointed at them either.

"Step away from my stuff," the wild boy commanded.

"Okay, no problem," Rex said, trying to hide the fear in his voice with a forced smile.

Leif took in for the first time the dull brown jumpsuit the boy was wearing. Or maybe it was once white. He also noticed a ragged, bloody bandage on the boy's hand, the one holding the squirrel kebab.

Rex didn't recognize the boy, which was odd, as everybody in Bleak Creek knew everybody in Bleak Creek. Especially everybody their own age.

"Uh, what are you doing out here? Hunting?" Rex convinced himself to ask.

"Well, this squirrel didn't impale itself on my spear. So yeah, hunting is one thing I'm doing," the boy answered, his eyes slowly moving between them. "Better question: What are *you* doing out here?"

"Uh, we were just leaving, actually," Leif said, convinced they'd crossed paths with a psychopath capable of killing more than just squirrels. "Sorry to bother you." He began to walk around the boy, who sidestepped to block his escape.

"I asked you a question," the boy said, his spear definitely pointing at Leif now.

"We come to this tree a lot," Rex said, trying to ease the tension.

"I can see why. This is an impressive specimen," the boy said. "White ash."

"Yep," Rex said after a pause.

Leif backed up, joining Rex at his side, then took an additional step in order to put his larger friend in between him and the spear wielder.

"You didn't know it was a white ash, did you?" the boy asked.

"We came here about a week ago," Rex said, ignoring the boy's question. "You weren't here."

"I was somewhere else."

"Are you, like, living out here?"

"I'm not dying."

"What about your hand?" Rex asked. "Seems like you might not be dying, but you're definitely getting hurt."

For the first time, the wild boy seemed unsure of himself as he briefly looked down at his bandaged hand. "Oh. That was from before."

"What was before?" Rex asked.

The boy looked around, including once over each shoulder, even though there was nothing surrounding them except trees and mosquitoes. He took another step forward, and, lowering his voice, said, "Can I trust you?"

Rex and Leif looked at each other and began a slow nod, not quite sure which of them was initiating their response, then let out a collective "Yes."

"I heard you say your friend is at Whitewood," the boy said.

Rex felt a flash of embarrassment, wondering how much of their conversation he had heard.

"I know things about that place. Your friend's in a lot of danger."

The boy's words hung in the air between them.

"What kind of danger?" Leif asked, his worry for Alicia suddenly doubling, momentarily eclipsing his concern for himself.

"Not sure I can tell you."

The boy raised his squirrel-on-a-stick and took a healthy bite, ripping a chunk of dark meat from one of the rear legs. He chewed it slowly, beginning to pace in an arc around them.

"I'll tell you what. If you can do something for me, I'll say what I know about the school."

"Okay," Rex said slowly.

Leif hoped he wasn't about to ask them to kill another squirrel. But he thought he could do it. For Alicia.

"Bring me a rake," the boy said matter-of-factly. Rex looked around. The ground around the Tree was mostly clear, a mix of dirt, moss, and patches of grass. Grooming it seemed unnecessary, but he didn't think this was the time to question the boy's reasoning.

"And a pack of hot dogs, three cans of Cheerwine. And a fire extinguisher. The carbon dioxide kind."

"Are you messing with us?" Rex asked.

"Do I look like the kind of person who messes with people?"

Rex declined to answer.

"You bring those things to me, I tell you what I know."

"Can't you get those things yourself?" Rex asked.

"Would I be living like a caveman in the woods if I could just stroll into the Piggly Wiggly?" the boy answered.

"All right. We'll get you what you're asking for," Rex said.

Leif shot appalled eyes at Rex. "Uh, we really should be getting back," he said. "It'll be dark soon." It wouldn't be dark for hours.

"Okay," the boy said as he took another bite of squirrel, though it seemed mostly for effect, as he came away with little to no meat. "I believe our business here is done anyway."

Rex stuck out his hand. "It was nice to meet you, uh . . ."

"Ben. The name's Ben."

"Nice to meet you, Ben."

"Likewise." Ben dropped the spear to his side, letting the blunt end rest on the ground, and extended his non-bandaged but still dirty hand, grabbing Rex's.

Leif was already backing away, hoping to avoid a handshake and wondering why Rex had found one necessary.

"Don't tell anyone I'm out here, or I'll have to kill you," Ben added, thrusting his spear toward them and winking.

It seemed like a joke and also not a joke.

Nobody laughed.

5

"CANDIDATUS," THE UNSMILING WOMAN AT THE FRONT OF THE classroom said.

She was staring directly at Alicia.

The woman wore a collared blouse, along with a skirt that struck just below the knee, revealing skin-colored hose several shades darker than her pale face. Her modest, fashion-backward style was not unlike what Alicia would expect to see on a teacher at Bleak Creek High School, the place she had been planning to start ninth grade in only a matter of days. There was one notable difference, though: Every article of clothing was a uniform beige. Even the woman's shoes. Her outfit alone was strange enough, but even more unsettling was how the woman blended in with the classroom itself, as its walls, floor, and ceiling were all painted the same shade of lifeless yellowish brown.

"Candidatus," she said again, this time overly pronouncing each consonant, the final, aggressive syllable rhyming with the word *moose*.

Was Alicia supposed to respond? She nodded, sitting up straight in her seat, giving the woman her undivided attention, but it didn't seem to be enough. Maybe somewhere in that depressing, barely furnished dorm room she'd been hurled into last night—every surface that now familiar beige—there was a student handbook that explained stuff like this. If so, she definitely hadn't found it.

She'd been too busy lying in that sad excuse for a bed—just stiff sheets laid over what felt more like a piece of plywood than a mattress—trying to sleep instead of crying, all the while doing her best to avoid eye contact with the only thing that broke the room's sad color scheme: a portrait of Mr. Whitewood that hung on the wall opposite her bed, reminding her of what she'd done to get herself here. It looked like the pictures she'd seen of Joseph Stalin in her world history book, complete with a similar non-smile and faraway look.

The woman continued to stare.

"Sorry," Alicia said. "I don't know . . ."

"You don't know *what*?" The woman jabbed the air with her words.

Alicia used her peripheral vision to survey the students in her immediate vicinity, hoping to find a helpful face, anyone who might throw her a line. There was no one. Every head was forward, all eyes glued to the teacher. That was more disturbing than the woman herself.

"I didn't know if you wanted me to respond," Alicia said.

"I'm looking right at you saying your name and you didn't know if you should respond?" The woman's face remained stern, but in her eyes was a trace of playfulness not unlike a cat's gaze as it toys with a mouse.

Alicia was confused. "Um," she said. "My name is Alic—"

"Your name," the woman barked, "is Candidatus. The same as every other student in this building. The name that Headmaster gave you. Isn't that right, Candidatus?" She stared at a short blond boy in the front row, who looked to be several years younger than Alicia. The class, she realized, was filled with kids of all ages. Were they all going to be taught the same material?

"Yes, Helper," the short blond boy said.

"You see?" the woman said, her head swiveling back to Alicia, who noticed the light reflecting off a silver pin—an upside-down seven-pointed star—attached to the woman's collar. She suddenly realized she recognized the woman. Alicia had seen her at the jewelry store next to the Twin Plaza movie theater.

"Do you think you and you alone deserve a different name?" she asked.

"No, ma'am," Alicia said, trying to demonstrate how quickly she was catching on.

"I am not 'ma'am.' I am Headmaster's helper. Do you understand?"

"Yes, um, Helper," Alicia said, recognizing the similarity to Hamburger Helper but not daring to laugh.

"Good. Do you think you can do whatever you desire in this world?" the woman asked.

"No, Helper."

"Do you think you know better than Headmaster?"

"No, Helper."

"Do you think your curly hair makes you unique? Special?" She spit out the last two words as if they were swears.

"No, Helper," Alicia said, even though the weirdness of this question caught her off-guard. And even though this, like her other answers, wasn't the truth. She loved her hair.

"Good, Candidatus," the helper said. "Headmaster would be very pleased."

Alicia held eye contact and ignored the itch on her shoulder from the scratchy, ill-fitting beige jumpsuit she'd been forced to wear, the same one every kid had on. She was just three minutes into her first class—if that's what you would even call this—and she already hated it here.

Not that she'd thought she would enjoy it, but she'd still been allowing for the possibility that maybe it could be good for her. That maybe she deserved it.

But no, this awful woman with her shoulder-length black hair who seemed like she could be one of Alicia's mom's friends, except missing a soul, left no doubt: This experience would not be good. If the blank faces on all sides were any indication, it was going to be very, very bad.

She couldn't believe her parents had actually sent her away.

"I know what you did, Candidatus," the helper said, eyes still locked on Alicia, "and it disgusts me."

"I'm sorry," Alicia said. She wondered how long this interrogation would last, how long she would be in this room. She had no sense of the day's schedule, which she suspected was by design. It was disorienting enough going to school on a Sunday, but as she'd learned from her roommate that morning—the only thing the freckled preteen had said to her—there were no weekends at the Whitewood School. Occasionally the students were given break periods, but they came without warning. And they would end just as suddenly as they'd begun.

"*Sorry,*" the helper said, finally looking away to address the entire class. "She says *sorry*. You should know, Candidati, *this* is the student who burned Headmaster."

The students quietly gasped. Alicia looked down at her desk, her face hot. It was becoming abundantly clear that her innocent tumble into Mr. Whitewood wasn't just disrespectful. It was blasphemous.

"Don't look down!" the helper barked at Alicia. "You look at me when I'm talking about you."

"Sorry, sorry," Alicia said, her head snapping up.

"Stop saying *sorry*!" It was a full-on scream, the woman's dark hair temporarily losing its shape as her voice shook. She composed herself, seeming to recognize that she'd lost control. "I don't need you to *say* it, I need you to *feel* it. I need to *see* it in your actions. I need to know that you will never disappoint Headmaster. That you will never again bring Headmaster harm."

"I will not disappoint or harm Headmaster, Helper," Alicia said, willing the tears in her eyes not to drop as she registered how ridiculous this conversation was. For the first time that morning, she allowed herself to think about Rex and Leif, to wonder what their take on all this would be. She knew how horrible they were probably feeling, and it gave her some comfort to know they were likely, even at this very moment, coming up with some ludicrous plot to save her. Probably sitting on those stupid rocks.

But she also knew there was no way they'd be able to pull it off. And even if they did, her parents would just send her right back.

"This is embarrassing for us," her mother had said in June, as Alicia had sat on her bed, staring a hole through the Salt-N-Pepa poster on her wall. Both of her parents had paced around, taking turns lecturing her for pulling down the pants of five mannequins earlier that day.

"Do you understand how this looks?" her dad had said. Alicia did understand. It looked like a teenage girl doing a mischievous prank you'd normally associate with a preschooler. The truth was, it had been an impulsive and cathartic expression of rage, her response to being left out—yet again—by the people who claimed to be her best friends. But Alicia knew the truth wouldn't help much with easing her parents' anger.

"It looks like you're a bad kid, Alicia," her dad continued. "But we know you're not a bad kid. You're a good kid."

"Can't I be both?" Alicia asked, sort of kidding, but also not.

That had stopped her parents cold. Her dad took slow steps toward her, which is when Alicia started to get scared. "You think this is a joke?"

"No," Alicia said.

"How many times do we have to talk about this? This town's hard enough on kids as it is, but you . . . *you* have to be extra careful."

"I know, Dad." This wasn't the first time he'd reminded her that in Bleak Creek, having a black father and white mother (not to mention being a girl with zero interest in acting like a young lady) meant that she would never be given the same margin of error as the other kids in town. She understood where he was coming from—she had watched how hard her father had worked to project strength and pride, even in the face of the whispered comments and snide remarks—but it was still exhausting to be on her best behavior every second of every day.

"Good. Because, Alicia, we're torn up about this. And we're not sure grounding you is working anymore." Her dad looked at her mother, who nodded after a moment, then stared out the window. "We didn't want to tell you this, but your mother and I have even started talking about . . . the Whitewood School."

Alicia internally shuddered as she looked to her mom, who again nodded solemnly. "Because of some pantsed mannequins?"

"It's not just that," her dad said. "It's your whole . . . attitude lately. Always talking back, rolling your eyes at everything we say. Or else you're holed up in your room, listening to that Nervous band . . ."

"Nirvana, Dad."

"Even worse," her mother said.

"What's wrong with Mariah Carey?" her dad asked.

"Or Amy Grant?" her mom added.

"Do you really think Nirvana made me pull down mannequin pants?"

"This is what I'm talking about!" her dad said, exasperated. "That tone!"

"And your little sister looks up to you so much," Alicia's mom said. "What if Melissa starts getting these same sorts of ideas?" Alicia knew her parents were using that as an excuse; her sister rarely crossed any lines, and when she did, it wasn't unusual to find her in her room praying for forgiveness.

"Okay," Alicia said. She respected her parents enough to take the threat seriously, though she still assumed they were bluffing. After all, pretty much every parent in Bleak Creek threatened to send their kids to Whitewood at some point. Alicia had always thought that was kind of the main reason the school existed at all. Like the hundreds of times her mom had said she was "going to go get the wooden spoon" if Alicia didn't stop some particular misdeed. She'd never seen her mom use that wooden spoon for anything other than stirring her infamous fifteen-bean soup, which her dad had always secretly called "ruptured spleen" soup due to its legendary gastrointestinal consequences.

What she wouldn't do for a spoonful of her mom's ruptured spleen soup now.

"Candidatus." The helper was suddenly very close to Alicia's face. "If I catch you daydreaming again, you're going to the Roll."

Alicia almost said sorry before remembering not to and simply nodding instead. She guessed the Roll was considerably less fun than this classroom, although it did sound like a ride she'd wait an hour to get on at the State Fair.

"Now, can you tell me what this sign says?" The woman walked back up to the front of the room and gestured to the wall behind her, which was mostly bare—not even a chalkboard—except for a portrait of Mr. Whitewood just like the one in Alicia's dorm room and a large white piece of paper with one word painted in red letters.

"Follow," Alicia said quietly.

"I can't hear you," the helper said.

"Follow!" Alicia shouted, finally accessing some of her rage.

"That's right, Candidatus. *Follow.* If you stick to this simple advice, you will do just fine here. If you don't . . . Well, I wouldn't advise that."

Alicia nodded again, though she no longer felt like crying. Igniting her anger had been helpful. It simmered in her chest, reminding her who she was. She thought again of Rex and Leif, and she suddenly knew where they'd stand on all this: They'd be terrified. Rex might be a little better at hiding it, but neither of them would stand up to the helper.

In the triumvirate, confrontation had always been Alicia's thing. Unlike Rex and Leif, she actually loved a good fight, mostly because it helped her deal with feeling stuck between the two worlds that her parents represented, two worlds that remained remarkably separated in Bleak Creek. Screw trying to fit in. She'd decided years ago that the easiest way to counteract ostracism was to stand out as much as possible. It still hurt to never feel completely at home, but at least she'd become pretty damn good at sticking up for herself.

So, no, Alicia decided: She wasn't going to *Follow,* and she wasn't going to wait for her best friends to rescue her, either. She was no Princess Peach, trapped in a castle hoping that two plumbers were coming to save her.

She was going to save herself.

"Are we clear?" the helper asked.

"Crystal," Alicia said, her lips turning to the slightest smile.

6

BIG GARY'S KIDNEY STONES WEREN'T AS VOMIT-INDUCING AS JANINE had been expecting. In fact, if she hadn't already known what she was staring at, she might have mistaken it for a jar of pebbles, something she would've kept on the shelf in her bedroom during her "collecting pointless things" phase.

"Now, don't forget this side," Big Gary said, turning the jar so Janine and her camcorder could capture every cubic inch of kidney stone. While the colossal man wore a nearly constant broad smile, his eyes betrayed the baseline level of skepticism he reserved for anyone from outside of Harland County.

"Great," Janine said, her eye pressed to the lens, zero emotion in her voice. "Really great." They were standing in the back of Li'l Dino's Pizza 'n' Subs, Donna behind them, already immersed in the process of washing dishes.

Big Gary had a habit of filling any gaps in conversation with a series of gentle but guttural noises, almost like he was tasting something he liked. The volume and frequency of these sounds increased as Janine racked focus across the jar. As she stood there, pointing her camcorder at a grown man's rock collection, birthed from his own urethra, listening to him say *mmm-mmmm* over and over again, she couldn't ignore the voice in her head screaming, *This is why you went to grad school? This is why you're thou-sands of dollars in debt? So you could do this?*

"I been waitin' so long for someone to film these," Big Gary said, staring at the jar with pride. Resisting the urge to say, "Seriously?" Janine zoomed out to capture Big Gary and his booger-green Li'l Dino's polo shirt in all its glory. She couldn't imagine any color looking worse on camera.

"That's why I keep 'em displayed on the counter out there. *This jar*"—Big Gary held it as close to the camera lens as possible, filling up the frame with a blurred nothingness—"is a symbol of all the pain I went through. Shows how tough I am. You know that expression *Look at the stones on that one?*"

Big Gary paused, as if he was waiting for Janine to answer.

"That's actually the bumper sticker on my car," she said, calculating that Big Gary wouldn't detect her sar-casm.

"Well, then, all right!" Big Gary said. "So you know what I'm gettin' at: Look at the stones on *this* one! *My* stones!"

Janine couldn't help but smile, though not for the rea-sons Big Gary thought. She turned to see if Donna was smiling too, but nope: She was sliding a rack of glasses into the industrial dishwasher and pushing it closed, initiating a loud splashing and humming.

"So tell me," Big Gary said, speaking louder to com-pete with the running dishwasher, "is this gonna be, like, in the movie theaters and whatnot?"

"Definitely," Janine said, doing her best to wipe the smile off her face as she lowered the camera.

"Wow," Big Gary said, nodding excitedly and releasing a barrage of *mmm*s. "That's—"

"Mr. Gary!" A panicked teen boy held the door to the kitchen open, his acne-riddled face resembling the generic pizza pictures scattered throughout the restaurant.

"Can't you see I'm busy, Tommy?" Big Gary said.

"Is she from the news?" Tommy asked. "Are we gonna be on the news?"

"No, it ain't the news. This lady's makin' a movie about me," Gary said, turning to Janine and smiling. "What is it, Tommy?"

"Uh, you better just come and see."

"It looks like we got a situation I need to attend to," Big Gary said to Janine, with a smile that failed to hide his annoyance. "But I'll be back in a hurry. Feel free to take the stones out and touch 'em. Just don't lose any."

"As tempting as that is, I think we're actually done," Janine said.

"That's it?" Big Gary said, seeming a little hurt.

"Well." Janine suddenly felt bad, imagining how disappointed Big Gary would be when his stones never made it to the big screen. She also knew the earliest flight she could book probably wouldn't be until tomorrow anyway. "Maybe I'll stick around to get a little more footage."

"Attagirl!" Big Gary clapped three times and let out his biggest *mmm* yet. "Hey, I'll have our cook fix you a personal pizza. On the house."

"Oh, you don't have t—"

"Ron!" Big Gary shouted as he waddled away through the kitchen. "I need one PP! Extra cheese!"

Janine wondered for the eighteenth or nineteenth time that day what she was doing with her life.

She was about to say something snarky about Big Gary to Donna, but caught herself when she saw how engrossed her cousin was in her work. Janine watched as Donna grabbed a plate, angled it toward the trash, dumped a couple of pizza crusts, blasted it with a powerful sink nozzle, and added it to a rack, all within a couple of seconds. She was remarkably efficient.

Janine was reminded that Donna had been doing this since she graduated from high school. So: ten years. As Donna joylessly grabbed the next dish, her two-sizes-too-big Li'l Dino's polo shirt damp from the splashing water, Janine could think of no starker contrast to the old Donna. If the twelve-year-old Janine had been present, she would have thought that Donna was simply acting, perfectly playing the role of "dejected dishwasher" in one of their movies.

"He's a character, huh?" Janine finally said.

Donna didn't respond. Janine couldn't tell if she was being ignored or if Donna was just in the zone.

"He's a character, huh?" she repeated, a little louder.

"Who?" Donna said without pausing in her work.

"Big Gary."

"Oh. He's all right." She aimed the power nozzle at the sink, creating fast-moving streams that picked up all the food scraps in their path and deposited them neatly in the drain.

He's all right? It was the most un-Donna response of all time. Janine remembered the man running Li'l Dino's when they were younger, with his thick glasses and an obvious toupee. Donna had ironically nicknamed him Fabio. She would always tell him how great his hair looked, and Janine could never keep a straight face.

It was surprising to Janine, even a bit embarrassing, to realize that some part of her was still holding out hope that her relationship with Donna could revert back to the way it had once been.

"We used to have so much fun together," she finally said.

Donna turned the power nozzle off. Janine's breath caught in her chest, though she wasn't sure if Donna had paused because of what she'd said or if she'd just happened to finish her task at that exact moment. Donna said nothing and kept looking straight ahead at the wall.

Janine pushed a little more. "You know, um . . . you're the reason I went to film school."

Donna put her power nozzle down. Her head still turned away from Janine, she said, "I used to like hanging out with you, too."

Janine didn't know how badly she'd wanted to hear those words. They meant she wasn't crazy, imagining a closeness with Donna that had never existed. "So what happened?" Janine asked, her voice tender.

Donna was silent for a moment. "A lot," she said quietly. "A lot happened."

"What— What was it?"

Donna's shoulders tensed up and she lowered her head. As Janine stepped forward to comfort her, Big Gary reappeared, holding a plate covered with a sloppy mess of sauce and cheese. Donna immediately resumed her work.

"Your PP's ready! And I'm ready for more quest—" Big Gary's eyes darted back and forth between Janine and Donna. "Everything okay back here?"

"Not exactly," Janine said, sniffing as she wiped her face, annoyed at Big Gary for interrupting right when she and Donna were finally getting somewhere. "It's that time of the month. For both of us. And it's *really* intense."

"Uh," Big Gary said, at a complete loss for words.

Janine thought she saw, for a millisecond, the slightest smile on Donna's face before it disappeared. "But also," Janine said, "I'm just . . . excited about the movie."

"Oh," Big Gary said, nodding, grateful for the subject change. "I get that. Like when the *Bleak Creek Gazette* named us best pizza restaurant in town. I was so proud, I cried. Just like you."

Janine was pretty sure Li'l Dino's was the only pizza place in town.

"Anyway, sorry about the delay," Big Gary said. "Those two troublemakers from yesterday just showed up. I'm sure you heard about it . . . knocked Mr. Whitewood right into his pig smoker."

"Oh," Janine said, remembering GamGam's excitement. "Only kind of."

"Wow, where you been? Under a rock?" Big Gary asked, though he was obviously delighted as he proceeded to lay out for Janine his version of what had gone down, breathlessly detailing the impudence of these "miscreants." "At least that girl they hang around with was sent away," he finally concluded, as if it was this story's equivalent of *And they all lived happily ever after.*

"Sent away?" Janine asked. "Where?"

"Where else?" Big Gary asked, this time disappointed that she didn't know. "To Mr. Whitewood's reform school."

"Wait," Janine said. "The guy they accidentally knocked into a grill also has a reform school?"

Big Gary turned to find Tommy or someone else with whom he could exchange a "This woman truly doesn't know anything, does she?" look, but came up empty. "Of course he does! That man is a hero to this town."

"But . . ." Janine looked to Donna to gauge if she had any opinion on this, but she'd walked off to some other part of the restaurant. "Sounds like it was just an accident. Why was the girl sent to reform school for that?"

"Oh, I don't know," Big Gary said, "maybe because *she was out of control*! Same with those boys, letting their dog run wild while the pastors were tryin' to say the blessing. If you ask me, all three of 'em should be sent away to that school. They shape kids up quick over there, quite an operation." Big Gary hitched up his pants. "Tell you one thing: If those boys try a stunt like yesterday in here, they're gonna be in for quite a surprise. That's for damn sure. Now, where were we?"

Janine had the sudden realization that continuing to film Big Gary would be far less satisfying than actively messing with him.

"Actually," she said, "I think I may want to interview those boys."

Big Gary stared at her as if he'd been whacked in the face with a flyswatter. "For the . . . for the movie?"

"Yeah, I think so." Janine tried hard to look serious. "Their story seems really interesting."

"Are you kiddin' me? I doubt those boys have passed a single stone!"

"Oh, good point," Janine said, seeing how relieved Big Gary was to have convinced her and letting that moment sink in before saying, "but maybe that makes them perfect for the movie. You know, provides a really nice contrast to your super-impressive stone collection."

Big Gary opened and closed his mouth, unsure how to argue with that.

"Can you point them out to me?"

—

"HEY REX. HEY Leif," Tommy Dowd said, looking particularly uncool in his Li'l Dino's shirt as they walked through the doors of the restaurant.

"Hey, Tommy," Rex said. He wanted to keep the small talk to a minimum, both because he and Leif were incredibly hungry and because conversations with Tommy were incredibly dull.

"Nice day, huh?" Tommy asked.

"I guess," Rex said, eyebrows furrowed.

Tommy took the hint and bent behind the welcome podium to get menus. "Just the two of you?"

Leif visibly flinched. He hadn't wanted to come here, and had tried to persuade Rex that getting a snack at the Short Stop made more sense, but Rex had been emphatic. "I gotta get protein to feed my scooter leg," he'd said. "Plus, I haven't touched my allowance this week, so it's on me." It was hard to refuse once Rex was paying, but Leif hadn't articulated what was actually bothering him, something that hadn't seemed to dawn on Rex: Nearly every time they'd gone to Li'l Dino's in the past year, it had been with Alicia. He knew Tommy hadn't been trying to dig a knife in the wound, but that's the effect his question had.

"Uh, yeah," Rex said. "Just the two of us."

"Great," Tommy said. "Follow me."

It was a busy day at Li'l Dino's, four or five tables already occupied, mostly by high school kids Rex and Leif recognized but didn't know. As Tommy led the boys to the orange booth in the back corner, the one they usually sat at, Rex could feel people staring, and he realized the whole town probably knew about Alicia.

Leif didn't take in any of the glares, as seeing their usual table had triggered a deluge of Alicia memories: her reaching across the booth to repeatedly flick at his ear, her insisting that he order a personal supreme pizza with black olives so she could pick them off individually, her cackling in Rex's face when he revealed he didn't realize that Shock G and Humpty Hump were the same person. Leif didn't know if he'd be able to get through this meal.

"Um," Tommy said, placing the menus on the table. "I heard about Alicia."

"Yeah," Rex said as Leif sat down and stared at the table. "Hey . . . what's it like in there?"

Leif looked up. He'd been so consumed by his thoughts that he'd forgotten Tommy had once gone to the White-wood School. And here he was, standing in front of them, a regular guy. Leif felt a little lighter, remembering he would see Alicia again, that all of this might turn out okay.

"Oh," Tommy said, thinking hard. "It's . . . Well, it's not, like, *fun*. But it was good for me. I was really out of control, you know? And now I stay outta trouble, I've got good grades, this job," he said, gesturing to the Li'l Dino's logo on his shirt, which featured a stereotypical plump Italian chef who had an accidental resemblance to Big Gary. "Sometimes I think everybody should go to White-wood. I'm sure it'll be great for Alicia."

Rex nodded. "Thanks, Tommy. That's good to hear."

"Yeah, thanks," Leif said. He desperately wanted to believe Tommy, but he still felt unsettled.

"No prob," Tommy said, walking away. "I'll be back to take your orders."

Rex leaned in. "Okay, so when are we taking that tree guy Ben the stuff he asked for?"

"What?" Leif said, slamming his menu shut. He had really hoped that Rex wouldn't bring this up. "How can we even be sure he's actually got information about the school?"

"Well, we can't. But what if he does?"

"He probably just said he did because he heard us talking about Alicia being at Whitewood and he knew it would be a good way to use us to get him some stuff."

"Okay. What if he *is* using us? Worst-case scenario, he was lying. All we lose is the time it takes to get what he asked for and take it to him."

"No, actually . . . worst-case scenario is he uses that spear—"

"What can I get you fellas?" Big Gary was suddenly looming over their table. Neither Rex nor Leif had ever seen him take an order.

"Um, I'd like a pepperoni personal pizza, please," Rex squeaked.

Big Gary focused his attention on Leif.

"I'll just do a turkey sub," he said. "No tomatoes, please."

Big Gary glared at Rex and Leif for a few moments before speaking. "Behave yourself, boys. You understand?"

As Big Gary stared at them, Rex and Leif began to instinctively nod, even though they did not, in fact, understand.

"Good." Big Gary turned away and shouted to Tommy, who was standing near the entrance to the kitchen. "Tell Ron I need a PPP and a turkey sub, extra tomatoes." He shot Leif a cold look.

"Yessir," Tommy said, disappearing into the kitchen, Big Gary following moments later.

"That was weird," Rex said. "Why couldn't Tommy just take our order?"

"There's no way that wasn't intentional, right?" Leif asked. "I asked for *no* tomatoes. Maybe he's really proud of his tomatoes and I just insulted him?"

"I'd find it hard to believe a man would be that defensive about his tomatoes. No, that seemed personal." Rex rubbed his chin the way he'd seen cops do on TV.

"I feel like I need to go up there and tell him to hold the tomatoes."

"Wait!" Rex said, grabbing Leif's wrist to stop him from getting up, even though Leif had made no moves to do so. "I figured it out. He's sizing us up. Because of what happened with Alicia."

"Really?" Leif looked down at himself, as if to assess

whether or not he seemed like trouble. "We don't even have our camera with us. Or Tucker. Does he think we're gonna push him into his oven or something?"

"Maybe!" Rex was excited. "I'm not used to people thinking I'm a bad kid. It's kind of exhilarating."

"I don't think it is at all," Leif said. "I feel like I'm being judged. And punished with tomatoes."

"Just take the tomatoes off."

"But they'll contaminate whatever they touch."

"With what?"

"Tomato . . . ness."

Rex rolled his eyes.

Leif sighed. If they'd gone to the Short Stop, they would have already eaten by now. He would've gotten his usual bag of pizza-flavored Combos and a blackberry Clearly Canadian, and they would've tasted amazing. Instead, he was waiting for a sandwich that wasn't even what he ordered because he was being tested. As if he hadn't already gone through enough in the past day.

"Act natural," Rex whispered.

"Huh?"

"Big Gary is watching us. He's with some woman."

"What?" Leif said, going totally still as if he'd just been told there was a bee on his shoulder.

"Yeah," Rex said. "Some woman I've never seen before. She looks kind of cool. Like, her jeans are ripped. And she's wearing a hoodie."

"Can I turn around and look?" Leif asked, only moving his mouth.

"Not yet. They're still looking. Oh, shoot, she's walking this way."

"Who? The woman?"

"Yes," Rex said, smiling and nodding at Leif as if they were deep in a conversation different from this one.

"Are we getting thrown out?"

"I don't know," Rex said. "She's holding a camera."

And then the woman was standing right next to them.

"Hey, guys," she said. "Sorry to interrupt whatever fun-fest you might be having, but I was wondering if I could ask you a few questions."

Leif swallowed extra hard.

—

THESE BOYS DID not look like troublemakers.

At least the one with glasses didn't. He just looked terrified, as if Janine were about to pull out handcuffs. The other one, who had the same side-part haircut as nearly every other male in this town, was trying to play it cool, but Janine saw through it. "What kinds of questions?" he asked. Something about him reminded Janine of Dennis, which was simultaneously endearing and irritating.

"Really deep and soul-searching ones," Janine said, catching a gratifying glimpse in her peripheral vision of an aggravated Big Gary, whom she'd told to hang back so as not to intimidate her interview subjects. "My name is Janine Blitstein. I'm a filmmaker, like you guys." She tagged that last part on so she could blow their minds a little bit. It worked. Both of their mouths dropped slightly open. "I heard about what happened yesterday. Sorry about your friend."

"Thanks," Side Part said. "I'm Rex, and this is Leif."

"Have you made actual movies?" Leif asked.

"Yep," Janine said. "Nothing you would have seen, though. I just graduated from NYU film school."

"Whoa," Rex said. "Seriously?"

"No, I made that up to impress you."

"Oh."

"Of course seriously! Why would I go around to teen-agers I don't know pretending that I went to NYU?"

The boys looked at each other, grinning in amazement at the sarcasm coming from this random woman they'd just met. If Janine knew anything in this world, it was that irreverence was the fastest way into an adolescent heart.

"But . . . why are you in Bleak Creek?" Leif asked.

"Well, Leif," Janine said. "I'm sorta trying to figure that out."

Leif and Rex laughed.

"Truth be told, I came here to make a documentary about the town. Would you be down to answer some questions about yesterday? And I can film you?"

Rex and Leif wordlessly checked in with each other before Rex said, "Sure."

Janine directed the boys to sit on the same side of the table, then plopped down across from them, gleefully noting that Big Gary was still by the door to the kitchen, practically hopping with anger. She hefted the camcorder up to her shoulder, looked through the lens, and pressed record. "So, okay, I heard that you were making a movie—"

"*PolterDog,*" Leif interrupted.

"*PolterDog.* Like *Poltergeist* with a dog?"

"Yeah," Leif said, seeming a little shocked that she'd gotten it right.

"Wonderful. Sounds amazing. And you were shooting at this fundraiser so that you'd have a full crowd reacting to what's happening?"

"Exactly," Rex said, similarly astounded at Janine's level of astuteness, which, from her perspective, seemed more like common sense.

The boys walked Janine through their version of the whole story, how Tucker had gone rogue, how Alicia had bashed into Whitewood, how Alicia's parents had called the Whitewood School, how Rex and Leif had witnessed her abduction.

"Oh my god," Janine said, realizing that somewhere during her fake interview, she'd become genuinely intrigued by what they were saying. "Did you get footage of her being taken?"

Rex closed his eyes as if he'd just been pied in the face. "No. We should have."

"Uh, don't be so hard on yourself. It sounds like you were a little busy trying to rescue your friend. But this Whitewood School sounds pretty terrible."

"I mean," Rex said, "it has a good reputation."

"You bet it does!" Big Gary said, startling Janine, who hadn't heard him walk over. "Now I think it's time to conclude this interview, as I don't think it's right for the movie anyway, and I've still got a whole lot more to say about these puppies." He banged his jar down onto the table between Rex and Leif, who both flinched.

Janine spun the camera toward Big Gary. "So you're saying the school has a good reputation, even though it sends men to abduct kids in the night?"

"Hey, hey, hey," Big Gary said in a quiet voice, looking around nervously. "Don't go ruinin' the school secrets like that. It's part of the process."

"Sounds like a pretty messed-up process if you ask me," Janine said. *This* was a side of Big Gary that she was delighted to film. She hoped Donna was watching.

"I don't care about the process, I care about the results," Big Gary said, an edge of threat now in his voice. "Why do you think every person who works here has gone to that school? Because it shapes young people into responsible human beings!"

Janine's brain went blank for a second.

"What'd you say?" she asked.

"I said I'll only hire kids who've gone to that school. Now turn that damn camera off before I do it myself."

Janine took the camera off her shoulder and stared at Big Gary.

"But . . . Donna . . ."

The room started to spin. Janine put a hand down on the table to get her balance, accidentally brushing into Big Gary's jar and knocking it off the edge. It shattered as it hit the floor, kidney stones fanning out across the linoleum.

7

REX BARRELED DOWN THE BLACKTOP OF JOHNSON POND ROAD, HIS
scooter leg bouncing off the pavement, propelling him at a
fraction of the speed of a bicycle.

The filmmaker woman's strange, shocked reaction to
learning that her friend (her cousin, as he'd later learned)
had gone to the Whitewood School had left Rex shaken,
convincing him that any additional information that wild
boy might have about the school was worth seeking out.
Most of the items on Ben's list were pretty straightforward
to acquire—except for the fire extinguisher.

Luckily, Rex had a connection.

As he passed the tilled-under tobacco fields that flanked
the country road on the way to his destination, he couldn't
stop thinking about how different freshman year would be
without Alicia. In the Triumvirate, she'd always been the
one who knew how to navigate the weird social pitfalls of
school. Now, he and Leif would have to face their most
daunting challenge yet—becoming high-schoolers—on
their own. And, thanks to him opening his big stupid
mouth about his feelings for her, he'd made everything
even worse than it already was.

Sure, Leif had given his blessing in the moment, but
things had been slightly off between them ever since. Rex
should've known that liking Alicia would be a threat to
Leif; the same thing had happened the summer between

sixth and seventh grades with Julie Adams. Rex had fallen
fast and hard, spending nearly all his time with her. They'd
even started calling each other "babe." Because Alicia had
spent a good portion of the summer in Virginia with her
sick grandmother, Leif had been alone a lot, taking up a
series of sad hobbies including metal detecting and soap
carving. Rex pictured Leif, alone in his bedroom holding a
duck made from a bar of Irish Spring, and felt like a jerk.

On top of all that, earlier that day, he and Leif had
made the gut-wrenching decision to pull the plug on *PolterDog.*

"But don't you think Alicia would want us to finish
it?" Leif had asked, standing in front of his bathroom mirror wearing a curly brown wig he'd found in the plastic bin
in his garage labeled PROPS. He was hoping Rex would
agree that he would make a suitable Alicia replacement for
the remaining scenes.

"Unless we want to write in a part for a bad Richard
Simmons impersonator," Rex had said, plucking the wig
off Leif's head, "I don't think it's gonna work."

"What if we find another girl to play her role?" Leif
had asked. "Like how Elisabeth Shue replaced Claudia
Wells as Jennifer in *Back to the Future Two*?"

"First off, you've always put that on your long list of
why the second movie sucked. Also, that's a switcheroo in
between movies. We'd be making the switch in the middle.
Wouldn't fly." Rex had directed his gaze down to the wig
in his hands. "Listen, Alicia won't be at Whitewood forever. We can finish it when she's out. We'll make Sundance
next year."

He hadn't really believed that. In truth, he'd developed
an abiding sense that nothing would ever be the same.

Rex now turned in to a gravel driveway, the small
wheels of his scooter grinding to a crunchy stop on the
loose rocks that led to the house of Travis Bethune.

Not only was Travis the nicest person Rex and Leif had ever met, seemingly never disparaging anyone, but he had an untold number of jobs: landscaper, septic tank pumper, chimney sweep, house painter, and, most important, volunteer fireman. He traveled from job to job on his bright red moped and wore a thick black leather belt that held a walkie-talkie, two beepers, a flashlight, a large bowie knife, and a giant key ring loaded with what looked to be thirty keys or more. The teenagers around Bleak Creek regularly referred to him as Redneck Batman. He didn't seem to mind the moniker, and Rex and Leif didn't know if that was due to his unwavering positivity or just the general allure of being compared to Batman.

They'd met Travis a couple of years earlier, during one of Rex's dad's barbecue exploits; his grill fire had gotten out of control, accidentally igniting a backyard tree, and Travis was on the team who'd shown up to put it out. Rex and Leif were outside filming the fire, thinking it could be incorporated into their first movie, a messy series of comedy bits—way less cohesive and ambitious than *PolterDog*— entitled *The Bleak Creek Boyz*. Once the blaze was extinguished, Travis struck up a conversation with them. Even though they were only twelve and he was in his thirties, Travis took them seriously as filmmakers and mentioned multiple times that he'd be down to do stunts if they ever needed someone. They took him up on it right then and there, filming him jumping out of several different trees once the other firefighters left. He'd been their stuntman ever since.

Suffice it to say, when Rex realized he needed a fire extinguisher, he'd immediately thought of Travis, who'd called Rex back three minutes after he'd beeped him.

Rex walked the rest of the way up to the single-wide trailer, which Travis referred to as his "ranch-style house," despite the wheels under the mobile home being only somewhat obscured by the wood lattice skirting. Travis opened the door before Rex even reached the front steps.

"Hey, man!" he said, flashing his signature grin. "Come on in. My casa, your casa!" Rex didn't often see Travis without his utility belt. He seemed smaller.

"Thanks, Travis," Rex said, hit with the smell of solder wire and bacon grease as he stepped onto the brown shag carpet. He'd only been to Travis's house once before, as he always seemed to be out and about.

Rex had decided to make this a solo trip. Over the years, he'd learned that the best way to get his often-tentative best friend on board with an idea was to just start doing it. He was confident that if he went through the trouble of gathering the items by himself, talking Leif into meeting up with Ben again would be that much easier. He'd already retrieved three of Ben's requests: a metal rake (from his dad's shed), hot dogs (from the meat drawer in the fridge), and Cheerwine (from the shelves of the Piggly Wiggly).

He could have walked into Thomble and Sons Hardware and bought a fire extinguisher with the Christmas money he still had stashed in his *Thundercats* Lion-O piggy bank, but given the scrutiny he and Leif were already under following the barbecue incident, Rex supposed that going to Travis, the volunteer fireman, was the wiser choice.

"Glad you're here," Travis said. Adopting a serious tone, he added, "You know, I ain't supposed to share the tools of the trade with laymen like yourself. But I'm willin' to make an exception for you. Now, whatta you need it for again?"

Even though he doubted Ben would *actually* kill them if the secret of his forest hideout was revealed, Rex still felt it was safest to honor the forest boy's wishes. "Uh, we're experimenting with some mild pyrotechnics," Rex said as genuinely as he could.

"For *PolterDog*?" Travis asked.

"Uh, no. A new project. We had to stop working on *PolterDog*," Rex said. "You know, because of Alicia."

"She quit or somethin'?" Travis asked.

"She got sent to Whitewood," Rex said, surprised he didn't know.

"Oh, shoot, that was her?" Travis was crestfallen. "She was part of that group makin' the movie? The ones who bumped Mr. Whitewood?"

"Yeah," Rex said, confused. "That group was us, Travis."

"What!" Travis's eyes bugged out. "Oh, wow. That's—I shoulda guessed when I heard the movie thing. Plus, you'd think I'da seen her at Whitewood."

Rex's knees weakened. "Why were you there?"

"Work there," Travis said, putting his hands on the back of one of the folding metal chairs surrounding his dining room table, looking off into the distance pensively. "I cut the grass. Once a week. I like it there. It's peaceful."

"What is— What's it like inside?" Rex asked. "You think Alicia's gonna be okay?"

"I don't go inside, but oh, yeah, she'll be good," Travis said, nodding. "It's tough, sure, but it does right by kids. Mr. Whitewood is a great man."

Hearing that Travis worked there and had no concerns about Alicia's well-being was by far the most reassuring thing Rex had learned about the Whitewood School.

"So what's the new movie?"

"Oh. It's, uh, kind of experimental."

"You mean, like, about chemistry or somethin'?"

Rex felt horrible lying to Travis, but it was just too easy. And necessary.

"Sort of. Yeah."

"You boys are so dang creative. A chemistry movie. That sounds awesome!"

"Yep . . ."

"You sure you don't just want me to come and keep an eye on things when you do the pyro?" Travis asked. "I live for that kinda stuff." He leaned in and spoke in a whisper, "To tell you the truth, that's why I'm a volunteer fireman. I love to watch stuff burn." Catching himself, he said loudly, "Of course, I love puttin' it out, too!"

"Uh, well I don't think you'd find this too interesting. Just sparklers," Rex said, adding another thread to his web of white lies.

"Hmm. Yeah. That ain't really even fire." Travis paused, looking at the fake-wood-paneled wall. "All right, lemme get it."

Travis got up and walked through a bead curtain to the back of his trailer. Rex stood waiting, surveying Travis's assortment of what looked to be about a hundred California Raisins figurines on the kitchen counter. There were lots of repeats. At least twenty of the one on the skateboard.

"They're cool as hell, huh?" Travis said, returning with an ancient-looking fire extinguisher.

"Yeah, pretty cool," Rex said.

"Smartest thing Hardee's ever did. I wish they'd bring 'em back," he said, shaking his head. "Anyway, here she is." He extended the fire extinguisher to Rex.

"Thanks, Travis. I really appreciate this," Rex said.

"My pleasure, buddy."

When Rex pulled back onto the road, he realized he'd failed to account for how difficult it would be to ride a scooter while carrying a fire extinguisher. He also wondered if scooting across Bleak Creek with a firefighting device was actually more conspicuous than just buying one at the hardware store. But it was too late to turn back now. At least he didn't have to go through town. He could get home by taking the slightly longer route on the dirt farm roads.

As Rex walked along holding the fire extinguisher like a baby, his now useless scooter slung over his shoulder, the handlebars bouncing off his lower back with each step, he was thankful Leif wasn't around to point out the inefficiencies of his mode of transportation. He was also thankful he hadn't run into anyone. He'd have to cross over Old Oak Road, but after that he'd be able to walk through the pine tree farm all the way to the back side of his neighborhood.

After he had walked for a half hour (and taken a dozen or so rest breaks for his weary arms), the sun was dipping behind the trees and Rex had almost made it to the road. Just ten steps more, and then across, and he'd be home free.

He heard the rumble of an engine.

Instinctively, he accelerated to a sprint, thinking he could make it across the road and into the pines before being seen. Midrun, he turned to look toward the headlights now cutting through the dusk. The roadside ditch was deeper than he expected, and his foot dropped suddenly, sending him into a tumble, the scooter flying over his head and skipping across the road. He caught himself before completely eating it, but not before he lost his grip on the fire extinguisher. The canister bounced off the asphalt, then rolled across the double yellow line.

He scrambled to pick up the scooter, then frantically kicked the fire extinguisher toward the ditch.

Before he had a chance to get out of the road, a monstrous diesel pickup was almost on top of him. The truck swerved into the left lane, just missing Rex, then skidded to a stop.

He looked into the cab, the driver hardly visible in the dying daylight.

The automatic window slowly rolled down.

Wayne Whitewood.

Rex swallowed hard.

Whitewood didn't appear alarmed or angry. He just sat there in his light blue dress shirt, staring blankly at Rex like he was sucking his soul out through his eyes.

Rex looked at the ground.

"I'm sorry, I just tripped," he said, an attempt to fill the painful silence.

He noticed Whitewood tightly gripping the steering wheel, his hands sheathed in white gloves that looked like the ones worn by the First Baptist hand bell choir.

"Also, I'm really sorry about what happened the other day," Rex said, continuing the one-sided exchange. "I hope you're doing okay."

Without taking his eyes off Rex, Whitewood released the steering wheel, then methodically took off each glove.

He held his hands up toward Rex.

Bright red streaks lined his palms and fingers, some spots blistered, others scabbed. It made Rex's stomach turn.

"Um . . . sir, I am so sorry about that." Rex had no idea what to do other than keep apologizing.

Whitewood slowly pulled his hands back down, then carefully put his gloves on. Finally, he released Rex from his stare and turned his eyes to the road, the oversized vehicle beginning to slowly roll forward.

Rex stood holding his scooter as he watched the taillights disappear around the bend.

He wanted to throw up.

Instead, he ran quickly across the road, scooped up the fire extinguisher, and disappeared into the pines.

8

"CANDIDATUS HAS NOT EMBRACED HER NEW NAME," ALICIA'S ROOM-mate said, all freckles and frowns as her index finger singled out Alicia.

Each day after lunch at the Whitewood School, the entire student body—what looked to be about seventy-five kids—crammed into the meeting hall for Reports, a seemingly endless session devoted to classmates publicly reporting any questionable behavior they'd seen from their peers.

"She has an *A* written on the wall above her bed," Freckles said. "Her old initial."

"What?" the helper asked, a woman in her late thirties Alicia had seen getting her hair done at Loretta's Beauty Salon. "You defaced school property?"

Alicia offered a shrug.

The helper turned red and snorted, like an angry bull in a cartoon. "How did you acquire a writing implement?"

"I didn't, Helper," Alicia said.

"What? Then how— What did you write with?"

"Blood," Alicia said, her heart pumping fast as she put on a face that said *Oops, is that bad?* She'd taken a staple from their only textbook—a Xeroxed stack of pages called *The Whitewood School Learning Guide*—to prick her finger, tracing her bleeding digit up, down, and across the wall to form an A. It was no *Perfect Strangers* poster, but it would have to do. She'd intended to write her whole name until she saw the blood was already getting thinner; she worried she'd only partially complete it, accidentally marking her territory with her least favorite nickname of all time. (Ali. She hated when people called her Ali.) Doing it this way was simple, powerful, and to the point. And, as she'd hoped, her roommate had noticed it right away.

The helper covered her mouth in disgust, then puffed out her chest and gave what appeared to be the evil equivalent of the Care Bear Stare before stomping over to the wall intercom and pressing a button. "Send any available helper immediately," she said. "We need transport to the Roll."

A few students gasped. Though Alicia had been expecting this, fear crept in now that it was actually happening.

"We have been trying to guide you, Candidatus," the helper continued through gritted teeth. "To help you. To warn you. But you don't seem to understand. Headmaster has had his eye on you since you set foot in this school, and you're treating it like some kind of joke."

"Well, it *has* been a real riot, Helper," Alicia said, only making the exasperated woman angrier. The door opened and in walked another helper, a burly, clean-shaven man with a flattop whom Alicia remembered working at Thomble and Sons Hardware.

"Sayonara, Candidati," Alicia said solemnly as Flattop guided her by the shoulders into the hallway, then past the cafeteria and through the locked-from-the-outside exit. This was Alicia's first time leaving the school since arriving a few days earlier, and she savored the late-summer air like she would a delicacy. It was a short walk to a row of small stand-alone buildings.

"Welcome to Thinking Shed Number One," Flattop said, nudging her through the door of the first building.

"You guys have a cute name for everything?"

"Watch your mouth, Candidatus."

The pleasant smell of the outdoors was replaced by the stench of rotten eggs, the same odor that would sometimes come from Bleak Creek plumbing after a big rain. The floor, walls, and ceiling of the Thinking Shed were covered in faded green tiles, making it not so much a shed as a giant walk-in shower. In the corner of the room sat a large tub filled with cloudy water, likely the source of the putrid bouquet.

Next to it was a large roll of carpet that may have once been blue. Flattop began unrolling it across the room. Once unfurled, the carpet—soiled with unknown stains in a streak down the middle—carried its own fragrance that mingled with the egg smell, creating a perfume of unholy funk.

"That's the Roll?" Alicia asked. She was honestly a bit disappointed in the Whitewood faculty's lack of imagination. After all the buildup, the steady stream of threatening references to "the Roll" from all the helpers, Alicia had almost started to look forward to being sent there, if only to see if reality matched the image in her head. She'd been picturing a human-sized hamster wheel, or at least something that moved.

"Lie down," Flattop instructed, ungraciously arranging her so that her head hung over the carpet's edge. "Keep your arms at your sides."

Once she was lying on the carpet, the smell was unmistakable. Stale urine. Flattop proceeded to push her across the room, her entire body tightly entombed up to the neck as he rolled her to the opposite wall. She came to a rest with her face pointing toward the ceiling. Alicia wished she'd inhaled as deeply as possible before being rolled up, as she immediately found it difficult to take a satisfactory breath.

"Snug as a bug in a rug," Flattop said, smiling at the quip he'd obviously made before, then placing his knee on the Roll right at her chest. Breathing became almost impossible.

"Good one," she said in a strained but defiant voice.

The helper grabbed a roll of duct tape from the corner and secured the carpet to itself, sealing her in place like the creme filling in some sadistic Swiss cake roll. "Didn't I tell you to watch your mouth?" He placed the heel of his work boot on the Roll and pulled it away from the wall, Alicia completing two and a half disorienting revolutions before stopping in the middle of the room, her face now toward the floor.

"Whee!" Alicia said, trying to push down her fear and the feeling that her chest was caving in.

"Wrong answer," Flattop said. He rested his foot on the Roll again, then thrust his leg forward aggressively, sending Alicia rocketing across the floor. After a few bewildering rotations, she slammed into the wall, what little breath she had squeezed out, her lunch of vegetable soup and creamed corn gurgling in her stomach.

"You done?" Flattop asked.

Alicia just looked at him, the room a spinning, jumbled mess.

"Good. Now take some time to think about what you've done. Oh, and if you tell your parents about this during your monthly phone call, we'll let them know you've developed a problem with lying. A problem that would definitely require more time here. I doubt you're interested in an extra year." When he closed the door, the room was still shifting.

Alicia attempted to move her body, thinking maybe she could somehow wriggle her way out. It wasn't happening. She was stuck here for as long as they wanted her to be.

Alicia finally allowed herself to cry.

As silently as possible.

Eventually, she fell asleep. She dreamt that she was with Rex and Leif on their island in the Cape Fear River, sitting on a third rock that was bigger than both of theirs. "Look, we hate to do this," Rex said, "but we have to re-cast you in *PolterDog.*"

"You can't do that," she said.

"No, we have to." Leif spoke in the form of a statement even though he was on the smaller rock. "Candace Cameron wants to play Jessica. This could be huge for us."

"D.J.? From *Full House*?" Alicia asked with disgust.

"Yup." Leif nodded smugly. "D.J. From *Full House*. And we were nominated for an Oscar!"

"Wait, how?" Alicia felt so confused. "We didn't even finish making the movie yet."

"We didn't have to," Rex said. "We got nominated for most original idea for a movie. It's a new category!" He high-fived Leif.

Alicia awoke, forgetting where she was until her eyes focused on the dingy green tiles all around her. The sunlight coming through the small frosted window in the door had dimmed considerably.

She desperately needed to pee.

Alicia began to wonder if she was going to join the ranks of Rollers before her who had given in and relieved themselves. Based on the stains and the smell, it had been quite a few.

She decided she could hold it.

As she lay there, unsure if she would be left overnight in this backwoods torture device, Alicia couldn't help but feel a little proud of herself for being here in the first place. It meant she was brave. Or idiotic. But still, she definitely hadn't seen any other students get sent to the Roll. She hadn't seen any of the other students do much of anything but follow, really. Given the state of the carpet, she guessed

some of them had been sent in the past, the impulse to disobey squeezed right out of them. She didn't want that to
happen to her. She didn't want to become like them.

At her first breakfast, Alicia had recognized Cindy
Fisher, who had been sent to Whitewood at the end of the
previous school year after her parents found a condom in
her bedroom. It didn't matter that it was unused—even
knowing that she was considering having sex—safe or
not—was enough for her parents to call up Mr. Whitewood. Though Alicia had never been close with Cindy,
she'd known her well enough to consider her kind, outgo-
ing, and even funny. But Alicia saw none of that in Cindy's
eyes when she'd sat next to her in the cafeteria, where they
were forbidden to speak as they ate. When Cindy had
looked at her, Alicia had raised her eyebrows to signal her
recognition; Cindy had quickly looked back down at her
Cream of Wheat.

There were a couple dozen other Bleak Creek kids that
Alicia knew, the youngest seeming around ten years old,
the oldest a high school senior named Todd something. But
the others—maybe forty students, as well as her
roommate—were complete strangers. Alicia had never really stopped to consider whether there were students from
out of town at Whitewood, but that was clearly the case.
However, none of them—whether Bleak Creekians or
outsiders—had made any effort to connect with her at all.
She figured this was just the way things were at Whitewood, but she also knew that her particular offense—
injuring the headmaster himself—had made her a special
brand of untouchable. She was the blackest sheep in a herd
of black sheep.

Maybe this stand she was taking was incredibly foolish. Maybe she should just follow, or at least pretend to.
But she felt like it was more important to not lose her grip
on who she was, even if it would ensure her a longer stay

in this hell. And she was still holding out a glimmer of hope that maybe, just maybe, bucking the system this way would allow her to find the school's Achilles' heel, which could be her ticket out of there. It was unlikely. But she had to keep believing.

The sunlight was gone now.

After another thirty minutes of resisting, Alicia finally let herself relax, warm urine spilling into her jumpsuit.

9

JANINE STROLLED DOWN WALNUT STREET, THE SIDEWALK STILL WET
from the previous night's thunderstorm. She passed an el-
derly lady sitting on her front porch, the old woman's head
swiveling to track her as she crossed the width of her yard.
Janine had always seemed to attract these kinds of stares in
Bleak Creek, a town with a knack for identifying outsiders.
Of course, she was making that a particularly easy task
with her camera bag, black leggings, cutoff jorts, combat
boots, and off-the-shoulder gray T-shirt that gave all Bleak
Creekians a pristine view of her left collarbone. She offered
a friendly wave to the woman, who reflexively waved
back, never losing her quizzical expression.

After Janine had learned that Donna was a former
Whitewood student, she'd made the decision to stick
around town. She had to learn more about this strange
institution, about what had happened there to transform
her cousin into a shell of her former self. Naturally, she'd
first tried to talk to Donna, striding to the back of Li'l Dino's even before her lightheadedness had gone away (and
before offering to help Big Gary clean up his stones), where
Donna made it clear that yes, she went to that school, and
no, she didn't want to talk about it.

Janine refused to be discouraged. Screw a movie about
old people's kidney stones. *This* was the film she needed to
make, whether or not her cousin was down to participate.

She'd asked Tommy, the pimply-faced server, if she could interview him, but Big Gary—still furious over his spilled treasures—had ordered her to get out of his restaurant before he called the cops, which had only confirmed Janine's suspicions that she was onto something. She'd slipped Tommy her number (well, GamGam's number) on a scrap of placemat, and, to her surprise, he'd called that night. Which is how Janine now found herself walking the quarter mile from her grandmother's house to the home of Tommy Dowd.

Janine pressed the doorbell and listened as it triggered a rising and falling sequence of chimes. Before the doorbell stopped ringing, Tommy answered the door.

"Uh, hi," the boy said, seeming surprised that she'd actually shown up.

"Hey, Tommy. Where should I set up?"

"Um . . ."

"My camera," Janine said, gesturing to her bag.

"Oh, uh . . . let's go to the backyard."

Janine followed Tommy around the side of the house, passing a large German shepherd chained to a pole, the dog growling but unwilling to deliver a proper bark. They finally arrived at two mildewed lawn chairs Tommy thought would be perfect for their talk.

"So, how long were you at the Whitewood School?" Janine asked once the camera was rolling.

"Uh, I . . . Well, I . . ." Tommy began, clearly uneasy. "I think it was about four months."

"Tell me about your time there. How are students . . . reformed?"

"It was, um, really good for me," Tommy said. "I learned how to, um, respect my, uh . . . elders." Janine noticed that Tommy's eyes were darting between the ground and somewhere on her clothes. *Just like Donna,* she thought. Unable to make eye contact. Then it hit her.

He's looking at my shoulder. Janine had failed to consider how something as innocuous as the collarbone of a mysterious older woman could derail a teen boy's thoughts. *That's why he agreed to this meeting.*

"But what happens specifically at the school? How do they . . . change you?" Janine pressed.

"Um, I'm sorry," Tommy began muttering, having now developed the courage to lock in directly on her shoulder. "I'd rather not talk about that. But like I said, it was, um, really really good for me."

Janine pulled her T-shirt up over her shoulder. Tommy's face reddened.

"Is that part of the deal? You're not supposed to talk about what happens at Whitewood?" Janine pushed further.

Tommy was squirming even more, and not just because his wandering eyes had been exposed. "I think I should go back inside. Thank you, um, Ms. Blitstein." He stood up abruptly and stiffly jogged back to the screened back door.

—

JANINE PULLED TO the side of the road, awkwardly reaching across the passenger seat of her GamGam's Grand Marquis to roll down the window. "Excuse me," she said to an older couple walking out of the post office. "Would you happen to know how to get to the Whitewood School?"

They stared at her. "You know parents ain't allowed to visit, right?" the man asked, adjusting his John Deere hat.

"Of course," Janine said, not missing a beat. "I'm just taking a look to see if I, uh, want to send my daughter there. She's being a real terror." Imagining herself as a mom freaked her out, but she tried to seem as normal as possible.

"It's a very good school," the woman said, eyeing the length of the car, then staring at Janine with more than a hint of skepticism about her ability to operate such a massive vehicle.

"I don't know what *seein'* it is gonna do," the man said. "You either want to send her or you don't. And you can't even really see it from the road anyhow."

"Well, a mother likes to know her child is gonna be okay. You know, get some peace of mind," Janine said, hearing how unbelievable she sounded.

"What kind of trouble is she in?" the woman asked.

"Gangsta rap," Janine said without thinking.

"Gang-ster rap?" the man asked.

"Yep. She listens to it nonstop. Ice-T, Ice Cube . . . all the Ices. She hates cops." Janine was almost cringing at this point.

"Oh my word," the woman said. "And you look mighty young, so she can't be that ol—"

"She's six," Janine said.

The couple was shocked. The man grabbed the bill of his hat and adjusted it right back to where it was.

"Yes, it's horrible," Janine added, laying it on thick.

"All right," the puzzled man said, ready for this conversation to end. "Just follow Main Street until it hits Creek Road. Take a right, and after a while you'll see the gate. They won't let you drive onto the premises, though."

"Great, thanks," Janine said. "I won't even try."

The man nodded without smiling. Janine rolled the window up and pulled the mammoth brown-and-beige automobile back onto the street. In the rearview mirror, she could see the couple still standing there, their furrowed brows watching her drive away.

Janine passed by the Bleak Creek landmarks she'd seen hundreds of times during her visits over the years: the red-brick First Baptist Church with its towering steeple, less than fifty yards from the light brown brick Second Baptist Church with its slightly taller steeple; Blanchard's Bait 'n'

Tackle, which she'd literally never passed without seeing the
WE'LL BE RIGHT BACK sign in the window; the THOMAS &
THOMAS LAW OFFICE in an imposing plantation-style house,
making it a rather ironic bastion of justice. She'd always
considered these places the staples of a polite southern small
town, but with her looming questions about the Whitewood
School, they seemed almost like a façade, carefully con-
structed exteriors hiding decidedly impolite truths.

She turned onto Creek Road and soon it was nothing
but lonely farms and woods dominated by pine trees. A
couple minutes later, she realized she'd arrived, rolling to a
bumpy stop on the road's weed-covered shoulder.

The beige sign read THE WHITEWOOD SCHOOL, COR-
RECTIVE CENTER FOR CHILDREN. Underneath the black
text, in smaller font, it read PROVERBS 23:13.

Janine stepped out of the car with her camera, her insides knotting up, and pressed record. She filled the frame
with the sign, curious as to what was said in that particular
Bible verse; she figured she'd write it out in a text overlay
in the final version of her film.

The old couple had been right. She couldn't see the
school, as a thick stand of trees lined the opposite side of
the tall chain-link fence that surrounded the property.
Three rows of barbed wire stretched along the top of the
barrier. Most people would assume a prison stood behind
those trees. Maybe that was the point.

Janine walked, camera in hand, up to the front gate.
Once there, she realized she could in fact see a portion of
the school down the long single-lane driveway. It looked to
be a three-story wooden building, painted a light beige,
trim and all.

Janine focused her camera on what she could see of the
school, strands of the chain-link fence blurry in the fore-
ground, obscuring the image as she panned left to right.
She listened carefully, thinking maybe she would hear kids

screaming or crying or something. There was only silence. She thought about young Donna in that building: scared, powerless, alone.

The camera landed on an object next to the building, the image in her viewfinder so grainy that she initially didn't recognize it for what it was: a person. It didn't help that the large, bored-looking man was wearing what looked to be some sort of yellowish-brown work suit that perfectly camouflaged him in front of the matching school.

"These people are really into beige," Janine said to herself. The man appeared to be standing guard outside one of the entrances. *Who do they think is going to try to break in?* she wondered, before realizing the concern was more likely about who they thought might try to get *out.*

She zoomed in, exhausting the capabilities of her camera, framing the man from the mid-thigh up. *Cowboy shot,* her film school word bank reminded her.

He turned and looked straight into the lens.

Janine ducked, but there wasn't anything to duck behind. She turned off her camcorder and crouch-walked to the car, quivering as she got back into the driver's seat and frantically peeled away.

———

JANINE PULLED OPEN the swinging glass door of the Bleak Creek Public Library, a place she had never had a reason to visit during her childhood summer trips. After her stop by the Whitewood School, she'd wanted to go straight home and wash away the image of that creepy dude with some of her GamGam's sweet tea, but she knew that gathering written resources was an essential part of any respectable documentary (if for no other reason than to have those cool shots of newspaper headlines she'd seen in Ken Burns's films).

As she approached the front desk, where a short, gray-haired woman sat reading a creased paperback of Agatha Christie's *Postern of Fate*, she felt the faint academic anxiety that always accompanied the musky fragrance of books. The woman didn't look up.

"Hello," Janine eventually said in her quietest, most library-ish voice.

"Oh!" the woman semi-screamed, "I didn't see you there. You're a sneaky one!"

"I'm sorry," Janine said.

"Don't worry about it. I could use some excitement around here!" She had not yet lowered her voice. "How can I help you!"

"I'm hoping to look at old newspapers," Janine said. "Like, local newspapers."

"Well, the only one we got is *Bleak Creek Gazette*," the woman said.

"Yes, that's perfect."

"Follow me."

Janine trailed the tiny woman through the library. As they entered the nonfiction section, a middle-aged man in suspenders over a white V-neck T-shirt looked up with sunken eyes from his XYZ volume of the *Encyclopedia Britannica*. Janine gave him a fake smile, the kind reserved for strangers you'd like to remain that way. The man stared back, trailing her with his eyes just like the old lady on the porch. Wishing she could walk faster, she continued to follow closely behind the librarian, stepping down a set of stairs to the even mustier-smelling basement.

"So, here's the microfilm reader," the librarian said when they arrived at a table on the far side of the dimly lit room, her powerful voice booming throughout the basement as she pointed to a machine with a large blank screen. "What years do you want, dear?"

"Uh," Janine said, "do you know what year the White-wood School was founded?"

The short woman paused before answering, her silence filled by the steady buzz from the lights. "Why?" she asked in a suddenly quieter, almost appropriate library voice.

Janine didn't think she should tell her the real reason. "Uh, I've been told that there were some great recipes in the lifestyle section of the paper that year," she said, contorting her face into an innocent smile, hoping to convince the woman of her ridiculous excuse—that she was just a good Bleak Creek girl who wanted to cook for her man.

"Hmm," the woman said, staring deeply into Janine's eyes as if trying to unlock an Agatha Christie clue. "Recipes, huh?"

"Yes, ma'am," Janine said, really turning on the charm.

The woman paused another second, then turned abruptly and walked away. Was she leaving to tell someone that there was a Yankee girl sticking her nose where it didn't belong, or just ignoring her request? Right as Janine was starting to wonder if maybe she should leave before drawing any more unnecessary attention, the woman reappeared. "Forgot the key," she said, walking over to a nearby cabinet and unlocking it. "I know the school opened sometime in the late seventies, so you could start in the 1975 to '79 section." She still hadn't returned to nearly shouting, which Janine took as her not completely buying her story. "I hope you find some good recipes." She went back upstairs, leaving the cabinet open.

Janine started with the 1977 microfilm rolls, scanning headline after headline for a mention of the Whitewood School, extremely grateful that the *Bleak Creek Gazette* was only a weekly publication. She let out a small yelp when she finally found what she was looking for in the August 27, 1979, issue:

THE WHITEWOOD SCHOOL OPENS, WITH
MISSION TO REFORM TROUBLED YOUTHS

The long-abandoned Bleak Family Resort, which served those wishing to soak in the mineral waters of Bleak Creek Spring from 1927 to 1961, will see new life as a reform school when it opens its doors to students in September. The Whitewood School is the work of Mr. Wayne Whitewood, a town newcomer, who will serve as headmaster. "It is easier than ever for young people to be lured off the straight and narrow by any number of worldly temptations. But once they go astray, we can't give up on them. The Whitewood School knows no lost causes," explained Mr. Whitewood, who has also become quite popular for his enthusiastic organ playing at Bleak Creek Second Baptist Church, having replaced Donald Jeffries after his tragic lawnmower accident last year.

Locals are excited about the prospect of a reform school. "Our children are being bombarded by rock music, drugs, alcohol, and, worst of all, sex," said Second Baptist Church secretary, Mary Hattaway. "Many parents have nowhere to turn. It will be nice to have a place to send young folks who are not responding to discipline at home."

The Whitewood School will be accepting students from Bleak Creek as well as surrounding areas. Mr. Whitewood promises that if he is able to get unruly young ones in his program before they become full-fledged troublemakers, there is hope that they will grow up to be responsible, normal adults. "Bleak Creek is such a wonderful place," said Mr. Whitewood. "I would hate to see it ruined by a few headstrong kids."

There were several articles that followed in the next month, mainly repeating the same information and celebrating the school. After doing some quick math, Janine realized Donna was probably one of the school's first students.

When she made it to the end of 1979, Janine was nursing a headache from the stagnant basement air, but she knew she had to keep looking. If someone told the loud librarian the truth about Janine's documentary, she might not give her access to the microfilm archives so easily. She had to dig further *now*.

She dumped more rolls on the table and began flying through the headlines. The school wasn't mentioned at all in 1980 or 1981. When she was nearing the end of 1982, she was convinced that the Whitewood School had become so inconsequential to the people of Bleak Creek that it didn't even warrant a mention in the homespun newspaper.

But then she saw it.

An article entitled "Teen Dies in Freak Accident at Whitewood School," dated December 18, 1982. Richard Stanley, a fourteen-year-old boy, had died after locking himself in the school's industrial oven during an unauthorized game of hide-and-seek.

Janine felt queasy.

The article wasn't clear as to how the oven had then been accidentally turned on, leaving the boy to be found by staff the next morning. Wayne Whitewood was quoted as saying, "The entire staff is devastated. We are deeply saddened that we lost this troubled young man. He was showing so much progress, but still had a wild streak. We honestly don't know what else we could have done."

It was tragic—and in this case, gruesome—for a student to die at a reform school. But it wasn't exactly scandalous. Even so, Janine noticed she was trembling as she read the article.

She kept going, grabbing the 1983 and 1984 microfilm rolls.

No mentions of the school.

Then, 1985.

A mention of Wayne Whitewood in May. Not about the school. He'd won a barbecue cook-off.

Then, June 12.

Oh my god.

"Girl Killed in Gas Explosion at Whitewood School."

The accident was similar to the first: a sixteen-year-old girl had been in the wrong place at the wrong time, doing the wrong thing (sneaking around to smoke a cigarette). The article included another heartfelt but blame-shifting quote from a grieving Wayne Whitewood.

Janine's mind was reeling faster than the knobs on the microfilm machine. Two students dead in a few years? Weren't the people of Bleak Creek curious? Did no one consider launching an investigation?

As she reached down to continue scrolling through the rest of 1985, she felt someone's presence.

"All those funerals were closed casket," a gravelly voice said.

Janine recoiled and turned to see the sunken-eyed man standing right behind her.

She thought of running for the exit.

"Sorry, ma'am," the man said with a voice reminiscent of an old car trying to start up. His dull gaze was locked on the microfilm display. He rocked back and forth slowly, his thumbs looped under his suspenders like he expected them to come undone at any moment.

"Wha . . . what are you talking about?" Janine asked, trying to catch her breath.

"The parents couldn't even identify the bodies. Sheriff had to use dental records."

"Wait a second . . . Did you say . . . *all* the funerals?"

"Yeah, I'll save you the trouble. There was another accident in 'eighty-nine."

"What . . . what happened?"

"Boy got struck by lightning out there on the property. Heard it was a pretty ugly scene."

Janine reached for the 1989 roll, already stacked next to the machine. She hurriedly exchanged the spools, then began whirling through the articles.

"What date?" she asked.

There was no response.

Janine turned around.

The man was gone.

10

REX AND LEIF WALKED INTO THE CAFETERIA ON THEIR FIRST DAY AT Bleak Creek High School, feeling Alicia's absence more than ever. This moment had been building in Rex's mind for years, ever since his older sister, Misty, told him that whoever you sat with at lunch that first day could determine your future. "Brad Stewart was the smartest guy in eighth grade," she'd said, "but he sat with the Gardner twins his freshman year, and now he drives an ice cream truck."

He, Leif, and Alicia had developed a plan: Instead of buying lunch, they would bring their own to avoid the hiccup of having to go through the line. Then they'd take their brown bags—lunch boxes were strictly off-limits, a sacrifice particularly challenging for Leif—directly to the spot of their choice, sit down, and wait to see who naturally joined them. The only rule they'd agreed on was that Mark Hornhat wasn't allowed. "If he comes over, I'll handle it," Alicia had promised. "I'll let him down easy. Don't worry."

Both Rex and Leif had serious doubts about doing all this without her.

But they didn't admit that to each other.

An initial scan of the room revealed that nearly every table was already taken, with very few students in line buying lunch. Maybe their plan wasn't so original after all. They walked around methodically, not talking, Rex doing his best to play it cool and blend in (not an easy task considering he towered over almost everyone), while Leif somehow forgot to move his arms as he walked.

After two and a half laps around the cafeteria, Rex looked at Leif and motioned with his head toward a table next to them. A handful of guys and girls they recognized as upperclassmen were deep in conversation, but there were three open seats.

"Mind if we sit here?" Rex asked.

"Huh?" a blond girl with a jean skirt asked.

"Go for it, Stretch," a guy with a Vanilla Ice *To the Extreme* T-shirt said before turning back to Jean Skirt and picking up where they'd left off.

"Thanks." No sooner had Rex and Leif sat down than they got a powerful whiff of Eternity. Mark Hornhat appeared beside them, as if he'd been perched somewhere waiting for them to decide on a table. A very Hornhat move.

"Hey hey, fellas," he said, taking his lunch out of his backpack. "High school is pretty rockin', huh? So many hot babes."

Rex and Leif just stared at him. They both realized that without Alicia, they stood little chance of repelling Hornhat. Freshman Lunch Plan 1992 was quickly falling apart.

"Oh, man!" he said. "What y'all did at the Second Baptist fundraiser was so rad. I can't wait to see *Ghost Dog* so I can relive it. Does Boykins have lunch this period? I want to congratulate her on her performance. Especially the part at the end, heh-heh."

Rex and Leif continued staring, coming to grips with the fact that Hornhat might be a permanent fixture of their cafeteria crew. Rex knew Hornhat's dad was a doctor, so at least eating with him on a regular basis didn't guarantee a future as an ice cream truck driver.

"What?" Hornhat said, responding to their silence. "Did Mr. Whitewood die or something?"

"No," Leif said. "But Alicia . . . she's not here. She's at Whitewood."

Hornhat's eyebrows shot up. "What?"

"Yeah," Rex said. "How have you not heard about this?"

"I've been in the Outer Banks with my family since the night of the fundraiser. You know, at our three-story beach house." Everyone knew about his parents' three-story beach house, seeing as Hornhat had a way of working it in to just about any conversation. "We got back yesterday. Oh, man, that sucks about Alicia . . ."

"It's not a huge deal," Rex said. "She'll probably be out in a few months."

"I don't know," Hornhat said, shaking his head. "Seems pretty serious to me. I mean, think about it. How many kids do we know who—"

"Shut up, Hornhat!" Rex said, his intensity surprising even himself. Vanilla Ice and Jean Skirt stopped talking to look at him. "Sorry."

Hornhat looked shell-shocked, caught off-guard by the scolding. "Okay."

"You gotta chill out, Stretch," Vanilla Ice said before picking up his conversation again.

"Yeah, uh, I will," Rex said, trying to reassert his coolness.

"Hey," Hornhat said excitedly, "you guys hear that Marky Mark is coming out with a new album?" Rex was always annoyed at Hornhat's tendency to bring things up at inappropriate times, usually in an effort to prove how in the know he was.

Rex looked down, trying not to explode again.

"Nope," Leif said. "Hadn't heard that."

"Yeah, just a couple more weeks," Hornhat said. "But honestly, I'm not too excited about it. I think the real talent in that family is Donnie. He's the most underrated member of New Kids on the Block, which is one of the most underrated bands of all ti—"

"Mark!" Rex said, almost yelling once more. "We've got some important business to discuss. You can sit here, but please don't interrupt."

"Okay, got it. Whatever you need, guys," Hornhat said, gesturing with a partially peeled banana. "Whatever you need."

"Thanks." Rex was already backfilling Alicia's role of speaking authoritatively to Hornhat. It felt better than he expected.

"One last thing," Hornhat said, his mouth filled with banana. "Leif, can I breathe on your shirt?"

"No." Leif crossed his arms over his purple Hypercolor.

"Gotcha. No problem." He set aside his banana peel and moved on to a tuna fish sandwich. The smell was overwhelming.

"What's the important business?" Leif asked.

"Remember the stuff that you-know-who asked for? Well, I've got it all. Even the fire extinguisher."

Leif stopped unwrapping the aluminum foil from his peanut butter and jelly sandwich. "You're not still thinking about going back to the wild boy, are you?"

"Actually, I am. I was thinking we could do it today after school," Rex said.

"This afternoon? I don't know . . ." Leif nervously sipped his Juicy Juice, even though Rex had strongly advised him not to bring juice boxes to high school. "I need time to prepare."

"Prepare for what?"

"Maybe . . . figuring out how to not get murdered in the woods?"

"I'm pretty sure he's not a murderer. Weird, yes. But not a killer."

"How do you know he won't hit us over the head with

the rake and then, like, throw the hot dogs and Cheerwine at us, and then spray us with the fire extinguisher?"

"I'd be very surprised if those exact things happened," Rex said.

"Pardon me for interrupting," Hornhat said, putting down his chocolate milk, "but I am quite intrigued by what I'm hearing and would love to join this mission if you'll have me. I have nunchucks, by the way."

Rex knew Leif was expecting him to immediately shut down Hornhat's offer, and that was his first instinct, but he stopped himself.

"Hmm," he said.

Leif stared at Rex, horrified. "Wait, you're actually considering this?"

"Maybe," Rex said. "I mean, since you're clearly not gonna come. He does have nunchucks." Hornhat nodded, pleased with himself.

"Well." Leif understood Rex was saying these things as a way of pressuring him to go, but he also knew Rex wasn't one to bluff. "I think no one should go," Leif said.

"All right," Rex said, shrugging, "I guess it's me and Hornhat then."

"Yes!" Hornhat said, pulling in his fist like he was doing an impression of Macaulay Culkin in *Home Alone.*

"Okay, I'm in," Leif said, the words busting out of him, almost involuntarily.

"Great!" Rex said. "Sorry, Hornhat. Leif is gonna go instead of you."

"Aw, seriously?" Hornhat said. "Why can't it be the three of us?"

"It's not that kind of mission, unfortunately," Rex said. "You're at the top of the alternate list, though."

"All right," Hornhat said. "That seems fair. But, hey, since I can't go on the mission, can I at least breathe on your shirt, Leif?"

Leif thought it seemed almost sacrilegious to let Horn-hat breathe on his Hypercolor shirt, considering that Alicia had always loved it, changing the purple to pink with her breath at least once every time he wore it. But he felt a little sympathy for Hornhat, considering he had just been deftly used as a pawn in one of Rex's schemes.

"Okay, fine."

"Awesome!" Hornhat's whole face lit up as he stood and approached Leif, then proceeded to bend down and unleash a cannon of tuna fish air. Leif held his breath and watched his left nipple area change color, trying to convince himself that this was a way of honoring Alicia.

—

AS LEIF WADED through the Cape Fear River holding a rake and a six-pack of Cheerwine, he was thinking he'd given in to Rex way too easily. There was a tight ball of fear in his gut, a genuine (if irrational) concern that they wouldn't make it home alive. "Let the record show that I think this is a mistake," he said as they stepped onto the far bank of the river, murky water spilling out of his yellow Asics.

They arrived at the edge of the small clearing around the Tree. Rex tiptoed out toward the giant trunk, Leif following with a couple of tiny steps. A small fire burned in the fire ring, but there was no sign of Ben.

"Hellooooo!" Rex shouted.

"SSSSHHHHHHH!" Leif placed his finger over his mouth and looked at Rex like he'd lost his mind.

"What? I want him to know we're here," Rex said.

"I think he's gone. Let's go home," Leif said, quickly turning around and beginning to walk back toward the river.

Before Leif could take one step, Ben jumped out from behind a smaller tree, landing in front of him, spear in hand. Leif peed a little, though it was unnoticeable in his already soaked Umbro shorts.

"You're back!" Ben said enthusiastically. He was still in the brown jumpsuit, a rabbit/possum pelt still slung over his shoulders and a bloody bandage still on his hand. "And you did it," he said, smiling. "You fulfilled the mission. Please, come in."

He walked past them back toward the fire. Rex turned to follow him, not sure what qualified as "coming in." Leif remained on the edge of the clearing, gathering himself. Ben seemed significantly friendlier this time around, despite his alarming way of welcoming visitors.

"I'm really glad you came through on this. I had a feeling you could be trusted. Would you mind passing me the rake and the hot dogs?"

Rex handed over the hot dogs, but it took Leif a few seconds to realize he was still holding the rake.

"Oh. Sure," he eventually said, walking up to Ben and carefully handing it over.

"I was in the middle of a game of tic-tac-toe if either of you is interested," Ben said, gesturing to the ground. "Feel free to use my stick."

"Thanks," Leif said, as if that was at all an appealing idea.

"I didn't catch your names last time," Ben said, tearing open the plastic package and methodically sliding a hot dog down each tine of the rake.

"Leif. And Rex."

"Leef? Not Layf?"

"My mom wanted to go with Layf, just like—"

"Leif Erikson," Ben interrupted, "the first person to discover North America, way before Columbus. Well, first white person."

"Yeah," Leif confirmed.

"And lemme guess. These nimrods around here kept

reading it and calling you Leef, so you just went with it to avoid the trouble of having to constantly correct idiots."

"Uh, yeah," Leif said. He'd never met anyone who had so bluntly (and accurately) stated the lifelong predicament with his name. "Pretty much exactly that."

"Well, I'm gonna call you Layf," Ben said. "Check it out." He smiled at them as the hot dogs roasted on the open fire.

"That's why you wanted the rake and the hot dogs?" Rex asked, in disbelief.

"Pretty great, right?" Ben said. "We're all gonna eat well tonight. Leif, would you mind taking over hot dog duty for a bit?"

"Oh," Leif said, thinking there was some kind of catch here, that maybe it was a trap. But it did look kind of fun to cook that many hot dogs at once. "Sure." He took the rake from Ben, who grabbed the six-pack of Cheerwine and stared at it.

"I only asked for three cans," he said.

"That's how they sell them," Leif said, dipping the rake into the fire and wondering why he'd never thought of using it in this way before.

"This is actually better." Ben placed the six-pack on the ground. "Rex, could I have the fire extinguisher?" Rex handed it over, and within seconds Ben had removed the pin and was spraying it at the cans.

"Whoa," Rex said, taking a couple steps backward. "What are you doing?"

"Do you know what the perfect soft drink temperature is?" Ben shouted over the sound of the carbon-dioxide-powered fire extinguisher.

"What?" Rex asked.

"It's thirty-nine degrees Fahrenheit. Three and eighty-nine hundredths degrees Celsius." A billowing white cloud surrounded the cans. "Now, we could attempt to get these cans there with a freezer. But we don't have one. And that would take about twenty-five minutes, anyway. A bucket of ice could do the job in about half that time. But we don't have that either. Lucky for us, and thanks to you, we do have this fire extinguisher, which will get these cans to the perfect temperature in less . . . than . . . one . . . minute." The spray ran out. Ben reached into the white cloud, his hand reappearing with a Cheerwine. He cracked it open and took a sip. "Ahh, perfect. I've been dying for one of these."

The spray dissipated, and soon Leif could again see past his nose. "We brought you a fire extinguisher so you could have a cold Cheerwine?"

"Yep, and I really appreciate it. You should both help yourselves to two of them. And I think you can take the dogs out. They're probably ready."

The longer they were with him, the more Leif became convinced that Ben wouldn't, in fact, murder them. He removed the rake from the flame and handed it to Ben as Rex cracked open two cans and handed one to Leif.

"This really is the perfect temperature," Rex said, wiping Cheerwine off his lips. "So, what do you know about the Whitewood School?"

Ben stopped chewing the first bite of hot dog he'd just taken directly from the rake.

"You should both grab a frank and join me in my quarters." Ben rested the rake on a log before walking into the crude lean-to he'd built against the Tree.

Rex and Leif looked at each other before each grabbing a hot dog and walking underneath the branches. Following Ben's lead, they sat cross-legged on the ground. It was a tight space. All their knees were touching.

"Since you did this noble act for me," Ben said, "I consider you my friends. And as your friend, I would like to entrust you with my secret."

Leif and Rex leaned forward.

"Last week, I escaped from the Whitewood School."

Ben took a long sip of Cheerwine.

"You . . . escaped?" Leif asked, his eyes wide.

"What do you mean?" Rex asked. "What were you escaping from?"

"Death, I believe," Ben said.

"What?" Leif was hit by a full-body shiver.

Rex didn't want to believe his story, but since Ben was already defying all reasonable expectations by living in the woods and cooling down Cheerwine with a fire extinguisher, he found himself shaken. "Death? Come on," Rex said.

Ben unwound the bloody bandage on his hand and showed them what was underneath. "Look."

Leif and Rex both felt queasy as they stared at a deep, still partially open wound traversing Ben's palm. "Oh my gosh," Leif said, covering his mouth. "They did that to you at the school?"

Ben nodded solemnly.

"You should go to a hospital, man," Rex said.

"I can't. I can't go anywhere."

"Okay, okay, hold on a second." Rex held his hands up in the air, more terrified than he wanted to admit. "What grade are you in? Maybe you went to Whitewood, but I don't remember you from our school before that. Do you, Leif?"

Leif examined Ben carefully. "I don't think so."

"I'm supposed to be entering ninth grade. But you wouldn't know me because I was homeschooled."

"So if you escaped," Leif said, "why don't you go back home?"

"Because my dad will just send me back to White-wood." Ben began to slowly wind the bandage around his hand.

"Not if you tell him they tried to kill you! And, like, cut your hand and stuff."

Ben looked deep into Leif's eyes. "He wouldn't believe me. The reason he sent me to the school in the first place was because of my . . . exaggerations."

"Huh," Rex said. He knew that Ben might just be a pathological liar, but Rex's highly sensitive BS meter was telling him otherwise, and there was something exciting about that, too. Horrifying, but exciting. He needed to be sure, though. "Wouldn't Whitewood report you missing?"

Ben laughed. "He'd rather get me back there without having to explain anything." He lowered his voice, suddenly serious again. "I've got no idea how deep this thing goes, but I know there are other adults in town helping him look for me. I've had to move twice already."

"So, our friend Alicia," Leif asked, trying not to shake, "are they gonna try to kill her, too?"

Ben took a bite of hot dog. "Very hard to say. You know about the other kids who died there, right?"

Leif bit down on his lower lip.

"Those were freak accidents," Rex said.

"You think they would tell the newspapers they murdered kids?" Ben asked.

"This is bad," Leif said, his arms wrapped around his knees. "This is very, very bad."

"I agree," Ben said, staring past them at the fire with a haunted look.

"Yeah. Okay. Yeah," Rex said, mainly to himself. He hadn't decided for sure if he believed Ben or not.

"Look," Ben said. "Maybe you think I'm making this up. I understand that. I can't guarantee I would believe me either, considering I referenced my history of embellishment less than two minutes ago. So meet me Friday night at midnight behind the old tobacco barn in the field near the Whitewood School."

"What will . . . what will happen then?" Leif asked.

"It's best if you come and see for yourself," Ben said.

"We'll be there," Rex said.

"No!" Leif shouted reflexively.

"Okay," Rex said, not wanting to get into another argument with Leif. "We'll think about it."

"This is . . . this is, like, nuts," Leif said. "Like totally nuts."

"We, uh . . . we should get going." Rex stood and helped Leif up as he continued muttering about how nuts this was.

"Think about my offer," Ben said. "Do it for your friend at Whitewood."

"We will," Rex said.

"Please take a Cheerwine for the road," Ben said, standing up. "They taste like motor oil when they're warm."

Once they were back in the river, Leif leaned toward Rex after a big gulp of soda. "Glad we'll never see *him* again."

"Yeah," Rex said. But he knew he would see Ben on Friday.

And he was pretty sure Leif would, too.

11

ALICIA HAD ONLY BEEN AT WHITEWOOD FOR A MATTER OF DAYS, BUT she'd needed just one meal to grow sick of the food. Knives and forks were forbidden, so anything that required cutting was blended into a spoonable slurry. Lunch was particularly unimpressive today. Even so, Alicia tried her best to enjoy it, shoveling a mystery stew into her mouth as she rubbed her sore neck with her other hand. It had been a couple days since her time in the Roll, but she'd developed an excruciating kink after sleeping an entire night with her head hanging out of the carpet cocoon.

Still, there was a perverse sweetness to the pain. It was like a battle scar, proof of her rebellion. They'd disciplined her, and she'd survived. She wasn't eager to visit the Roll again, but she was proud of how she'd handled it.

One thing was for sure: Her time in the Roll definitely hadn't helped her standing among her peers. If she had been a pariah before, now she was practically toxic. A small part of her had wanted to believe her defiance would serve as inspiration, a spark to resistance, but it was clear that her fellow students had been trained to distance themselves from mutiny. She tried not to let it bother her; no one at the school was talking to anyone else anyway, so what did it matter if nobody sat next to her at meals, that she seemed surrounded by a bubble at all times?

As she finished one of her two Saltines and pulled back

the foil of her applesauce, the girl beside her—well, not so much *beside* her, since there were two empty seats separating them—slid her tray several inches in Alicia's direction. Alicia ignored it, assuming it had nothing to do with her, until the girl slowly slid it even closer. Alicia took a quick glance at her. The girl, who had long black hair and thick eyebrows and looked close to her age, was staring straight ahead while gently wiggling the tray, as if to direct Alicia's attention there.

Alicia looked. The girl had mostly cleaned her plate, but left behind some peas.

Was she offering Alicia extra peas? If Alicia was going to the Roll again, it wasn't going to be because she broke the food-sharing rule for peas. If the girl had been offering an extra cupcake, that might have been worth considering. But there were no cupcakes at Whitewood.

Alicia really missed cupcakes.

She stared forward the way the girl did, subtly shaking her head that no thanks, she didn't need the peas.

The girl coughed, one hand over her mouth, then slid her tray an inch closer to Alicia, who was starting to get annoyed. Why was this girl so obsessed with sharing her peas? Was she mentally unstable? Or was she *trying* to get Alicia in trouble? Alicia glanced down at the plate once more, and that was when she saw it:

J.

The peas were arranged to form the letter *J.*

The girl saw Alicia receive the message. Still staring straight ahead, she patted her chest twice and gave the smallest of smiles.

Alicia understood; it was a nod to the *A* that Alicia had written in blood on the wall, the very act that had gotten her sent to the Roll. This girl didn't want to go by Candidatus either.

Alicia had gone so many days without genuinely connecting with anyone that the interaction invigorated her, giving her a warm feeling in her chest like a favorite T-shirt she'd discovered buried in a drawer.

J slid the tray back to its regular position and spooned some peas into her mouth.

Alicia kept J in the corner of her eye through the rest of the meal, but she made no further attempts to communicate.

—

TWO DAYS WENT by before J made contact again.

Not that Alicia was counting or anything.

The cafeteria exchange—if you could even call it that—had affected her more than she'd first realized. Knowing that she wasn't alone—that she had an ally at Whitewood, maybe even a *friend*—made her all the more determined to hold on to her Alicia-ness.

And weirdly, knowing there was someone she wanted to run into again inspired Alicia to be, for at least a brief time, obedient. She held her tongue and kept her head down, hoping she wouldn't be sent to the Roll again before she'd communicated with J.

Opportunities to connect, however, proved rare, and the wait was excruciating. Though Alicia saw her every day at lunch, she couldn't bring herself to sit at J's table. She didn't want to inadvertently reveal their connection to the helpers, who might stamp out the friendship before it even started. No, J had to be the one to make the next move.

Which she finally did. In the Leisure Room.

The students of Whitewood had two options for spending their limited break time: their dorm room or the Leisure Room. In the latter—which was really just a small library, complete with built-in bookshelves on three of the walls—Candidati were allowed to sit on the worn wooden floor and read from the sparse collection of old books. Alicia hadn't found anything written after 1960. There was one entire wall of Bibles (all King James Version) along with other religious writings and, randomly, about a dozen primers for learning Latin. The other two walls' shelves were full of classic literature that Headmaster had apparently deemed acceptable for young, impressionable minds.

During her first stint in the Leisure Room, Alicia had picked up *The Pilgrim's Progress*, having heard her grandfather talk about it before, but three pages in she found it impenetrable. And so she had chosen to spend her remaining time in thought, imagining what her first week of freshman year at Bleak Creek High would have been like. She wondered if Rex and Leif had successfully pulled off their plan to avoid sitting with Mark Hornhat at lunch. *Probably not without me,* she thought.

Now, during her second visit to the Leisure Room, she planned to bypass the books altogether and simply sit, letting her mind take her on a journey. But as she entered the room and looked over the twenty or so students who had already found a seat on the floor, she caught a glimpse of those thick eyebrows.

She didn't want to make her interest in J too obvious, so instead of facing her, she took a seat about ten feet away and turned ninety degrees, placing her new friend in her periphery.

Then she waited.

For a few minutes, J remained motionless, not looking up from her copy of *Treasure Island*. Alicia started to lose hope, thinking J had changed her mind about continuing their secret connection.

But then J coughed.

Alicia turned her head slowly to see that J was looking just above the giant book in her hands, directly at her.

Alicia then looked over at the helper assigned to the Leisure Room, a skinny guy with Luke Perry sideburns who Alicia had decided must be newer, as he didn't seem that much older than the students. He was deeply engrossed in a Hardy Boys novel.

J coughed again. She subtly lifted her chin, as if pointing to something. When Alicia tracked her eyeline, all she saw was the same FOLLOW sign that hung in every room.

J slowly stood, then walked to the helper and asked if she could go to the bathroom. He nodded without looking up from his book, and J left the room.

Alicia was confused for a second before she understood.

FOLLOW.

"Helper, may I use the restroom?" she asked, getting to her feet.

"Somebody just went, Candidatus," the helper said, still not looking up. "You can go when she gets back."

"I really have to go," Alicia said. "Like, really really."

The helper looked at her over the pages of his book, skeptical but also clearly wanting to get back to those Hardy boys. *They must be on a very exciting case,* Alicia thought. "Fine. But make it quick."

"Thank you, Helper," Alicia said, but he was already back with Frank and Joe.

Alicia headed out into the beige hallway and saw J's dark hair turning the corner all the way down at the other end of the hall. She'd passed right by the girls' bathroom. Alicia picked up her pace to try to catch up.

Her heart beat extra fast, knowing that if she was caught roaming like this, she'd almost definitely end up in the Roll again.

It was worth it, though.

When Alicia turned the corner, J was hovering about twenty steps ahead. She nodded at Alicia and then stepped into the wall. Alicia half believed some kind of magic had occurred until she reached the spot where J had been and saw that it wasn't actually a wall, but a beige curtain that she'd never noticed. She looked around nervously before threading her body past the curtain to find . . . another hallway.

J was about halfway down, standing next to an open door, gesturing with her hand like *Come on come on come on quickly come on.*

Alicia suddenly worried. Was this a trap? But even if it was, it couldn't make things worse than they already were. The words of the helper rang in her ears: *Make it quick.* She speed-walked the remaining distance to J and went through the open door.

What she saw took her breath away.

She'd been assuming this was J's dorm room, but it was immediately clear that she'd been wrong. The room was huge, at least three times as large as the cramped space Alicia shared with her roommate. But the most startling part was the colors. The walls were covered with a pink, blue, and violet floral-patterned wallpaper, while the white four-poster bed was draped with a deep purple comforter and topped with fluffy tasseled pillows of multiple patterns and a worn blue crochet toy frog that looked homemade. Across from the bed stood a teal desk with an orange mug filled with pens and pencils of every shade. Having spent a week seeing little other than beige throughout all of the school, the colors overwhelmed Alicia, seeming to spill into her other senses.

As she caught her breath, she registered that this was a little girl's bedroom. But something was a bit off. While the room was clean, as if someone still lived there, the decor had a noticeably dated feel. It reminded Alicia of the girls' room from *The Brady Bunch*.

"Whose room is this?" she whispered once J had come inside and carefully closed the door behind her.

"Hers," J answered, pointing at a picture hanging on the wall near the desk. "I think she might have been one of the students who died."

Alicia quivered, then took a cautious step toward the picture. She was walking with her hands close to her side as if she were exploring a museum exhibit. In the faded picture sat a young girl, maybe seven or eight years old, holding what appeared to be the same blue frog from the bed. She had blond pigtails, a forced smile, and sad eyes lined with dark circles.

"She looks sick," Alicia observed.

"Yeah, maybe that's why they gave her this nice room," J reasoned.

Over the desk hung a bulletin board with crayon drawings of flowers, dogs, a dragon, and a family of three. The pictures were signed, in the sloppy fashion of a small child, *Ruby*.

"We don't have much time. Take a seat." J motioned toward the perfectly made bed. Alicia sat down softly, keeping most of her weight in her feet as if she didn't trust it to support her.

"The J is for Josefina," J said.

"The A is for Alicia," Alicia replied.

"I knew it! You don't look like an Allison. Or an Amy. And definitely not an Amber."

"Thanks, I guess?"

Josefina was strange. In a good way.

"I'm Guatemalan," she said.

"Oh, okay."

"I kinda have a habit of telling people that because

they always ask. Anyway. Nice to meet you, Alicia." She extended her arm.

"Nice to meet *you*, Josefina." Then, still not completely sure what was happening, Alicia grabbed her hand. The simple touch of another human—after days of feeling so isolated—seemed to raise her body temperature. She felt her face flush.

"So, how did you find this place?" Alicia asked in an effort to hide her embarrassment.

"Sneaking around is kinda my thing," Josefina explained. "I know where your dorm room is too."

Alicia stared, not sure what to make of that.

"It's not creepy," Josefina said. "Just practical. Anyway, thank you."

"Thank you?"

"Yeah. Before you came, I was starting to lose hope. Lose myself. You snapped me out of it."

"Oh," Alicia said. "Uh, yeah. You're welcome."

"After what you did to Headmaster, you've got a bright red bull's-eye on your back. And you act like it's no big thing. I admire that. Reminded me what it means to fight."

Josefina's words made Alicia feel like her resilience had been worth it. She smiled.

"We should get back," Josefina said, rising from her chair. "I'll go first, then you follow after a minute."

"That's it?" Alicia said. She knew Josefina was right, but she desperately wished they had more time. Even just another minute.

"For now," Josefina said. "We'll meet again soon. Try to keep each other sane. Next time we're in the Leisure Room together, follow my lead. If that doesn't happen, get here right after dinner, during those fifteen minutes of study time before lights out."

"Are we safe to be in here, though?" Alicia asked, getting to her feet.

"Doubt it," Josefina said. "But it's all we have. We'll be careful." She gave Alicia a final nod before opening the door a crack and sliding out into the hallway.

Alicia silently counted to sixty before following.

—

OVER THE NEXT twenty-four hours, Alicia replayed her conversation with Josefina again and again. Especially the parts where she'd been told how inspiring she was. She parsed every line, every gesture, every inflection, wondering if Josefina had some larger plan in mind. Whatever it was, Alicia was on board.

Unfortunately, she didn't make it to the Leisure Room that day, or even to dinner, as she ended up back in the Roll. She hadn't even been trying to disobey.

Alicia had just finished participating in a class activity, a sort of deprogramming during which students would share a hobby or interest and their classmates would list all the ways that particular passion could corrupt them. After she'd mentioned that *Cheers* was one of her favorite TV shows, the class had somehow managed to make a case that continuing to watch it would set her on a surefire course toward alcoholism.

This had been immediately followed by a deeply unsettling slideshow of people who'd fallen victim to various worldly vices: mangled bodies in drunk driving accidents, blue-faced overdosers, and half-naked murder victims. Alicia had involuntarily looked away from the stomach-turning images.

Candidati were not allowed to look away.

Her experience in the Roll was again horrendous, but a hair less this time, both because she'd been through it before and because it provided her with so many undisturbed hours to think about her new friend. In Josefina, there was hope.

When Alicia was released from the Roll a day or so later, a new kink in her neck and her beige onesie freshly soiled with urine, she was far from broken. After she was given clean clothes, she was delighted to realize it was already dinnertime, which meant, yes, she could put food in her brutally deprived stomach, but also that she might be able to make it to the bedroom behind the beige curtain to see Josefina.

That night, once dinner ended, she again walked to the bathroom, hid in a stall for a few minutes, peeked into the hall to make sure no helper was patrolling, and made a beeline for the secret bedroom. She knew what she was doing was reckless, that to be taken back to the Roll now would be devastating, but she had no choice. She *needed* to see Josefina again.

And sure enough, Josefina was already there when Alicia walked in. She was sitting in that same desk chair, holding close the blue stuffed frog from the bed.

"Hey," Alicia said, feeling buoyant even as she gripped her sore neck.

"Oh no," Josefina said, standing up and dropping the frog, maybe a little embarrassed. "They sent you to the Roll again, didn't they?"

"Yeah. But it's okay."

"The Roll is the worst," Josefina said. "I've only been there once and that was enough for me."

"You're missing out. It's *so* much better the second time," Alicia said.

Josefina released a small *heh* sound, which Alicia echoed. She'd forgotten how good it felt to laugh.

"So what else have you learned sneaking around here?" asked Alicia.

"This is gonna blow your mind," Josefina answered, "but this whole place used to be a resort."

"A resort?"

"Yep. I found some old brochures in a storage closet. People would come to that mineral spring outside so it could, like, heal them. And then some of the water would get pumped to those private bath houses."

"The Thinking Sheds."

"Exactly."

"Hard to believe anyone could have a good time in there," Alicia said.

"For real," said Josefina.

"So, how long have you been here?"

"At Whitewood? I don't even know." Josefina sat back down in the chair. "It has to be at least six months, but hard to say."

Alicia nodded and sat down gently on the bed, suddenly wanting to learn as much as she could as quickly as possible. "Why did your parents send you?"

"I killed my sister," Josefina said, staring at Alicia without blinking.

It wasn't what Alicia was expecting. She tried to get this new information to add up, to process that her only ally in the building was a murderer. "Wow," she said. "That's—"

"I'm joking," Josefina said, breaking into a smile. "I don't even have a sister. Sorry. I've always been bad at jokes."

Alicia exhaled. "Oh. Well. It would have been okay if you had. Done that."

"Really?"

"I don't know. Maybe not."

Josefina laughed. So did Alicia.

"Honestly," Josefina said, "it wasn't one thing that got me sent here. I mean, I've put my mom through a lot."

"Yeah?"

"My dad left when I was little, and she raised me by herself. And we fight. A lot. Like, full-on shouting matches. I think she just needed a break. And she had no idea this place was as nuts as it is."

"That sucks," Alicia said. "I'm sorry."

Josefina shrugged. "Thanks, but I'm looking forward to making her feel pretty guilty about it when I get home."

Alicia laughed again before getting sad thinking about her own parents and needing to change the subject. "Really, though, what is this room?" She stood up and looked at one of the framed photos on the wall. "Who is this girl? Ruby."

"I don't know, but we should go," Josefina said. "Lights out is in five minutes."

"Yeah," Alicia said, transfixed by the little girl's long blond hair and slightly crooked smile, thinking she recognized her from somewhere.

—

"YOU KNOW, I'M pretty sure a kid escaped from here," Josefina said the next night at their third meet-up. "Like, from the school, I mean."

"What?" Alicia said, propping herself up from the bed with an elbow.

"Yeah," Josefina said. "Not even that long ago."

"Wait, what do you mean?"

"I mean, there was this kid who was here. And then one day he was gone."

"You keep track of everybody here?" Alicia asked, one eyebrow raised.

"Well, no, but he was sort of my friend. He was a sneaker like me. I found him in the basement one time and we promised not to tell on each other."

"This place has a basement?"

"Then he told me there was weird stuff going on at the spring behind the school. Like weird ceremonies or something. I'm pretty sure he was just trying to seem cool."

"Huh." Alicia sat up, swinging her legs off the side of the bed. "How do you know he escaped? Maybe he just got to go home. Maybe he was *reformed . . .*"

"No way. The helpers hated him. He was sent to the Roll at least twice, one of those times like a week or so before he disappeared."

"But isn't it possible that he . . . ?"

"Died?" Josefina said. "Yeah, that's what I thought. But then, on my phone call with my mom, she didn't bring it up."

"So what?"

"Well, if a kid died in school, it would have to be in the news, right? That's what happened with the kids who died here in the past."

"I guess . . ."

"But if he escaped," Josefina said, spinning back and forth on the rolly chair, "they wouldn't want to put that in the news. They'd probably just be trying to catch him and bring him back before they'd have to tell his parents anything."

"And, if he went back to his parents—"

"They'd have just sent him back here."

"So how do you think he escaped?"

—

ALONE AT THE table as usual, Alicia finished off a bland bowl of grits, slid her tray onto the rack, and left dinner at the same time as everyone else. This after-dinner ritual had become a routine, her favorite part of the day by a long shot, and she tried not to smile as she headed down the hall to the girls' room.

Since the night before, she hadn't been able to stop thinking about the idea of escape. She was convinced that if she could just get to her parents, it would be different. In person, she'd be able to convince them that this school was a horrible place where no kid deserved to be sent. Whatever method that boy had used to escape likely wouldn't work twice. Whitewood and the helpers weren't idiots. But it meant there *was* some crack in the school's defenses, and that alone produced so much hope.

She waited in the bathroom the customary three minutes, then headed down the hall, past the curtain, and to the Secret Bedroom.

"I think I have a plan," she said as she walked through the door.

"Great. I can't wait to hear it," a voice said.

Wayne Whitewood stood from the rolling desk chair and walked toward her.

12

"OH, LORD, I DIDN'T KNOW YOU MEANT AN INTERVIEW THAT WOULD be filmed with your camera," Aunt Roberta said, nervously playing with her wedding ring as she watched Janine unpack her tripod on the kitchen floor.

"Oh," Janine said. "Is that . . . a problem?"

"Well, no," Aunt Roberta said, smiling. She had the same sunny disposition as GamGam and the same determination to maintain it at all costs. Janine's mom—and, by extension, Janine—must not have gotten that gene. "It's not a *problem*. I just . . . Well, I thought you'd be takin' notes to write an article for a newspaper, somethin' like that."

"Nope," Janine said. "I'm making a documentary." She had to stop herself from unleashing any sarcastic barbs that might further ruffle her aunt. But, come on: Aunt Roberta knew Janine went to film school. Why would she be writing a newspaper article? She felt a pulse of shame, realizing that she was blood related to someone who could be so dense. That was followed by a bigger pulse of shame as she recognized that she, in turn, could be so judgmental.

"Oh, wow, so you've been filming people? In town?"

Again, Janine bit her tongue. "Yes, Aunt Roberta. That's what you do when you make a documentary."

"Who have you been talking to?" Aunt Roberta seemed jumpier than usual, even as she kept up her shiny, happy façade. Janine didn't want to make her nervous, but she didn't want to put her completely at ease, either. What she wanted was answers. She knew that the string of deaths at Whitewood had begun after Donna's time there, but surely Aunt Roberta had an opinion about them. And there had to be a good reason she'd never told Janine about Donna attending the school. She was determined to find out about it.

But now, standing in the house that Roberta and Donna shared, watching her aunt fidget and flutter like a hummingbird, Janine felt more inclined to gently pry than ruthlessly interrogate. She reminded herself that Roberta probably never expected Donna to come back from the school as broken as she had, and also that Uncle Jim had been dead for almost ten years, leaving her aunt to deal with the new Donna all alone. Suddenly Janine felt terrible for her. *Damn you, empathy.* It was much easier to just be pissed.

"I've only spoken to a couple of people so far," Janine said.

"And what is it exactly that you're interviewing people about?" Aunt Roberta said now. "I think GamGam mentioned you're asking folks about kidney stones . . . ?"

Janine couldn't put her finger on it, but there was something about Aunt Roberta's clueless questions that tipped her off. Aunt Roberta was *deliberately* deceiving her.

"I was at first, yeah," Janine said, humoring her aunt, thinking she should wait to reveal the truth until the camera was on, and then deciding it would be kinder not to. "But now I'm interviewing people about the Whitewood School. I believe you're familiar with it?"

"Oh, really? That school on the edge of town?"

"I know, Aunt Roberta," Janine said. "I know that Donna went there."

Aunt Roberta kept smiling, even as something in her eyes crumpled.

"And you never told me," Janine added.

Her aunt's smile slowly wilted, and she began to shake.

"Are you okay?" Janine wasn't sure what was happening. "I didn't mean to . . . It's okay, we don't have to do this right now."

Aunt Roberta silently beckoned her to come closer.

As Janine walked forward, she looked into her aunt's eyes and saw it: pure, paralyzing fear. "You can't make this movie," Aunt Roberta said, her voice only slightly above a whisper.

"Why not?" Janine asked, the hair on her neck rising to attention.

"Just . . . don't."

Janine had the sense she was on the verge of pulling back the curtain on the Whitewood School, if she could just keep Aunt Roberta talking. "Is there a reason," she asked, with as much tenderness as she could, "that you never told the family Donna went to that school?"

Aunt Roberta covered her eyes. "I . . . We were embarrassed." She began to sob. "We just wanted to help her . . . We didn't think it would . . ." She sniffed and wiped her nose. "But I'm serious, Janine. You can't make this movie. I won't let you."

Janine felt both compassion and rage. "But what happened to Donna? What did they do to her that made her change so much?"

Aunt Roberta just looked away, shaking her head.

"And what about the kids that have died?"

"Please," she said, again covering her face with her hand.

"Aunt Roberta!" Janine couldn't help but raise her voice. "Don't you want to stop this from happening again?"

"We tried!" Aunt Roberta shouted, causing Janine to involuntarily take a half step back. "Your uncle and I tried to do . . . everything you're saying. And it wasn't worth it. I don't want to see you get—I just can't let you do that to yourself."

"But if you knew something happened," Janine said, "why didn't you at least go to the police?"

Aunt Roberta's eyes went cold.

"Jim did," she said, staring past Janine. "He told Sheriff Lawson there was somethin' wrong with that place."

"And what did he say?" Janine asked, realizing she was finally getting somewhere.

Aunt Roberta lowered her head, her eyes welling up with tears. "I don't think it was an accident, Janine. You understand what I'm saying? What happened to Jim . . . So that's why you need to stop all this. You understand me? You just can't—"

There were three loud knocks at the front door. Aunt Roberta's head snapped toward the sound, looking panicked, as if ready to escape through a window if necessary.

"Are you expecting anybody?" Janine asked.

"Helloooo!" a woman's voice chirped from the other side of the door.

Aunt Roberta stared into space, the gears in her brain spinning.

"Do you know who that is?"

"Mary Hattaway," she said, more to herself than to Janine.

Mary Hattaway . . . where do I know that name from? Janine thought.

Aunt Roberta wiped her eyes and took a deep breath. "Let me do the talking," she whispered.

"Um. Okay." Janine watched as her aunt crossed the room and opened the door.

"Hi, Mary!" Aunt Roberta said, suddenly back to her sunny self, a way more convincing performance than her earlier one. "What a nice surprise—come on in."

"Thank you, Roberta," Mary Hattaway said as she stepped into the house. She was tall and blond, in her forties, wearing a blue suit with giant gold buttons and shoulder pads that rivaled an NFL linebacker's. She looked like a real estate agent that ate other real estate agents for breakfast. Janine instantly disliked her. "I was just in the neighborhood and thought, *You know who I haven't seen in a while? Roberta!* I hope you don't mind me poppin' in like this."

"Not at all," Aunt Roberta said.

"Oh darlin', your makeup," Mary said, slightly horrified. "You been cryin'?"

Aunt Roberta froze for a moment before making a quick recovery. "Well, yes. We were just watchin' *Steel Magnolias*. Probably my tenth time seein' the thing, but it still gets me."

"Hmm," Mary said, her attempt at being sympathetic. "Dolly Parton should've never gotten mixed up in Hollywood, if you ask me." She flashed her white teeth at Janine. "And who might you be?"

"I'm Roberta's niece, Janine," she said, still trying to recover from the whiplash of greeting a guest moments after learning her uncle had likely been murdered.

"Hi, Janine. I'm Mary Hattaway." She extended a bony hand, which Janine had no choice but to shake.

"Mary's the secretary over at our church," Aunt Roberta said.

Oh, right. The secretary at Second Baptist. The one in that Gazette *article who said that kids were being . . . what was it? Oh yeah, "bombarded by sex."*

"You bet I am," Mary said. "What brings you to town,

Janine?" The woman's piercing eyes made the conversation feel unnecessarily intense.

"Just visiting," Janine said, knowing it was what her aunt wanted her to say.

"Would you like to join us in the kitchen, Mary?" Roberta asked. "I was just about to make some coffee."

"Oh, that's sweet, but I only have a minute before I have to get back to work. Is that your camera, Janine?" She pointed into the kitchen, where the camcorder still sat on the table.

"You bet it is," Janine said.

Mary smiled coldly, picking up on the echo of her own words. "How cute," she said. "My daughter Tammy likes playing around with cameras too. Just got her a Polaroid for her birthday. She's been havin' a ball with it."

Janine wished she could keep her mouth shut and go with the flow for her aunt's sake, but she knew it wasn't happening. "Oh," she said, "I don't play around with my camera."

"No?" Mary cocked her head to the side like an inquisitive spaniel.

"Not at all," Janine said. "I'm making a documentary."

"You sure you don't want to stay for some coffee, Mary?" Aunt Roberta said as she went ahead and loaded up the Mr. Coffee machine, her veneer of sunniness again starting to feel manufactured. "It should only take a minute."

"What's it about?" Mary asked, ignoring the question and taking a step closer to Janine, who held her ground even though she wanted nothing more than to leave the room.

"Well," Janine said. She could feel Aunt Roberta looking at her, desperately hoping Janine would say the right thing. But Janine was pretty sure Mary already knew what the movie was about—that it was, in fact, why she'd stopped by in the first place—so she felt fine throwing her off the scent a bit. "It's about architecture."

"Oh. How interesting." Janine could tell Mary wasn't expecting that. "In our town?"

"In lots of towns," Janine said. "I've been filming buildings and structures all over the country." The word *structures* seemed like an odd choice once she'd said it, but Mary didn't seem to notice.

"Hmm. Fascinating." Mary kept holding eye contact with Janine, as if she were scrutinizing her soul. "I bet my daughter would love to see this little movie when it's finished."

"Yeah, I'll bet," Janine said coldly.

After a few moments, Mary finally looked away. "Well, guess I should be gettin' back to work!" she said. "Roberta, I hope you'll be bringin' Janine with you on Sunday. We'd love to see you there."

"I'm Jewish," Janine said to Mary, knowing full well she could have just nodded and smiled. "We don't really do Sundays."

"Oh, gosh," Mary said, genuinely surprised for the second time that visit. "That's . . . just fine." She shook her head. *That's too bad* is what she'd been about to say. Janine was sure of it. She'd forgotten about this aspect of her Bleak Creek visits—how people never really knew how to hide their mix of fascination, prejudice, and sympathy for those unlike themselves—but it all came flooding back to her.

"My sister married a Jewish man," Aunt Roberta explained.

"Well, Janine, you're still welcome to come by anyway." Mary looked very proud of her own benevolence. "If you'd like."

"I doubt it," Janine said, smiling. "But thanks."

"I understand."

"You need to put that camera away and start makin' plans to get back to New York."

Janine nodded politely, knowing full well that she wasn't headed to New York anytime soon. After suffering through a cup of horribly weak coffee and labored small talk, she hugged Aunt Roberta one last time and headed out the door, then walked under the huge oak tree toward the street. As she approached GamGam's car, parked at the curb in front of the house, she froze.

Scrawled in red paint across the passenger side doors were two words:

Leave Bitch.

Mary stared at her a beat. "See you Sunday, Roberta.
She opened the door and was gone, leaving an offensiv
trail of White Diamonds by Elizabeth Taylor in her wake

Aunt Roberta walked into the kitchen and sat down ;
the small brown table. She looked tired. "I told you to l̪
me do the talking," she said.

"I know," Janine said, sitting down across from he
"I'm sorry."

Aunt Roberta let out a defeated sigh. "I meant what
said about Jim. These people . . . I don't think you unde
stand who you're dealing with here."

Janine was suddenly overcome by the magnitude (
what her aunt was saying, the sheer awfulness of it. Fc
lack of knowing what else to do, she stood up and walke
behind her aunt's chair, draping her arms around her in a
awkward hug.

"I miss my family," Aunt Roberta said, starting to cɪ
again. "Donna. The old Donna. Jim. I miss them so much.

"I know. Me too."

"Not a day goes by that I don't wish we'd never seɪ
Donna to that school. Not a day."

Janine wasn't sure if this was the right moment for
question, but she tried anyway. "Why *did* you send her?

Aunt Roberta sniffed a few times. "She . . . smelled liḷ
beer one night. Jim and I got scared."

Janine couldn't believe how ridiculous that was, tha
all of this tragedy had happened because Donna had onɕ
smelled like beer. Who knows if she'd even been the oɪ
drinking it.

But Janine knew it would do no good to point that ou

"I'm sorry, Aunt Roberta. So sorry for everythin
you've been through."

"Thank you, honey."

Her aunt turned to look Janine in the eye. "Now, I'ᴠ
got nothin' else to say about that place. I mean it."

13

"SEE? HE'S NOT HERE," LEIF SAID IN THE DARKNESS, HIS BACK AGAINST a long-abandoned tobacco barn near the Whitewood School property. "He was messing with us the whole time. Let's go home."

"What time is it?" Rex asked.

Leif found it annoying that Rex so often made fun of his Casio calculator watch but still regularly asked him for the time (and to do math). "It's 11:58," he said, illuminating the digital watch face. "He's not coming."

An owl loudly hooted from the nearby trees, as if to emphatically agree with Leif.

"Ben will be here," Rex insisted.

"It just changed to 11:59 as you said that."

"Okay, fine, whatever. But let's give it till at least 12:01."

"He said midnight."

"You can't give it one extra minute?"

"Not really!" Leif was tired of terrifying situations. His life had become a steady drumbeat of fear, worry, manipulation by Rex, and then more fear and worry. When Rex had said he'd meet up with Ben whether Leif came along or not—that Alicia was "depending on them to follow every lead, to help her however they could"—well, of *course* Leif was going along too. But he wasn't thrilled about it. He couldn't shake the feeling this was all going to end very badly.

Leif startled as the owl hooted again. "Welp, it's midnight," he said, pointing to his lit Casio. "Let's go!"

Rex tried to remain composed, but Leif was frustrating when he got like this. And a tiny part of him wondered if maybe Ben *was* going to stand them up. "Look, we have to wait until *at least* 12:01, because every second of 12:00 counts as midnight."

"That's not true," Leif said. "Every second after midnight is the next day. He said Friday night at midnight. It's Saturday!"

Before Rex could continue the argument, the owl hooted again, louder than ever, followed by what sounded like an animal landing in the grass at the tree line. Rex and Leif froze in place as they stared into the inky dark, listening as the thing crept toward them. The creature came closer, the gibbous moon making it obvious—much to Leif's simultaneous relief and disappointment—that it was human. A chunk of pale hair poked out from under a misshapen fur hat. Ben hooted again once he was next to them.

"The owl in the tree was you?" Leif asked.

"Yes," Ben said. "I was the owl in the tree."

Ben looked dirtier than usual. His entire face was caked with mud, as was his jumpsuit. Leaves, pine straw, and twigs were stuck to his torso and limbs in various spots.

"It's camo," Ben said, noticing Rex and Leif staring. "I shouldn't even be this close to the school, so I need to take every precaution."

"Yeah, but we shouldn't be this close to the school either," Leif said. "Whitewood knows who we are. If we're caught out here, he'll probably just, like, grab us and take us to the school without even asking our parents."

"That's not how it works," Ben said.

"Yeah," Rex agreed.

"But . . . shouldn't we also have camo?" Leif asked.

"There's plenty of dirt," Ben said, sweeping a leafy arm toward the barren patch underneath the buckling barn's awning. "Help yourself."

"I'll pass," Rex said.

Leif contemplated for a moment, then slowly crouched down and tried to dig his nails into the earth. It was cement-like, compacted by cattle traffic. He moved his hands around, hoping to find a softer spot. His fingers entered what felt like a pile of mud.

"Ah, shit!" Leif whisper-shouted.

"You said it," affirmed Ben. "I was gonna tell you to watch your step for cow pies out here, but I didn't think I needed to tell you to watch your, uh, hands."

Leif stood up, thankful the night was covering his blushing. He took a step into the grass, careful to avoid making his situation worse by stumbling into another bovine deposit, and knelt down, running his soiled hand through the thick blades.

"At least you'll smell like a cow. That's a form of camouflage, I guess," Rex said, snickering as he pulled his backpack over one shoulder.

"Funny," Leif said.

"So, uh, Ben, what is it you think we're gonna see here?" Rex had brought his dad's camcorder, thinking whatever they observed might be worth documenting.

"It's not here, actually," Ben said. "We've got to go onto the Whitewood School property to see it. And we should get going. It usually happens about quarter after twelve."

"What? No!" Leif protested. "Go on the school property? Are you nuts?"

"Possibly," Ben answered. "My uncle once told me I was 'uniquely challenging,' which sounds like a nice way of saying nuts."

Rex took a step toward Leif and adopted his serious voice, which registered about a half octave below his usual speech. "You need to decide right now if you're going with us."

Leif knew he was cornered. Rex had purposely said *us*, a clear indication that Leif would have to stand alone in this creepy cow pasture—or, worse, walk home alone in the middle of the night—if he didn't tag along.

"Fine," Leif said. "But what are we supposed to do? Climb that fence?" He pointed toward the ten-foot chain-link fence topped with barbed wire running just behind the barn.

"No need to climb," Ben said, starting to walk. "Follow me."

Rex immediately strode after Ben.

Leif paused, sighed loud enough for Rex to hear it, then followed.

When Ben reached the fence, he squatted down and placed both hands on it, moving them around like a mime outlining an invisible box until he found what he was looking for. He pushed forward to reveal a part of the fence was cut, giving them a gap to squeeze through, about fifteen links high. "You guys first," he whispered.

Rex appreciated the polite gesture. Leif thought it might be a trap. "No, that's okay, you go first," he whispered.

"Okay," Ben said with a shrug, sliding one leg through the gap, then his head and torso, followed by the other leg. A few twigs fell off him, but it was an otherwise smooth passage.

Rex went next, first popping his backpack through before his towering frame, sliding through the fence using

Ben's technique (though failing to make it look as easy as Ben had). Leif, perhaps in subconscious protest of this midnight mission, took a different approach, turning around and backing his way through the fence. The tail of his Coke shirt got caught, sending the fabric up and over his head, halting his progress. Before Leif could ask for help, Rex unhooked his shirt and the rest of him popped through the fence.

"You're welcome," Rex said.

Leif scowled at him, but his tall and currently irritating friend was already catching up with Ben.

They moved through the woods as silently as they could, each of them highly aware they were now on the grounds of the Whitewood School.

They had walked for a minute or so up a small hill when Ben stopped at a medium-sized tree with a trunk that, just above his head, forked into two. "This is the spot," he said, crouching down and encouraging Rex and Leif to do the same.

Leif peered around the two-trunked tree. From the top of this crest, he could see they were only a couple dozen yards from the edge of the woods behind the school. At the bottom of the hill, glistening in the moonlight, was a pool of water about forty feet across, a creek slowly flowing away from it across the school grounds.

"Is that," Rex whispered excitedly, "Bleak Creek Spring?"

"Yep," Ben answered. "That's where Bleak Creek begins, and it's also where the action's gonna happen."

"I've lived here my whole life and I've never seen it," Leif said, the wonder of seeing his town's hidden namesake momentarily distracting him from his fear.

Beyond the sparse trees on the opposite side of the spring, they could see the school itself, a featureless pale rectangle in the darkness. It stood less than a hundred yards away, along with a row of four tiny buildings, all surrounded by a large lawn, the same lawn that Travis cut each week. An interior light shone from a first-floor window, a translucent curtain obscuring any details within.

"So . . . what happens now?" Rex asked, camcorder in hand.

"Now, we wait," Ben said, gazing out at the spring.

"How long?" He didn't feel as antsy as Leif, but he was again relying on the ol' punching-bag-in-bed trick to keep his parents from realizing he was gone, and the off-chance of them checking his room left him uneasy.

"Just a bit," Ben said.

As they crouched in silence, watching and waiting, they noticed the cicadas belting out their pulsing songs around them, making the forest seem alive, like it had a giant, beating heart. "I'm kinda hungry," Leif said. Terror and hunger were often interchangeable for him.

"Here." Rex dug around in his backpack and chucked a huge Ziploc bag over to Leif. "Brought some trail mix."

"Thanks," Leif said, instantly comforted by a familiar snack.

"You can have some too, Ben," Rex said.

"I'm okay," Ben said. "Still pretty full from my three-squirrel dinner."

"Uh, all right," Rex said, as he noticed Leif taking out individual peanuts from the bag and consuming them one by one. He was tempted to say something, but he was well acquainted with Leif's pickiness—his aversion to olives, mushrooms, and pepperoni had sabotaged many a pizza order—and either way, this was no time to bicker over trail mix etiquette. Then Leif popped another peanut in his mouth, chewing so loudly, the sound began to rival the cicadas.

"Hey, Leif, don't—Let's not . . . let's not do it like that."

"Like what?" Leif asked.

"Like eating all the peanuts and nothing else."

"But I don't like M&M's or raisins. I'm avoiding them."

"Yeah, but you're throwing off the whole ratio. My mom had a specific mix in mind."

"You think your mom is gonna be upset about me eating the peanuts?"

"No," Rex said, growing more flustered, "but when you eat trail mix, you're supposed to take a handful. Everybody knows that. What you get is what you eat!"

"Maybe quiet down a bit," Ben said from between them.

"Sorry," Rex said.

"Yeah," Leif said, depositing yet another peanut onto his tongue. "You offer me a snack and then you're telling me how to eat it. Makes it kinda hard to enjoy."

"Okay," Rex said, reaching his arm across Ben, "gimme back my mom's trail mix."

"No," Leif said, holding the bag close, "you—"

He didn't finish his sentence, because that's when the chanting started.

Just outside the school, about a dozen people were walking across the grass toward the spring. Their words were indecipherable but sounded to Rex like Latin. Or at least how he imagined Latin would sound. Two individuals holding torches led the procession; the others walked two by two behind them. All wore full-length hooded robes and walked slowly in step with one another.

"What is this?" Rex asked, hitting the record button on his camcorder and placing his finger over the red light to maintain their cover.

"See?" Ben whispered. "I told you you'd want to check it out."

"Is it the KKK?" Leif asked. "I've heard they're still around."

"Nope," Ben said. "KKK's got white robes. These are light blue. Plus, they've got open hoods, not the pointy ones with eyeholes."

"Yeah, they look more like Druids or something," Rex said.

"Might just be, like, a nighttime choir group," Leif said, gripping tight to the Ziploc of disproportionate trail mix. "You know, like Christmas carolers. Is there such a thing as Labor Day carolers?"

"Just keep watching," Ben said.

As the group reached the edge of the spring, their chanting hit a crescendo. They were now close enough for the boys to hear the foreign words clearly: "Vee-tah ehst ah-kwa, vee-tah ehst ah-kwa."

"Maybe they're Episcopalian?" Leif asked, barely able to get the words out. "I think they do weird stuff like this."

The pairs split, making way for an individual to walk down the newly created aisle between them. In addition to the light blue robe, this person wore a white stole draped over his shoulders with what looked to be some sort of star symbol embroidered at each end. Rex got a glimpse of the face under the drooping hood, the torchlight illuminating his features. "Is that . . . Whitewood?" he asked in disbelief.

"Bingo," Ben whispered.

Leif couldn't fully process what he was seeing.

Whitewood lifted his arms, and the torchbearers placed their fiery sticks into two stands near the edge of the water. The chanters fanned out, forming a semicircle around the spring. They all kneeled and began to chant more quietly.

"Are those students?" Rex asked.

"Unlikely," Ben said. "I never wore a robe."

"Wait, so they're *teachers*?" Leif asked.

Ben shrugged.

Whitewood signaled with his hand, and the group bent

down, bringing their faces to the surface of the water to drink.

"Gross!" Leif whispered. "There's gotta be like, amoebas or something in there."

After they'd had their fill, the followers lifted their heads and resumed the chanting.

He then began to slowly and deliberately walk counterclockwise along the row of chanters, his left hand extended to hover over each head, like some perverse game of duck duck goose. When he reached the end of the line, he turned around and walked back the other way, now holding out his right hand over the kneeling subjects. He then abruptly stopped and gently placed his hand on one of the heads.

The goose stood, and they both stepped forward to the spring as the chanting increased in volume. Whitewood reached into the folds of his robe and produced a knife, which he held aloft like the Statue of Liberty's torch.

The chanting grew louder.

Leif took a deep breath. "Maybe they're just practicing for Hallow—"

"It's a cult!" Rex said, having trouble keeping his voice at a whisper. "They're not carolers or Episcopalians, and nobody practices for Halloween! It's clearly a cult." Leif looked very much the way he had looked in second grade after Rex had told him the truth about Santa Claus.

They watched now as the robed woman chosen by Whitewood—at least, Rex was fairly sure it was a woman—extended one hand, palm up, from her robe. As the chanting intensified to near shouting, Whitewood slowly lowered the knife to the woman's hand, then pulled back sharply across her palm. She shouted out in pain but also sustained a specific pitch, as if it were a continuation of the chant.

"What the crap!" Leif said, covering his eyes. "Did he cut off her hand?"

"No, it was just a slice," Rex said, horrified but also

grinning. Sometimes he inexplicably smiled when awful things happened.

Remembering the nasty, bloody bandage on Ben's hand, Rex asked, "Is this what they did to you?"

"Pretty much," Ben said. "Just watch."

Leif reluctantly parted the fingers he held over his eyes just in time to see the woman kneel by the spring and dip in her wounded hand.

"That's a great way to get an infection," Leif said.

"Shut up and watch!" Ben whispered firmly. "This is the best part!"

The woman kept her hand in the dark water as Whitewood stood on the bank of the spring, motionless. The cult continued their chant. It seemed like they were waiting for something.

A faint blue light began to glow from deep under the water.

A few bubbles floated to the surface, as if some underwater creature were being stirred. Slowly, the light began to fill the pool as more bubbles rose. Within a minute, the spring was glowing bright and bubbling like a boiling cauldron.

"Holy shit," Rex and Leif said in unison. Normally one of them would have said "Jinx." But not today.

The woman rose and receded back into line as one of the other chanters stood and approached Whitewood, assisting him as he unfastened and pulled off his robe. Underneath, he wore an old-fashioned one-piece swimsuit. His untoned body spilled out of it, while his white mane of hair-sprayed locks held their ground in the gentle night breeze. None of the boys said a thing. The weirdness had reached a level that rendered snarky remarks about an old man's body untenable.

Whitewood waded into the blue spring. He stepped forward methodically, sinking deeper as he made his way to the center. But instead of beginning to swim, he slowly marched forward until his head disappeared completely under the water.

Rex was expecting Whitewood to come up quickly, a brief dunk.

But he didn't.

A minute passed.

"What the hell . . . ?" Rex said.

The chanting continued, but Leif noticed that the words had changed. *"Elect-us in-trot ah-qwam sank-tum,"* they now droned.

Another minute passed. Whitewood did not reappear.

"Did he go into a cave or something?" Rex asked.

"I think we just watched a dude drown," Leif said.

"Just wait," Ben said.

Another minute.

Leif tried to distract himself by picking out some more peanuts from the bag he'd been gripping, but he'd entirely lost his appetite.

By the time five minutes had passed, Rex was more confused than ever.

Finally, Whitewood's head broke the surface and he slowly came toward the water's edge, not swimming but instead moving as if he was being propelled by an under-water motor. When he reached the shallows, he groggily stood up to walk out of the spring. His perfectly shaped bouffant had wilted, his wet hair hugging his skull, making him seem almost feeble. He stumbled onto the shore, then bent over and began to heave. A massive amount of spring water spewed out onto the ground, Whitewood repeatedly convulsing, ejecting fountain after fountain onto the muddy bank.

After he'd emptied himself completely, the blue light faded to nothing and the chanting stopped. Two of the robed people grabbed Whitewood under his arms to steady him. He said something weakly to the group, though it was hard to make out what it was. Rex thought he heard the word *prophecy*.

The torchbearers took the torches from the stands and led Whitewood and his followers back toward the school.

"I just . . ." Rex said. "What the hell did we just witness?"

"That's what I've been trying to figure out," Ben said.

"I mean, that can't be real, right?" said Rex. "The glowing water, the bubbles? I mean, like, he's rigged some lights and air tubes or something under there . . . It's like a big Jacuzzi."

"I don't know . . . seemed pretty real to me," Leif said. "I think this is some straight-up evil stuff. Like when Pastor Mitchell played Led Zeppelin backward and it said 'my sweet Satan.'"

Rex noticed that Ben was staring silently out at the now-dark spring.

"What do you think, Ben?" Rex asked. "It's not real, right?"

"I think they were trying to sacrifice me," he said without emotion, not looking at them.

"What? No," Leif said.

"This ceremony had no students. Therefore no death. But after they cut *my* hand, I could have sworn they were going to drown me. Those kids who died . . . I think they were sacrificed."

Rex's eyes widened. All traces of fear had been replaced by exhilaration, like after the first time he'd ridden the Big Bad Wolf at Busch Gardens. Whether or not the spring was Satanic or just some wild illusion cooked up by Wayne Whitewood, Bleak Creek had just been transformed from a dull town into a genuinely interesting place. They'd stumbled onto something huge. And he had it all on tape.

"How *did* you get away?" Leif asked, completely terrified by everything that had transpired in the past twenty minutes.

"I did some moves," Ben said. "Martial arts stuff. Jean-Claude Van Damme saved my life."

"Wow," Leif said.

"People need to know about this," Rex said. "We can show them the footage." He held up the camera and was horrified to see that it wasn't recording. *Oh no.* He'd committed the cardinal sin of videography: stopping the recording when you think you're starting it. He would later realize that he'd accidentally hit the record button when passing through the fence, and the only thing of interest he'd captured was an argument about trail mix.

He didn't think Leif or Ben noticed. "But not right away," he backtracked. "Maybe . . . yeah, maybe we'll wait on showing them the footage."

"Definitely," Ben agreed, getting to his feet, seeming eager to leave. "We shouldn't assume we can trust anyone. Only each other."

"Right," Rex said. "That's what I was thinking."

"I don't want Alicia to be sacrificed," Leif said quietly.

"We won't let that happen." Rex was completely serious, and yet he could feel it: He was still smiling a little. He dug a hand into the trail mix Leif was still holding and threw a bunch into his mouth, thinking it might suppress the smirk. It did, but that was mostly because he realized he was chomping down on nothing but raisins and M&M's.

14

ALICIA COULDN'T BREATHE.

Wayne Whitewood's gloved hands were gripping her neck.

It took everything she had not to panic, to resist the water from pouring into her nose as the headmaster leaned her back, her face just below the surface.

This was her third time in a Thinking Shed, but instead of being compressed in the unforgiving coils of the Roll, she was now immersed in a grimy basin filled with the so-called healing waters of Bleak Creek Spring.

"Are you ready to follow, Candidatus?" Whitewood asked after lifting her out of the water. Alicia coughed and sputtered, her curls heavy and matted to the sides of her face. Then she just stared at him.

Whitewood dunked her again.

Alicia's brain was still racing to catch up to her new situation. She'd been forced to one-eighty so quickly from the anticipation of seeing Josefina to the dread of encountering Whitewood that it hadn't sunk in yet.

And almost worse than the abuse she was currently suffering was the thought that had occurred to Alicia moments after she'd entered the bedroom:

Did Josefina set me up?

Was that what their friendship was the whole time? A con?

It was too painful to contemplate. Could it be that the only real human connection she'd made since arriving at Whitewood wasn't real at all, that she was even more alone than she'd imagined?

Just when she thought she might gasp in a lungful of water, Whitewood lifted her up.

"*Now* are you ready to follow?" His tone remained calm, but Alicia thought she saw a flash of desperation in his face. She stayed silent, though she was beginning to question how long she could keep it up.

Whitewood shook his head slowly, tightening his grip on her throat, and pushed her down once more.

Aside from the horrible smell coming from the cloudy water, the sinewy hands pressing on her windpipe, and her arms being tied behind her back, it wasn't too unlike her actual baptism, performed by Pastor Mitchell when she was ten. Just like back then, she was in waist-deep water with a fully clothed man who wanted to hear some very specific words. Pastor Mitchell had told her ahead of time that he would be asking a number of questions about Jesus, and all she had to do was say yes to each one. Whitewood hadn't mentioned Jesus once, but he seemed to be after a similar answer. She wondered now, as she had then with Pastor Mitchell, if the best strategy was simply to go along with what the adult was looking for.

As Whitewood again lifted her from the water, her head woozy and vision blurry, she questioned how much it would really hurt to just say, "Yes, I will follow." She could spend the rest of her time at the Whitewood School in hushed defiance.

"Candidatus," Whitewood said, his voice oozing with charm even as his eyes conveyed the exact opposite, "I have to say, I'm glad we're gettin' this chance to talk. Had my eye on you since you got here. Every day I'm wonderin' if you'll see the light. If you'll let us save you. But that doesn't seem to be on your agenda."

Alicia didn't know how to respond, but it didn't matter, as it was evidently just a dramatic pause. "You feel these gloves on my hands?" Whitewood asked.

Alicia nodded.

"You know why I have to wear these?"

She nodded again.

Whitewood smiled. "Of course you do. I have to wear these while my hands heal. Because of what you did to me. Let me ask you, Candidatus: Do you know how difficult it is to play the organ with gloves on?"

Alicia shook her head, a genuine response.

"Pretty darn difficult," Whitewood said. "You can still do it, sure, but you lose the subtleties, the nuances. I can convey the basic message of the music to all the congregants, but it's like I'm . . . It's like my music is screamin' the whole time. And sometimes I don't want it to scream. Sometimes I want it to talk. To converse. To whisper. You understand?"

Alicia didn't. But she nodded anyway, water dripping from her hair into her eyes.

"And you've taken that from me," Whitewood said. "Because you think the rules don't apply to you. That you're . . . *special*. So what I want to know is . . . Was it worth it? *Is* it worth it?"

It was a very good question. But Alicia couldn't fully consider an answer because she was transfixed by Whitewood's flawlessly coiffed hair. The way it maintained its signature swoop despite the strained expression on his face, it almost looked fake.

"Well, I'll tell you," he said. "*It's not.* So I hope you're ready to fall in line. Are you? Are you ready to follow?"

Whitewood stared coldly, his hands still wrapped loosely around her neck. "I asked you a question, Candidatus."

Alicia was on the verge of saying yes.

She decided to split the difference between rebellion and submission.

"Whose room was that?" she asked. "Who was that girl, Ruby?"

A cloud of rage passed over Whitewood's features as he dug his thumb into her neck, his face reddening. He scream-grunted through gritted teeth as he again shoved her underwater.

Alicia immediately regretted asking. She should have just said yes.

But it was too late. Whitewood was screaming things above the surface.

For the first time since arriving at the Whitewood School, it hit her: She could die here. Is this what had happened to the students who'd been in those freak accidents over the years? Had they just pushed Whitewood too far?

When he brought her to the surface again, she would say yes. It was time. She would rather be a living Alicia with a compromised sense of self than a dead Alicia with no self at all.

But Whitewood was still yelling, showing no indication that he'd be lifting her anytime soon.

Her entire body was flooded with the panic she'd been holding back since the moment she'd seen Whitewood in that room instead of Josefina. She squirmed, twisted, and thrashed her legs, striking Whitewood's shins and calves, which only inspired him to stiffen his grip.

She realized with horror that she might have missed the moment to save her own life.

And then, suddenly—just like she'd seen in movies but had always doubted could actually happen—her thoughts became a patchwork of disjointed memories.

She remembered her family watching *Honey, I Shrunk the Kids* on movie night, her mom and sister cracking up the whole time, her dad bemoaning the irresponsible parenting of the Rick Moranis character.

She remembered daring Leif and Rex to shoplift a Krackel bar from the Short Stop and neither of them being able to go through with it.

She remembered the day earlier that summer when she'd gotten so angry at them, the day she'd decided to show up uninvited at their island of stupid rocks in the Cape Fear River—the one place where their group friendship didn't seem to extend to her, a reminder that no matter how close the three of them became, Rex and Leif would always have their own special, impenetrable thing— and overheard them coming up with the idea for *Polter-Dog*, laughing and high-fiving and congratulating each other on their brilliance. Another genius plan that the boys' club had devised without her input. She'd lost it, getting back on her bike and pedaling furiously away. Then, when she'd seen the dopey mannequins in ridiculously puffy pleated khakis in the storefront of the Belk and realized they vaguely (ever so vaguely) resembled Rex and Leif, she'd gone inside and pantsed the crap out of them. And three others, too. It had felt very cathartic.

But even the most frustrating parts of her friendship with Rex and Leif were a billion times better than everything that had happened since she'd arrived at the Whitewood School.

She was going to miss them.

And there was something else, too.

About Leif.

She was finally allowing herself to think it. Seconds away from death—the world around her beginning to blur into hues of yellow—but still.

It had started that summer as they froze in position, Rex figuring out camera angles for the scene where Jessica tells her father that Mr. Bones has been run over. They were staring at each other so Rex could get the eyelines right, and Alicia was struck by Leif's eyes. Had they always been so blue? Leif gave a goofy grin to break the inherent awkwardness of holding eye contact for so long, and Alicia smiled back, horrified by the part of her brain that was imagining what it might be like to kiss him. She'd pushed the thought away, then and always, for a billion reasons, one of which was that Leif definitely didn't reciprocate the feeling, as he'd started to seem very irritated every time she was around. It was a ridiculous idea anyway. And now Leif would never kn—

Her head was lifted up out of the water.

Air.

She tried to consume as much as her lungs could handle, loud, greedy gulps that still weren't enough. Her head pounded.

It took her at least a minute to even understand where she was, that Wayne Whitewood was still holding her by the neck, that she was alive.

She was alive.

Whitewood was saying something.

". . . to follow?"

Alicia stared at him.

"Come on, Candidatus! I said: Are you ready to follow?"

She'd been given a second chance.

She nodded. She said, "Yes."

Whitewood looked surprised. "What?"

Alicia nodded again, as vigorously as she could with hands clamped around her throat. "Yes," she said for the second time.

Whitewood didn't seem satisfied; he seemed taken aback. "Well, you— It's too late!" He dipped Alicia back into the water, a quick dunk this time, but shocking nevertheless.

He wasn't understanding her. Alicia must be miscommunicating somehow. She tried to get her mouth working, to tell him as clearly as she could: "I . . . will . . . follow."

"No!" Whitewood practically screamed into her face. "You're too late! It's done, all right? It's done!"

Alicia didn't understand. What kind of a heinous mind game was this? Maybe she was dead. Maybe she was dreaming. Maybe her brain had been severely compromised by her time underwater. "But . . . I'm . . ." She searched for the right words, in case she wasn't dead yet. "I . . . will follow."

Whitewood looked at Alicia, really looked at her for the first time, and took his hands off her neck. He began to quietly giggle to himself, more unhinged than ever. "Well, that's very sweet, but again: You're too damn late." He shook his head, as if thinking fondly about a scene from his favorite sitcom. "You think this school is all about reforming kids, helpin' out 'troubled youth.' "

Alicia's head still throbbed. She was fairly certain Whitewood had lost his mind.

"It's about so much more than that—you have no idea," he said, one last chuckle before he flipped back to rage. "Now let's do this again, and this time you ain't gonna give in. You understand?"

Alicia didn't. She really didn't. But she nodded anyway.

"Are you ready to follow?" Whitewood asked.

Alicia nodded.

"No!" Whitewood screamed. "You've come this far, and now you're just givin' up? What about your friend, your little trespassin' buddy, who's in the Roll right now? You're gonna let her down?"

Josefina. It hadn't been a setup.

Why was Whitewood telling her all this?

He looked like he might cry.

"Here," he said, reaching behind her and struggling with the twine for a minute before he got it untied. "You're free. What're you gonna do? Escape? Hit me? You wanna hit me?"

Alicia had no idea what was happening. Her wrists burned and her arms ached and all she wanted to do was nestle up in the cozy purple bed in Ruby's room.

But she wasn't dead.

And Josefina hadn't betrayed her.

And Wayne Whitewood was encouraging her to hit him.

"Come on," he said. "Shove me like you shoved me into that grill. Wouldn't that feel good?"

"I . . . I don't know what you want from me!" Alicia said.

Whitewood grunted again before charging at Alicia, his hands back on her neck, this time choking her above water.

With her hands free.

She still had no idea what to do, but she knew she wanted to live.

Her adrenaline surging, she dug her nails into Whitewood's face as hard as she could.

He removed his hands from her neck and smiled, a thin streak of blood appearing on his cheek. "That's more like it," he said. "Now: Are you ready to follow?"

"Guess not," Alicia said. If playing along with this lunatic's mind games was what it took to stay alive—to see her family again, Rex, *Leif*—then that was what Alicia would do.

"Good," Whitewood said, grinning as he placed his

hands back on her neck. He thrust her under the water, pushing her all the way to the bottom of the tub.

Alicia hadn't gotten a good breath, and after only a few seconds she felt herself beginning to black out.

The darkness closed in on all sides.

15

LEIF GROANED AND KEELED OVER ONTO HIS SIDE, HAVING JUST BEEN hit with a Nerf basketball in the groin.

"Yeah!" Rex said, laughing and lifting his arms in triumph.

"Aw, man," Leif said, in the fetal position on the carpet of Rex's bedroom. "I really feel that in my stomach."

"That's because I'm very skilled at this. You ready to forfeit?"

Still shaken by what they'd witnessed at the spring—not to mention constantly worrying about what might be happening to Alicia at that twisted school—Rex and Leif were trying to distract themselves by playing a game they'd made up during elementary school. It didn't have a name, but it involved sitting six feet apart with their legs spread and throwing a Nerf basketball at each other's testicles as hard as possible. The only rule was that you couldn't protect your testicles.

Leif reached out an arm, grabbed the soft orange ball, and pushed himself back into sitting position. "I don't even know how to spell 'forfeit.'" He flashed Rex a sly grin, then froze in thought. "Actually, I *really* don't know how to spell it!" They both laughed.

Since their expedition Friday night, Rex and Leif had devoted hours of time to figuring out what they'd seen, what their next steps should be. It was now Monday, and they'd walked to Rex's house together after school. Above his desk, Rex had repurposed his cork bulletin board for the cause; it was covered in Post-it notes with words and phrases in black marker: CULT, BLUE LIGHT, BLUE ROBES, STAR SYMBOL, SPRING, ABDUCTION, SACRIFICE, BEN'S ESCAPE, BEN'S SQUIRREL CONSUMPTION.

Leif lifted the Nerf and focused hard, steadying his breathing the way he'd learned in the one archery class he'd taken before dropping out of Cub Scouts. "Get ready," he said, winding up. "This one's gonna be especially nutty."

"I'll believe it when I feel it," Rex said.

The words were innocuous enough, but the way Rex said them triggered something within Leif. They reminded him how he'd been letting Rex take the lead on everything, constantly pushing aside his own reservations—even his own *crush*—to go along with what *Rex* wanted. He harnessed that resentful energy and flung the orange sphere toward Rex's crotch harder than ever before.

Direct hit.

"Ohhhhhh," Rex said, eyes bugged out and mouth literally forming an O—a genuine response, even though it seemed like he was mimicking something he'd seen on *America's Funniest Home Videos*. He slowly tipped over onto his side, like a huge oak tree toppling toward the forest floor.

Timber! Leif thought, feeling immensely satisfied with himself.

"Wow," Rex said, letting out a mix of groaning and laughter. "Didn't know you had that in you."

"There's a lot you don't know about me," Leif said in a jokey voice, even though he sort of meant it.

There was a knock at the bedroom door.

Rex winced as he quickly got himself back upright. Leif closed his legs. This had been known to happen during their Nerf-to-the-nuts game, an interruption from an infuriated grownup—usually Rex's dad—wondering what the hell was going on up there. He didn't often concern himself with formalities like knocking on doors, though.

"Uh, come in," Rex said.

It was, indeed, Rex's dad. Both boys braced themselves for his wrath; it usually came in a quick, powerful burst and then disappeared, like a brief afternoon thunderstorm. No wrath was coming, though, and when Rex looked up he was surprised—shocked, even—to see his father on the verge of tears. His mom had come into the room, too, fully in the act of crying, her makeup splotched and runny.

Rex had pushed it too far. He and Leif had been told repeatedly to stop making a game of hurling foam balls at each other's jewels, but they'd never listened. His parents' worries about his future infertility had finally come to a head. "I'm sorry," he said. "I'm so sorry. We will never throw the ball at each other's . . . balls . . . again."

"Yeah, sorry, Mr. and Mrs. McClendon," Leif said. "Never again."

"What?" Rex's dad said. "No, we're not— That's not . . . that's not why we came up here, boys." He put an arm around Rex's mother.

"Oh," Rex said, looking to Leif, as if he might understand why Rex's parents were both crying. "Why did . . . What's goin—"

"It's Alicia," Rex's mom said in between sobs. "We just heard from the Boykinses. She's passed, boys. Alicia has passed."

The words didn't make sense to either Rex or Leif. She's passed what?

"Like . . . a test?" Rex asked.

His mom's face crumpled further, her entire body sagging into Rex's dad, who hugged her to keep her from falling to the floor.

"No, Rex," Rex's dad said. "She's passed away. Alicia is . . . dead."

Alicia is dead.

Alicia.

Is.

Dead.

Alicia. Dead.

Rex couldn't comprehend the words, no matter how he arranged them in his mind.

"Oh God, oh no." Leif thought the voice was Rex's but realized it was actually his own. He couldn't stop. "Oh God. Oh no. Oh, God."

"I know," Rex's mom said, crouching down to hug Leif. "I know, sweetie. It's so awful."

Rex still couldn't register what he was hearing. "What happened?" he asked.

"There was a fire," his dad said, shaking his head, as he sat next to Rex and put an arm around him.

"Oh God," Leif said, covering his mouth with his hand, realizing he was incapable of doing anything other than using the Lord's name in vain over and over again. He figured God would give him a pass under these circumstances. It was as if he'd entered some alternate dimension, like he was in someone else's dream. Alicia couldn't have died. She was the most full-of-life person he'd ever known. "Oh God."

As Rex stared blankly around the room, deep in shock, the word SACRIFICE screamed out from the Post-it in his own handwriting.

It practically knocked the wind out of him.

Ben was right.

They'd sacrificed Alicia. And here was their pathetic cover-up.

Rex wanted to weep, but instead he got angry. "What do you mean, a fire?"

"Son," Rex's dad said. "There was a fire in a small building on the school property that they use to . . . you know, to discipline kids. Seems Alicia was in there and somehow . . . a fire started. They think she may have started it herself and wasn't able to get out. Apparently she was having a lot of trouble at the school. But we don't really know much."

Leif pictured flames rapidly spreading, surrounding Alicia.

Rex scoffed at their barely plausible story. This didn't sound like the Alicia he knew. Sure, maybe she was capable of burning down a small building in some act of defiance, but she'd never make the mistake of getting caught in the fire herself. "We should find out," he said. "That's all you were told?"

Rex's parents looked at each other, then gave him a sad shrug.

"But that can't be what happened!" Rex shouted, jumping to his feet. "Something is really wrong with that school!" He made eye contact with Leif, who seemed to have been buying the fire story until this very second.

"I agree," Rex's dad said. "They obviously need to update their safety standards. Probably hasn't changed since it was that old resort."

"No, not . . ." Rex wanted to tell his parents about everything listed right in front of them on the bulletin board—Ben, Alicia's violent abduction, what he and Rex had seen at the spring—but he also knew they wouldn't be pleased that he and Leif had repeatedly been sneaking out past midnight. Now was no time to invite tighter surveillance on his nighttime activities; he needed to tread with caution. "I mean, they're doing bad things to those kids. They did something bad to Alicia."

"Sit down, honey," Rex's mom said, gently pulling at his hand. "You're in shock. We all are."

Leif's hand was over his mouth again. Ben's sacrifice theory. Could that really have happened to Alicia? Up until last Friday, he would have said *No way, of course not, it's a SCHOOL.*

But now he thought: *Yes. Yes, it definitely* could *have happened.*

Rex sat back down. He knew that nothing he said to his parents right now would make any difference.

"Look," Rex's dad said, rubbing his son's back, "when something terrible like this happens, it's impossible to comprehend, and so we try to come up with all kinds of explanations. But the truth is, when God says it's your time, it's your time. All we can do is pray. For Jean and Bill. For Melissa."

That's not all *we can do,* Rex thought, allowing his rage to simmer, mainly because he knew the alternative involved losing control. "Has anyone seen her body?"

Rex's mom and dad looked at each other.

"Well, I'm sure *someone* has," Rex's dad said.

"But, like, her parents? Have her parents seen the body?"

"Sweetie," Rex's mom said after blowing her nose, "you don't need to concern yourself with morbid details like that right now. I think you're just gonna get yourself more worked up."

"So that's a no?" Rex asked.

"It's okay, Rex," Leif said, not thinking this line of questioning would lead anywhere productive.

"Oh, is it, *Leif*?" Rex looked at him. "Alicia is dead. She's *dead*."

"I know," Leif said, taking off his glasses to wipe away tears. "I know."

"Are we doing her funeral?" Rex asked his parents, milliseconds after the thought occurred to him.

Rex's dad sighed and grimaced. "I'm afraid not. Shackelford already offered the Boykinses a funeral on the house. Free service, free coffin, free everything."

"Well, you should offer that too! Alicia was *my* best friend, Dad. The Boykinses aren't even that close with Shackelford!"

"Rex, come on, you think I don't know that? Of course I offered. I was going to either way, but Shackelford beat me to the punch."

"That's true, honey," Rex's mom said.

Rex's dad shook his head. "Jean and Bill had already signed the paperwork with Shackelford. I wasn't gonna press 'em on it. They're out of their heads right now, don't know up from down, and I don't blame 'em, either. Sorry, son."

Rex clenched his jaw, then picked up the Nerf basketball and hurled it against the wall.

—

"IT DOESN'T FEEL real," Leif said.

It was the first thing either of them had said in at least ten minutes. They were on their island, sitting on their rocks, not bothering to decide who would sit on which boulder, not adhering to the rules of statements and questions, maybe because they were too in shock to remember to. Or maybe because in a world where their best friend could be around one second and gone the next, those rules now seemed pathetic and meaningless.

"I know," Rex said, staring out toward the woods where Ben lived.

"Remember when Alicia wore a cape for three weeks in fifth grade?" Leif asked. "And when people asked which superhero she was, she would say, 'None of them, I'm just a girl in a cape.'"

"Don't do that," Rex said.

"Do what?"

"Start talking about her in the past tense. Like, reminiscing. I'm not ready for that."

"Okay. Sorry." Leif wasn't necessarily ready either, but he couldn't help himself. He felt an obsessive need to remember every little detail he could about Alicia, that if he didn't do that *right now,* the memories would all fade, like a vivid dream that evaporates as soon as you lift your head from the pillow.

He'd thought about that time, only a few weeks after she'd moved to Bleak Creek, when Alicia invited herself to a sleepover he and Rex had already planned. Rex told her it would be weird to have a girl spend the night, and Alicia told him, "*You're* weird for saying that." He'd also remembered when, in sixth grade, Jeremy Hawkins found a toad on the playground and proceeded to organize an impromptu game of "frog baseball." Before the first pitch was thrown, Alicia took the wiffle ball bat from Jeremy and said, "How 'bout we play some Jeremy baseball?" She then proceeded to clock him repeatedly in the head with the plastic bat until the PE teacher intervened. She was sent to the principal's office, but Jeremy never touched a toad again.

And now Alicia was gone.

She was never coming back.

She and Leif would never sit together near a cozy fireplace, or work on crossword puzzles, or make beautiful offspring that were perfect combinations of all of their best respective features. He wouldn't even get to tell her how he felt. He would spend his whole lifetime never having told her.

That seemed impossible.

"I really don't think there was a fire," Rex said, still not looking at Leif. "Don't you feel that too?"

"Honestly," Leif said, "I don't know what to think."

"I bet Ben will have an opinion on this." Rex scanned the woods. Ben didn't seem to be home. Probably out squirrel hunting.

"Well, sure, we all know what that will be," Leif said, sounding more sarcastic than he'd intended.

"What do you mean by that?" Rex asked.

"I mean . . ." Leif felt like the tension between them could reach a breaking point at any moment, like his animosity toward Rex might combine with their grief and quickly combust. But he didn't care. "He already said that he thinks kids are being sacrificed. So he's obviously gonna confirm your theory about . . . you know, about that happening to Alicia."

"You don't agree?"

"I already told you, I don't know what to think."

"So you'd prefer to believe their dumb-ass story about Alicia accidentally burning herself up over—"

"I'd prefer that she wasn't dead at all!" Leif shouted, surprising himself but feeling empowered by his anger. "That's what I'd prefer! Whether we know how she died or not, dead is dead!"

Rex looked stunned, as if he'd just been slapped. "All right." He nodded a few times. "That's fine. If you don't care enough about Alicia to want to figure it out—"

"What'd you just say?"

"I said if you don't—"

"You seriously think you care more than me?" Leif had been carefully protecting his affection for Alicia for so long, not wanting it to come between him and Rex and, if he was being honest, afraid of how vulnerable it might feel to reveal it. But now his rage was overriding his fear. "You have no idea how much I—"

"Rex! Leif!" Travis Bethune was wading in the river toward them, utility belt and all. "Thought I might find you boys here."

"Oh, hey," Rex said, his tone gentler.

"Yeah, I just . . . Gosh, man, I'm so sorry about Alicia," he said, stepping up onto the island in his enormous work boots.

"Thanks, Travis," Leif said, coming down from his fury.

"Yeah, thanks," Rex added.

"She was a really great person." Travis didn't seem to know what to do with his hands, and ended up planting them on his hips. "You know, the reason I . . . Well, I should say . . ." He looked at the ground and shook his head. "The day it happened, I was paintin' a house over on Brewster. I got the call on my radio, and by the time I got over there in my gear, it was all . . . it had already burnt down."

The color drained from Rex's face. "You saw it?"

"Well, yeah . . . what was left of it. Wasn't pretty, that's for sure. I keep thinkin' if I had been there cuttin' the grass that day, I woulda . . . I don't know. Maybe I coulda done somethin' to help her."

Rex hadn't imagined Whitewood would go so far as to actually burn down a building to legitimize his cover story, but of course he would. Otherwise, it would be obvious that it had been a lie. "I don't know that you could have done anything, Travis," he said, "but thanks, man." There was so much the poor guy didn't know.

"Oh, right, so, yeah . . . When I got there, I found this." Travis dug around on his belt, pushing aside keys and reaching behind his measuring tape, coming up with something small and black pinched between his thumb and index finger. "The rest of her stuff went to her parents, of course, but . . . I thought you might want it."

Rex and Leif stared at Travis's hand, unsure of what they were looking at.

"It's a button," Travis said. "From her jumpsuit. Burnt, but . . . you know. Hers."

"Oh," Leif said.

"Do you . . . ?"

"Yeah, yeah." Leif put out his palm and received the sacred piece of blackened metal.

"Huh," Rex said, standing up from his rock and leaning over to see.

Something about the button made the situation that much more real for Leif—having an object on his skin that had so recently been so close to Alicia—and he began to cry. "Thanks for this, Travis," he said. "This means . . . this means a lot."

"Least I can do," Travis said, his hands back on his hips. "Really. You boys shouldn't have to go through somethin' like this, at so young an age. I just . . . yeah. But remember, you'll see her again one day."

"Right," Rex said. This was something he'd heard the pastor say at every funeral he'd ever attended. He wanted to believe it was true—that he'd get to hang out with Alicia on a cloud, telling her all the things she'd missed on earth—but he had his doubts.

"Anyway, I'm gonna get goin'," Travis said. "But if you boys need anything, anything at all, you know who to call."

Rex and Leif nodded, genuinely appreciative as Travis walked back into the river.

"Though," he said, turning back, "my answering machine broke, so. If it keeps ringin', that means I'm out. In which case, call my beeper. My second beeper. First beeper's for business only. Y'all got that number, right?"

"Yep," Leif said. "Thanks, Travis."

Travis gave them a thumbs-up and waded away.

Rex held out a hand toward Leif. "Can I . . . ?"

"Oh, sure." Leif didn't actually want to part with the button, but he was touched by Rex's sincerity. He passed it over, continuing to stare at it even after it was in Rex's hand.

Rex didn't know what to make of it. It felt good to hold, though. His gut still told him that even if this had been a fire, it certainly hadn't been Alicia's fault. None of it was. In fact, she wouldn't have even been at that school if it weren't for him and Leif and *PolterDog*.

So it was their fault.

Their best friend was gone, and it was all their fault.

16

JANINE LOOKED INTO THE SIDE-VIEW MIRROR FOR THE SEVENTH TIME in the past minute.

She was sitting in the passenger seat of GamGam's Grand Marquis as her grandmother steered them toward the airport, and she couldn't shake the feeling that they were being followed. Or that GamGam's brakes were going to suddenly give out. Or that something else horrible would happen.

The paranoia had been with her for days, ever since her visit to Aunt Roberta's. Learning that her uncle's fatal car accident had likely been a murder—that there were people in town (including the sheriff, for God's sake) so desperate to hide whatever was happening inside that school that they would kill another human being—had been jarring, to say the least. It was a level of cruelty she hadn't anticipated, and she was ready to heed the message so gracelessly scrawled on the side of the vehicle she was currently in.

So that's what Janine was doing.

She was leaving Bleak Creek.

It hadn't been a snap decision. As rattled as she'd been after talking with her aunt, she'd been incredibly angry, too. At first she'd let that fuel her, imagining her documentary could uncover the truth, not only about what had happened to Donna but also about her uncle's death. It quickly became clear, though, that word had spread about Janine. Most people she approached, from parents to teachers to other students, wouldn't even entertain the idea of speaking with her.

The only interviews she'd successfully conducted were with a couple of Donna's other coworkers from Li'l Dino's, twenty-one-year-old server Gabriel Rodriguez and sixteen-year-old hostess Sandy Dillon. Both of them had provided variations on the responses she'd gotten from Tommy Dowd: that the Whitewood School had really helped them out, that they'd deserved to be sent there and were glad it happened, that it had put them on a path to living a successful life. As soon as Janine's questions got even slightly probing, they'd shut down. (Once their interview was done, Gabriel had revealed his true motivation for being there, awkwardly asking Janine out for coffee. Sandy, meanwhile, had asked Janine to sign a form indicating that the interview would count as an hour of community service for Key Club.)

After unsuccessfully attempting to talk to both Donna and Aunt Roberta once more about the school and what had happened to Uncle Jim, Janine had reacquainted herself with an old friend: self-doubt. She was putting her life—and possibly her aunt's and cousin's and grandmother's, too—in serious jeopardy, and for what? She couldn't even get any good interviews. If she was killed, people would find her footage and think, *Why was she even down here? To film boring conversations with her grandmother and some teenagers and a fat man bragging about his kidney stones?* Janine had no business making a documentary, and she wasn't quite sure why she'd ever thought she could.

But all that didn't explain why she'd finally decided to leave, not entirely.

No, there was one more thing.

Dennis.

The night before, after Janine had come home from her scintillating interview with Sandy, she and GamGam had been sitting on the couch eating cold fried chicken and watching *Wheel of Fortune* when the phone rang. Gam-Gam had toddled off to get it while Janine tried to decide if Vanna White had the best job in the world or the worst. Moments later, with a *You're never gonna believe this* tone in her voice, GamGam called out, "It's for you, Neenie."

Janine had trudged toward the phone, fully expecting it to be Gabriel Rodriguez asking her out again, and she was actually considering saying yes, thinking maybe his persistence was the universe's way of helping her officially hit rock bottom. But all thoughts of Gabriel had disappeared once she heard the voice on the other line.

"Hey," Dennis said.

Janine froze, thinking Bleak Creek had officially caused her to lose a grip on reality.

"Janine? You still there?"

It was really him. His voice conjured up a million feelings at once, as if she wanted to shriek and swoon at the same time. "Yeah. I'm here."

"Good."

"How did you find me?" Out of all her questions, this was arguably the least important, but it was the easiest to ask.

"It wasn't that hard," Dennis said, obviously grinning. He hadn't actually answered her question. "I miss us."

Though it was wonderful to hear him say those words, it was also infuriating. "Oh, really?" Janine said. "Does Lola know that?"

"She and I are done. She's not a very . . . creative person. Compared to you, anyway."

Janine smiled. It was a very satisfying answer. She couldn't let him off the hook yet, though. "Aren't you still living in L.A.?"

"Nah. L.A. sucks, man. They wouldn't know good filmmaking if it bit 'em in the ass."

"Oh. Wow."

"Yeah. This one executive said *The Boy Who Became a Man* was just a rip-off of *Big,* which is so insulting I don't even know where to begin."

Janine couldn't help but smile again, mainly because she'd thought the same thing more than once as they'd worked on it—that Dennis had made an artsy version of *Big* except without the funny parts.

"What a dick, right?" Dennis said. The rhythms of their relationship came back to her, and she knew what her line was supposed to be: *Yeah, such an asshole. What he said isn't true at all.*

"Well, it's just one executive, isn't it?" she said instead.

"Yeah, I guess. But then everyone else stopped returning my calls too. And now I have writer's block. I'm telling you, those people suck. NYC is where it's at. We need to start Dennine. For real this time."

Janine had imagined this scenario so many times she'd lost count, and now it was actually *happening.* Dennis had tracked her down all the way in Bleak Creek. For a guy who hated doing any kind of tedious legwork, anything he didn't deem "creatively stimulating," it wasn't nothing.

"And," Dennis continued, "I, you know . . . I'm sorry about the way I acted. I was an idiot. You're, like, the best thing that ever happened to me, and I don't know why I couldn't recognize that."

Janine knew what was happening here—Dennis's charms were once again dismantling her defenses—but she was on the verge of joyful hyperventilation anyway. "Thank you for that," she said, wishing he was in the room so she could kiss him. She annoyed herself with how easily she was falling for him again. But he really seemed sorry.

"When are you coming back?" Dennis asked. "I need you, babe."

Maybe, Janine thought, *this is a nudge from the universe after all.* She'd tried to go it alone, and it hadn't worked out. She had barely any usable footage, and rather than making the world a better place with her art, she'd succeeded only in becoming a magnet for death stares and *Leave Bitch* warnings, in making life *worse* for her Bleak Creek family members.

And Dennis *needed* her.

"Tomorrow," Janine said. "I come back tomorrow."

She'd booked the flight as soon as she got off the phone, and for the first time in days, she had breathed easy. It felt right.

"Gosh," GamGam said now, as they passed the IT ONLY GETS BLEAKER WHEN YOU LEAVE BLEAK CREEK! sign. "I sure am gonna miss having you around, Neenie."

"I'm gonna miss you too, GamGam," Janine said. She meant it. There wasn't much she would miss about that screwed-up town, but she'd never felt this close to her grandmother, and it was a bummer to think that the next time they spoke, they'd be hundreds of miles apart.

Naturally, Boyz II Men's "End of the Road" came on the radio right at that moment.

A little on the nose, universe, Janine thought as she teared up, her gaze flitting to the side-view mirror out of habit, where this time she saw genuine cause for concern. Several cars back, a vehicle was moving way faster than the speed limit, wildly weaving in and out of the oncoming traffic lane as it passed a car at a time.

Janine shuddered. It was possible it was just a reckless driver who had nothing to do with her. After all, she'd already left Bleak Creek, just like she'd been told.

But once the red car was almost directly behind Gam-

Gam's Grand Marquis—only one vehicle remaining as a buffer between them—Janine felt confident that whoever was driving it intended to do her harm. To make sure she wouldn't blab to the world about the Whitewood School. The way Uncle Jim had tried to.

"You might have to drive a little faster, GamGam," Janine said, her voice shaky.

"Didn't you say your flight's at 2:30?" GamGam asked. "We got plenty of time, darlin'."

"No." Janine tried to swallow, but her mouth was too dry. "I think . . . I think there's a car following us."

"Huh?" GamGam looked into the rearview. "Oh my word! It might be that crazy Wendell Brown. Sometimes he steals a car and goes on a joyride."

"I don't think so," Janine said. After learning the truth about Uncle Jim, Janine had quickly determined that this theory had never been shared with GamGam. She'd considered telling her grandmother herself but ultimately thought it wasn't her place. Now, of course, she wished she had, as it would have made their current predicament much easier to explain. "People weren't happy about my movie, GamGam."

"Well, I thought that movie *Basic Instincts* was a piece of trash, but that don't mean I'm about to go drivin' down the highway after Mikey Douglas!"

"Can you just . . . Can you just speed up a little? Try and lose 'em?"

"For you, Neenie? Anything." GamGam pressed down on the gas, and Janine's head was thrust back into her headrest.

GamGam had never been a good driver, and Janine immediately felt like she'd put her life into more danger by asking her to speed, but even with GamGam's erratic swerving, Janine was relieved to see the car fading into the distance and then turning off the road onto a side street.

"Wow, GamGam," Janine said. "They're gone. Nice work." She exhaled and tried to relax, though she knew she wouldn't fully feel better until she was taking off in that plane.

"Woohoo!" GamGam shouted into the rearview. "Eat my dust! I wish your Grandpa Chuck was here to see this."

"Me too, GamGam," Janine said, picturing her late Grandpa riding along with them, his eyes bugging out in terror as GamGam traveled well above the speed limit. Janine then had the morbid thought that even if Grandpa Chuck had somehow survived his heart attack in 1981, being here for GamGam's wild driving might have finally killed him.

"I tell ya, I think I owe my drivin' skills to Burt," Gam-Gam said. "You know he did all his own stunts in *Smokey and the Ban*— Aaaahhhhhh!"

Janine joined her grandmother in screaming as the red car shot out ahead of them from another side street, screeching to a halt and blocking their lane. GamGam slammed on the brakes and desperately cut the wheel to the right as she brought the Grand Marquis to its own, far less skillful screeching halt.

Janine's first impulse was to grab her things and make a run for it, but she didn't want to abandon GamGam. So instead she would stay. She would fight.

"Good Lord," GamGam said, trying to keep a sense of humor even though she was obviously as shaken up as Janine. "All this over a movie. Some people are too sensitive."

Janine couldn't even speak. Horns blared behind them, as both their Grand Marquis and this strangely familiar Corolla were completely blocking the road. Her mind raced. She was about to be murdered in the middle of a country road, all for thinking it would be cool to make a movie about kidney stones. What a legacy.

She watched the door of the red car open, ready to duck in case the driver had some kind of weapon. When she saw who had been behind the wheel, though, her brain short-circuited.

The person who had been chasing Janine was . . . her cousin?

Donna, in one of her trademark flannel shirts, quickly reached back into the car and then held up a piece of white posterboard—styled just like the Gnome Girls title cards she used to make—with two words written on it:

Stay Bitch

Janine slowly opened her door and stepped out of the car.

"You . . . can't leave," Donna said.

"I don't . . . What . . ." Janine was trying to make sense of what she was witnessing. Her painfully reserved cousin had stopped her from leaving town with some sort of stunt-driving move, and now she was holding up an ironically hilarious sign.

"Donna, that was very dangerous," GamGam said, joining them on the street. "Are you drunk?"

"No, GamGam," Donna said. "Janine, that girl was killed. Alicia. She died in a fire at the school."

"Oh my god," Janine said. Another dead Whitewood student. Who conveniently happened to be the one kid who had personally injured Whitewood. That girl had barely been there a week.

"How awful," GamGam said.

"Quit blockin' the damn road!" a woman shouted from behind them.

"But . . . I don't think that's the full story," Donna said.

"No, of course not," Janine said. She was almost as shocked by Donna putting together complete sentences as she was about Alicia Boykins's death.

"This ain't book club—move your daggone cars!" a man shouted.

"So, uh, why are you . . . leaving?" Donna asked. Janine could see that her cousin was growing more comfortable speaking with every word. It was like watching someone beginning to walk after an accident.

"It's complicated," Janine said. "I wasn't getting anywhere with my movie. And, well, Dennis . . ."

"That asshole?"

Janine stared at Donna in wonder and confusion.

"GamGam told me the deal," she said.

Janine looked to GamGam, who shrugged.

"He sounds like a piece of crap who doesn't deserve to be mentioned in the same breath as you," Donna continued. "Let alone *date* you."

"Oh." Having Donna, of all people, say that to her was not unlike being splashed with a bucket of ice water.

"I know I haven't been myself for . . . a while now. But I'm tired of being afraid. It's hard to . . . It's hard to talk about what . . . happened to me." For a moment, Janine saw the distance enter Donna's eyes, that same disconnectedness she'd seen for years. But then she looked right at Janine, and the detachment was suddenly replaced with resolve. Janine felt as if she was looking at fifteen-year-old Donna. "But watching you with your movie, and remembering my dad . . . and now hearing what happened to this girl . . . You can't leave. Because you might actually be able to do something about this. And I want to help."

Janine understood then that she was running away from Bleak Creek, just as her mother had done so many years before. She saw herself becoming yet another person who sees a problem and then leaves town to let somebody else deal with it.

"Okay," Janine said, wiping tears away. "I'll stay."

Donna rushed over and hugged Janine for the first time since they were teenagers.

"Aw, geez, you girls are making *me* cry now," Gam-Gam said.

"If I'd wanted to watch my soaps, I would have stayed at home!" a woman shouted.

Janine held tight to Donna. "Nice touch with the sign," she said through tears.

"Thanks, bitch," Donna said as dozens of cars continued to honk.

17

"I HATE IT HERE," REX SAID. "ALICIA WOULD HATE IT TOO."

"Yeah, maybe," Leif said.

Crammed next to each other in the next to last pew of the Shackelford Funeral Home, they were lucky to have a seat at all. The room was packed, a crowd three rows deep already standing behind them. Rex had never set foot inside what his family referred to only as the Competition, and while the olive green carpet and stained-glass windows of its chapel were probably purchased from the same wholesaler that the McClendon-McClemmons Funeral Home used, he couldn't help but think it felt cheaper.

"These pews suck," Rex said. "Probably fake wood."

"Seems pretty real to me," Leif said.

Rex glared at him. "Whatever."

Leif was wearing a tight blue suit he hadn't tried on since his Uncle Terry's wedding two years earlier, and Rex was in the black suit he wore whenever he helped his parents out at funerals. It was wrinkled and slightly smelly, as he'd accidentally left it lying on his closet floor with other dirty clothes for a few weeks.

"It doesn't even make sense," Rex said, getting more fired up, his scooter leg jittering nonstop. "This should be happening at the church. You only do it at the funeral home when it's small. Like for old people who have no friends because they're all dead."

200 RHETT McLAUGHLIN & LINK NEAL

"Shhh," Leif said. He didn't disagree, but it still felt disrespectful to talk that way as they publicly mourned their best friend. Especially when a lot of people were likely already judging them for getting Alicia into this situation in the first place.

"You want to know what I think?" Rex whispered.

"I already kno—"

"This couldn't happen at First Baptist or even at my parents' funeral home. Because then Whitewood would lose control of the situation. Here, he can do whatever he wants; he and Shackelford are like best friends. And so maybe there was actually a fire—or they made it look like there was one—but that doesn't mean we're not still right about everything else."

"Yeah, definitely," Leif said as he patted his right pants pocket, making sure Alicia's button was still there. He'd been the one to take it home after Travis had given it to them, and Rex hadn't seemed to mind. The little blackened piece of metal had been a source of immense comfort, making Leif feel like he was carrying Alicia around with him everywhere he went.

"And," Rex continued, "the fact that it's a closed casket only further pro—"

"I'm so sorry, homies." Leif and Rex both winced. The last thing they needed right now was Mark Hornhat. But here he was, standing in the aisle hovering over them. In a tux, no less.

"Thanks, Mark," Leif said.

"I can't believe it. I just can't believe it."

"Uh-huh," Rex said, barely making eye contact. He'd been hoping that sitting down for the service would temporarily put a stop to the awkward condolences from classmates.

"Boykins is *gone*. Wow. It's like, *please don't go girl*."

"What?" Leif asked.

"That's one of my favorite New Kids songs," Hornhat said. Leif looked away, unable to hide his disgust. "But really, I wish she didn't go. I remember one time I was telling Boykins about my family's three-story beach house, and she said the most hilarious thing. She was like—"

"Mark," Leif said, somehow finding the fortitude to cut him off, "maybe we could talk about this some other time?"

"Oh." Mark blinked at him in that Hornhat way of his. "Yeah, for sure. Hey, is there any room in this row for me to squish in?"

"Absolutely not," Rex said.

"Okay. Cool, cool. Either of you dudes want an Airhead? I have blue raspberry or mystery."

"No," Leif said, desperate for Hornhat to walk away. "We're good."

"I'll take one, actually," Rex said, reaching a hand past Leif. He had an involuntary reflex for accepting free food, regardless of the circumstances. "Mystery sounds good."

"You got it, dude," Hornhat said, nodding and smiling as he passed over the long white package, almost as if he'd forgotten that he was at his dead friend's funeral. His face went somber, though, as the mournful sound of an organ began. He turned and walked quickly up the aisle.

As Rex ripped open the Airhead, he looked to the front of the room, and sitting there playing the opening progression of "Blessed Assurance" was none other than Wayne Whitewood himself.

"No," Rex whispered. "No way does this guy get to play the organ at Alicia's funeral!" Whitewood was wearing a black suit and his white gloves, and looking very sad. Fake sad. "We should be at First Baptist right now, with Tanya playing the organ, like Alicia would have wanted. Man, I hate everything about this."

"Me too," Leif whispered back. "At least Pastor Mitchell is here."

Seeing the genuinely distraught look on their pastor's face as he stood up front, singing his way through the hymn, was sobering for Rex. Once the opening song was over, he could hear the sound of sniffling all around them. The loudest came from the front row, where Jean and Melissa Boykins were sobbing, Bill holding an arm around each of them, his mouth pursed stoically.

Pastor Mitchell walked to the podium, his George Michael beard looking especially well trimmed. "We are gathered here today to honor and celebrate the life of Alicia Michelle Boykins," he said. "A vibrant soul who we've lost too soon. Far too soon."

That was it for Leif. He quickly joined the rank of the criers, barely able to pay attention to a thing Pastor Mitchell was saying. Or what Bill Boykins was saying after him. ("All we wanted was to protect our Alicia. Keep her safe. But it didn't matter. It didn't matter . . .") Or Melissa Boykins next. ("She was my hero. She'll always be my hero.") Or Alicia's New Agey aunt from Oregon after her. ("Do you feel Alicia's energy in the room right now? Because I sure do!") He didn't even realize that Pastor Mitchell had asked if anyone else would like to share a few words until Rex was standing and gently nudging him, saying, "Hey, we're still doing this, right?"

They'd decided beforehand that they would go up and say some meaningful things about Alicia, but now Leif worried he'd be crying too hard to speak. He had to get up there with Rex, though. It was the least he could do.

When they arrived at the podium, Rex made eye contact with Whitewood, who returned a kind smile. Rex didn't smile back.

Leif stared out at all the people crowded into the room, devastated that Alicia had exited this world being so misunderstood by so many in Bleak Creek. She would forever be remembered as a troublemaker whose bad decisions had resulted in her own death, all because of something that he knew was largely his and Rex's fault. It hit him that he should say something to change their minds. To help them remember the *real* Alicia.

Leif looked to Rex as if to say *I'll go first,* but Rex either misinterpreted or ignored the cue, as he leaned in to the microphone and said, "Hi, everyone."

Leif stepped back and straightened his clip-on tie, hoping that listening to Rex talk about Alicia wouldn't cause him to explode into a full waterworks display before he was able to say anything.

"I'm Rex, and this is my best friend, Leif, and we're best friends with Alicia." Rex was suddenly struck by the feeling that he couldn't trust anyone in the pews. They all looked perfectly normal and perfectly sad, but so did Wayne Whitewood. "Uh, were"—he corrected himself— "We *were* best friends with Alicia." Rex looked to Leif, inviting him to speak. Apparently this would be somewhat of a tag-team speech.

Leif took a deep breath and forced himself to begin. "I know," he said, "that some of you think Alicia was 'troubled' or 'a bad influence' or, you know, something like that, but I never saw it that way. Alicia is one of the most amazing people I've ever known."

"I agree," Rex said, even as he felt a paranoia gripping his chest more tightly by the second. "Alicia was the greatest. So smart and funny. And weird! But not bad weird, like 'doing magic tricks in your room by yourself' weird, but good weird, like 'doing a magic trick that's not even a magic trick because that's the joke' kinda weird." He scanned the audience, simultaneously questioning why he'd decided to use magic as a gauge for weirdness and thinking he'd somehow know the faces of Alicia's murderers—assuming members of Whitewood's cult were out there—when he saw them.

Meanwhile, Leif was interpreting everything Rex was saying as an attempt to one-up him, to try to out-honor Alicia. He knew this wasn't a competition, and sure, they both missed her, but what he had felt for her was more profound than Rex's admiration of her lips. "Even more than all that," Leif said decisively, "Alicia had a huge heart. You could see that with every person she met."

"That's for sure," Rex said. "She could make anyone—" His eyes landed on Mary Hattaway, the secretary over at Second Baptist Church, sitting there in the fourth-row aisle seat. More specifically, his eyes landed on her hand.

Her carefully bandaged hand.

He looked at her face, where her cold eyes burned into his, even as she made it seem like she was genuinely mourning Alicia. He quickly looked away. "Sorry," he said into the mic, clearing his throat. "Sorry."

Leif glanced at Rex, who seemed to have gotten so choked up about Alicia that he'd needed to stop talking. He related, but why did Rex get to be the one to have the public emotional breakdown about her? If that was going to happen to anyone, it should be him!

"You know," Leif said, before he'd even made the decision to do so, "I've never told anyone this, but I . . . I really . . . Since this past summer, I've had . . . feelings for Alicia. Like, more-than-friend feelings." Leif heard his mom gasp as he took in the expressions of everyone else in the audience: some surprised, some sweetly moved. He couldn't believe he'd just said that.

"What?" Rex asked, off-mic.

"I never got a chance to tell her how I feel," Leif continued, ignoring Rex, "but I wish I had. You can't waste a moment, you know? Because, if you do, the person you care about might, you know . . . they might be gone."

The crowd was silent, as if absorbing the profundity of what Leif had just said.

"Whoaaa," Mark Hornhat said from the back of the room.

Rex was absorbing Leif's words too. He'd recalled their conversation about Alicia back on the rocks. Why hadn't Leif said anything then? Their friendship had always been built on honesty. That's what made it work. He was stunned. He couldn't really dwell on that at the moment, though, because seeing the Boykinses' devastated faces reminded him there was something more important to address.

"He's right," Rex said into the mic. "We can't waste a moment. Which is why we need to tell you what *actually* happened to Alicia."

"What?" Leif said off-mic, now his turn to be surprised.

"Everybody praises Mr. Whitewood and his school for saving the town or whatever, but I don't see what's so praiseworthy about murdering kids."

Leif's mom gasped again, as did Rex's and the majority of the other people sitting in the pews.

"I mean, how many 'freak accidents' can one school have?" Rex continued. "Four dead kids in, like, a decade? Doesn't that strike you as at least slightly disturbing? Right, Leif?"

"Uh," Leif said into the mic, not quite understanding how even a soul-baring moment like the one he'd just had could be wrested away by Rex. "I agree that it seems a little fishy."

"It's more than fishy!" Rex said. "This man is a killer!" He pointed at Whitewood, and the crowd again gasped. Rex hoped it was the sort of gasp you'd hear at the end of a murder mystery, but he had the feeling it was actually disgust at his insolence. He couldn't stop, though. "And we're just gonna let him play the organ at the funeral of the girl he killed? That's not right! You'll never believe what we saw at the spri—"

"Now, now, that's just about enough," Wayne Whitewood said, standing up from the organ. He'd shouted the words, but he didn't look angry. In fact, he seemed to be radiating warmth and kindness.

"See?" Rex said into the mic, terrified but knowing he needed to press on. "He doesn't want us telling you—"

Whitewood stepped between Rex and Leif and covered the microphone. He lifted his hand, adjusting the mic to his level before putting an arm around each of the boys. Rex and Leif stayed completely still (or as still as they could while trembling), convinced they were about to be murdered in public.

"I'm truly sorry to interrupt you fellas," Whitewood said into the mic in a quiet, gentle voice, "but I don't think your words are really appropriate for the occasion. Trust me, I get it. As most people here know, I understand grieving very well. I lost my wife and my daughter." There were tears in Whitewood's eyes. "And just like you, I wanted to blame someone. When grief takes ahold of you . . . well, it's not pretty. But I promise you boys . . . it will get better. Time makes everything better."

"Bless you, Mr. Whitewood," said a man from the crowd.

Whitewood nodded and smiled. "Now, why don't you fellas get back to your seats? You said some beautiful things about your friend, and I know her family appreciates it."

For lack of any other options, Leif and Rex stepped back from the podium and walked wordlessly to their seats, careful not to make eye contact with anyone, especially their parents. They stared forward as their sixth grade teacher, Mrs. Crawford, began to talk about what a joy Alicia had been to have in class.

—

AS JANINE AND Donna walked side by side across the lobby of the Shackelford Funeral Home, weaving through clusters of people and looking for the teenage boys Janine had met that day in Li'l Dino's—the ones who had just bravely called out Whitewood during their best friend's funeral service—Janine couldn't help but feel a tinge of satisfaction.

The Gnome Girls were back.

Well, not entirely—Donna still wasn't saying a lot and seemed to sporadically regress back into the aloof version of herself at unpredictable moments—but it was certainly a start.

With Donna by her side, Janine almost didn't mind the stares and frowns that had been aimed in their direction all afternoon. Their attire certainly wasn't helping. Since she, understandably, hadn't packed anything funereal, Janine was wearing one of GamGam's dresses, a matronly black number that was so baggy she'd had to pull it back in various places with safety pins. Donna didn't have that excuse, but she'd opted to wear a puffy-shouldered black dress over a pair of torn blue jeans and black Chuck Taylors. They looked like Addams Family rejects.

Janine hadn't known if Donna would be game to come to Alicia's funeral, thinking it might be traumatic for her, but Donna had insisted. As they had stood in the back during the incredibly sad service, Janine had snuck glances at her cousin to make sure she was okay. Even though Donna had spent most of the time with that zombie look on her face—a protective instinct, Janine figured—a hint of determination flashed across her face when Rex began to rail

against Wayne Whitewood. Janine's resolve had strength-
ened too; she recognized allies when she saw them.

Because Rex was right. There seemed to be something
ominous under Wayne Whitewood's smiling, organ-playing
exterior.

The interview Donna had done with Janine once they
returned to GamGam's after their dramatic highway encounter had only confirmed that fact.

"They tried to drown me," Donna had said, eyes aimed
squarely at the floor, clearly not enjoying having a camera
pointed at her but enduring it for the sake of the greater
good.

"Drown you?"

"Well. First they cut me," Donna said. She held out her
right hand to the camera, where a faint scar could still be
seen across her palm.

"Are you sure Whitewood was involved?"

Donna had paused a long moment before nodding.
"He was the one who cut me."

"Oh my god," Janine had said. "I'm so sorry, Donna."
She'd been tempted to turn off the camera, to hug her
cousin, but Donna said it was okay and seemed determined
to keep going. "Can you . . . can you tell me about the
drowning?"

"They carried me into the spring and—"

"Wait, what spring?"

"Bleak Creek Spring. Next to the school."

"Oh. Right. From the resort days. Okay."

"They carried me in, and I was . . ."

"You were what?"

Donna shook her head back and forth at least a dozen
times, and the distant look came back, and Janine had
known that this time they were indeed done for the day.

"There," Donna said now, pointing past the line of

people waiting to offer condolences to Alicia's parents and sister, to where Rex was in an intense-seeming conversation with two adults who had to be his parents.

"Perfect," Janine said, but before she could take another step, a brittle hand landed on her arm.

"Still here, huh?" It was that awful woman Mary Hattaway, in a dark version of the many-buttoned outfit she'd been wearing the first time Janine met her. She spoke brightly but wasn't smiling.

"Yup," Janine said, looking Mary right in the eyes. "Still here." She wasn't sure if Mary herself had been the one to paint the profanity on GamGam's Grand Marquis, but Janine was certain she'd been involved.

"That little architecture movie sure is taking a long time. And, Donna," Mary said, "what a nice surprise to see you out and about."

Donna grunted.

"Still keeping the dishes clean at Li'l Dino's?"

"Go screw yourself," Donna said under her breath, looking at the floor.

"Well, bless your heart," Mary said. Janine guessed that meant Mary had heard Donna loud and clear. Leaning in toward Janine and lowering her voice, Mary added, "I think it might be a good idea for you to leave town, sweetie. They have lots of interesting 'structures' in other places."

As Janine tried to think of a snarky response, she was distracted by Mary's right hand, which she'd noticed was wrapped in a bandage, more or less in the same place where Donna's scar was. "What happened to your hand?" she asked.

Mary's face turned a deep shade of red. "Oh . . . I, um . . . I broke a glass," she seethed. "It's fine." Realizing she'd lost her composure, she pivoted sharply and marched off.

Janine turned to Donna, who looked like she was receding into herself again. "I'm sorry, we don't have to stay here. We can leave."

"No," Donna said, as she nodded over Janine's shoulder at Rex, who had broken off from his parents and was heading for the front door.

"Rex," Janine said more loudly than she'd intended.

"Huh?" he asked, walking over to them, blinking as if she'd just woken him up.

"It's me, Janine. The filmmaker?"

"Oh. Yeah. Hey."

"And this is my cousin Donna."

Donna gave a small nod while staring at her shoes.

"I'm so sorry about Alicia," Janine said. "You're right, you know. What you said up there. About the school. You're totally right."

"Oh," Rex said, both relieved and validated. "Well. My parents don't think so. But . . ."

"Let's go over here for a minute," Janine said, leading them to a large fake potted plant they could comfortably speak behind without drawing too much attention. "I've read about the deaths at the school. So I know it doesn't add up. In every single case, the body was too disfigured to have an open-casket funeral. Just like with Alicia."

"Yes! Right?" Rex sounded shocked, as if he couldn't believe anyone would actually agree with him.

"When Donna went there, they . . . Well, are you okay if I tell him?"

Donna nodded.

"They cut her hand and tried to drown her in the—"

"Spring!" Rex said.

"How do you know that?" Janine asked.

"Oh, man, that's . . . because that's what almost happened to our friend Ben. He . . . Well . . ." Rex looked around to make sure no one was listening, and got distracted by the sight of Leif walking past them with his mom. "Hey!" he whispered.

Leif's head spun toward them, seeming for a moment as if he thought the plant itself was talking to him. When he saw that it was Rex, though, his expression hardened. "What do you want?" They were clearly in some kind of fight.

"Just . . . come here for a second. It's the filmmaker lady. From Li'l Dino's."

Leif seemed to have a private battle with himself before sighing, telling his mom he'd only be a minute, and joining them.

"She thinks I'm right," Rex said. "About the murders at Whitewood. I was just about to tell her and her cousin Donna what we saw at the spring."

"Okay," Leif said, unimpressed.

Rex shook his head in frustration, deciding to continue the story rather than letting Leif have a piece of his mind. That could wait. "So, we were at the spring the other night and we saw this . . . like, this ritual. Like, a cult ritual."

The word *cult* caught Janine off-guard, even after hearing Donna's story. "Are you sure?"

"Pretty sure," Leif chimed in. "They were wearing light blue robes, and they—"

"Don," Janine interrupted. "Were they wearing robes when they . . . ?"

"No," Donna said. "At least, I don't think so."

"Okay." Janine hoped these kids weren't adding fantastical details just for the hell of it. "So what happened at this ritual?"

"Whitewood cut some woman's hand," Leif said, getting more into it, "and then the water lit up this weird blue."

"I remember that," Donna said.

"The water . . . lit up?" Janine asked.

Donna nodded.

"Wow. All right."

"Yeah, and then Whitewood walked into the water," Rex said, "and stayed under there for, like, a long time. Not even sure how he did it. Probably some kind of breathing tubes or something."

Janine's skepticism was kicking into overdrive as the details grew more sensational, but watching Donna as she absorbed the boys' story was enough to keep her disbelief suspended.

"I've been thinking about what to do next," Rex said. "We should probably tell Sheriff Lawson, right? Because this is huge. He's the one over there talking to Alicia's parents. We could pull him aside and—"

"Can't do that," Janine said. "We need to be incredibly careful." She saw the confusion on Rex's and Leif's faces, the inability to process the idea that being careful would mean *not* going to the police, but she didn't want to explain the entire situation with Donna's father to them. Not here, anyway. "I think the best thing for us to—"

"I think the best thing for y'all to do is to head on out," a deep voice said. They turned to see Leggett Shackelford in his black suit and mammoth mustache framing the same unwavering smile as Mary Hattaway's. "I'm sorry to interrupt your meeting, but this place is full of grieving folks, and I believe you've already made enough of a scene today," the big man said, locking eyes with Rex before turning to Janine.

"Hi, I'm Leggett Shackelford," he said, extending a large paw for Janine to shake, "and this is my funeral home." She tried not to noticeably freak out when she saw a raised scar along his palm.

"So nice to meet you," she said, with zero warmth in her voice as she shook his hand.

"I'd love to say the same, but I've heard about the unfortunate movie you're makin'. Big Gary told me he's still missing three stones. Such a shame." He spoke with an unnatural congeniality, that sappiness the people of Bleak Creek so often adopted when ripping you a new one. "And now, to show up at this young woman's funeral, after all you've done to upset people here? Seems pretty impolite, if you ask me."

"Well, nobody's asking you," Janine said, unwilling to play his game of fake friendliness. "Though I could, if you'd be down to be interviewed for my documentary."

Leggett held his grin in silence, surprised that a young woman would talk to him that way.

"Okay, ma'am, I think we're done here," he finally said. "Now, if y'all could make your way home I'd appreciate it."

"Gladly," Janine said, giving a quick nod to Donna, Leif, and Rex before making a beeline for the exit, hoping they would follow.

Once she was outside, she saw that Donna and Rex had followed, but Leif had reconnected with his mom. Rex's parents were walking out the door, so she tried to speak fast.

"You need to take us to that spring."

18

AS REX AND LEIF LED JANINE AND DONNA THROUGH THE DARKNESS—Janine with a camera bag slung over her shoulder and Donna holding a tripod duct-taped to a long aluminum pole—both boys were silent. This was partly because they were once again sneaking onto the Whitewood School property, but mostly because, other than a perfunctory phone call about logistics, they hadn't spoken since the funeral.

Rex still felt betrayed by Leif for keeping his crush to himself all summer, while Leif was still fuming at Rex, not only for upstaging his confession, but for putting their lives in danger by publicly accusing Whitewood of being a murderer. Leif didn't even want to come back to the spring, but as was the case with most everything that had happened in the past couple weeks, he was doing it for Alicia.

As they reached the tobacco barn, a familiar hoot came from the trees.

Rex had taken a solo trip to the Tree earlier that day, letting Ben know that Janine wanted to film the spring for her documentary about the school, that her cousin was a Whitewood alumna who had nearly drowned there. "I love this idea," Ben had said while munching on the Moon-Pie Rex brought him. "But I'll sit this one out—no amount of camo will protect me if I'm that close to the school. Let me know when you're going, though. I'll stay in a tree. Be your watchman."

Rex now returned Ben's all-clear hoot with a hoot of his own, which sounded less like an owl and more like a sick horse. "All right, we're good," he said, finding the cut part of the fence and holding it open. "Once we're all through, we'll find the two-trunked tree from before and regroup there." He gestured toward Janine and Donna. "Ladies first."

"Why do you get to decide who goes first?" Leif whispered, simmering with resentment at yet another display of Rex trying to take charge.

"Wow, okay. I was just being nice," Rex said.

"No, you were doing what you always do. Trying to be in the driver's seat. Just like the funeral. I was having, like, a nice moment up there, talking about Alicia, and you couldn't deal with it, so you had to make it about you!"

"That's not what I was doing!"

"Oh yeah, right. And here you go doing it again. Ladies first, my ass. What if I think the gentlemen should go first? Huh? What about that?"

"Dude, you're not making any sense."

"*You're* not making any sense!" Leif shouted in frustration, realizing he might not be making any sense.

"Guys!" Janine whisper-shouted, a finger to her lips. "We really don't care who goes first. Either go or stop blocking the way."

Rex and Leif looked surprised, as if they'd forgotten they weren't alone.

"Oh, sorry," Rex said, sure that Janine was second-guessing going on a mission—after midnight, on a Thursday—led by two kids she hardly knew. "We were just . . . working some stuff out."

"That's great news," Janine said, "but maybe you

should do it some other time when we're not about to investigate a magic murder spring."

"Good point," Leif said, stepping aside. "Ladies first."

They all passed through the fence, then marched in silence up the hill into the woods. Rex scanned the forest for the two-trunked tree. It was notably darker tonight, an overcast sky obscuring the moon, and he couldn't spot it. As they continued walking toward the spring, Rex noticed that they were all tiptoeing like the four members of Mystery, Inc., from *Scooby-Doo. Maybe Leif should have brought Tucker along to help us get to the bottom of this,* he thought, as he looked left and realized they'd missed the double tree by a good fifty feet.

"Shoot," he said. "Um, follow me." He motioned to Janine and Donna and caught a sour look on Leif's face. "I mean, follow *us.*"

Once they arrived at the tree, Rex grabbed his goggles out of his pocket and put them around his neck. "So, there it is," he said, pointing through the sparse woods to the spring, shivering as he realized he'd be in it in a matter of moments.

"Yup, okay," Janine said, pulling out her camcorder, which she had thoroughly covered with clear plastic wrap, every part of the camera sealed, including the tripod mount itself. It was a camera waterproofing technique she'd employed while shooting one of Dennis's crappy short films called *The Man Who Met a Mermaid.*

"Cool," Rex said. "So that's gonna work?"

"It should. I'm not interested in ruining my camera." Janine grabbed the homemade extended tripod contraption from Donna and carefully fastened the camcorder to it. "Okay, all set."

Rex nodded, and the troop began slowly descending the hill toward the spring. When they neared the edge of the tree line, Leif stopped.

He pointed across the spring, beyond the grassy expanse on the opposite side, to the Whitewood School. On the near side of the school, next to a row of three little buildings, they could see a small, blackened concrete slab where a fourth building had stood.

"That's . . ." Leif said, his voice cracking. "That's where she . . . died."

Rex placed a hand on his shoulder. "And that's why we're here. So no one else will."

Leif nodded and wiped his face.

"I'm gonna go ahead and start filming," Janine said. She pressed the record button through the plastic wrap, looked in the viewfinder to confirm she was rolling, then awkwardly raised the camera to her face, not an easy task given that the length of the aluminum pole taped to the tripod was nearly her height.

Janine pointed the camera toward the school. She guessed it was about a hundred yards away. *Far enough to get the hell out of here if someone comes outside,* she thought. A single porch light shone next to the back door.

Seeing the school from the rear gave her the sense that she was somewhere she shouldn't be, like being on the wrong side of the barrier of the lion exhibit at the zoo. She shuddered, then noticed Donna staring at the spring and trembling.

"You okay, Don?" she asked her cousin.

"I don't know," Donna said quietly.

"I told you, you don't have to be here. I completely under—"

"No," Donna said. "I need to do this."

"All right, here we go," Rex said. He stepped out of the woods into previously uncharted territory, feeling naked once he was out in the open; the spring was only a few dozen steps away, but without the cover of trees, it seemed like miles. Rex was grateful for the clouds, as this brazen trespassing would have been much dicier on a bright night. He looked toward the school. No signs of life.

They reached the water's edge and were hit by a pungent stench.

"Whew. Was that you, man?" Leif whispered to Rex.

"No," Rex said. "It's the spring. Sulfur, I think."

"Oh," Leif said. "Right."

Now that Leif was standing next to the dark, slow-moving water where they had seen things he still couldn't explain, he felt a tightness in his chest.

Rex snapped his goggles on. "I'm going in."

Even though Leif had only minutes ago been complaining about Rex's need to lead, he didn't object. Rex was the better swimmer anyway.

Janine panned the camera across the premises, then looked back to Donna, who'd stopped about ten steps earlier than the rest of them. "You sure you're all right?" Janine asked.

Donna gave a slight nod, her arms wrapped around herself, her eyes locked on the spring, captivated and terrified.

Rex found Donna's look of dread more than a little disconcerting, but he had to press forward. He reminded himself that this was all some sick scam masterminded by Wayne Whitewood. Granted, it was technologically impressive, involving some sophisticated engineering to turn a natural spring into a giant hot tub with bubbles and lights, but a scam nonetheless.

He took a few steps into the spring, the water warm around his knees. He bent his face down to the surface, dipping his goggles in. Nothing but darkness. Obviously. He came up and wiped the water away with his arm, hoping he didn't smell like farts now.

"Didn't you say the water lit up?" Janine asked, pointing the camera at Rex.

"Uh, yeah," he said.

"But you don't know how to make it do that?"

"Uh, not exactly. But, I'm gonna do a couple dives, see if I can find a switch," he said, trying to sound confident.

"A switch?" Janine asked.

"To turn the light on." It sounded stupid as soon as he said it, but Rex didn't know what else to do, so he strode deeper into the spring, just as Mr. Whitewood had done. Once the water reached his waist, he pushed off and started to swim.

As he moved farther from shore, the black Hanes V-neck he'd borrowed from his dad's drawer began billowing up around his midsection. Without the reassuring underfooting of the creek floor, Rex instantly felt uneasy. The water was a temperature somewhere between bath and hot tub that should have been soothing, and yet . . . he felt cold, too. As if a pocket of chilly air had cocooned around him.

He continued toward the center of the spring, swimming in a slow, deliberate breast stroke, when he was suddenly gripped with another, more disturbing sensation: that feeling he sometimes got at the beach when he swam out farther than he'd intended and couldn't shake the thought that a shark was lurking in the depths below.

The feeling he was being watched.

He had trouble convincing himself to drop his head below the surface, but he needed to find *something* underwater for Janine to film; footage of a goggled teenager doing laps around Bleak Creek Spring at night wouldn't prove anything.

He inhaled deeply, then dove down, his eyes breaking into the darkness. As water filled his ears, he was struck by the sheer quiet. No muffled whooshes from his arms paddling. No gentle rumble of water flowing into the mouth of the creek. No sound at all.

He looked around, seeing pure blackness in every direction, the filtered moonlight unable to pierce the murk. There was no way he'd be able to spot an underwater cave, if that was indeed what Whitewood had gone into. He'd at least been hoping to see a glint in the water—of steel, or some other metal—but there was nothing other than uniform, lightless deep.

He felt his arm brush against something and realized he'd collided into one of the spring walls. He moved his hands across a wide patch of it, thinking maybe he'd feel some pipes or cables, but it was only rocks and dirt.

The water suddenly got colder—frigid, even—and Rex had the ominous thought that he was somehow closer to whatever was watching him. Or, more precisely, like he was swimming *inside* it.

Rex frantically kicked his legs to return to the surface, guessing it was only inches away, a foot at most.

But he didn't emerge.

He looked up, only to see more blackness. Was that even up? What if this was some kind of Bermuda Triangle he would never escape?

He began to propel himself wildly, hoping he'd eventually hit the side or the bottom of the spring, which might orient him. Just when his breath was running out, he felt the night breeze on his face as his head broke through.

Gasping, he looked out toward the creek bank and saw no one. Oh no. Had they left him here?

"Hey!" he heard Leif call from behind him. "What'd you see?"

Rex tried to hide his terror while swimming toward Leif as quickly as possible, feeling profound relief when his feet brushed the rocky bottom.

"Couldn't find anything yet," he said, lifting his goggles to his forehead and stepping out onto the creek bank, water dripping from his cargo shorts. He wanted to tell them what he'd just experienced but was unable to find words that didn't sound ridiculous. "It's too dark."

"My camera has a light on it," Janine said. "But I'm not sure I can get to the button with the way I've wrapped it. Dammit. Didn't think about tha—"

"Blood," Donna said, still ten steps away.

"What?" Janine asked.

"It has to be blood."

Rex had been slightly creeped out by Donna all night, and this didn't help.

But Leif understood. "Oh, right!" he said. "The spring didn't light up until that woman dipped her bleeding hand in."

"Wait, for real?" Janine asked.

"Yes," Donna said.

No one spoke for a moment. For the first time that night, Rex noticed the ever-present hum of the cicadas. "Anybody have something sharp?" he asked.

"My house key . . . ?" Leif said, taking it out of his pocket.

"That could work." Rex extended his hand toward Leif. "Scratch me. As hard as you can."

"Really?" Janine asked, tempted to stop filming. "This is what's happening right now?"

Leif placed the uneven side of the key on Rex's palm.

"You ready?" Leif asked.

"Just do it," Rex said, closing his eyes.

"Okay, three . . . two . . . one!" Leif jabbed the key sharply down and dragged it across Rex's palm.

"Ow!" Rex shrieked, holding his hand and hopping in place. "That was good, that was good." But when they examined the hand in the faint light, it wasn't. "You didn't even break the skin!"

"I think the palm is too meaty," Leif said. "We should do it to the *back* of your hand."

"Oh my god," Janine said, shaking her head. "I don't think I can stay here for this."

"Okay, try it," Rex said, extending his hand palm down and biting his lip.

Leif skipped the countdown altogether, whacking the key's teeth down and across Rex's knuckles with a focus of purpose and energy not unlike his direct hit on Rex's testicles earlier that week. Doling out this physical punishment was apparently releasing some of his anger. "Geez!" Rex said, gritting his teeth and flapping his hand wildly back and forth.

"I think that one was good," Leif said.

Rex held his hand close to his face and identified a thin line of red along his knuckles. "I'm bleeding. I'm bleeding!" He waved his hand around triumphantly.

"Congratulations," Janine said.

"All right, I'm gonna do this," Rex said to himself, walking toward the water, Janine begrudgingly keeping her camera trained on him.

Donna took a few more steps away from them as Rex crouched down at the edge of the spring—trying not to shake from the combination of pain and terror still coursing through him—and dipped his hand in, just as he'd seen the robed woman do.

He stared at the water.

"Does it feel like anything's happening?" Leif asked.

It felt like his slightly bleeding hand was surrounded by water.

"Nah," Rex said.

He hadn't really been expecting it to work.

Janine pulled her eye away from the viewfinder and sighed. "Not to be a buzzkill," she said, "but I don't think . . ."

"You don't think what?" Leif asked.

"It's working," Janine said, her eyes glued to the middle of the spring, which had begun to light up from below just as Rex and Leif had described: a blue glow, pale at first, then brighter as it expanded outward.

"Yeah," Rex said, still staring down at the spot where his own hand was submerged. "I don't think this is how it works."

"No," Leif said. "Look."

The bubbles had started, and within ten seconds, the entire spring was at full gurgle, illuminating a bright, otherworldly blue.

Rex jerked his hand out of the water.

"Wow," Janine said. "This is . . . wow."

"Shouldn't you be filming this?" Leif asked.

"Oh, right. My bad." Janine hastily pulled the camera back to her eye.

Rex was shocked, his mind racing to find a logical explanation for what had just transpired. But from this close, he couldn't see any sources of light in the spring. It was like the glow was coming from the water itself.

This wasn't just a cult with fancy technology. This was something bigger. Something unknowable.

There was a stifled sob from behind them, and they all turned to see Donna stumbling back toward the woods. "Oh, shit," Janine said. "I should . . . Yeah, I should go check on her." She started to run before remembering what was in her hand. "Watch this for me for a second," she said, handing the pole and camcorder over to Rex. "Just keep rolling!" She ran after Donna.

Leif looked to Rex, who continued to stare at the water in disbelief.

"Do you . . ." Leif began. "Do you think we should start filming under the water?"

"Sure," Rex said, shaking his head like he'd just been awakened from a dream.

He turned the pole over, the camera now upside down,

just off the ground. He leaned over the edge of the water and dipped it below the surface. It hit bottom before the lens was even submerged.

"I think you're gonna have to get in the water," Leif said. "Take it a little deeper."

Rex looked at him, his face a portrait of dread.

Leif had never seen Rex like this before. If *he* was scared to get back in the water, then Leif *definitely* didn't want to go in.

But then he remembered Alicia. They were here to make sense of her death, to potentially save other kids. And, at this moment, with his normally brave best friend paralyzed with fear, he was the only one left to do anything about it.

"I'll go," he said, surprising himself. "Gimme the camera."

Rex looked at Leif, wide-eyed. "Really?" he asked.

"Yes." Leif reached down to take the camera pole.

"Okay, yeah. All right," Rex said, handing it over. "Just . . . be careful."

Leif didn't like the sound of that, but he took a step into the bubbling spring without looking back. He lowered the camera into the water, barely a foot deep. He pivoted it around in a half circle, doubting that he was filming anything other than bubbles, seeing as he was still so far from the middle of the spring, where Whitewood had descended. He decided to walk farther out, slowly and methodically panning the camcorder back and forth like he was operating a metal detector, the muscle memory kicking in from the many hours he'd spent doing just that during the lonely summer before seventh grade.

I can't believe I'm doing this, he thought as the water reached his chest. But somehow he wasn't that scared. He bounced off the bottom of the spring, only a few yards from where they'd seen Whitewood disappear. Soon his feet moved freely through the water. Too deep to touch. He hadn't thought through how he would swim while holding the camera pole, but the rising bubbles made it relatively easy to float in place. Relieved he wasn't sinking, he swiveled the camera around in a slow circle. *I'm gonna be the one who captures the game-changing footag—*

He felt a tug at the camera.

Startled, Leif pulled at the pole for a few seconds, and it loosened up. He exhaled. Maybe it had just gotten caught on some underwater plants or something. He pulled the camera higher, then started another swivel.

"Everything okay?" Rex shouted, sounding far away as he competed with the gurgle of the bubbles.

"Yeah, it's fine," Leif shouted. "I think the camera just got caught on some—"

He screamed as something yanked the camera pole down sharply, nearly pulling him underwater.

It was no plant.

Rex stood frozen in terror as he watched Leif struggling in the water.

He was snapped out of it by an owl hoot.

Then another one.

Ben. Signaling them.

Rex looked over to the school, where a light had turned on in a first-floor window. "Oh crap," he said. "Somebody's coming! Leif, somebody's coming!"

Leif heard Rex shouting something but he had no idea what. He was somehow still holding on to the camera pole, barely keeping his head above water as he played tug-of-war with this invisible force.

He had to hold on. He could almost hear Alicia telling him not to let go.

There was a sharp tug, and the pole was pulled completely out of his hand.

"We gotta get out of here!" Rex yelled from the shore.

"But . . . the camera!" Leif said between heaving breaths.

"Forget about it!" Rex said. "We got bigger problems!"

There was another owl hoot. Then three more in quick succession.

Leif looked toward the school, where he saw a figure, holding a torch, steadily walking in their direction. He began a mad paddle back to shore.

"What's happening?" Janine asked in a panic as she returned from the woods without Donna. "And where the hell is my camera?"

Leif tumbled out of the water onto the muddy bank. "I'm sorry," he said, catching his breath. "I—"

There was a violent splash from the center of the spring as the camera pole, with camera still attached, shot out of the water and landed nearby in the shallows.

"There it is," Rex said.

"Fuck," said Janine, her astonished mouth hanging open.

Rex saw the person was about fifty yards away, now trotting and closing the distance quickly.

Janine grabbed her camera from the water, and the three of them sprinted back to the woods.

"What's the rush?" a voice shouted from behind them.

Rex burned forward, the first to make it to the woods, where he shouted ahead to a petrified Donna: "Go! Go! Go!"

She ran side by side with him, twigs crunching under their feet as they darted through trees and dodged branches.

The fence came into view. Rex found the gap and practically dove through, landing on his knees in the damp grass before holding it open, first for Donna, then for the camera and its lengthy pole, then for Janine, and then for . . .

"Where's Leif?" Rex asked.

"I don't know," Janine said. "I thought he was right there with us."

Rex began to freak out and was climbing back through the fence when he heard someone running through the woods. Leif materialized out of the darkness. "I slipped," he said. He was holding his side, completely out of breath as he came toward them—more of a jog than a run, really—but he was going to make it.

Rex pulled the fence back.

"Come on, Leif!"

As Leif kneeled down to slide through the hole, Rex saw another silhouette.

Wayne Whitewood was only a few yards behind, in full sprint.

Leif. Come. On.

Leif began to slide through the fence but was abruptly jerked to a stop.

His shirt was stuck.

Rex reached down, grasping at Leif's collar, trying to rip the fabric. They locked eyes as Leif lurched backward.

Whitewood had him by the leg.

"Let go of me!" Leif said, writhing back and forth.

"I'm afraid I can't do that," Whitewood said.

Rex started to pull the fence back and go through, imagining that together, maybe he and Leif could somehow fend Whitewood off.

But then Whitewood pulled out his knife.

"Come on over," he said. "I'll take both of you."

Rex didn't know what to do.

So he did nothing, watching as Whitewood tied Leif's hands behind his back and walked him deeper into the woods. "Don't worry, I'll see you again soon," Whitewood said.

"Rex!" Leif shouted. "Help! Please!"

Rex desperately wanted to, but he knew that if he had any real hope of helping him, he couldn't be captured too.

"I will," he yelled, slowly backing away from the fence, "I promise!"

19

REX WAS JARRED OUT OF A DEEP SLEEP BY THE PHONE RINGING IN the kitchen.

He'd forgotten to close his bedroom door.

Understandable, considering the night he'd had.

He'd also neglected to remove the decoy punching bag from under his covers, which meant, once again, his five or so hours of restless attempts at sleep had been spent crammed onto one half of his extra-long twin bed. He leaned in to the massive bag, pushing it off the edge of the mattress. It slammed to the floor, making more noise than he'd expected and taking his top sheet and comforter along for the ride. He lay there in his Teenage Mutant Ninja Turtles boxers, which were still slightly damp with the mysterious waters of Bleak Creek Spring.

The phone rang again. He buried his head beneath his pillow.

It wasn't just the phone he wanted to block out.

It was any thought about what had happened last night. He felt the way characters in movies looked when they had a hangover. Like he'd been run over by a truck.

The minuscule amount of sleep he'd gotten had been dominated by dreams of Leif, Rex abandoning him in every single one—riding away on a bus that Leif had just missed, seeing Leif drowning and doing nothing to help him, releasing Leif's hand and watching him plummet off a cliff.

They were dreams it didn't take a psychologist to interpret.

Leif had been taken by Whitewood, and Rex hadn't even put up a fight.

He knew he'd probably done the right thing, that taking on a grown man who had a knife wouldn't have ended well, but that didn't prevent him from feeling more guilt than he'd ever experienced. He couldn't stop cycling through the night's events, questioning each disastrous decision. He should never have let Leif go into the spring to begin with. It was supposed to be him.

At the very least, he should have made sure Leif—who'd just exhausted himself tussling with that thing in the spring—was following him to the fence. But no. He was too selfish to even look back. *What an asshole.*

And now what?

What had Whitewood done with Leif?

He couldn't just keep him there. Admission to the school required parental consent, and Leif's mom wouldn't agree to that, would she?

Then it dawned on him. The ringing of the phone.

It was Whitewood calling. Of course. He was gonna tell Rex's parents that he was also there last night, trespassing.

They would both end up at the Whitewood School.

This was the worst-case scenario.

But no. Whitewood wouldn't push to get Rex into the school so soon after the public accusation at the funeral. Too obvious.

It hit him. The real worst-case scenario: Whitewood had *already* killed Leif. He was a madman, after all. Maybe he'd dragged him right back to the spring and drowned him, then called Leif's mom saying there had been an accident.

"Are you up?" Rex's mom said, peeking through the doorframe in her nightgown, seeing him lying there uncovered. "Is everything all right? Where are your covers?"

"I was hot," Rex said in a sleepy voice, trying to hide his full-blown panic attack.

Rex's mom stepped into his room, shutting the door behind her.

"I just got off the phone with Leif's mom."

Rex shot up in bed so fast the room spun a little. He was having the worst kind of déjà-vu, remembering his parents walking into this same room to break the news about Alicia.

"It seems Leif got caught trespassing on the Whitewood School property last night. You wouldn't happen to know anything about this, would you?"

Rex exhaled as his entire body relaxed. Leif wasn't dead. Thank God.

"Rex?" It was clear his mom knew, or at least strongly suspected, he'd been there. He decided to stall anyway.

"Trespassing?" Rex asked in his most incredulous voice.

"Cut the act," Martha said, her eyes looking furious even as they filled with tears. "I just . . . What in the world were you thinking, Rex? First saying all that nonsense at the funeral, and now, even after your father and I warned you about it, you're gallivantin' around in the middle of the night on Mr. Whitewood's property? This has to stop!"

"I'm sorry," Rex said.

"You know Bonnie got called out to that school at two in the morning? Mr. Whitewood strongly encouraged her to send Leif to the school, and she agreed right there on the spot. Just as I—"

"She *agreed?*"

"Of course she did! And you better believe your father and I have talked about it too! I don't know why you can't seem to understand how serious—"

"How could you even consider that after what happened to Alicia?"

"Rex, that was an accident! And it looks like it was her own fault. You've got to stop with these ridiculous stories—"

"I can't believe you're that stupid!" Rex yelled, jumping out of bed. "You want me to die there too?"

His mom looked taken aback. Rex had never spoken to her like this. She steadied herself on the doorframe, her expression quickly transforming from shock to anger. "What do you think your father would think about you talking like that?"

Rex knew he'd gone too far. Things never turned out well once his mom asked that question.

"I'm sorry, Mom," he said. "I'm really sorry. It's just ever since Alicia died . . ." He had the thought that he should make himself cry to garner sympathy, but then realized he was already crying. He sat back on his bed, his face in his hands.

His mom's face softened. "Oh, sweetie," she said, sitting down next to Rex and putting an arm around him. "I know how hard this is."

Rex leaned in to the snot and the tears and the mess of it all. "I just miss her so much, Mom. And now Leif is gone too . . . I didn't mean to misbehave. Leif didn't either, I swear. We just . . . we don't know what to do, so we come up with these stories. I'm so sorry." It was both a performance and not a performance, as most of what he was saying—and all the underlying pain—was more or less true.

"I understand," Martha said. "I'm sorry I was so harsh with you. But you understand why you can't keep behavin' like this, right?"

"Of course. Of course I do."

"Good. Now, Dad's already over at the home—got a

THE LOST CAUSES OF BLEAK CREEK 233

rush job funeral this afternoon that I need to get over there and help him with—but are you gonna be okay gettin' to school?"

Rex stared at his mom and, again, the emotions were all there to support his case. "Is it . . . Is it all right if I stay home today?" he asked between sniffs. "I just . . . I feel so awful."

"Rex, now, I don't want people talkin' when they hear that Leif has been sent to that school and see that you're absent too." Rex nodded as he let out a sob. "But then I don't want people talkin' when they see that you're a total mess, either." Martha puzzled it out for a moment. "All right, you can stay home, but you are *not to leave this house,* you understand?"

Rex nodded.

Martha hugged him. "All right then," she said as she stood. "You take it easy today, okay? Call us if you need anything."

"Thanks, Mom."

Martha walked out of the room, and Rex gingerly rolled over and laid his head on the pillow, immediately beginning to brainstorm ways to take down the White-wood School and save Leif's life.

—

REX DIDN'T KNOW he'd fallen back asleep until he was again abruptly awakened.

It wasn't the phone this time.

It was a tapping. At his bedroom window.

Rex tried to steady his breathing even as an internal voice said *oh shit oh shit oh shit oh shit.*

He suddenly understood why his mom had been so easily convinced to let him stay at home.

His parents *were* sending him to the Whitewood School

and the goons in coveralls were outside his window, moments from crashing into his room to abduct him.

How could he have been so stupid?

There was the tapping again.

Rex stepped out of bed—as quietly as he could—thinking his best bet would be to grab a baseball bat from the garage.

Just as he was about to leave the room, though, he heard a voice.

"Rex! Are you in there?"

It wasn't the voice of a goon in coveralls.

"Ben?" Rex asked, cautiously lifting the shade, not quite believing that the wild boy from the woods was standing in the shrubs next to his bedroom window.

"Can you let me in?" Ben asked. "No one else is home, right?"

"Uh . . . yeah. But do you want to go around and use the front door?"

"Not really," Ben said. "I've had too much exposure as it is. Can you just open the window?"

"Sure, sure." Rex slid the window open and helped Ben negotiate his way over the sill. He was still in the dirty jumpsuit and, without the woods as a buffer, his stench was much more apparent. Rex left the window open but pulled down the shade. "What are you doing here?"

"Who's your favorite?" Ben asked.

"What?"

"Your favorite Ninja Turtle. I see you're a fan," Ben said, gesturing to Rex's underwear.

"Oh. Can we discuss that later?" Rex grabbed a pair of jams from his drawer and slid them on. "Why are you here?"

"Yeah, okay. Well, as you know," Ben said, "I saw everything that happened last night."

"Yep, thanks for the hoots."

"I did what I could. And it still wasn't enough." Ben shook his head, as if feeling deep regret. "So I thought it was time for me to . . . emerge. To help." Ben picked up a book from Rex's desk. "*Deep Thoughts*. I love these. Jack Handey is hilarious."

"Uh, yeah, definitely. How did you know where I live?"

"The phone book," Ben said. "They had one at the Short Stop."

"Weren't you worried about being seen?"

"Desperate times."

"Yeah."

"Only one person saw me. A woman power walking. I told her I was going duck hunting."

"Smart."

"So. Whitewood took Leif," Ben said, shifting his voice into "let's get down to business" mode. "Which means Leif could be the next sacrifice."

Rex was grateful to have someone to talk everything out with, but even with the window open, Ben's smell was overpowering. "Hey," Rex said. "Do you want to maybe take a shower?"

"Oh," Ben said. "Is that an option?"

"Yes, definitely. You can borrow some of my clothes, too. Maybe ditch the jumpsuit."

"That is incredibly generous," Ben said.

Thirty minutes later, with Ben looking and smelling like a regular human being, outfitted in sweatpants and a baggy orange 1990 rec-league basketball T-shirt and fresh gauze on his hand, the two of them stood in the kitchen, staring at the contents of the McClendon family fridge.

"Really, help yourself to whatever," Rex said.

Ben's eyes greedily roamed over everything before grabbing a carrot from the produce drawer.

"That's what you want?" Rex asked.

"I've missed carrots so much," Ben said, taking a huge chomp.

Rex was mid-shrug when he heard a car pulling into the driveway. "My parents!"

He rushed Ben and his carrot into his bedroom closet and ran to the front window to see if it was his mom or his dad.

It was neither.

It was a Grand Marquis with a red stripe of paint on the side.

Janine bounded out of the car, camera bag in hand, and by the time she made it to the front doorstep, Rex was waiting for her. "Hey," he said. "How'd you know I was staying home from school?"

"Oh, right. School," Janine said. "I didn't even think about that. Can I come in? There's something you need to see."

"Yeah, definitely," Rex said. "So Leif is officially a student at Whitewoo—"

"Where's your TV?" Janine asked, already striding past him into the house, unzipping her camera bag.

"Uh, in the living room," Rex said, pointing. "Hey, Ben," he called back to his bedroom. "It's not my parents, it's Janine. The filmmaker."

When Ben made it to the living room, Janine was crouched down by the TV, pulling random cords out of her camera bag as Rex paced around, biting his nails, wondering what they'd caught on camera. He had a feeling it wasn't the underwater machinery of a fancy hot tub.

"Why is your TV so weird?" Janine asked, trying to figure out which colored holes on the back of the television were the right ones to attach the camera cords to.

"It's not weird," Rex said, feeling oddly defensive about his parents' choice of electronics. He took the cords from her hand and quickly plugged them in, as if to prove his point.

"Oh, that worked," Janine said, as the otherworldly blue of the spring filled the television screen, the camera on pause.

"I haven't seen a TV in ages," Ben said, still working on the carrot.

"Who the hell are you?" Janine asked.

"I'm Ben." He gave a small wave with his bandaged hand. "I was the hooter."

Janine cocked her head.

"In the tree," added Ben. "Making owl noises."

"Oh, yeah," said Janine. "Hi."

"Thank you for joining the fight," Ben said. "Most adults think it's bullshit."

"No problem," Janine said, eager to show them the tape. "Okay, so, um . . . I rushed over here as fast as I could. Because this is . . . Well. I mean. Yeah. I'm gonna hit play now."

Rex and Ben nodded.

It was hard at first to tell that the footage was no longer paused, as the screen remained bright blue even as the camera panned back and forth. Then, the frame shifted violently, the picture dimming for a moment.

"That was whatever was pulling on the camera?" Rex said.

"Yeah," Janine said. "You never see anything other than that darkening. But just keep watching."

The camera began to swing around again, a wall of roots and rocks coming into view as Leif panned the camera farther to the right. Janine paused the camera.

"There," she said.

"There what?" All Rex saw was the rocky wall of the spring. Was there more to see than that?

"Oh," Ben said, his eyes bugging.

What were they seeing? *Is there an especially interesting rock?* He was embarrassed to ask.

But then Rex saw.

And he felt faint.

Sticking out from the dense, mossy wall was a head. A curly-haired head.

Alicia.

"That's not all," Janine said. She pressed play again and Rex saw it, just before the camera moved left.

Alicia opened her eyes.

20

THE MOMENT HE WALKED IN THE DOOR, WAYNE WHITEWOOD KNEW something was wrong.

He set Ruby down in front of the television, unable to shed the sudden feeling of panic, like a bat fluttering around his rib cage. He began calling his wife's name, inviting her to come enjoy the banana split they'd brought back from the Dairy Queen.

"Hey, honey," he said as he walked down the hall to their bedroom, hoping that if he kept behaving like everything was okay, then it really would be. "You better get in here before this thing melts!"

Judith was in bed, but she wasn't asleep.

She'd left a note next to the empty bottle of pills: *It's too hard. I'm sorry.*

Word traveled fast through their small town of Plumland, North Carolina, even faster than normal, given Wayne Whitewood's story was one of bad luck piling on bad luck, the kind of story that opened your heart wide even as it made you exhale with relief that your own troubles seemed mild by comparison. "Oh, no," people would gasp. "And after everything that poor man's gone through with Ruby . . ."

Wayne and Judith's daughter had been sick since she

was three, an unforgiving illness that had gripped their family and refused to let go. At first, they'd thought it was the flu, and their pediatrician had agreed; what else would leave an exuberant, bouncy toddler like Ruby completely sapped of energy? But, two weeks after following Dr. Robinson's recommendations to the letter—rest, hydration, and plenty of orange juice for Vitamin C—Ruby had been as fatigued as ever. And disturbingly frail, too. She'd ended up with bruises up and down her leg just from bumping into a chair in the kitchen. Another time she'd tripped in the living room on her beloved blue crocheted frog, and somehow broken an arm. She also bled easily—even a slight nick from safety scissors could break skin. When they'd returned to Dr. Robinson, he'd examined Ruby and said, "You sure she's been gettin' enough orange juice?"

Wayne and Judith took Ruby to several other doctors, including one at the nearby university hospital. Even the big shot doctor had no idea what was wrong with their precious little girl, despite running a battery of unpleasant tests on her. They returned home, having become disillusioned with medical professionals altogether. It was then that Judith had suggested they turn to God.

Wayne, up to that point not a particularly religious man, agreed to join the local Pentecostal church that Judith had attended as a child. He'd always been skeptical of that crowd, with their tales of healing and miracles. But given the circumstances, it seemed like the perfect fit. After they shared their situation with the church, everyone lovingly gathered around Ruby, devoting an entire Sunday service to laying healing hands on the little girl and pleading with the Lord to take the sickness away. Ruby came home that day with more energy than she'd had in weeks, giving them hope that their prayers had been answered. The next morning, however, when Ruby awoke, her listlessness was back in full force.

It was then that Wayne saw his wife change. Judith retreated to a grim place, refusing to discuss further treatment for Ruby. She continued to carry out her motherly duties, but she did so distantly, like a robot following a program. The love was gone from her eyes. She'd grown cold.

When Ruby was five, Wayne made the difficult decision to enroll her in kindergarten at Plumland Elementary School, where he had served as principal for the last ten years. He thought this could provide a badly needed break for Judith, and he figured he'd be able to keep an eye on his fragile daughter at school. On her third day, though, two boys in a shoving match collided with her and broke a couple of her ribs. Wayne wanted to have the boys expelled; the vice principal convinced him that was unreasonable. Wayne pulled Ruby out of school instead. It would be up to Judith to teach her at home.

Two miserable years later, his wife was dead and his seven-year-old daughter was as ill as she'd ever been. The grief was unrelenting. A day barely passed when he didn't feel that same pull toward hopelessness that had overtaken his wife. Ruby remained the only reason he was able to get out of bed each morning. He couldn't lose her as well.

Wayne leveraged his unenviable circumstances into a yearlong sabbatical—something elementary school administrators weren't typically granted—so he could devote himself entirely to his daughter and her health.

This time he turned over all the stones, taking Ruby to anyone within a hundred-mile radius who he thought might be able to help: doctors, healers, homeopaths, practitioners of New Agey crap that he would have never considered before. An old woman in thick glasses stuck leeches all over Ruby's back. A master of Eastern medicine made meticulous adjustments to Ruby's chi. A lazy-eyed German man zapped her with a giant electromagnet.

Wayne was optimistic each time, thinking maybe this was it, they'd finally figured it out, but then a month would pass and Ruby's situation would be unchanged. In a way, these days of chasing unlikely remedies were the most bittersweet of his life, as spending so much quality time with his daughter brought him profound joy in the midst of his crumbling hopes. He'd started teaching her how to play piano, and those moments together at the keyboard were the only ones in which he could truly lose himself, his routine of misfortune sloughing off like a snakeskin.

"You know, it's a shame that spring ain't open anymore," Wayne's friend Hank said one night as they downed a couple of Budweisers on Wayne's porch, Ruby fast asleep in her room.

"What spring?" Wayne asked. Hank had been his mentor at Plumland Elementary before retiring and handing Wayne the job. The older man seemed to enjoy maintaining that knowledge-bestowing dynamic.

"That healing spring over in Bleak Creek. You never heard about it?"

Wayne shook his head.

"Oh, yeah, at one point people were comin' from all over to bathe in that spring, get healed." Hank took a long sip of his beer, like an ellipsis at the end of his sentence. "Even had a whole resort set up next to it."

"Healed from what?" Wayne asked.

"Everything, I guess." Another long sip. "I remember people goin' for smaller stuff—gout, kidney stones, rashes, that sort of thing—but Patty's cousin still swears it wiped out his leukemia."

Wayne laughed. Hank didn't.

"I'm dead serious," Hank said. "He was gettin' his will together and everything. But then his wife convinced him to go to the spring."

"I don't know," Wayne said. "I'm not sure I believe in that sorta thing."

"Wayne, there's a lot out there that don't fit into our boxes, you know?" Hank said. "Just because I can't explain it don't mean it ain't true."

"Okay, I guess. But if this spring can work so many miracles, then how come it's closed?" Wayne asked.

"Well," Hank said, finishing off his beer and placing it with a dramatic thunk onto the coffee table. "The owners of that resort, the Bleak family, one of their kids drowned in it. About fifteen years ago. A four-year-old boy. He and his twin brother were playin' around and . . . Well, one of 'em went too deep. The Bleaks shut it down after that."

Wayne nodded and took a gulp of his beer. "But the spring's still there . . ."

—

"COME ON, BABY," Wayne said, gently shaking Ruby awake in the back seat. He'd intentionally left Plumland at bedtime, knowing she'd sleep the four or so hours it would take to drive to Bleak Creek. Either way, arriving at night was a necessity, since they were technically about to trespass.

"Where are we, Daddy?" Ruby asked, her eyes not yet fully open.

"Remember I told you we were gonna have a fun adventure? Goin' swimmin' at night?"

Ruby closed her eyes. "I don't want to do that anymore, Daddy. I'm tired."

"I know you are, Ruby Jane," he said, brushing blond strands of hair away from her face. "That's why we have to do it. But don't you worry—I'll carry you over there." He scooped her into his arms and shut the car door with his hip.

He'd had to drive around for at least half an hour before he even figured out how to gain access to the spring; the main entrance was gated and locked up with heavy chains, more than the simple wire-cutters he'd brought could handle. Eventually, he'd off-roaded his beige Ford Fairmont, slowly cutting across a tobacco field with his headlights off and parking near a chain-link fence that, if he could cut through it, seemed to offer a clear path to the spring.

He bent with Ruby in his arms and grabbed the wire-cutters from the trunk of the car along with a flashlight, which he flicked on as he walked toward the fence. It was a warm May night, and for that he was grateful.

"All right, Ruby-girl, gonna put you down for a seco—"

"No, Daddy, no!"

"Shhh!" Wayne said. "We can't be loud, baby. Please don't be loud."

"I don't want you to put me down."

"But . . ." *Dammit,* Wayne thought, nervous enough breaking the law on his own, let alone with his kid. "Okay, here, let's do piggy." He readjusted his daughter in his arms and hoisted her onto his back, a move he'd taken pride in perfecting over the past few years. "There we go."

"Thanks, Daddy."

He positioned the flashlight near his feet, pointing it upward at the fence, and began to cut the first link, which was challenging with a forty-pound human on his back. By the time he'd cut two links, he was sweating bullets. *What the hell am I doing here?* Wayne thought, suddenly regretting every stupid hoop he'd forced his unwell daughter to jump through. He'd come this far, though.

After a minute, he'd cut a large enough gap in the fence for him and Ruby to awkwardly slide through. From there, it was a short walk through the woods, and then: There it was.

The moonlight shone down on the spring invitingly, and Wayne's doubts began to melt away. This was right. He could feel it.

"Doesn't it look fun, baby?" he asked Ruby.

"I don't know."

He walked across the dirt and stopped about ten steps from the water. "I'm gonna put you down now, darlin', and please don't argue with me." Wayne gently set down Ruby, who decided not to protest. He undressed himself down to the blue swim trunks he wore under his slacks. Before leaving, he'd convinced Ruby to put on her green one-piece underneath her dress. "Okay, honey, now you get down into your bathin' suit and we'll go swim. How does that sound?"

"I don't wanna take off my dress," Ruby said.

"But you'll get it all wet."

"I don't wanna, Daddy!"

"Okay, you can keep the dress on," Wayne said, guessing that agreeing to her request would get her in the water. "When do you ever get to swim at night in your clothes, right?" he asked, unable to hide how truly hopeful he was. Tonight might change everything.

"You're a goofus," Ruby said.

Wayne laughed, a little louder than he'd intended. "I am, baby. I sure am." He took her hand and they took a few steps toward the spring, placing their feet into the shallow water along the bank.

"It feels nice," Ruby said.

"I think so too," Wayne said, already imagining the water working its miracles.

In his overexcitement, he took a few more quick steps to go deeper.

"Daddy, slow down!" Ruby yelled. "Owww!" She'd clipped her heel on a rock. "I hurt my foot!"

"Shit!" Wayne said, a rare moment when he was unable to catch the swear before it left his mouth.

"Bad word, Daddy!" Ruby said, as Wayne lifted her foot out of the water, the moon illuminating a thin stream of blood.

"You're right, Rubes. I'm sorry. And I'm sorry about your foot, baby. That was my fault."

"It's okay." Ruby had grown so used to little cuts like this that she rarely cried over them anymore. She gave her father one of her classic slightly crooked smiles, and it just about melted his heart.

Wayne took her hand again, and they walked forward more slowly, the water now at Ruby's waist.

"Look, Daddy!"

Beneath the water, there was a blue glow, pale at first, then steadily brighter as it spread throughout the spring.

"Oh my Lord!" Wayne said. It *was* working. The water all around them began to bubble. Wayne began to laugh, unconcerned about disturbing anyone who might be within earshot.

Ruby laughed too. "This really is fun!"

She pushed off the bottom, beginning to swim. Wayne was careful not to let go of her hand.

That didn't matter, though.

As soon as she dropped her face below the surface, Ruby was violently sucked down into the water.

Her hand slipped from her father's.

"Ruby!" he yelled. "Baby!"

He frantically dove after her.

The moment he went under, he could feel water forcefully pressing on his mouth and nose. Like the spring itself was trying to invade him.

He watched through the blur as Ruby spun away from him, as if she was being pulled by an invisible chain. She was yanked to the side of the spring, which seemed to come to life, a layer of dirt and rocks creeping across her body, trapping her.

Horrified, Wayne swam toward the wall, but he could no longer resist the water, now streaming powerfully into his nose and pushing apart his lips, filling his lungs. Drowning him.

As his field of vision began to darken, the end almost near, he was wildly catapulted out of the water—as if by a dozen invisible hands—soaring through the air and landing on the dirt.

Then he began to retch.

Violent, full-body spasms as he vomited up water, so much water.

When—five or ten minutes later—his body seemed to have finished, Wayne rolled over onto his back, utterly spent. *Ruby,* he thought, as he passed out.

—

IT WAS APPROXIMATELY three seconds after he felt the sun on his eyelids that Wayne began to panic.

He jumped to his feet and ran into the now-sunlit water, madly swimming down to where he remembered seeing his daughter get trapped. There was only a bare wall, just rocks and dirt. *Was it all a bad dream? Had he really seen Ruby pulled into the rocky wall?*

The events from the night began to crystallize in his head. It *was* real. His beloved baby girl was trapped. He had to get to her.

Wayne went up for air, then came back down again, his heart racing as he tore at the sharp rocks where'd she gone in, scooping away handfuls of earth in his determination to free her. The jagged edges lacerated his hands, but he continued to grab, dig, and pull, the blood from his tender fingers mixing with the stirred mud.

He felt an effervescent tingle on his face, then saw that the spring was once again filling with the blue glow.

There was a shift in the rocks, and suddenly she was there.

His Ruby, her head sticking out from the wall. Her eyes were open but unfocused.

Wayne reached out to touch her sweet face, but the water was already forcing its way into his nostrils and mouth. Again he tried to fight it, but the persistent water easily passed his lips and overwhelmed him. He waited for everything to turn dark, bracing himself for the violent ejection.

It never came.

Instead, the darkness intensified until he saw only blackness.

For a moment, he experienced nothing at all. No sound, no light, no sensation of any kind. He had no idea how long this lasted.

Slowly, he began to feel his body, like coming to after a fainting spell.

His eyes adjusted to the darkness.

It seemed he'd been transported to an entirely different place: a vast ocean, endless in every direction.

He was submerged deep in the boundless watery expanse, but felt no impulse to breathe.

Wayne knew, of course, that he hadn't actually been transported anywhere.

He was dead.

He hadn't expected it to feel like such a relief.

"You're not dead, Daddy."

Wayne's heart jolted as Ruby appeared next to him, her

white dress floating around her. She was as blurry as the rest of his surroundings, radiating a strange light.

"And I'm not either," she said.

"Ruby," Wayne said, finding he could somehow speak underwater. "We're not dead?"

"Nope," Ruby said. "Want to meet my new friend?"

Before he could respond, another glowing body floated up next to Ruby.

"This is Timothy," Ruby said.

Timothy, a little boy he guessed to be four or five, came closer. He wore a white polo, khaki shorts, and a blank look that made Wayne's skin crawl.

"Nice to meet you, Timothy," Wayne said.

The boy just stared.

"He's been down here for a while," Ruby said, as if it was very impressive. "But he's not dead either."

"I have a twin brother," Timothy said. "Eli."

"Oh," Wayne said. "Is he . . . down here too?"

Timothy shook his head. "I miss my family," he said, his voice devoid of emotion.

"I'm sorry," Wayne said, suddenly becoming aware of another presence hovering around them. This one wasn't a body, and it wasn't glowing. It was more of a . . . shadow. It was even more unnerving than Timothy, appearing right next to them, then farther away, then somewhere else, impossible to pin down, accompanied by a sort of buzzing scream.

"That's the Keeper," Ruby said.

"Oh," Wayne said.

"He says he's willing to let me go. And heal me. If you do something for him."

"What's that?"

"Bring him seven more."

Wayne's insides went cold. "Ruby . . ."

"But the Keeper only wants young, strong ones."

Timothy nodded along confidently.

"I don't understand . . ." Wayne said.

"The Keeper needs the ones who won't follow," Timothy added.

Wayne looked at his daughter as the Keeper pinballed from location to location faster than before.

"Can you do that, Daddy?"

"I . . . I don't know . . ."

"You don't love me?" Ruby suddenly looked and sounded distressed.

"Of course I do, baby."

"Then please! Do what the Keeper asks, Daddy!"

"I . . ."

As he stared at his daughter, everything blurred to black as her words blended with the buzzing scream, getting louder and louder and then abruptly cutting out.

Wayne was back to looking at the dirt wall of the spring, the water mercilessly pressing in on him from all sides. Rather than rudely flinging him away, Wayne felt himself deliberately lifted to the surface and lightly shoved toward the shore.

The retching was just as terrible as it had been the night before, maybe even worse. When it was done, Whitewood lay in the dirt in his blue swim trunks, trying to make sense of what he'd just experienced.

His daughter was gone.

But there was a way to get her back. Fully healed.

He propped himself up on one elbow as he noticed a boarded-up building about a hundred yards away.

—

THE WHITEWOOD SCHOOL opened in August of 1979, just four months after Wayne Whitewood first visited Bleak Creek.

It filled a need the people of Bleak Creek didn't even realize they'd had, finally getting the kids in town to fall in line.

It was an immediate success.

—

"WHERE ARE THE ones who won't follow, Daddy?" Ruby asked.

"I'm trying, Ruby-girl," Whitewood said.

It was the fall of 1982, and the new year had just begun at the Whitewood School. While Whitewood felt like he'd aged a decade in just three years, even his hair going prematurely white, Ruby hadn't changed at all. She was still the sweet seven-year-old she'd been when the Keeper had taken her. He was now seeing her monthly, his body unable to visit more often, as each violent invasion of the spring water took him days to fully recover.

"The Keeper says you're not trying hard enough."

"I've given him a few kids now, and he spit 'em all out! And they all ended up . . . well, changed. Like the life had been taken right out of 'em."

"He says they weren't strong enough."

"I don't know what else to do," Whitewood said, growing frustrated. "None of those kids would not bow to my authority. I pushed them so hard."

"Sorry, Daddy, you need to push harder."

"I just . . . You gotta tell the Keeper this is gettin' ridiculous! I just want you back!"

Whitewood heard the familiar buzzing scream, the shadowy form coming close and pulsing near his head.

Suddenly Ruby began to shriek, her face stretching out like taffy, as if it were being yanked. "Daddy! Help me! Daddy!"

"Stop that!" Whitewood yelled. "Right now!"

Ruby's face returned to normal. "The Keeper says he's going to hurt me if you don't bring him one very soon."

"Okay, baby, okay," Whitewood said. "I just . . . I don't know if I can do this alone."

"Then get help!" Ruby shrieked. "Do whatever you have to do!"

"Calm down, Ruby!" Whitewood said.

The black shadow presence of the Keeper enveloped Ruby, the dark cloud seeping through her nose and mouth. Her face grew angular, demented.

"The Keeper is growing impatient!" she said, the voice a mix of Ruby and the grating buzz of the Keeper.

Whitewood felt like he was going to freeze.

The freakish version of his daughter shot toward him, her face inches from his, the inky residue of the Keeper leaking from her obsidian eyes.

"He thirsts for those who will not follow!" she/it screamed.

Whitewood cowered. "I need time," he said sheepishly.

"How much time do you require!" it yelled.

Whitewood hadn't expected a negotiation.

"I don't know . . ." Whitewood said. "I'll have to come up with a cover story for any child the Keeper accepts. Explain to the town what happened to 'em. I'm no good to you if I'm locked away."

"How much time!"

"Uh, ten years?" Whitewood said reflexively, guessing his suggestion would be met with more screaming. Or worse.

Suddenly, the black cloud enveloping Ruby receded into the distance, his daughter's face her own once again.

"The Keeper says you have ten years," she said.

Whitewood felt sudden relief, but it was quickly followed by a sinking weight of dread, realizing what the coming years would look like.

"Okay, Ruby. I can do that. I *will* do that. For you."

"Thank you, Daddy. I love you."

"I love you, too, baby girl."

—

WHITEWOOD NERVOUSLY TAPPED his gloved fingers on his desk and looked at the calendar: September 1992.

It had taken him close to a decade to find four acceptable individuals for the Keeper. He'd done unspeakable things—and gotten others to do even worse by convincing them that it was all for the good of Bleak Creek, and the world—just so he could be reunited with his beloved Ruby.

He had just over a week to find three more kids. Even for a man who had successfully made himself the prophet of a bogus cult, that seemed impossible.

But there was hope. Leif Nelson had practically offered himself up on a silver platter earlier tonight. He had a feeling that meant Rex McClendon would soon find his way to the school as well. And he still had people on the lookout for the one who had escaped, not to mention the new crop of students he was just beginning to break.

Three more.

It could happen.

It would have to happen.

After all, he'd come this far.

21

LEIF WAS PRETTY SURE THE SOUR-FACED LADY AT THE FRONT OF THE classroom was looking at him. He was also fairly certain she'd gotten some bad information, because she had just called him something that sounded nothing like Leif or Nelson.

"Yes, you, Candidatus," she said.

"Oh," Leif said. "That's, uh, not me."

The helper smiled, which was actually worse than when she didn't. "How sad you don't know your own name."

The past twelve hours had been—by a long shot—the most difficult of his life.

After confronting some kind of invisible monster in the spring, he'd been chased down by an all-too-visible monster, who'd caught him and then somehow convinced his mother that he needed to be sent here, to this terrible place.

"For your information," the helper continued, "*Candidatus* is Latin for 'candidate.' Because you, just like each and every student in this room, are a *candidate* for reform. *If* you decide to . . ." She tapped the large sign on the wall that said FOLLOW. "Do you understand, Candidatus?"

"Yes, ma'am," Leif said.

"Yes, *Helper*!" she said. "You call me Helper."

Leif thought, as far as titles of respect went, *ma'am* carried more dignity than *helper*, which was a designation he remembered coveting back in kindergarten. But he wasn't going to say that. "Okay, Helper."

She narrowed her eyes in disgust. "You're just like her," the woman said with a hushed intensity before redirecting her attention to the whole class. "Candidati, you should know that not only was Candidatus caught by Headmaster trespassing on school grounds in the middle of the night, but he also aided and abetted that student— may she rest in peace—who injured Headmaster's hands." Everyone quietly freaked out, though it seemed more like a performance than a genuine response. "He is a complete disgrace. Now please open your Whitewood Learning Guides to page four hundred and sixteen."

In spite of everything Leif knew about the Whitewood School and its headmaster, he couldn't help but feel ashamed. He was accustomed to being singled out in class, but that was because he usually had the answer the teacher was after. Now, he felt completely in over his head. Rex should be here instead. He'd know what to do. Probably come up with some completely outlandish plan that would somehow totally work out.

But there was an even better question than *What would Rex do?*

What would *Alicia* do?

Or, rather: What *did* Alicia do?

Leif tried to picture her here, her first day. He was sure she'd handled herself like she always did in difficult situations, with that natural poise. She'd probably seemed brave regardless of how she felt. She'd probably even summoned the nerve to talk back to the helper.

And then Whitewood had killed her.

Leif shuddered, for the first time fully acknowledging that truth.

And now the same man was featured in a huge portrait in front of him, as if murdering Leif's best friend was a virtue to aspire to. Leif felt himself shaking. He assumed it was more of the involuntary sobs that had been erupting from him for hours, but then he realized it was something else.

He was shaking with anger.

Anger that this righteous organ-playing psychopath had taken from Leif one of the people he loved most in this world. Had forced his mother to turn on him. Had even driven a wedge between him and Rex.

It wasn't okay.

Leif knew in his gut what Alicia would do.

She would run toward her anger, not away from it.

Embracing his rage, he felt it transforming into courage.

He was speaking before he had time to second-guess it.

"Hey, teach," he said. "I was wondering: Are you part of Whitewood's cult that sacrifices students or is that, like, a separate department?"

The blood drained from the helper's face as she stared at Leif in shock.

"You just earned yourself a trip to the Roll," she said.

The students were shocked again, but this time it seemed genuine.

———

AS HE LAY on the floor of Thinking Shed Number Two wrapped up in a cheap carpet like an enchilada, Leif considered his options.

Following his rude introduction to the Roll, during which he'd believed that his head might legitimately twist off his body like a mistreated G.I. Joe figure, he questioned if open rebellion was worth it. What exactly did his smartass outburst accomplish other than giving him a chance to marinate in his own pee?

Sure, it had felt amazing to go against his passive in-stincts. It was intoxicating to swim out into the spring when Rex was frozen in fear, and calling out the helper in class was electrifying, like he'd tapped in to some sup-pressed inner rebel. But where had that gotten him? Right here in this moldy room, struggling to breathe.

Yeah, it was probably best to just hunker down and wait. Save the boat-rocking for someone else.

—

LEIF SHUFFLED THROUGH the cafeteria with his tray of mush—which, after going so long without food, actually looked appetizing—and sat down by himself for lunch. The relief he experienced once he was let out of the Roll had con-firmed his earlier decision to simply do as he was told. It wouldn't be hard. There was only one rule around this place: Follow. He was sort of an expert at it.

As he was convincing himself that he legitimately liked the flavor of the lukewarm paste that matched the color of the walls, he was startled by someone knocking into him, dropping her entire bowl of mush into his lap.

"I'm sorry, I'm so sorry," a girl about Leif's age with dark hair and thick eyebrows said as she bent over to pick up her bowl and tray.

"What's going on over there?" a young helper with sideburns that reminded Leif of Jason Priestley said as he rushed toward them.

"I tripped," the girl said. "I'm so sorry, it was an acci-dent. I'll clean it up."

"It's okay," Leif said, as he wiped the mess off his legs and onto the floor.

"It's not okay!" the helper said, two more helpers hov-ering behind him in case backup was needed. "There's no talking during mealtime!"

The girl began to stand up, but as her face passed by Leif's ear, she whispered, "Shoe."

"Come on, let's go, Candidatus," the helper said, practically pushing the girl along. "Headmaster doesn't appreciate clumsiness. Sit by yourself over there. And I hope you aren't expecting a replacement meal."

"Of course not, Helper," the girl said, sitting down all the way across the room.

"Quiet!"

Leif kept his head down as he wiped the remaining glop from his legs, confounded by the entire incident. What had she even tripped on?

As he went to wipe some flecks off his beige Keds, Leif noticed a small piece of paper sticking out of the left one.

Shoe.

Leif's heart beat faster as, after a quick glance in both directions to make sure no helpers were nearby, he slid the paper out of his sneaker.

He hid it in his fist and rose to the table before bending back down, pretending to notice one last bit of the girl's lunch on his jumpsuit.

He unfolded the paper with shaking fingers. It was a note in purple ink on a piece of stationery with a unicorn on the top.

Alicia was my friend, the note said.

So you are too.

Keep fighting.

J

———

LEIF WAS AMAZED at the power ten words could have.

They proved to him that Alicia had made a mark on this place. In her short time here, she'd inspired J. And who knew who else.

As Leif walked to the Leisure Room that afternoon, he reached into his jumpsuit pocket and rubbed J's note between his fingers. He was overcome with a deep shame for giving up so easily, for so quickly retreating to his tendency to defer.

Since his arrival, Leif had wanted to believe that Rex was coming up with some kind of plan to save him, to expose the school for what it was. But Leif was the one with the advantage of being on the inside. If he could get through to even just some of his peers, could convince them that they too could choose not to follow, it might have a ripple effect. Maybe they could be the ones to change things around here. Maybe they could take down the whole school.

He found himself thinking that Rex would be proud, but then he realized that's probably not how leaders thought.

This wasn't going to be easy.

—

LEIF TOOK A seat in the corner of the meeting hall and watched his schoolmates quietly file in for Reports. He'd spent most of his day—including a four-hour lecture on the evils of pop culture (the two C's in C&C Music Factory, they'd been taught, actually stood for crack and cocaine)—resisting the voice in his head telling him that leading a rebellion would be foolish.

As he surveyed the defeated faces in the room, all of them looking down at their feet, he was reminded just how strong the spell was. These students had been conditioned to follow for weeks or months. Why did he think he'd be able to change their minds in a few days?

But then he saw J walking in.

She cracked the slightest, shortest smile.

Once everyone was present, the female helper from his first class spoke. "Welcome, Candidati. Does anyone have anything to report?"

Sweat dripped from Leif's underarms.

After a young redheaded boy reported an older girl for longingly looking out the window for an extended period of time, and a tall teenage girl outed her roommate for asking her how she was doing, the helper prompted again, "Does anyone else have something to report? No infraction is too small."

Leif heard himself swallow.

He looked over at J.

She locked eyes with him.

Keep fighting.

He shot up from his seat without thinking.

"Hey, everybody," he said, immediately wanting to sit back down and pretend it hadn't happened, but knowing it was too late for that.

So he kept speaking.

"My name is Leif Nelson—not Candy Datoose or whatever—and I want you all to know: There's some truly evil stuff going on in this place."

"Stop that!" the helper shouted as she started marching toward him from across the room, weaving through the crowd, stepping over those seated.

Leif tried to speak faster, knowing he had minimal time. "And I'm not just talking about being rolled up in a carpet. Kids are being murdered!" His heart was pounding so hard, he felt it in his ears. "But guess what? There's more of us than there are of them! So we don't have to follow!"

Flattop and Sideburns were now making their way to Leif along with the woman, pushing students aside. Not one of his peers was showing any indication they were hearing him.

But then J stood up.

"He's right! We don't have to follow!"

The female helper, already feet away from J, turned to grab her, affording Leif a few extra seconds to speak.

"They can't put us all in that carpet at once, right?" he said. The two male helpers reached him, hooking him by the arms and beginning to drag him out of the room.

But he kept talking.

"Don't follow!" he shouted, trying not to get disheartened by the complete lack of a response from anyone other than J.

"Don't follow!" he repeated.

"Don't follow!" J joined his chant.

The female helper grabbed J by the arm, but she and Leif continued shouting, leading their defiant, two-person mantra from the unhappy clutches of the helpers, the rest of the students silent and staring down.

"Don't fol—"

Everything went black as Leif was whacked in the head with something hard.

———

WHEN LEIF OPENED his eyes, he was covered by a cushy purple comforter.

He blinked a few times, adjusting to the light. Even without his glasses, he could see the room was decorated with bright splashes of color, and the bed was about a hundred times more comfortable than the one in his dorm.

"Well, there you are."

Leif almost screamed when he saw that Wayne Whitewood was practically next to him, sitting at a desk, writing.

"Your glasses are here if you want 'em." He pointed a gloved finger toward the corner of the desk, which was almost close enough to the bed to serve as a nightstand.

Leif sat up, reaching out a trembling hand to retrieve them.

Was this how it ended?

Was this where it had ended for Alicia, too?

With glasses back on, it became clear he was in a little girl's bedroom. Maybe that should have been comforting, but in the context of a school where every other room was that same insipid beige, Leif found it chilling.

The door was closed.

"You could try to run," Whitewood said, as if reading Leif's mind, "but I wouldn't recommend it." Leif didn't know whether that meant there were helpers standing guard outside the door, or if Whitewood himself would pummel him if he stood up. Either way, his head was still aching—pounding, really—from whatever had knocked him unconscious earlier, so he had little choice but to lie there.

Whitewood put his pen down and held up a stack of paper. "See this? It's the names of all my students, their *real* names, along with a record of what they did to get here and how they've behaved since arriving." He placed the stack on the desk. "I've been lookin' at this list a lot."

Whitewood paused as if waiting for Leif to respond, but he was too scared to speak. This was the man who killed Alicia. Those three other kids. Sure, he'd be stupid to kill Leif, but he could still *harm* him.

"That was quite a little speech you gave," Whitewood said, now turning his rolling desk chair so he faced Leif head-on. "I liked it. Very much."

Leif nodded, unable to say thank you.

"You see, that kind of thing only makes my job easier." Whitewood stared at Leif for what felt like a full minute before standing and starting to pace around the room. "Now, what I did *not* like was that comment you made in class, the one that got you sent to the Roll. What was that word you used . . . ?" Whitewood turned back to Leif. "Oh right. *Cult.* I hate that word."

Leif nodded again.

"It's got such a negative connotation." Whitewood stepped toward the bed and sat down on the edge, inches from Leif's feet. "What I have is a *group.* A group of people who help me accomplish what I need to accomplish. And you know what's funny, Candidatus?"

Leif gave a small shake of his head.

Whitewood leaned toward him and said in a low voice, "This group doesn't even actually know what it is that they're helpin' me do. Not really." Whitewood laughed to himself.

Leif felt vulnerable sitting in bed under the covers, like it would be hard to defend himself if Whitewood decided to attack. Maybe that was the point.

"I know what you think of me. You and your friend are just so sure I'm a bad man." Whitewood looked at Leif with disappointment in his eyes. "Shoutin' about me in funeral homes. Cafeterias. Did it ever occur to you that maybe it's not so simple?"

Leif blinked.

"Let me ask you this: Have you ever loved someone so much you would do just about anything for 'em?" Leif didn't respond, but his presence in this school right now attested to the fact that he had. "That's who this room is for, you understand? It's for my daughter. This is all for my sweet, sweet Ruby."

Leif had no idea what Whitewood was talking about, but the man seemed genuinely heartbroken.

"Look," Whitewood said, suddenly getting to his feet and pointing to a photo of a blond girl on the wall. "This is my baby. Just look at her. Who wouldn't do what I've done for that face?" Whitewood shook his head in pride and despair, his back turned to Leif. "I'm so close, Ruby!" he shouted at the photo.

Leif wasn't sure what was happening, but he noticed that Whitewood's pen was nearly within reaching distance.

A pen could be very helpful.

In a number of ways.

Leif quietly reached out his hand and wrapped it around the pen, pulling it under the covers.

"I will make this happen," Whitewood said, his voice now steely. "No matter what it takes." He turned around. "Now give it to me."

"Huh?" Leif said, trying to play dumb.

"Gimme the damn pen."

Leif put the pen into Whitewood's gloved hand.

"Thank you for being so helpful, Candidatus," White-wood said, placing the pen in the orange mug on the desk.

He walked to the door and opened it, for three helpers entering with the Roll.

They picked Leif up and rolled him in the carpet once more, taping it closed with even more layers of thick duct tape than the first time.

"Don't worry, you won't be in there too long," White-wood said. "I've got bigger plans for you."

Leif felt cold dread in his heart as the helpers left him on the floor and filed out of the room.

Whitewood was the last to leave.

"See you tonight," he said, before flicking off the light and shutting the door.

22

"Y'ALL SURE YOU DON'T WANT ANY MORE SNACKS?" GAMGAM ASKED, poking her head into the shed in her backyard where Janine, Donna, Rex, and Ben were gathered.

"I think we're all set," Janine said, feeling like a twelve-year-old as she gestured to the grapes, pretzels, and goldfish her grandmother had just set down in bowls on a wooden bench. She could've really used a tequila. "But thanks, GamGam."

"Okay, Neenie. If you change your mind, just give a holler! This is so excitin'. My girls, makin' a movie together again!"

"Yup," Janine said, nodding awkwardly, camera on her shoulder, intent on making sure GamGam didn't suspect they hoped to do much more than just make a documentary.

"It's starting to rain out here!" GamGam said as she ambled away. "My gout's gonna go nuts . . ."

They stood listening to the rain beat down on the shed's corrugated roof, inhaling the smell of mulch as they waited for GamGam to move out of earshot. Donna took sips from a can of Diet Pepsi. Rex grabbed a handful of goldfish.

"All right," Ben said, suddenly all business, "so as I was saying—"

"Hold up, kiddo," Janine said. "Let me get the camera

going." She wasn't sure how all this would play out, especially now that they were dealing with more than just a cult. They'd uncovered some kind of sick supernatural kidnapping scheme, and Janine had decided it would be wise to record as much of the planning as possible. If it didn't result in a film, it could at least be evidence.

"Oh, sure, of course." Ben subtly readjusted his expression, as if he had a specific face he thought would look best on camera. It was hard for Janine not to laugh, as Ben—paranoid that Whitewood still had people out searching for him—had disguised himself with Rex's help. He was in a T-shirt, sweatpants, the brown curly wig Leif had worn when he thought he'd replace Alicia in *Polter-Dog*, and red sunglasses that Rex had gotten for free at last year's middle school dance. Ben didn't seem to have any idea how ridiculous he looked. "All set?"

"You got it, Curly Sue."

"Excellent," Ben said. "So as I was saying, our focus needs to be on getting Alicia out of the spring. If we—"

"But we still agree," Rex interrupted, "that if Alicia's down there, that means all the other kids reported as dead are probably alive down there too, right? Like, trapped in the dirt walls?" Rex still couldn't believe how crazy this whole thing was.

"Most likely," Ben said. "But taking into consideration the small window of time we'll actually have to do this, it behooves us to focus on Alicia first."

"Okay," Rex said, not sure what "behoove" meant or why Ben found it necessary to use such words. He was pretty sure he was doing it for the camera. "But we also have to save Leif from the school."

"That's not our focus either," Ben said, somewhat sternly. "Look, if we can rescue Alicia from the spring and show everyone that she's alive, Whitewood's plan will be exposed and the school will be shut down, thereby allowing us to go back and save those other kids, including Leif." Ben crossed his arms and looked at Rex. "Cause and effect."

"Hmm," Rex said, nodding, not wanting to fully agree. Somehow Ben had taken the mantle as leader, which seemed all wrong. Leif and Alicia were *his* best friends; he should be the one planning the rescue. He was sticking his neck out enough as is, lying to his parents that he was at a classmate's house for a school project (almost true), so he should at least retain control of how this all went down. And if he *were* going to cede leadership to anyone, it would be to Janine, the experienced filmmaker in her twenties, not the homeschooled weirdo dressed like Screech from *Saved by the Bell*.

"It's our best shot," Ben said. "I've been at the school, I know how it works."

Rex, who hated nothing more than being told he didn't know about something, couldn't accept that. "What about posters, though?" he asked, not entirely sure where he was going with it.

"What do you mean?" Janine asked, pointing the camera at him.

"Just, like . . . what if we took a still frame of Alicia from that underwater footage and put it on a flyer that says, you know, like: *Alicia Boykins is alive! In Bleak Creek Spring! All the other "dead" kids are there too! Whitewood School is a scam!* And put it on telephone poles and stuff. Around town." Rex muttered the last two words, as he'd realized about halfway through what a terrible idea it was.

"What would that accomplish?" Ben asked.

"You know," Rex said. "Just . . . gettin' the word out."

"Will people even be able to tell that's a picture of Alicia?" Donna asked.

"I mean . . . probably." Rex reached for some more

goldfish to try and diffuse his discomfort. "It's just another option. Maybe we can come back to it later."

Everybody gave sort of a half nod, then looked back to Ben. As much as Rex hated it, he had no choice but to let Ben assume the role of leader, at least for now. He finally understood Leif's frustration with always taking the back seat. When they got him out of the school, he'd make sure to apologize.

"All right," Ben said, gesturing like a tour guide, "before we get into the details of our rescue mission, I'd now like to turn things over to Janine, who's done some great research for us."

Again, Janine had to hold back a laugh. Though she'd more or less gotten used to working side by side with fourteen-year-olds, there were still moments when she was struck by how surreal her life had become. "Thanks, Ben," she said in a peppy newscaster voice. "Let me just . . . Here." She passed the camcorder to Donna. "Could you film for a sec?"

"Oh," Donna said, receiving the camera with reverence and care, as if she were holding a newborn. "Yeah." Janine knew this was probably the first time Donna had held a camera since their teenage movie-making days.

"So," Janine said once Donna had started filming, "when I went back to the library, I found . . ." Janine picked up a large book from the ground and dropped it onto the snack bench with a thud. "This."

Donna zoomed in on the cover, which read *Paranormal Phenomena.*

"Out of everything I read during the, like, eight hours I was there, this one seemed to have the most helpful info for our situation." Janine picked up the heavy book and began leafing through the pages. "I was trying to read about everything water related, and I found this whole section about . . . Yeah, here it is." She put the open book back down on the bench, pushing aside the snack bowls to make room. Everyone huddled around.

"Pretty sure we're dealing with a *cursed spring*," Janine said.

Rex sneezed. It was a dusty book.

"Feel free to read all the tiny print," Janine said, "but for now, I'll give you the Cliffs Notes: There's this idea in Celtic folklore that springs can be cursed. And once they're cursed, lots of weird shit goes down."

There was a huge crash of thunder, bizarrely well-timed for dramatic emphasis. They all silently acknowledged it before Janine continued.

"So, the idea is that every spring has a spirit within it. And the spirits are thought to be capable of doing different stuff: They might heal people, or give them knowledge, and sometimes—in the case of a cursed spring—do bad things, like collect people, so to speak, storing them . . . alive."

"Storing them for what?" Rex asked.

"It's not clear, but it seems like the spirit feeds on the people in some way. Like, absorbs their souls or something."

Janine realized that Donna had stopped filming, the camera held down by her side, a look of terror on her face.

"What's wrong, Don?"

"I met the spirit," Donna said.

The thunder boomed again as Rex, Ben, and Janine stared at Donna, unsure what to say next.

"So, like . . ." Janine said, trying to be delicate with her words. "How come you, uh, never . . . mentioned this?"

Donna shrugged. "Didn't want to sound crazier than I already seem, I guess. Also it's not the most fun thing to talk about."

"That's . . . awful. I'm sorry," Janine said, reaching to take the camera from Donna, realizing this might be good to film.

"It's not like I really *saw* it or anything," Donna said. "I never even had a word for what it was until I just heard you say that. It was more of a feeling, like I was being surrounded by something. Some*one*. Who was, like, inspecting me or something."

"I felt that too," Rex said. "When I was swimming. I mean, probably not nearly as intensely as you did, but I know what you're talking about."

"And that's what must've grabbed the camera," Ben said.

"And what the cult is worshipping," Rex added.

"What else does it say in there?" Ben asked.

Janine continued to film, now focusing on the open book as she spoke. "Blood is required for the spirit to collect someone," she explained.

"Oh, man," Rex said. "Like the blood that made the spring light up and bubble."

"That was the spring opening up," Ben said, putting it together.

"Exactly," Janine said. "Once there's blood in the water, that seems to create, like, a gateway."

The rain suddenly intensified to a downpour, forcing them to speak louder.

"And if it's a gateway in," Ben said, "it could be a gateway out, too."

"Maybe . . ." Janine said.

"Okay, wait." Ben began to pace around the shed. "This could be good. This could be very good. If we put blood in the spring, like *a lot* of blood, maybe it'll open the gateway even wider and longer for us to extract Alicia."

"Yeah," Rex said. "It could, like, loosen the spirit's hold on her."

"Again, that's a huge maybe," Janine said. "It doesn't say anything about the amount of blood."

"Anything else relevant in there?" Ben asked.

"Just something about how a curse can alter and reverse the properties of the water," Janine said. "Not sure that really—"

"Kidney stones," Ben said flatly.

Everyone stared at him.

"Bleak Creek Spring was once known to heal people, right?" He continued. "That's why the Whitewood School used to be a resort. So if the curse reversed the properties of the water, then maybe—"

"But it's not like people like Big Gary are out swimming in the spring," Rex said, thinking he had a good point.

"No, but the creek is the town's main water supply," Ben said.

"Oh. Right." Rex reached for some grapes.

Janine couldn't believe it.

Somehow she'd ended up right back where she started. With *The Kidney Stoners.*

"Hmm. It also says that 'those of us who drink of the waters shall be persuaded by the waters,'" Rex said, squinting as he leaned over the giant tome with a mouthful of grapes.

"Oh my bod," Janine said. "Maybe that's why people in town are willing to ignore the deaths at the school."

"And why Whitewood's followers will do whatever he asks," Ben added. "They drink *directly* from the spring."

Rex's eyes bugged out, signaling a sudden revelation. "We gotta stop drinking the town water! And get our parents to stop too!"

"Okay, okay . . ." Ben said, holding his hands up like a conductor. "Let's not get ahead of ourselves. For now, we need to focus on the task at hand. Here's what I'm thinking."

Ben's plan was fairly straightforward. He and Rex would tie ropes around themselves, which the others would hold from the shore. Then they'd go into the spring—ideally in scuba gear—and release a very large amount of blood, overwhelming the spring and opening the gateway long enough for them to rescue Alicia. They'd use a couple of hammers to chip away at the rocks and dirt holding her in the wall, and once they'd gotten her free, they would tie her to themselves and all three of them would be pulled out of the water.

Rex had to hand it to Ben; this was way better than posters.

"Now," Ben went on, turning toward Janine and Donna, "we want to be absolutely sure we can pull Alicia out of there, so we're probably going to want to bring on a third puller to help you two ladies. Ideally a man."

Janine and Donna stared at him.

"Sorry." Ben shrugged. "But males are stronger. That's just a biological fact."

Rex internally cringed and cheered, delighted to finally see their fearless leader make a misstep, one he liked to think he never would have made.

"First of all, never say that again," Janine said. "And second of all, I want to film everything, so yeah, it would probably be best to have someone—not necessarily a man—help Donna pull."

"I got a guy, or, um . . . a person who just so happens to be a male," Rex said, happily filling his role as Second Fiddle Who Changes the Subject When Necessary. "Travis Bethune. He actually mows the grass at the school."

"Wait a second," Ben said, lowering his sunglasses. "He works there? You trust him?"

"Well, he just cuts the grass. He doesn't go inside. He's a good friend. And he cared about Alicia. Plus, he's strong and has a lot of tools."

"Okay. Sounds like he may at least have some insights if he's that familiar with the school grounds . . ." Ben scratched his wig, considering the proposition. "I'm fine with it if the group agrees," he said, looking to Janine and Donna.

Janine gave a thumbs-up as Donna barely nodded her head.

"Done," Ben said. "Now we just need one more person to serve as lookout and we're set. Anyone know anybody?"

Janine considered GamGam for a brief moment before realizing she couldn't say that because it was insane.

Rex had an idea, but he was desperately hoping someone else would speak up first.

Nobody did.

"Yeah, I think I got someone for lookout, too," he said, already anticipating how annoying his conversation with Hornhat was going to be.

"Fantastic!" Ben said. "We've got a squad."

"A squad," Janine said, panning the camera around to film all of them. "That's adorable."

"Indeed," Ben said, nodding so hard that his wig almost flew off. "Main thing we need to figure out now is: Where can we get *a lot* of blood?"

They were all silent, the rain still coming down.

"Rex," Ben said, "didn't you say your parents have a funeral home?"

Rex slowly nodded, even as he cursed himself for not thinking of it first.

23

AS LEIF WAS HASTILY EXTRACTED FROM THE ROLL, THEN BLIND-
folded, gagged, and walked down the hall with his hands
tied behind his back, he had the distinct sense that his theory about Whitewood not killing him had been incorrect.

This feeling had started, really, as soon as Whitewood
had left the room, that ominous *See you tonight* echoing in
Leif's head for however many hours he'd been wrapped up.

And it continued now, as Leif heard the whoosh of a
heavy door.

They crossed a threshold and he was pelted with rain.
He knew that he'd somehow—in only a matter of days—
managed to become the next sacrifice. He'd pushed too
hard. Just like Alicia.

The helpers walked him a short distance, heavy rain-
drops soaking his jumpsuit through in less than a minute.

"Thank you," a woman's voice said from ahead of
him, projecting to be heard over the downpour. Leif was
passed on by the helpers, four new hands gripping him so
tightly, it felt like they were leaving fingerprint-shaped
bruises. The saturated fabric of robes brushed against him.

The cult.

Or, as Whitewood preferred: the *group*.

"Are we ready to begin?" the woman asked, and this
time Leif identified her. Mary Hattaway. The intense lady

from Second Baptist whose hand had been bandaged at the funeral.

"Master should be here shortly," a man's voice said, this one harder to place.

Leif saw light flash through his blindfold, followed not too long after by a clap of thunder that reverberated for at least ten seconds. Why were they doing this tonight, during a thunderstorm? He found himself worrying about being struck by lightning before realizing how ridiculous that was. If anything should terrify him, it was the invisible presence in the spring that had yanked Janine's camera away.

"Let's begin," Wayne Whitewood said as he joined them.

Leif barely had time to register the profound dread Whitewood stirred before the chanting started. As he was marched away from the school, Leif subtly moved his shoulders back and forth, testing to see if escape would be possible. After all, Ben had done it, right?

"Don't even think about it, son," a voice said, two of the hands on his arms clamping down even harder. It was Sheriff Lawson. *Even the police are involved.* Leif's hopes of getting away were wilting fast.

His heart started pounding as he comprehended how soon he was going to die.

He thought of his mom—his wonderful, hardworking mom. He didn't want to leave her.

He didn't want to leave Rex, either. He hated that their friendship would be ending on such a weird note. Hopefully Rex would remember the good times—drawing contests, stupid messages passed back and forth in church, laughing so hard tears streamed down their faces—and not the pointless arguing from the last month.

"Vee-tah ehst ah-kwa," the cult chanted over and over

again, still in competition with the rain. He felt the ground under his feet change from grass to rocky mud. They were nearing the spring.

All four hands gripped Leif in place, and he realized everyone had stopped walking.

The chanting ended abruptly. Whitewood began to speak.

"Tonight is very special," he proclaimed. "For we will be saving not just one Lost Cause, but two!"

Two? Leif thought, as his blindfold was pulled off and he saw, standing not ten feet away with two cult members at her sides, J. It was like a slap in the face, as he of course felt responsible. As they made eye contact, there were no silent entreaties to *Keep Fighting.* J was as petrified as he was, which Leif found comforting before it quickly became soul-crushing.

"A dark, rebellious spirit has been gaining strength amongst our young ones," Whitewood continued, his swirl of white hair sticking out from under his hood and quickly losing its battle with the rain. "It has been spreading like a virus, infecting souls in a way never before seen. But we have been shown the way! We have found the waters that can purify these wayward souls!"

"We thank you, Master, for showing us the purifying waters that will deliver these young ones," Mary Hattaway said, her eyes fixed on Whitewood like she was staring at a natural wonder.

"Yes, Master," the others repeated.

"And let us not forget," Whitewood said. "If the One Below accepts our two offerings tonight, we will be just one Lost Cause away from seeing fulfilled what has long been foretold . . ."

They all began speaking in unison. "When the last Lost Cause is given to the waters for purification, the Seven Lost Causes shall be cleansed of their rebellious spirits and emerge as the Seven Shepherds. These holy ones shall lead our youth into righteousness, teaching them to submit to the precepts of the old and wise."

Leif could only see some of the cult members' faces—four were kneeling at the edge of the spring in front of him, and he assumed more were doing the same behind—but their huge, beatific smiles were enough to clue him in that for them this was a very big deal.

"Let us begin!" Whitewood shouted up to the heavens, raising his arms.

The chanting started again, Leif's stomach flipping as he saw that one of the cult members walking J over to Whitewood was C.B. Donner of C.B.'s Auto Parts. He took out her gag and untied her hands from behind her back.

Leif knew all too well what was going to happen next.

C.B. Donner held out J's right hand as Whitewood brought down his knife and sliced her palm.

The sound of her crying out was among the worst things Leif had ever heard.

She writhed in place as C.B. and another man restrained her.

Whitewood turned to Leif, whose gag was removed as he felt his hands being untied.

I don't want to be here I don't want to be here I don't want to be here, he thought, trying to imagine he was somewhere else, *anywhere else,* even as he felt Sheriff Lawson forcing his hand out toward Whitewood.

Leif was with Rex on their island. He was on the Small Rock, and he had a very important question: *Why was all this happeni—*

The pain was blinding, all-consuming.

Leif stared in shock at his hand, his poor hand, as he felt himself being walked toward the water.

This was his last chance.

He pulled his arms away from Sheriff Lawson as sharply as he could, but the man's rough hands wouldn't let go. Leif jabbed his knee into the other man, making solid contact with his hip.

"Dammit, boy!"

Leif heard an explosive thud as the man slapped him on the ear. It was both painful and disorienting, followed by a ringing that wouldn't stop. The men dragged him into the spring, warm water spilling into his school-issued shoes as he stepped into the shallows. There would be no escape.

"We will immerse both at once! On my signal!" Whitewood said, and moments later Leif's hand was underwater. The chanting got louder behind them—*Ah-miss-um in-trot ah-qwam sank-tum*—as Leif half noticed the start of the glowing and the bubbling, how it seemed brighter and more intense than the other two times.

Soon he was being walked deeper into the water, side by side with J.

His hand was still screaming, his ear was still ringing, and he thought he might faint.

He felt Sheriff Lawson's hand clamp down on the back of his neck, pushing his head toward the surface.

Leif took a panicked breath before going under.

The second his face entered the spring, water began streaming into his nose and mouth, pushing its way in with undeniable force. No amount of struggling seemed to make a difference, and the discomfort of being literally filled by the spring was so much worse than his cut hand or clocked ear. The bitterly cold water coursed through his body, its icy tendrils seeming to race down his veins into his core. He was overwhelmed with the feeling that something, or some*one*, in the frigid water was scanning him, evaluating him.

Judging him.

He was suddenly, violently pulled toward one of the spring's walls.

As everything around him began to blur and blacken, he knew he would be dead soon. He even thought he saw Alicia's face sticking out from the dirt, as if waiting to greet him.

Hi, Alicia, he thought during his last few seconds of consciousness.

It was a wonderful hallucination to go out on.

—

SO THIS WAS death.

Blackness.

Nothingness.

For all time.

Or . . . wait.

Leif slowly began to feel his body again, at the same time that his surroundings came into view, as if someone were very gradually raising a dimmer switch.

He was in an endless ocean, where breathing didn't seem necessary. He held his hand out in front of him. Glowing faintly in the dreamy haze, it appeared to no longer be injured.

"Hello," a voice said from his right. Leif somehow shifted his floating body so that he was looking at a boy his age, also suspended in the water, emanating the same dull light as his hand. The boy had a hockey haircut—a mullet fanning out behind his head—and wore a jumpsuit similar to, but not quite the same, as Leif's.

"Hey," Leif said, discovering he could speak underwater.

"I'm Rich," the boy said. Leif couldn't tell if his mouth was actually moving. "Who're you?"

"Leif." He pronounced it *Layf.*

"And who's she?" Rich asked, pointing behind him.

Leif was surprised to see J floating toward him.

"I'm Josefina," she said.

Leif was glad to finally know her full name.

Rich narrowed his eyes. "How'd you both get here at once?"

Leif shuddered instead of responding, as he'd just made eye contact with an unsmiling little boy in a polo shirt who'd floated up next to Rich.

"What?" Rich asked, before noticing the little boy. "Oh. Timothy, don't stare! We talked about this."

Timothy looked down, then began to stare again.

"Is this Heaven?" Josefina asked.

"Uh, no," Rich said. "You're not dead. You're in the spring."

"What do you mean?" Leif asked, excited to not be dead but also very confused.

"We're all in the spring. Physically, at least. Our *bodies* are still alive, but our minds, or souls, or whatever you want to call 'em, are here, in this place. We call it the Void. It's actually quite extensive once you look around. You'll meet the others eventually. They're busy now."

"What year is it out there?" the stone-faced little boy asked.

"It's 1992," Leif answered.

"Wow. Still 1992," Rich said. "That's the same year Alicia joined us."

Leif's heart—or whatever one would call it in this strange place—practically stopped.

Alicia was here.

"What— Why— How did—" Leif couldn't make a sentence.

"What do you mean, *still* 1992?" Josefina interrupted. "Alicia was kill— Uh, put here, like a week ago."

"Yeah," Rich said. "But we don't really have weeks

here. Or days. Or years. Or even minutes. Time is sort of irrelevant."

Leif didn't understand, and trying to do so made his not-dead brain hurt. "Can we see her?" he asked instead. "Alicia?"

"Hold on." Rich and Timothy appeared to dissipate into the water.

Leif found it hard to believe he might actually see Alicia again, but he couldn't help but feel incredibly excited.

"So," Josefina said as they floated awkwardly on their own, "this is pretty weird."

"Yeah," Leif agreed. "I'm, um, sorry you ended up down here with me."

"Not your fault," she said.

"I really appreciated how you, you know, helped me. At the school."

Josefina shrugged. "I really appreciated that you were willing to stand up to those people."

"Thanks," Leif said. "I just can't believe we're—" He was distracted by a dissonant noise, like an incessant whirring, as he noticed a shadowy presence moving all around them. Moving wasn't quite the right word, as it seemed almost to jump instantly from one point to the next, one moment twenty feet away, the next moment jarringly close to his face.

It gave Leif that same feeling he'd had right before he'd drowned. Like he was being judged.

Then it was gone, just as abruptly as it had appeared.

After a few moments of pure stillness, Leif saw a distant point of light moving toward them at a great speed. As it drew near, it became clear it was a person.

Alicia.

She stopped mere feet away, the soft glow surrounding her and her jumpsuit only accentuating her awesomeness, like some otherworldly version of Glamour Shots.

"Alicia!" Leif said. He'd never been happier to see someone. He wished he could hug her, but physical contact didn't seem possible, so he just smiled as big as he could as she came closer.

Alicia seemed perplexed, her eyebrows furrowed like she was trying to solve a riddle.

Leif was seized with panic. Did she not recognize him?

"It's me . . ." he said, hoping she would interrupt before he had to tell her his name. She didn't. "Leif."

She stared at him a few more moments—it felt like an eternity—before a twinkle of recognition finally registered in her eyes. "Leif!" she shouted.

"Yes!" he said, feeling profound relief. "I can't believe you're alive! This is— We all thought you were dead, and it was . . . I just . . . I missed you." He felt his face contort into a cry, though he couldn't feel any tears falling.

Alicia smiled, a bit more uncomfortably than Leif would have liked, before turning to Josefina. "Have we met too?"

"Yeah. It's J. Josefina. From Whitewood."

"Right," Alicia said, in a way that made it clear she still had no idea who J was. "I'm sorry," she said, frustrated. "My life before here is just . . . cloudy."

Leif was very freaked out. "It's only been a week," he said, desperate to further jog her memory. "Remember? It was summer . . . We were making *PolterDog* . . ."

"Polter . . . Dog?" Alicia said. She might as well have driven a dagger through Leif's heart.

"You shouldn't do that," Rich said, suddenly appearing next to them with Timothy.

"Do what?" Leif asked.

"Ask any of us about our life up there. It begins to fade quickly, and it can be difficult, even painful, to try to remember."

Leif looked at Alicia, who seemed very confused. He'd

heard what Rich said, but he couldn't help himself. "Do you remember Rex? Our other best friend?"

Alicia looked down at her hands, as if maybe she'd scrawled the answer there in pen.

"Tall guy?" Leif prodded. "Hilarious and great? Likes to boss people around?"

"I don't know," Alicia said, putting her hands on her head. "I don't know!"

"I told you not to do that, man!" Rich said.

"I'm sorry, I'm sorry!" Seeing Alicia this distressed made Leif want to implode. To make things worse, he realized that even if he finally got up the nerve to tell her how he felt, it would mean absolutely nothing to her.

"It's okay," Rich said. "Just . . . don't do it again. You'll understand soon enough. Especially after He . . . visits you."

"Who's He?" Josefina asked. "Who are you talking about?"

Before he could answer, the buzzing shriek came back, louder and more intense than before, and the shadowy presence began to pinball among them. Leif was disturbed to see a little blond girl by the shadow's side, moving in tandem everywhere that it went.

Suddenly Rich, Timothy, and Alicia were screaming in agony, enveloped by wisps and tangles of the dark shadow, the little girl giggling as their bodies seemed to be stretched out like Silly Putty.

"Oh my god," Josefina said, as she and Leif watched in horror.

The little girl appeared inches from Leif's face. "Nice to meet you," she said, laughing. "Now the Keeper only needs one more!"

"One more what?" Leif asked, but the girl didn't answer.

Instead, he was enveloped by the shadow.

Then there was only pain. Unfathomable pain.

His limbs felt like they were being ripped away at the joint, his ligaments stretching beyond any natural limit, his bones bending past the breaking point.

It was unbearable.

And endless.

As Rich had said, time was irrelevant here.

Finally, and without warning, the shadow was gone.

Leif felt like a deflated balloon, as if the dark figure had fed on him. Josefina floated nearby, clearly having also been through it.

Leif's mind was a blur. He thought back to the time before. It seemed so distant. He remembered that he'd been at the Whitewood School. But for how long?

He had no idea.

Rich floated up next to him.

"You'll get used to it," he said. "Everyone does."

24

"NOW, REMEMBER," BEN SAID, STANDING NEXT TO THE CHAIN-LINK fence in the curly wig, the red sunglasses, and Rex's over-sized black T-shirt, illuminated by Janine's camera light as she filmed. "If we stick to the plan, we should be able to get in and out within twenty minutes or so."

Oh, sure, Rex thought. *We're only dealing with an angry spirit that stores humans and feeds on their souls. What could possibly go wrong?* Even as he knew this plan represented their best (and probably only) option, he also knew there was a high likelihood that by the time this night was done, he and Ben would both be students at the White-wood School. Or worse.

The risk was worth it, though, if it meant they might save Alicia. And Leif.

And maybe even bring down Wayne Whitewood and his twisted school, once and for all.

Ben looked at each of them gathered in the dark by the old tobacco barn—Rex, Janine, Donna, and Travis—doing a silent count, as if they were a much larger group of people. "Your lookout person is still coming, right?" he asked.

"Yeah, yeah," Rex said. "He'll definitely be here." If Hornhat no-showed, Rex would never speak to him again.

"With the scuba gear too? That's essential so we can stay underwater as long as we need to."

"I know," Rex said, trying not to get annoyed by Ben's

patronizing tone. "Don't worry, he's bringing it." Hornhat had been all too eager to offer up the equipment his family took every summer to their three-story beach house.

"He's bringing scuba gear?" Janine asked. "How is he getting here?"

"He said he had his own ride," Rex said, realizing how bizarre it would be if Hornhat's parents dropped him off at a cow pasture late at night on a Monday. "But—"

All heads turned as a small, almost silent vehicle pulled up right next to them.

"Hey, dudes!" Hornhat said, waving as he came to a stop. "Say hello to the Horn-cart."

Of course the Hornhats had a golf cart. And of course they named it the Horn-cart.

"This baby's top of the line," Hornhat continued, running his hand down the candy apple red exterior as Janine shined her camera light on him and Travis nodded appreciatively. "'Ninety-one model, built-in stereo. My dad even put in a subwoofer."

"Uh. Okay," Rex said. He hoped his choice of Hornhat for lookout wouldn't get them all killed.

"Sorry I'm late, by the way," Hornhat said. "Thought there would be clearer signage." He stepped out of the cart, guilelessly introducing himself one by one—"Mark Hornhat, nice to meetcha"—to Janine, Travis, Ben, and Donna, who seemed particularly appalled.

"Do you have the scuba gear?" Ben asked.

"Oh, do I ever," Hornhat said. He walked to the back of his cart, where, strapped in next to a bag of golf clubs, were two diving tanks, along with masks, fins, and breathing regulators. "Are y'all gearing up here?"

"Yes," Ben answered. "Best to get fully prepped here to minimize our time at the spring."

"Rad," Hornhat said as he went to work, strapping the

tanks over Rex's and Ben's backs and explaining how everything worked, Janine filming the whole time.

"I gotta say," Travis said, wearing a black tank-top that, along with his utility belt, brought out the Redneck Batman even more than usual. "I'm still in shock about what you said Mr. Whitewood's been doin' with these kids. I mean, dang, you think you know somebody . . ."

"Yeah, well, thanks for being here," Rex said, sitting on the back of the cart as Hornhat helped slide fins onto his feet. "I know that if we succeed tonight, you'll be out of a job."

"Aw, that's no problem," Travis said, fiddling with some of the keys on his belt. "I got some stuff to fall back on."

"All set, amigos," Hornhat said.

Rex stood up from the cart, the weight of the tank on his back making all of this feel more real. They were actually going through with it. He and Ben looked at each other in all their equipment, almost as if they were peering into a mirror. "This is good," Ben said, his mask hanging off his neck. "Nice work, Mark."

Hornhat gave a salute.

"It's almost go-time. Let's grab the blood." Ben led Rex back toward the fence, where they'd dropped their blood bags, the collection of which had been an ordeal unto itself.

The body of Rex's eighty-two-year-old barber, Harold, was at his parents' funeral home, waiting to be embalmed the following day. Rex had seen his father drain blood from deceased people dozens of times, but he'd never tried it himself. With Ben's surprisingly enthusiastic help, they'd drained the old man, an awkward and messy affair consisting of over two hours of poking tubes into a dead naked guy who used to hum along to Johnny Cash as he cut Rex's hair. When all was said and done, they'd collected less than a gallon of blood. "I thought there'd be more," Rex had said, right before scrawling a note for his dad (*Drained him already. Hope that's helpful!*) and placing it on Harold's belly. Ben had then suggested they supplement by getting pig's blood from Riley's hog farm, which sold pork directly to the public. It'd taken about ten minutes. And they'd gotten a lot.

"I have an idea," Ben now said after picking up the bag of Harold's blood. "Let's cover ourselves with this."

"What?" Rex asked. "Why?"

"Because we know human blood will open up the gateway. Pig's blood isn't a sure thing."

"No, I mean why are we covering ourselves with blood at all?"

"Oh," Ben said. "Because once we get down to the spring, we don't know what's gonna happen. We might drop our blood bags. We might be short on time. Lots of variables. But this way, we can take control of the situation and guarantee we have at least—"

"Yeah, yeah, okay, fine," Rex said.

They took turns dipping their hands into the bag and rubbing layer upon layer of barber's blood all over their clothes. The rotten metallic smell was absolutely heinous. They each stopped at least four times to dry heave.

Without saying a thing, Ben took a blood-dipped finger and decorated his face like he was preparing for war. Rex had no desire to follow suit, but he didn't want to seem like he wasn't committed. Holding his breath, he put two random lines of blood on his face.

"This is really disgusting and I don't want to keep filming," Janine said. "But I will, because I'm dedicated to my craft."

"I hate this so much," Donna said, covering her nose with her sweatshirt.

Hornhat reached into the bag without asking and streaked blood on his face, too.

"Y'all are nuts," Travis said, smiling.

"Okay," Ben said, knotting the rope around his waist. "To recap, once we get to the spring, Rex and I will jump in, poke holes in our pig's blood bags, and start digging out Alicia. Janine will film. Donna and Travis will have the other end of this rope, and once we get Alicia out of the wall, we'll loop the rope around her and give it three tugs. That'll be the signal to start pulling the three of us back to land."

Travis and Donna nodded.

"Mark, you'll hang back in the woods as lookout. If you see anyone—and I mean *anyone*—heading toward us at the spring, give us a signal. Can you do a good owl hoot?"

"Definitely." Hornhat made an unsettling noise that reminded Rex of his late Grandpa Mack's smoker's cough.

"Yeah, no," Ben said. "If you see someone coming, just shout at us."

"Got it."

"Anyone have any last questions?" Ben asked.

Why is my heart beating so damn hard? Rex wanted to ask.

"Good luck out there, you guys," Janine said from behind her camera.

"Let's save Alicia," Donna said. "And take down those assholes who killed my dad."

Janine had never heard Donna talk about her father's death, let alone refer to it as a murder, and she found it oddly moving. "We're going to," she said.

They crossed through the gap in the chain-link fence one by one. Rex's right scuba fin momentarily got stuck as he went through, and of course he couldn't help but think of Leif. It reminded him that he was exactly where he needed to be, doing exactly what he needed to do. And also that it was very challenging to walk in scuba fins. They probably could have waited to put these on.

"Wonder if Mr. Whitewood knows there's this big ol' gap in his fence," Travis said as he passed through last.

That was the last thing any of them said, as once they'd all made it to the other side, Ben held a commanding finger to his lips. Rex's heart continued to pound as they moved through what was now familiar territory: the woods, the two-trunked tree with a view of the spring, the thirty or so exposed steps down toward the water. A sense of calm settled upon him as the group approached the water's edge; with his hammer in one hand and bag of pig's blood in the other, Rex was ready to do whatever it would take to save Alicia from this cursed spring.

That calm only lasted a few seconds, though, as a row of torches suddenly lit up in front of them.

25

"WELCOME BACK," WHITEWOOD SAID FROM THE FAR SIDE OF THE spring, dressed in his light blue robe with the white stole over the shoulders, the rest of the cult fanned out behind him with torches. "Nice to see you again, Candidatus."

Rex didn't know what that meant, but he did know their plan had fallen apart before they'd even started. Somehow they'd timed their rescue incredibly poorly, choosing the same night as this ritual, which looked to be particularly horrifying. Just beyond the cult—on the lawn between the school and the spring—about twenty or so students were lined up, hands tied behind their backs, ankles bound. Rex did a quick scan for Leif but didn't see him.

He wondered if he and his squad might be able to run back to the hole in the fence. But as he turned his head toward the woods, he saw that four more robed cult members had emerged from the tree line.

There was no escape.

Had Whitewood known they were coming?

"I'd like to extend a special thanks to my Employee of the Month, Travis Bethune," Whitewood said, "for letting us know about this little mission and making all of this possible."

Rex felt woozy. He should have known dim bulb Travis would accidentally reveal their secret.

"I'm sorry, guys," Travis said. "But what Mr. White-

292 RHETT McLAUGHLIN & LINK NEAL

wood is doin' here is real important. It's what our town needs. I can't let y'all mess it up."

"Wait," Rex said, trying to keep up, "you're a part of this . . . thing?"

"Yeah, man," Travis said, growing excited. "I been wantin' to tell ya, it's *good* that Alicia's in the spring! She's gonna be one of the Seven Shepherds. And one of y'all might be too!"

"That's exactly right, Travis," Whitewood said, spreading his arms dramatically, his robe billowing around him. "Tonight is our last night to offer one final Lost Cause to the One Below!"

"The Seven Shepherds shall rise!" shouted Leggett Shackelford, standing next to Whitewood.

"The Seven Shepherds shall rise!" the cult repeated.

Rex still had no idea what the hell they were talking about, but he was fairly certain he had no interest in being one of their weird shepherds. And that Alicia wouldn't either.

Apparently Ben felt the same way, because he was already awkwardly bolting toward the spring in his flippers.

"Come on!" he shouted.

Rex started to run after him, hammer and bag of pig's blood in hand, but the fins made it challenging. After only a few steps, Travis grabbed him by the shoulders.

"No!" Whitewood yelled. "Let them go! If they want to offer themselves to the One Below, don't stand in their way!"

Travis did as he was told. Though Rex wasn't exactly encouraged by the idea that he and Ben were making an offering of themselves, he knew if they had a chance to save Alicia, they had to take it.

He followed Ben into the spring, watching as he pulled his mask down.

"We won't have any pullers!" Rex realized.

"We'll figure it out!" Ben said, putting the regulator in his mouth and diving under.

Rex did the same, submerging his blood-covered body and watching as a pale blue glow spread all around him, bubbles percolating on the surface above. Using the back of his hammer, he tore a hole in his bag of pig's blood, then watched the red fluid commingle with the bright blue of the water, breaking down into smaller strands as it dissipated throughout the spring. It was oddly beautiful.

Seconds later, the water got so bright it almost hurt Rex's eyes, with bubbles so large and violent, they were actually creating waves. He tried to swim forward, but the entire spring had become a churning, roiling cauldron.

And that wasn't all.

Rex felt the spirit.

It was watching him, as it had that first time.

Rex tried to ignore it, to focus on getting to Alicia, but that became impossible as he felt the dark presence completely envelop him.

He began thrashing his limbs in the water, as if he could somehow fling it off, like it was a bee.

His efforts were unsuccessful.

How could he have been so stupid? Whatever this "One Below" was, he and Ben had willingly walked into its lair. Once it took them, not only would they not save Alicia, but they would also need someone to come save *them*.

Rex gave a few last, desperate flails.

It worked.

The spirit was gone.

He pushed through the water, only to feel it return moments later, surrounding him once again.

This time, though, Rex had a minor revelation: the spirit was in distress. *Maybe the unusual amount of blood is overwhelming it.*

Whatever the cause, the presence around him seemed

fragmented somehow, there one moment and gone the next. He felt the water squeezing his face, desperately pushing on his regulator and mask, then relenting.

It was almost as if the spirit couldn't find a way in.

Screw you, One Below, Rex thought, realizing it no longer had enough of a hold to keep him from moving. *I'm saving my best friend, whether you like it or not.*

He battled forward through the water—finally, the fins were helpful—until he caught sight of Ben next to the spring wall, where Alicia's head was sticking out just as it had on the video.

They could actually do this.

He expected Ben to immediately start digging her out, but instead he was pointing emphatically past her.

Holy shit.

Leif's head was sticking out of the wall too.

Rex felt a billion things at once, all of which he pushed aside in order to begin using the back of his hammer to hack away at the rocky mud wall holding in Leif, as Ben did the same for Alicia.

The rocks were loose enough to dislodge, but most of Leif's body was covered.

This might take a while.

—

THOUGH JANINE WAS considerably caught off-guard by the turn of events their night had taken, she wasn't at all surprised to learn that Mary Hattaway was part of the cult.

"Was my message on your grandmother's car not clear enough?" Mary said brightly into Janine's ear, gripping her right arm so she couldn't go anywhere.

"Oh, it was perfectly clear," Janine said. "I just don't take orders from human sludge."

Mary reached toward Janine's left arm—the one Travis

was holding with a firm but gentle pressure—and yanked the camera out of her hand.

"Give that back," Janine said.

"I don't think so." Mary looked into the lens as if she was testing it out. "Might give it to my Tammy—she'll think it's a riot. Or maybe . . ." Mary let the camera slide out of her hand and clunk onto the dirt. "Oopsy."

Janine wanted to scream, but she didn't want Mary to see how much anger she was inspiring.

"Oh, I'm sorry about that, dear." But instead of bending down to pick it up, Mary stomped on the camera three times with her white Nike running shoe.

"No!" Janine said, feeling like she'd lost a limb.

The VHS cassette fell out, raw tape spilling on the ground in chaotic coils.

"Oh, come on, Mary. You didn't have to do that," Travis said. "That camera wasn't hurtin' nobody."

"Shut up, Travis!" Mary snapped.

"You are a terrible fucking person," Donna said, restrained by two other men next to Janine.

"Your mother would be ashamed to hear you talk like that," Mary said.

"My mother thinks you're a bitch."

Mary lost her fake smile.

Whitewood, meanwhile, seemed euphoric. "We have been blessed tonight!" he proclaimed. "Those boys offered themselves to the purifying waters without us having to lift a finger. If the One Below accepts either of them, the seventh Lost Cause will have been delivered and the Prophecy will be fulfilled!"

The cult members shouted in celebration, several of them beginning to cry. This was even more screwed up than Janine could've guessed.

"Thank you, Master!" one of the men holding Donna shouted, causing her to turn her head in recognition.

"Dr. Bob?"

"Hi, Donna," Dr. Bob said, pulling off his hood to reveal his glistening bald head and round, frameless glasses. He had the same caring face he'd had during each of Donna's appointments over the course of her lifetime. "I know it's hard to understand, darlin'. But this spring is gonna save our town."

"You're right, I don't understand," Donna said, remembering the darkness she'd encountered under that water. Her muscles tensed under Dr. Bob's grip. "I don't understand why my dad had to die."

"Oh, Donna," Dr. Bob said, reminding her of his response years ago when she'd gotten up the nerve to tell him that she thought she was depressed. "That was just a car accident. And I'm still truly sorry for your loss, sweetheart."

"Don't call me sweetheart." Donna jerked her neck back, slamming her head into Dr. Bob's nose.

As he cried out in pain, Janine took advantage of the brief commotion, jabbing her elbow into Mary Hattaway's stomach, knocking the wind out of her.

Janine was just about to use her free arm to bury a fist in Travis's stomach when Leggett Shackelford—who'd been restraining Donna along with Dr. Bob—folded his monstrous arms around her, and Donna, too, effectively locking them both in place.

"Don't try anything like that again," he said.

Mary stood up slowly, gathering herself. "Down here," she said, bringing her face close to Janine's, "we teach our girls not to hit." She spit, the viscous substance reeking of stale cigarettes as it streamed down Janine's cheek. "You're lucky the One Below isn't interested in Lost Causes your age. Because if He was, I'd throw you in that spring myself."

Janine squirmed in Shackelford's vise-like grip, wishing she could get loose and knock Mary in the stomach a couple dozen more times.

"What's takin' so long?" Whitewood said, seeming slightly panicked as he leaned out over the wild, bubbling water. "Those boys should have been accepted or rejected by now."

The cult was silent, watching their leader like a hawk, absorbing his anxiety as if it were their own.

"Master," Mary Hattaway said after a long moment, "do you think their masks might be . . . preventing the One Below from his evaluation?"

Whitewood's head jerked toward Mary, his eyes trembling in their sockets.

"Or maybe not," Mary said, bowing her head.

"Dammit!" Whitewood screamed at the spring. "We're running out of time! Start untying some of the Candidati." He gestured to the line of terrified kids. "We *must* have one more accepted before midnight, or all of this will have been for nothing!"

—

REX HELD TIGHT to his hammer—continuing to chip away at the last of the spring wall holding Leif in place—as the spirit tried to rip it from his hand.

He and Ben had been dealing with this near-constant interference the entire time they'd been digging, the spirit seeming to get stronger and more focused as time passed. Their bags of pig's blood were now empty, but they'd nearly finished the job.

Rex tore away one last particularly large rock and felt a burst of joy as Leif's body sagged forward. Rex reached out to hold him, grabbing the rope that Ben had already tied around Alicia and gently looping it around his best friend's waist.

Gotcha, buddy, Rex thought as he looked at Leif.

Leif's eyes were open but unfocused, his jaw agape.

I know, Rex thought. *I missed you, too.*

Ben double-knotted the rope around Leif and Alicia and tested it with a few sharp tugs. He pointed toward the side of the spring opposite Whitewood and the cult, grabbed the rope close to Alicia, then began kicking his fins, pulling their helpless cargo along. Rex understood: since they had no pullers waiting on the shore to haul them in, they'd have to tow their friends back themselves. Rex grasped the rope and started kicking.

They hadn't made it five feet before the darkness engulfed them, violently dragging Leif and Alicia—and Rex and Ben with them—back to the spring wall.

Rex's hopes came crashing down as he realized just what the spirit was capable of. He and Ben stared at each other, both obviously thinking the same thing:

How the hell are we going to do this?

There was a splash from above.

About fifteen feet away, Rex saw a young boy in a jumpsuit plunge down into the water.

The spirit left the four of them immediately, darting to the boy and enveloping him.

Rex was thinking they should go help him before he realized:

This was their chance.

He and Ben began kicking their fins again, moving Leif and Alicia through the water as fast as they possibly could. They made it a little less than ten feet before they saw the boy in the jumpsuit launched out of the spring, as if the spirit had decided it had no use for him.

Moments later, the spirit returned to them, Rex and Ben kicking with everything they had, barely making a dif-

299 THE LOST CAUSES OF BLEAK CREEK

ference as the frenzied shadow towed them back almost to their starting point.

Another splash.

Then another.

A teenage boy and girl came plummeting down together. Rex suddenly understood that the cult was throwing these kids in, offering them up to "the One Below." *Insane.*

He couldn't think about it too hard, though, because the spirit sped away again, and he and Ben resumed their exhausting rescue. Rex was running on sheer adrenaline at this point; he wondered how much longer he could keep it up.

The spirit, meanwhile, bounced between the boy and the girl, seeming confused as to whom to engulf first. It finally settled on the girl, wrapping her up in its blackness.

Rex and Ben made it back to the spot where the spirit had last stopped them and kept going, Leif and Alicia still drifting behind them.

The girl was propelled toward the spring wall.

The spirit had decided she was worth keeping.

Rex and Ben kicked harder.

By the time the spirit was violently ejecting the teenage boy from the spring, Rex and Ben had managed to get Leif and Alicia a few feet from the shallows. Just a bit further and they'd be able to walk out of this hellscape.

But the spirit had other ideas, wrenching them back toward the wall.

Rex was ready to concede defeat. There was no way he'd be able to swim all the way across the spring again.

Before they'd even been pulled halfway, though: another splash.

Then two more.

And another.

Whitewood and the cult must have been getting desperate, throwing in several students at a time. Ben and Rex took full advantage of the diversion, somehow finding the energy to zoom forward.

A young blond boy was accepted and pulled along to the wall, the three other students ruthlessly catapulted to the shore, all of which gave Rex and Ben more than enough time to pull Leif and Alicia all the way to the shallows.

As their heads broke the surface of the water, Alicia and Leif lurched to life, coughing and gasping like newborn babies torn from the womb.

They'd made it. Rex wanted to pass out.

—

"WHY IS NOTHING happening!" Whitewood screamed. "The Keeper has accepted two more! That makes eight!"

On the opposite side of the spring, he saw the reason his math was wrong: two of his rebellious souls were no longer with the Keeper.

Ben and Rex were helping Alicia and Leif to shore, where the two freed captives both collapsed onto all fours and began, with a series of terrible retches, to purge the spring water.

"Get them!" Whitewood yelled. "We only need one more Lost Cause!"

Mary Hattaway, Travis, Dr. Bob, and Shackelford raced toward the escaped Lost Causes, abandoning Janine and Donna. Seizing the opportunity, Janine immediately ran to help the tied-up kids. Donna followed.

"Well, this isn't good," Ben said, seeing the four adults headed in their direction.

Rex knew neither of them had the energy to fight off the cult members. "Do you have a plan?"

"Let me think," Ben said, silent for a few seconds. "No."

This definitely wasn't good.

But then Rex heard something. A sound both foreign and familiar.

Oh-Oh-Oh-Oh-Oh

"Do you hear that?" he asked Ben.

They looked across the spring, where the Horn-cart was barreling through the grass toward the cult, and suddenly Rex knew what he was hearing.

New Kids on the Block.

Mark Hornhat sat behind the wheel, one triumphant finger in the air, nodding his head to "Hangin' Tough" as it blasted from the golf cart speakers. He was upon the cult in a matter of seconds, not slowing down before crashing into two of the robed figures holding torches.

They fell to the ground in a daze, and Hornhat steered the still-speeding Horn-cart toward Sheriff Lawson, who was unable to dodge it before his legs rolled up under the bumper, the electric vehicle running him over, knocking him unconscious.

"Don't cross our path 'cause you're gonna get stomped!" Hornhat sang along with NKOTB as his back wheels made a speed bump of the sheriff. He drove over to the line of students waiting to be thrown into the springs, where Janine and Donna were already untying two kids.

"Now you guys untie the others!" Janine told them, and the students sprang into action.

"Stop them!" Whitewood screamed, spit flying from his mouth as he watched his plan unraveling. A small crew of cult members who had been tossing students into the water ran toward Janine, Donna, Hornhat, and the newly unbound kids.

"Here!" Hornhat parked his cart and passed two golf clubs from the back to Janine and Donna. He then grabbed more for the students who'd been freed before reaching into the cart one last time and emerging triumphantly with

302 RHETT McLAUGHLIN & LINK NEAL

his nunchucks. "Time to party," he said, swinging them around indiscriminately in the air, just barely missing Donna's face.

The small group of cult members was closing in, led by C.B. Donner of C.B.'s Auto Parts. "Get yer hands off the Candidati!" he shouted, charging straight at Janine, an unhinged look in his eyes.

Janine reared back with Hornhat's Big Bertha driver—accessing the one golf lesson her dad had given her when she was eleven—then swung the club around at full force, the bulbous metal head connecting with C.B.'s "fuzzy dice."

"Fore," Janine said as the howling man fell over.

The other cultists were upon them, trying to restrain whomever they could, but the kids held their ground next to Janine and Donna, wildly swinging their clubs. None of them was really hitting their targets, but they were still enough of a threat to keep the cult from tying any of them back up. And they were more effective than Hornhat, in any case, who was currently doing nothing but grimacing after having nunchucked himself in the thigh.

Across the spring, Alicia and Leif were still retching. Rex and Ben removed their tanks, fins, and masks, preparing themselves to become a human blockade as Travis, Mary, Shackelford, and Dr. Bob stepped toward them.

"I hate that it turned out this way, y'all," Travis said, placing his head in his hands. "I really do."

"Shut up!" Mary said. "Just throw them back in!"

Travis took a reluctant step forward, followed by the less reluctant Leggett Shackelford.

Rex and Ben raised their hammers.

"Don't do this, Travis," Rex said, still out of breath.

"I'm sorry, bud," Travis said. "You'll thank me one day."

He lunged at Rex, who immediately swung his hammer down. Travis caught his arm, and the two of them tumbled to the ground, Travis easily pinning Rex and prying the hammer away.

Ben was only slightly more successful; he struck Shackelford's shoulder, but it barely slowed him. The huge man knocked the hammer from Ben's hand and wrapped him in a bear hug. "Get it done," he said to his fellow cult members.

Rex writhed in Travis's grip as he watched Mary and Dr. Bob run to Alicia and Leif, their path clear.

—

WHEN SHERIFF LAWSON regained consciousness after his dance with the Horn-cart, he saw the brawl unfolding between the cult and the now-weaponized golf gang. He was astounded that the kids seemed to have the advantage over the adults, who cowered as the metal clubs whipped back and forth, some of the students loudly chanting "Don't follow!" over and over again.

This ends now, he thought, reaching into his robe and pulling out his service revolver.

"Gun!" Janine shouted, seeing the sheriff's six-shooter glinting in the torch light as he pointed it at them.

"Drop the clubs, kids," Sheriff Lawson said before aiming his weapon at a terrified Hornhat. "You're gonna regret driving that thing over me, you little punk. This'll teach y—"

From behind the sheriff, a teenage girl with freckles swung her pitching wedge up into his hand.

The sheriff screamed, grabbing his stinging knuckles as the gun flew through the air and landed in the thick grass.

The girl with the freckles directed a second swing to the back of the sheriff's head, the club catching his robe but still delivering a dazing blow.

Across the way, Shackelford locked Ben in his firm grasp.

"Ain't gettin' away this time," he said, hoisting Ben over his shoulder and stepping off the bank into the shallow water.

Ben flailed his limbs madly, making himself a perfectly uncooperative payload. As Shackelford adjusted his grip to steady himself, Ben grabbed the hood of the man's cumbersome robe and yanked it down over his face.

"You little bastard!" Shackelford slammed Ben down into the shallow water.

Mary and Dr. Bob had been struggling to lift the limp, barely conscious bodies of Alicia and Leif, but they'd each finally found a good hold and were starting to drag them the few steps to the water.

In his exhaustion, Rex had given up fighting against Travis, who still had him pinned, but seeing his best friends being carried back to the spirit's lair gave him a second wind.

He twisted his body, retracting his legs beneath Travis and kicking out as hard as he could.

"Oof!" Travis said as he was knocked to the ground.

Thank you, scooter leg, Rex thought, scrambling to his feet and charging toward Mary and Dr. Bob. He made a mad leap, tackling their ankles just as they were about to drop Alicia and Leif back into the water, all five of them landing in a tangled heap.

Wayne Whitewood looked to both sides of the spring, years of careful plotting culminating in this utter fiasco— the inept pile-up happening on the far side of the spring, his usually subdued students ruthlessly attacking his followers on the near side. He needed just one more Lost Cause for the Keeper, or else he would never be reunited with his sweet Ruby. The *real* Ruby. In the flesh. Emptied of that terrible spring water and no longer in the menacing grip of a dark spirit.

If you wanted something done, sometimes you just had to do it yourself.

Whitewood pulled out his large ceremonial knife and walked toward the few students who remained tied up. He quickly assessed them, choosing a boy with a crew cut, who, even though he was shaking like a leaf, seemed to have a rebellious look in his eyes.

"Your time has come," Whitewood said, cutting through the boy's rope with a swift flick of his blade and bending down to lift him up. "The less you struggle, the easier this will—"

"Stop!" someone shouted from behind him.

Whitewood turned. Donna was about fifteen steps away, pointing the sheriff's gun at him.

He stopped.

The entire cult did too, even those across the spring, all eyes on their Master.

Hornhat and the other students also stopped, their clubs frozen in the air.

"Okay now, little lady," Whitewood said, slowly raising his gloved hands. "Why don't you just put that thing down?"

"No," Donna said, the gun trembling in her hands.

"All right." Whitewood shifted his eyes from the gun to her face. "Hey, now, aren't you . . . one of my first students?"

He took a step forward.

Donna said nothing, instead taking a shaky breath.

"Yes!" Whitewood said. "I know you! My very first Lost Cause. Well, I'll be." He smiled at her, as if this were a friendly run-in at the dry cleaner's. "Except the One Below didn't agree, did he? He knew the truth about you."

He took another few steps toward Donna.

"He knew you weren't really a rebel. You were a good little girl. A girl who does as she's told."

He was now only feet away from Donna, the gun bouncing in her quivering hands.

"You've hurt so many people," she said, on the verge of tears.

"That's not true," Whitewood said, just a step or two away from being able to rip the pistol from her hands.

Donna cocked the gun.

"You're just confused. And listen: This isn't you. Pointing a gun at your old headmaster? Come on now. You're still a good girl. A follower."

"Follow this," Donna said.

The barrel flashed like a firework.

Whitewood grabbed his chest, staring in shock as a bloodstain blossomed on his robe.

"No!" Mary Hattaway shrieked, madly dashing to Whitewood as he fell to his knees.

"But Ruby," he said, looking toward the spring. "I was . . . just about to . . . finally . . ." He struggled to his feet, blood already dripping from his mouth. He reached the spring's edge, barely able to keep himself upright, then stumbled in, tripping over his flowing robe and dropping on all fours in the shallow water. As the bloody fabric touched the water, the spring—which had been calm for minutes, only lightly glowing and bubbling—began to gleam brightly. Whitewood continued his labored crawl, eventually reaching deeper water and doggie-paddling toward the center.

"I'm coming, Ruby!" he strained, blood pooling around him, causing the spring to bubble even more fiercely, the surface of the water like a wind-whipped lake. He gurgled one last time before his face fell under the water. After a few weak strokes, he stopped struggling, his motionless body floating in place.

"We have to save him!" Mary said, running out into the spring, Travis and Dr. Bob right behind her.

They didn't get far, though, before the water whisked up ferociously, waves splashing about, knocking the three followers down. On the far side of the spring in the shallows, even the massive Shackelford, somehow still holding Ben after all this, was blasted over by a wave. Ben was finally able to break free and began to shuffle his way back to the bank.

Rex saw what Ben didn't, though: an especially dark wave rising high above the surface of the water, accompanied by a loud, buzzing scream.

It darted furiously across the surface, spiraling toward Ben, who had just placed one foot on the shore.

"Ben!" Rex yelled. "Behind you!"

Ben turned his head in alarm right as the black wave engulfed his body, streams of gravity-defying water wrapping themselves around him and dragging him along the surface of the spring.

Ben screamed.

The black wave rocketed to the center of the spring, where it enveloped Whitewood's body, then suddenly dove down, sucking both Whitewood and Ben beneath the surface.

A second later, the spring went dark and calm.

No blue glow.

No bubbles.

Not even a ripple where the wave had descended.

Everyone standing on shore—Janine, Donna, Hornhat, the remaining students, the cult—stared in confusion at the now placid water. Even the low hum of the cicadas sounded perplexed.

Rex knew what to do.

He picked up his hammer and dug its sharp end into his left palm as hard as he could, then once again for good measure.

When the blood came, he dove in, hammer in hand.

He made his way through the darkness, waiting for the water to start glowing.

He wasn't sure why it was taking so long.

His hand had definitely been bleeding.

Dismayed, he jabbed the hammer into his palm again, ignoring the searing pain. The fresh cut streamed more blood into the spring.

Nothing. It wasn't responding.

He swam desperately to the side of the spring, then dove down, feeling the rocks, frantically running his hands across the wall.

No signs of Ben.

No signs of anything.

A horrifying thought occurred to him:

What if the spring never opens again?

What if the gateway is closed . . . forever?

He pushed the thought away, trying to will the spring back to life.

Any moment now it would start glowing.

Any moment.

Rex gripped his hammer tight.

He waited.

26

"IT'S VERY CLEAR NOW," SHERIFF LAWSON SAID, SPEAKING TO A crowd of reporters and concerned citizens outside the Bleak Creek Police Station, "that Wayne Whitewood was not the man we thought he was."

"Well, that's for darn sure," Martha McClendon said, her arm wrapped tightly around her son as if she intended to never let go. She sat with Rex and her husband on the couch, all eyes glued to the television screen.

"After a tip from an inside source at the school," Sheriff Lawson continued, "we were able to uncover the truth about what Mr. Whitewood had actually been doin' all these years, taking certain students captive and, in some cases . . ."—the sheriff shook his head, seeming genuinely mournful—"murdering them."

Rex's mom clutched him tighter, her lower lip trembling. "I just can't believe it," she whispered.

"I made the same mistake as everyone else," Sheriff Lawson said. "I trusted this man." He grimaced, like he had a bad taste in his mouth. Rex was impressed; the sheriff's acting chops were nearly as honed as Whitewood's had been. "That won't happen again. Even though Mr. Whitewood was able to elude our grasp last night, I have full faith that we'll find him. Justice will be served." Rex wondered how long Sheriff Lawson would be able to sustain a fake manhunt. He pictured concerned Bleak Creekians combing the woods around town, destined to find nothing. "And I do have some good news," the sheriff continued. "Mr. Whitewood had announced Alicia Boykins to be deceased—with a cover story just like the ones he'd concocted for his other victims—but that turned out to be another lie. Last night, we were able to save her." He nodded solemnly as some of the crowd applauded. "Don't get me wrong—he put that girl through hell, keeping her isolated and carrying out his sick 'punishments.' That poor young lady is still in a place where she doesn't know fantasy from reality. But now she can start to get better."

"I'm sorry, son," Rex's dad said, the first words he'd uttered to Rex since they'd driven him home from the Whitewood School the night before (after having been awakened by a call from Sheriff Lawson himself). "I'm sorry we didn't believe you. I might never forgive myself." He put his arm around Rex and kissed the side of his head, something he hadn't done since Rex was little. "From now on, whatever you tell us, we will take you at your word. I promise you that."

"Thanks, Dad," Rex said, still numb as he continued to watch Sheriff Lawson lie on television to thousands of people. There was, of course, a ton that he wanted to tell his parents. And maybe they truly would have believed him, but he cared about them too much to take that chance.

By the time Rex had finally emerged from the spring—once it was obvious that there would be no more glowing and bubbling, that Ben and the others were just . . . gone, Sheriff Lawson had started to explain to everyone gathered on the shore what was going to happen:

Whitewood would be blamed for everything.

All the students—minus the Seven Lost Causes down in the spring—would be returned safely to their homes.

The Whitewood School would be shut down.

None of them would ever again speak about the cult, about the spring, about anything other than Whitewood being a mentally unstable murderer.

"But . . . we can't taint Master's name like this," Mary had said. "He's with the One Below now, but what if he comes back?"

"We don't have a choice," Sheriff Lawson insisted.

"Can't we at least wait for the Seven Shepherds to come out before makin' any decisions?" Travis asked. "I mean, the One Below's got all the Lost Causes He asked for. It should happen any minute. Everybody will be *thankin'* Mr. Whitewood once they understand what he did for all of us."

"Master never told us how long the Purification would take," Mary said. "It could be days. Weeks."

"Right," Sheriff Lawson said. "Which is why we need to stick with my plan."

"You can't stop us from talking about this," Rex said.

"Oh no?" Sheriff Lawson took two menacing steps toward him. "Who do you think people will believe? A bunch of kids who have been tortured and brainwashed by a psychopath, kids who were already troubled to begin with? Or a dozen respected pillars of the community?"

"Guess we'll just have to wait and see," Janine said.

Sheriff Lawson looked to Mary Hattaway. "You destroyed the tape in that camera, right?"

Mary nodded.

"Good. Now, if any of you want to challenge me on this," Sheriff Lawson had said, staring deep into Rex's eyes, "I promise: I will make life very hard for you. For your friends. For your families. I wouldn't recommend it."

As Rex now felt the warm weight of his parents' arms on his back, he knew for sure he couldn't say anything. Sheriff Lawson and his crew had killed Donna's father, and even if they weren't willing to murder again, there was no shortage of horrible things they could do. They held such sway in the town; who's to say they wouldn't come up with a reason to encourage everyone to boycott his parents' funeral home, crushing their livelihood in one fell swoop? No. Rex couldn't do that to them.

"Unfortunately," Sheriff Lawson continued at the press conference, "four students are still unaccounted for: Patrick Small, April Li, Josefina Morales, and Ben Merritt."

Rex took deep breaths through his nose.

"Oh, baby, are you friends with any of them?" Martha asked.

Rex nodded. His parents held him tighter.

"We believe that Mr. Whitewood snuck these four students out of the school sometime in the past month," the sheriff said. "He had been keeping them captive somewhere off the premises. They may still be at that location, or he may be moving them as we speak."

"Sheriff Lawson," a tall woman from the *Raleigh News and Observer* asked, "was the school staff aware of what Mr. Whitewood was doing?"

"We will be thoroughly questioning everyone who worked at the school," the sheriff answered. "For now, though, Wayne Whitewood is our only suspect."

The brazen lying was hard to take. Rex wished he could go back to the spring right now, this time with more blood, tons of it, to again try to activate the spring and dig out Ben and all the others. But it would have to wait, at least a day or two.

"I assure you," Sheriff Lawson said, "we have our entire squad, as well as several in neighboring towns, scouring every square inch until we can find these kids and return them to their families."

Rex desperately needed to talk to his best friends. He'd called Leif twice that afternoon; both times he'd been sleeping. He'd called Alicia and was told by Mrs. Boykins that she hadn't started talking yet, "but Lord, wasn't it a miracle that she survived?"

"And then," Sheriff Lawson said, his tone more dramatic, "we will find this deranged killer and put him where he belongs: behind bars. We're gonna find these kids, and we're gonna find our suspect. And once we do, we can all move past this terrible stain on our town's history."

Rex extracted himself from his parents' embrace and walked out of the room.

—

JANINE SAT IN the darkened theater, incredibly nervous.

Donna was to her right and GamGam to her left, which was a definite comfort, but she knew that once their movie had finished screening, her and Donna's lives—possibly GamGam's, too—were very likely to change.

And not necessarily for the better.

Though Mary Hattaway had destroyed the tape from that awful night, Janine still had the other ones—including evidence of Alicia being held in the bubbling, glowing spring—stored back at GamGam's. Almost immediately, she and Donna had thrown themselves into sifting through the footage. Janine had worried it might be too much for her cousin, but, weirdly, it seemed to have the opposite effect, giving Donna a project, a distraction from the reality that she'd taken a man's life. A very evil man, yes, but a man all the same.

And this project would, for better or worse, reveal to the world the truth about what had happened.

So Janine had stayed in Bleak Creek, taking regular

trips with Donna to Raleigh, where one of Janine's NYU friends had a friend who had a friend who had a hook-up with the NC State film department, which gave them access to an editing bay. They'd worked nearly nonstop, their old teenage rhythms reemerging—cutting together footage, writing and recording voiceover, grabbing talking head interviews with Rex, Leif, Hornhat, and even a quick one with Alicia—until they'd finished a cut, just barely making the deadline for the Durham Film Festival.

Sitting in the Durham Arts Council theater, Janine couldn't tell what the audience of about seventy people was thinking. No one had walked out, which seemed promising.

Whatever happens, she reminded herself, *we're going to be okay.* In less than a week, she'd be heading back to New York City, and Donna was coming with her, finally escaping that mess of a town. They would live together in her tiny East Village apartment and make more movies with their newly formed production company: Donnine.

As the large screen filled up with the image of Alicia underwater in the spring, Janine heard several gasps, the loudest one belonging to GamGam. Donna reached over the armrest and took Janine's sweaty hand. Janine squeezed tight and didn't let go the rest of the movie.

As the final, eerie shot of the spring faded to black, Janine's heart wouldn't stop pounding. She wanted to sprint out of the theater and not stop running until she made it to New York.

Then the applause started.

And it wasn't just the polite kind.

Janine and Donna looked at each other in shock as people all around them got to their feet.

A standing ovation.

Tears sprang involuntarily to Janine's eyes.

They'd done it.

"Wow," the emcee, a balding man in glasses, said into a microphone at the front of the theater as the applause continued. "Just . . . wow. I'd love to invite the filmmakers, Janine Blitstein and Donna Lowe, up here for a brief Q and A."

As Janine and Donna side-stepped out of their row and headed up the aisle, the clapping surged even louder. Janine felt completely out of body.

"Ladies and gentlemen," the emcee said as Janine and Donna sat down in folding chairs. "I present to you the directors of *The Lost Causes of Bleak Creek.*"

Janine nodded and smiled politely through a final round of appreciation, her heart still thumping in her ears.

"First of all, congratulations," the man said. "We're honored to be debuting this stunning work."

"Thanks. Thank you," Janine said quietly.

Donna nodded her agreement.

"I think the film speaks for itself, and we've got another screening in just a bit, so let's get right to it and open up the floor for questions." Janine felt thrilled and terrified by the dozen or so hands that shot up. "Yes, you."

"Uh, hi," a long-haired twenty-something guy in a Homer Simpson T-shirt said. "I really loved your movie."

The emcee passed his microphone down to Donna, who passed it to Janine like a hot potato, the cord dragging on the ground. "Thanks," Janine said.

"Yeah," the guy continued. "So my question is . . . Like, what was the budget? Because I thought it was really amazing, like, how you could get such realistic visual effects on what otherwise seemed to be a pretty shoestring budget, you know? So . . . Uh, yeah. How did you do that?"

"Oh," Janine said, exchanging a dry look with Donna as she wondered how to answer without making the guy feel like an idiot, even though he obviously was one. "Those, um, weren't effects."

The guy stared at Janine for a second, mystified, before a slow smile broke out on his face. "Ohhh," he said, chuckling. "Of course they weren't. Ha, that's so cool. Well played."

"No," Janine said, "I'm serious."

"Oh, I know," the guy said, nodding knowingly as he sat down. "So am I."

Janine barely had time to process this odd exchange before the emcee pointed to someone else.

"Hello," an older woman said. "While I deeply appreciate the craft and storytelling on display, I think we need to address the elephant in the room. You've taken a set of horrific real-life murders of children and used them to create this horror film."

Janine looked to Donna, this time very unsettled.

"It's unquestionably entertaining," the woman continued, "but, considering this is a very recent event, it seems—to me, at least—in poor taste. Could you speak to that a bit?"

Janine gripped the microphone, stunned. "Of course," she said. "This is definitely *not* a hor—"

"I don't see it like that at all," a skinny dude wearing a suit vest over a T-shirt stood up to say. "I see this film as a tribute to those deaths, as a heightened metaphor for what they went through. And honestly, I think it's a beautiful achievement."

As some other people shouted their agreement, the whole room began to applaud again, and Janine's stomach dropped. She and Donna stared at each other in horrified disbelief.

Nobody in the audience thought it was real.

Well, that's not true. Janine locked eyes for a moment with GamGam, whose cheeks had gone an ashen gray. She knew it wasn't pretend.

"Come on, stand up, you two!" the emcee said. "Take a bow, you deserve it!"

Completely overwhelmed, Janine and Donna tried to let the moment pass, but it was no use.

They got to their feet and took an awkward bow as the applause continued.

—

"I DON'T KNOW if I'm ready," Alicia said, standing in between Rex and Leif, staring down at the slow-moving water of the Cape Fear River.

"We totally get it," Rex said, hands in the pockets of his Hornets Starter jacket. "We can just go somewhere else."

"Yeah," Leif said. "Definitely."

The Triumvirate was attempting to make their way to the tiny island, where they could sit and talk and pretend things were just as they'd always been, that their lives hadn't been irrevocably changed by what they'd been through.

This was not their first attempt.

Alicia had, unsurprisingly, developed an aversion to water. Thankfully, this spot was upstream from where Bleak Creek emptied into the river, so they could at least avoid contact with the tainted waters of Bleak Creek Spring (waters they were avoiding as much as possible these days, taking fewer showers and never drinking from the tap).

"No," she said now, a cool November breeze blowing past them, "I need to get over this. Leif can do it; I should be able to too."

"Yeah," Leif said, "but I was in the spring for barely any time compared to you. And I *was* totally freaked to go back into water at first. It would make sense that it would take you longer because—"

Alicia grabbed Leif's hand, and his heart jolted in his chest.

Over the past couple months, there had been no hugs, no playful shoves, no half nelsons, no physical contact whatsoever. Leif knew that was to be expected, as Alicia had gone through an extraordinary trauma—and he also knew how selfish it was to be wondering about her feelings for him in the midst of everything else she was dealing with—but it still hurt.

To feel her skin touching his was electrifying, like a flashback to a better time.

The spark faded as Leif watched Alicia grab Rex's hand, too.

"We'll go at the same time," she said. "Okay?"

"Yep," Rex said.

"Just say the word," Leif agreed.

Alicia nodded and took a deep breath. "The word."

They splashed their worn-out sneakers into the bracingly cold water at the same time, Alicia's eyes immediately clenching shut, her shoulders lifting to her ears.

"One step at a time," Leif said. "You got this."

Alicia whimpered.

"Do you want to go back?" Rex asked.

Alicia shook her head.

"All right," he said, "then we gotta go forward."

A few dozen steps later, Rex and Leif encouraging Alicia for every one of them, they made it onto the island.

"You take the Big Rock," Rex told Alicia as he and Leif helped her sit down.

Leif saw Rex release her hand, so he did too, even though he wanted to keep holding on.

"Oh, wait, aren't there some rules or something?" Alicia asked.

Leif and Rex exchanged a quick look. Alicia of before had known the rules of the rocks very well, as she had mocked them constantly. This was yet another thing in a long line of things that Alicia didn't remember from her old life. No matter how many times this happened, Leif was always a bit shaken (and grateful all of his memories had returned more or less intact).

"There were," Leif said. "But now the only rule is that when you're on the island, you can talk about whatever you want. Especially the stuff that, off the island, makes people look at you like you're some kind of damaged weirdo."

"Good rule," Rex said, clearly making a conscious effort to support what his best friend said and not point out some way to improve upon it. He'd been apologizing to Leif for being a selfish dick more or less nonstop since he'd rescued him from the spring. Leif had been appreciative at first, but lately he'd found himself longing for the way things had been; sure, Rex had been annoying sometimes, and it was nice to have him acknowledge that, but these new contrite vibes didn't make for the most fun friend dynamic.

"Yeah," Alicia said. "I can get behind that."

"You take the other one," Rex said to Leif, gesturing to the Small Rock.

"Really?" Leif asked.

"Sure!" Rex said, awkwardly lowering himself to a third, much smaller rock, his long limbs jutting out at strange angles. "This is actually pretty comfortable."

Leif saw how hard Rex was trying to sell this lie, how intent he was on making life okay for his two best friends, and this time, he felt deeply moved.

Then he started cracking up. "That's just stupid, man."

Alicia laughed too. "There's no way that's comfortable."

"Yeah, no," Rex said, joining in the laughter. "It's a lot more painful than I thought it would be."

"Come on, get up," Leif said, helping Rex to his feet so

that he could take the medium rock and Leif could take the tiny one.

Laughing had opened something up within all three of them, as if allowing them to fully access the sacred space of the island. Once they'd settled on their respective rocks, Alicia spoke first.

"Are we gonna feel like this forever?" she asked.

"Like what?" Rex asked.

"Bad."

"I hope not," Rex said, staring out toward the woods, toward Ben's Tree.

"I hate that we can't tell anyone the truth," Alicia said. "I hate that so much. And I hate the way people look at me."

"I know," Leif said. "I hate that people all feel so sorry for us, but they don't even know what actually happened. And if we told them, they'd think we were nuts."

"I hate that there's nothing left we can do," Rex said. "That we can't save Ben. And your friend Josefina. And the other kids. Maybe I should try again."

Leif sighed. "But why? There's still nothing there."

It was the horrible truth. Rex and Hornhat had returned to Bleak Creek Spring multiple times, with the scuba gear and more blood—pig's, human's, even goat's—hoping they'd open the gateway, reveal the heads of children and teens protruding from the spring wall, and get to work digging them out. But it never bubbled and glowed the way it once had.

The spring was never anything more than a spring.

"Yeah, but . . ." Rex shook his head. "So they're just stuck down there forever? In the Void, or whatever you guys called it?"

Alicia shivered on her rock, wrapping her arms tightly around herself.

"Maybe," Leif said. "Who knows."

They sat in silence for a moment.

"Still can't believe Janine and Donna's movie won the audience award," Leif said. "It's mind-blowing that everybody thinks it's a giant stunt."

"I know," Rex said. "I wish my parents would've let us go see it."

"I don't," Alicia said. "Then we would've had to listen to everybody tell us what great actors we are."

"Yeah," Leif said. "That woulda sucked."

"Should have been our movie at that festival," Alicia said, staring down into the water.

Leif and Rex generally refrained from ever mentioning *PolterDog*, seeing as they still, consciously or not, held it responsible for all the terrible things that had happened. But hearing Alicia mention it now, on the very island where the idea had first been conceived, was actually nice.

"I agree," Leif said.

"For sure," Rex said. "Hornhat still really wants to see it."

"Who's Hornhat?" Alicia said.

Leif and Rex looked at each other, alarmed.

"I'm kidding, guys," she said. "I remember Mark Hornhat. We see him literally every day at school."

"Oh, too bad," Leif said. "I was gonna say this was the one case where it'd be advantageous to forget someone."

"Come on," Rex said, laughing. "Hornhat is cool now! He helped save our frickin' lives."

"Yeah, but he's still very annoying," Alicia said.

"Also true," Rex said.

As the three of them again burst into giggles, Leif realized it didn't matter if Alicia never felt about him the way he did about her. Because sitting there laughing with the two people he loved most in the world, he suddenly felt so lucky.

They were still here.

Still alive.
Still together.
And maybe that was enough.
Leif adjusted his body on the tiny rock.
It really was quite uncomfortable.

EPILOGUE

"LATER, GUYS," ALICIA SAID, PEDALING AWAY IN THE DUSK AS THEY broke off at their usual spot, the corner of Creek and Pritchett. Alicia had overcome her fear of the water, the Triumvirate having now visited their island nearly every day for a few weeks, each time helping Alicia to piece together her life from before the Void.

They'd determined that this would be their last trip until next year, the depth and temperature of the river having made reaching the island nearly impossible. Rex and Leif had asked, as they always did, if she wanted them to escort her home, and, as she always did, she'd told them no.

She was actually somewhat relieved to part ways, both because she and Leif had to slow down considerably for Rex to keep up on his scooter, and because she'd come to relish riding around town by herself on her bike. Something about the constant motion, the not having to talk to anyone, made it the place where Alicia felt most at ease in her new life. She always stayed out till the very last minute of her parents' strict sundown curfew, exploring random streets, enjoying the solitude.

She noticed the last bit of sun dripping down below the horizon, and she knew she was pushing it a little too far this time. She picked up her pace, hoping to rocket through the last few blocks before home.

As she approached Fulkins Park on her right, she noticed something lying in the road ahead of her.

Maybe roadkill.

She got closer and started to steer around it, relieved to see it was just a stuffed animal.

A blue frog.

She experienced a jolt of recognition and turned her head, catching something in her peripheral vision.

She almost fell off her bike.

Standing in the near-darkness of the park, staring at her, was a little blond girl in a white dress.

A little blond girl with sad eyes and a slightly crooked smile.

Alicia had no trouble remembering her.

"Hi, Alicia," the girl said, her smile getting wider. "Everybody misses you."

Alicia pushed down the scream lodged in her throat.

She pedaled away quickly.

ACKNOWLEDGMENTS

Like everything in our career, we couldn't have done this alone. Well, maybe we could have, but it would have sucked.

Thank you to:

The South in general and Buies Creek, North Carolina, in particular. We are who we are because you are the way you are.

Lance Rubin, our sherpa in the adventures of novel-writing. Your talent, insights, and contributions were absolutely indispensable.

Our wives, Jessie and Christy, for supporting us in yet another entirely new and daunting endeavor, as well as tolerating us as we talked incessantly about this story. You are our hearts.

Our kids, Lily, Locke, Lincoln, Shepherd, and Lando for helping us stay connected to our own childhood through the vibrant ways you experience yours.

Our parents, for encouraging us to think big but never forget we're from a small town.

Stevie Levine, our CCO and creative partner, for your input, ideas, notes, and guidance, as well as your management of our many other simultaneous projects.

Matt Inman and the whole team at Crown, for your tireless commitment to excellence and meaningful involvement throughout.

Ward Roberts, Daniel Strange, Jessie McLaughlin, Nica Halula, Helen Kim, Britton Buchanan, Lily Neal, Mike Feldman, Jenna Purdy, and Cole McLaughlin for your detailed feedback on our first draft.

Our amazing staff at Mythical Entertainment. Your incredible work on *Good Mythical Morning* and beyond allowed us to give this novel the attention it deserved.

Marc Gerald for daring us to write a novel.

Brian Flanagan, our COO, for holding down the fort at *Mythical* while we threw ourselves into this book.

Byrd Leavell, Brent Weinstein, Ali Berman, and the team at UTA.

Adam Kaller, Ryan Pastorek, and the team at HJTH.

Our childhood friend Ben Greenwood for leading us into constant adventure and fearlessly embodying Mythicality in all that life held for you. You gave us the Tree, the Rocks, and the River.

Each and every Mythical Beast who has supported our creative aspirations. We consider it a privilege to be on this journey with you. Keep on being your Mythical best.

ABOUT THE AUTHORS

Rhett McLaughlin and Link Neal, raised in North Carolina and best friends since the first grade, are an L.A.-based comedy duo known for creating the Internet's most-watched daily talk show, *Good Mythical Morning;* the narrative series *Rhett & Link's Buddy System;* the award-winning weekly podcast *Ear Biscuits;* and the instant #1 *New York Times* bestseller, *Rhett & Link's Book of Mythicality.* Their YouTube channels have a combined subscriber base of over 24 million people with 7 billion total views. They have been featured on and in *The Tonight Show Starring Jimmy Fallon, Live with Kelly & Ryan, The Conan O'Brien Show, Variety, USA Today, The Wall Street Journal, Vanity Fair,* and *The New Yorker.*